THE

DEATH SHIP

THE STORY OF AN AMERICAN SAILOR

B. TRAVEN

Lawrence Hill Books

Library of Congress Cataloging-in-Publication Data

Traven, B.
  [Totenschiff. English]
  The death ship : the story of an American sailor / B. Traven ;
foreword by John Anthony West. — 2nd ed.
      p. cm.
  Translation of: Totenschiff.
  ISBN 1-55652-110-3 : $12.95
  [PT3919.T7T613 1991]
  813'.52—dc20   91-25293
                                                                      CIP

©1934 by Alfred A. Knopf, Inc. and B. Traven,
renewed 1962 by B. Traven
Foreword by John Anthony West, ©1991
Reprinted with the permission of Rosa Elena Lujan by
Lawrence Hill Books, Brooklyn, New York, 1991

Printed in the United States of America
Second edition
First printing
Published by Lawrence Hill Books, Brooklyn, New York
An imprint of Chicago Review Press, Incorporated
814 North Franklin Street
Chicago, Illinois 60610

FOREWORD

In 1934, B. Traven's first novel, *The Death Ship*, was published in English. It had already appeared in German and in a dozen other translations to enormous acclaim. Its reception in English was no different.

"The finest modern sea story I have read. Indeed, I think it unique, for it is the first *real* book about the lives of men for'ard of the bridge. . . . This book gives us their lives, and we are grateful to Mr. Traven for it. It is dreadfully real, horrible, fantastic but disgustingly true. . . . No better description of a ship's stokehold and the strange beings in it has ever come my way"—James Hanley, *The Spectator*. "Not Gorky himself has more authentically described the bottom dogs. This is real proletarian literature, with genuine proletarian dirt and smells and cruel, ribald wit"—Lewis Gannet, *The Literary Digest*. "The book is not primarily a sea-story . . . it merely uses a tramp steamer as a by-product and illustration of certain phases of industrialism. . . . In its own way [it] is a challenge to pretty much everything in the modern world"—Lincoln Colcord, *The New York Herald Tribune*.

With near unanimity, critics praised *The Death Ship* for its hypnotic power, timeliness, universality, and authenticity. It provoked comparisons to Melville, Conrad, Gorky, and Dana. A story circulated (impossible to prove now but not out of character) that Albert Einstein had named *The Death Ship* as the book he would take with him to a desert island.

But following its initial success, an unprecedented literary situation arose. The author of *The Death Ship* refused to divulge even a scrap of biographical information about himself. He said he believed a writer should be known for his work, not his personal life—surely a defensible point of view. We know little about Shakespeare's life, and it neither enhances nor detracts from his work. By contrast, we know everything about Kafka, and what of it?

Although *The Death Ship* was followed by a stream of haunting, powerful novels, among them *The Treasure of the Sierra Madre*, the trail to their author ended at a post office box in Mexico City. Unable to discern the wide and luminous line that separates legitimate investigative reportage from an invasion of privacy, the literary world reacted as though to an absconding politician or mafioso. The bloodhounds of journalism were dispatched to track Traven down, to no avail, and amazing legends grew up—some perhaps fostered by Traven himself, in self-defense, out of amusement, or both. As a result the writer who insisted on remaining anonymous and on letting his work speak for him became world-famous mostly for his genius at remaining anonymous, a reputation that persists posthumously.

Many articles and several books have been written about Traven since his death in 1969. Most of them dutifully cite his wish to be known for his work and then go on to shortchange or patronize the work, while dwelling on the mystery. One book that actually focuses on Traven's work sets out with a perfectly straight face to psychoanalyze him (the ship is a womb, the smokestacks phallic symbols) and reads like one of Nabokov's Freudian parodies.

This is not to say that Traven was ignored. His work was widely published and often enthusiastically reviewed. "Traven is a very great writer, and . . . his work must be read," wrote James Herndon in *The New York Times Book Review*. His aficionados included eminent writers and statesmen, and, though resolutely anonymous, he was something of a national hero in Mexico. He was even nominated for a Nobel Prize. But to put the matter into perspective: While the film of *The Treasure of the Sierra Madre* is a classic, people aren't always aware that Traven wrote the book; for all they know Humphrey Bogart did. A new Traven novel might not make the front page of a major literary review, but some new clue to his identity would.

Traven is usually described as a gifted storyteller with radical political views—anarchist, anti-capitalist, anti-Communist, anti-bureaucrat, champion of the underdog. All these labels apply, but miss the essence. Behind the gripping adventure of a Traven novel, there runs the theme that motivates much of the rare literature that may age, but never dies: the ability of the human spirit to withstand and ultimately to transcend every onslaught made upon its inherent nobility—whether engineered by the caprices of the gods, or by the diabolical ingenuity of man himself. It is in *The Death Ship* that this theme finds its fullest expression.

Bruce Catton called the book "a startling novel about the horrible things that can happen to a man in the cockeyed post war world of Europe if he can't prove he is who he says he is. . . . Our sailor is entangled in a world gone mad, a world in which justice and sanity have simply ceased to exist." We are now post a few more wars, and the world is no less cockeyed, and no more just or sane. As a story, as a metaphor, *The Death Ship* is no less startling than when it was written. Yet it elicits peculiarly little literary notice. Even the red herring of the Traven "mystery" does not quite account for that. But I think that I know why.

Later Traven novels are models of craft and precision, simply and classically wrought. By contrast, *The Death*

Ship looks jagged, headlong, excessive, with its grim, wild humor, harrowing physical detail, and rambling philosophical digressions. Using conventional criteria, it is impossible to explain the source of its power. But the unkempt appearance is deceptive. Almost nothing in *The Death Ship* can be cut, edited, transposed, civilized, or otherwise "improved" without doing damage. *The Death Ship* obeys rules, but they are rules not usually associated with literature but with ancient liturgical dramas and epics, Eastern sacred music, and, above all, alchemy.

The true alchemist was not a deluded proto-scientist out to turn lead into gold for gain. His rituals with lead, mercury, and sulfur served as mnemonic aids in the quest for spiritual self-perfection. As the carnal became spiritual on the inner plane, so—according to the medieval theory of hierarchy and correspondences—the gross would become fine on the physical plane. Though the method may not wash as science, it is singularly apt when applied to art. All art is alchemical in the sense that it distills the raw stuff of experience into something rarer and finer. Understood metaphorically, every real artist is an alchemist. In this ancient discipline, the repetition of the experiment, the constant application of fire, eventually prepares the material for transmutation. In Eastern music and ancient epics, the endless repetition of a phrase or refrain served a similar function. In *The Death Ship,* Traven uses the actual methodology of alchemy. That use is instinctive—there is no indication that Traven was a student of alchemy—but it is unerring.

The time is the 1920s, after what Traven calls "The Great War for Freedom." Gerard Gales, an American sailor, is stranded in Antwerp, Belgium, without papers or money. Without papers or money, Everyman becomes Noman and Ulysses is destined to wander ever farther from home.

As Gales is kicked around Europe by the authorities of various countries, it is not the variety of adventure and the ingenuity of the comic invention that produce the laughter, as in most other great satires *(Pantagruel, Don Quixote, Gulliver's Travels)*; it is the essential sameness— the shaggy dog story carried beyond the limits of endurance. It is a risky way to go about comedy, but the exasperated hilarity that repetition provokes has a compelling quality. And as an indictment of the bureaucracy that knows no national or ideological frontiers, this first section of *The Death Ship* has few equals.

It takes shock to break the rhythms induced by repetition. A lesser writer, having exhausted the possibilities of purgatory, would introduce his hero directly into hell. Traven first lets him taste paradise. Gales wends his way through France and over the border into Spain. Spain has not fought the Great War for Freedom, and therefore people are still free. In pre-Franco Spain no one asks if he has papers or money, because no one has papers or money. When a policeman accosts him, sleeping on a park bench, it is to tell him to move under cover since it is about to rain. People give him leftovers without insulting his dignity. He can fish for dinner off a pier in the harbor.

Then the *Yorikke* appears, the most decrepit and absurd craft ever to sail the seas. Gales spends seven glorious, hyperbolic pages ridiculing her. But when he is offered a job, he takes it. Nothing on earth could induce him to ask for a job; not on the *Yorikke,* and not in "sunny Spain." But sailor's honor and superstition will not permit him to turn down a job he has been *offered.* This would be tempting the gods.

With this masterstroke of irony, a door clangs shut. The card of destiny has been thrown onto the table, satire has been transmuted into horror. The *Yorikke* is a gunrunner. When her numbered days are up she will be sunk to collect "the holy insurance" (hence *The Death Ship*). Meanwhile, with her ragtag crew, she is a floating Foreign Legion, Blake's "dark satanic mills" and *The Flying Dutch-*

man rolled into one. There has never been a writer who excelled Traven at describing trial by toil; the effect of forced physical labor carried beyond the limits of endurance. It is not so much that the story moves forward; rather, the heat intensifies. Again, a risky literary device, but straightforward alchemy.

One masterstroke of irony puts Gales onto the *Yorikke;* another now gets him off. Instinct tells him it is time to try his luck elsewhere. In remote Dakar, he sees the shiny, new *Empress of Madagascar* incongruously docked. He applies for a job and is refused: no papers. Later, he and his fellow coal stoker, Stanislav, beg a meal on a Norwegian freighter. They are told that despite her appearance, the *Empress* has a terminal engineering defect and is unfit even to run guns. She will be scuttled this trip for the insurance. Suddenly the monstrous but still functioning *Yorikke* acquires the glamour of a new lover. Gales and Stanislav are returning to her, singing her praises, when they are set upon and shanghaied. They wake up aboard the *Empress of Madagascar.* As putative stowaways they can be signed on the books without papers. Later, the insurance company cannot quibble. "All legal."

The *Yorikke* was hell, but hell on earth, crewed appropriately by living demons. Aboard the *Empress* all are zombies, and the stage is set for shipwreck. (In alchemy, the "death" and dissolution of matter precede the final transmutation.)

The skipper and mates have an escape plan. But the plan goes awry. Only Gales and Stanislav survive, clinging to the wrecked *Empress,* tipsily wedged aloft on a reef and dining on caviar and Chablis from the captain's locker. Finally, a storm dislodges the ship, and the two are abruptly reduced to hanging onto a bit of raft, without food or water, beneath a burning sun, adrift in a stretch of African ocean hundreds of miles from a shipping lane. Raving and delirious, Stanislav thinks he sees the *Yorikke* standing by to rescue them. He cuts himself free of the ropes that lash him to the raft, leaps into the still, empty ocean, and sinks like a stone.

In the literature of alchemy, there are supposedly authenticated instances of transmutation. I am in no position to verify or disparage such claims. But there can be no doubt that, correctly applied to art, the principles are valid. Stanislav's death instantly brings Gales to his senses. He needs only a few sentences to commend his vanished comrade to "The Great Skipper." But these sound a note as decisive as a gong. With no apparent effort, *The Death Ship* slips out of the realm of the hallucinatory and into the sublime. After almost 400 harrowing, hilarious pages, it ends in that "peace which passeth all understanding"; the equivalent in literature of the alchemist's gold.

John Anthony West
Saugerties, New York
April 1991

SONG OF AN AMERICAN SAILOR

Now stop that crying, honey dear,
The Jackson Square remains still here
In sunny New Orleans
In lovely Louisiana.

She thinks me buried in the sea,
No longer does she wait for me
In sunny New Orleans
In lovely Louisiana.

The death ship is it I am in,
All I have lost, nothing to win
So far off sunny New Orleans
So far off lovely Louisiana.

THE FIRST BOOK

THE FIRST BOOK

I

We had brought, in the holds of the S.S. *Tuscaloosa*, a full cargo of cotton from New Orleans to Antwerp.

The *Tuscaloosa* was a fine ship, an excellent ship, true and honest down to the bilge. First-rate freighter. Not a tramp. Made in the United States of America. Home port New Orleans. Oh, good old New Orleans, with your golden sun above you and your merry laughter within you! So unlike the frosty towns of the Puritans with their sour faces of string-savers.

What a ship the *Tuscaloosa* was! The swellest quarters for the crew you could think of. There was a great ship-builder indeed. A man, an engineer, an architect who for the first time in the history of shipbuilding had the communistic idea that the crew of a freighter might consist of human beings, not merely of hands. The company who had ordered the ship to be built had, somehow, made the great discovery that a well-treated, well-fed, well-housed crew is worth more to the welfare of a ship and its ability to pay high dividends than a crew treated like bums. Everything was as clean as a Dutch girl. Showers whenever you wanted them. Clean bed-sheets and clean pillow-covers twice a week. Yes, sir. Everything was solid like rock. The food was good, rich, and you could have as much as you could pack. The mess-gear always polished like in a swell hotel dining-room. There were two colored boys to attend to our quarters and mess to keep them spick and span like a peasant home in Sweden at Whitsunday. All for no other reason than to keep the crew in fine health and in high spirits. Yes, sir.

I second mate? No, sir. I was not mate on this can, not even bos'n. I was just a plain sailor. Deck-hand you may say. You see, sir, to tell you the truth, full-fledged sailors aren't needed now. They have gone for ever, I think, with the last horse-drawn cab in New York. A freighter of today isn't a ship at all. A modern freighter meant to make money for the company is only a floating machine. You may not know very much about ships, sir, but, believe me, real sailors wouldn't know what to do with a modern ship. What such a ship needs is not sailors who know all about rigging; what she really cries for is men who are good engineers, mechanics, and working-men who know machinery when they see it. Even the skipper has to be more of an engineer than a sailor. Take the A.B., the able-bodied sailor, who used to be more than anybody else a real sailor; today he is just a plain worker tending a certain machine. He is not supposed to know anything about sails. Nobody would ask him to make a proper splice. He couldn't do it for a hundred dollars. Nevertheless he is as good a sailor on a modern freighter as his grandfather was on a three-mast schooner. Yes, sir.

All the romance of the sea that you still find in magazine stories died long, long ago. You would look in vain for it even in the China Sea and south of it. I don't believe it ever existed save in sea-stories—never on the high seas or in sea-going ships. There are many fine youngsters who fell for those stories and believed them true, and off they went to a life that destroyed their bodies and their souls. Because everything was so very different from what they had read in those alluring stories. Life on the sea is not like they make it out to be and it never was. There is a chance, one in a hundred, maybe, that at some time romance and adventure did exist for skippers, for mates, for engineers. You still may see them singing in operas and making beebaboo in the movies. You may find them also in best-sellers and in old ballads. Anyway, the fact is that the song of the real and genuine hero of the sea has never yet been sung. Why? Because the true song would be too cruel and too strange for the people who like ballads. Opera-audiences, movie-goers, and magazine-readers are like that. They want to have everything pleasant, with a happy ending. The true story of the sea is anything but pleasant or romantic in the accepted sense. The life of the real heroes has always been cruel, made up of hard work, of treatment worse than the animals of the cargo get, and often of the most noble sacrifices, but without medals and plaques, and without mention in stories, operas, and movies. Even the hairy apes are opera-singers looking for a piece of lingerie.

I was just a plain deck-hand. What you might call a handy man aboard. I had to do every kind of work that came my way or that was pushed my way. In short, I was just a painter and brass-polisher. The deck-hands have to be kept busy all day long. Otherwise they might fall for some dangerous ideas about Russia. On a modern ship, once under weigh, there is little to do outside of the engine-holds. Sometimes repairs have to be made on deck or in the holds. Holds have to be cleaned or aired. The cargo has shifted, perhaps, and has to be put back into place to keep the ship from hanging down a fin. Lamps have to be cleaned. Signal flags set in order. The life-boats watered and inspected. And when nothing else can be done on deck, the hands paint. Always there is something to be painted. From morning to night.

There comes a day in the deck-hand's life when he feels convinced that there are only two kinds of people on earth, those who sail the high seas and those who make paint. You feel a sort of gratitude towards those good people who make all that paint, because should they ever stop, the second mate would surely go mad wondering what to do with the deck-hands. The deck-hands can't get paid for just looking around the horizon or watching the smoke of another ship coming up. No, sir.

The pay was not high. I have to admit that. The company could not have competed with the German and the Italian freight rates had they paid us the wages of the vice-president of a railroad. They say the whole trouble is that sailors don't know what to do with their pay; otherwise they might easily own, after a couple of years, five or six seagoing freighters. For my part, not being under the influence of the success stories of the builders of our nation, I reckoned like this: if I would not spend a cent of my pay for twenty-five years and I would tuck it away in a trust or bank and if I would never have, during these twenty-five years, one week without pay, but work hard all the time, even then I could not retire and live on my dividends. Still, after another twenty-five years of equal pay and of equal good luck in always having a ship, I might by then call myself a useful and honest citizen and a member of the lower middle-class, ready to buy a gas-station somewhere on a highway. A fine and noble prospect—it convinced me to stay a plain sailor for a good long while and so prepare myself for the bread in heaven and leave for others the cake here on earth. . . .

The other guys had gone ashore. I didn't care to see the city. I don't like Antwerp. There are too many beachcombers, bums, worthless sailors, and drunken ships'-carpenters around anyway. One should not mix with such people, being a sailor on a smart American freighter, and a freighter from New Orleans at that. Besides, I told Honey I wouldn't play around with any dames. At least not on this trip. No, sir. I mean, yes, sir.

I have learned that it is not the mountains that makes destiny, but the grains of sand and the little pebbles. Sounds philosophic, but it is the truth.

I was alone in the foc'sle. Everybody else had gone ashore to get a bellyful of port life before going home to be dry again. I was sick of reading true confession stories and ranch romances. I couldn't even sleep any more, which was strange, because I can sleep anywhere and any time. I didn't know what to do with myself. We had laid off work at noon, when the watches were assigned for the trip home.

I wandered from the quarters to midship and back again. Five hundred times or more. I spit into the water and speculated on how far the rings might go before they died. I threw crumbs of bread into the water to feed the fishes.

It made me so very miserable to look at the offices and buildings along the docks, by now all empty and closed. Office windows after closing hours make the same impression upon me as bleached human bones found in a desolate place in the open sun. From the height of the ship I could see right into the offices, where on dull desks were piled up all kinds of papers, blanks, bills. Blanks too can make me sick; they remind me of questions I have to answer to some official to whom I would like to say whose son I think he is.

All and everything about the docks and the buildings and the offices looked so utterly hopeless, like a world going to pieces without knowing it.

In the end I got a craving to feel a solid street under my feet. I wanted to see people hustling about. I wanted to make sure that the world was still going on in the usual way, doing business, making money, getting drunk, laughing, cursing, stealing, killing, dancing, falling in love, and falling out again. I really got frightened being alone there.

"Why didn't you come earlier in the afternoon like the other guys did?" the mate said. "I won't give you any money now."

"Sorry, sir, to bother you, but I sure must have twenty bucks advance. I have to send it home to my mother."

"Five and not a cent more."

"I can do nothing with a five, sir. Prices are high here in Belgium since the war. I need twenty, not a cent less. Maybe, sir, I mean I might be very sick tomorrow. Who do you expect would paint the galley then? Tell me that, sir. The galley has to be ready when we reach home."

"All right. Ten. My last word. Ten or nothing. I'm not obliged to give you even a nickel."

"Well then, sir, I'll take the ten. But I think it's lousy the way they treat us here in a foreign country."

"Shut up. Sign here for the ten. We'll write it in the book tomorrow."

The truth is I didn't want more than ten in the first place. But if I had asked for ten I wouldn't have got more than five. The fact is I couldn't even use more than ten. Once in your pocket and out in town, the money is gone, whether you have ten bucks or two hundred.

"Now, don't get drunk. Understand. There'll be plenty of work tomorrow and you've got to be ready to go on hand when we're putting out," the mate said.

Get drunk? Me get drunk? An insult. The skipper, the other mates, the engineers, the bos'n, the carpenter haven't been sober for six consecutive hours since we made this port. And I am told not to get drunk. I didn't even think of Scotch at all. Not for a minute.

"Me get drunk, sir? Never. I don't even touch the cork of a whisky bottle, I hate that stuff so much. I know what I owe my country in a foreign port. I am dry, sir. I may be a Democrat, but I am dry. Ever seen me drunk, sir?"

"All right, all right, I haven't said a word. Forget it."

"Thank you, sir."

Ashore.

2

It was a summer twilight, beautiful and dreamlike. I was in full harmony with the world as it was. I could not understand how anybody on earth could be displeased with life. Communists, reformers, and hell-drummers ought to be kicked out of this beautiful world of ours. I strolled along the streets, looking at the windows where the riches of the world were on display, calling to be bought and carried away. All the people I met seemed so satisfied with themselves and with everyone else. The girls smiled at me, and the prettiest were the ones who greeted me best.

I came to a house that had a fine gilded front. It looked friendly, inviting, and very gay. The doors were wide open, and they said: "Come in, good friend. Come in and be happy with the happy. Just drop in here, and forget all your worries!"

I had no worries. Yet I felt fine that somebody should call me and remind me that I might have worries. In I went. There was a jolly crowd there. Singing. Music. Laughter. Gay talk. Everything friendly.

I sat down on a chair, at a table. Immediately a young man came, looked me over, and said in English: "How do you do, mister?" He put down a bottle and a glass. He filled the glass and said: "Drink to the greatness of your country!" So I did.

For weeks I had seen only the guys of the bucket, and water and more water, and stinking paint. So I thought again of the greatness of my country. And again. There is really too much water on earth. And most of it is salty, at that. And paint is no perfume. Well, to the greatness of my country!

There was foggy weather around me. The longer I sat at the table, and the more I thought of my country, the thicker became the fog. I forgot all the worries I could remember ever having had during my life.

Late at night I found myself in the room of a pretty girl. She was laughing and friendly. She was sweet.

Finally I said to her: "Now look here, Mademoiselle whatever your name may be, you're a piece of sugar. That's what you are. Tell me, what time is it now?"

With her sweet laughing mouth she said: "Oh, you handsome boy—" Yes, sir, that's exactly what she said to me. "Oh, you handsome sailor boy from the great and beautiful Amerique land, you want to be a cavalier, don't you? A real cavalier. You wouldn't leave a little defenseless lady alone in her room at midnight, would you? Burglars might come and rob me or take me away to dark Africa. They might even murder me or sell me as a slave to the wild Arabians. And I am afraid of mice, I am."

"I am not afraid of a mouse," I said.

"Oh, you bad sailor man! That's what you are," the pretty lady said. "Please don't leave me alone here at midnight. I am so afraid of terrible burglars."

I know what a real red-blooded American must do when he's called to rescue a defenseless lady. It was almost a daily sermon from the time I was a kid: "When a lady asks you to do something, you jump up and do what she says, even if it should cost you your life. Just remember that every woman is a mother or may be a mother some day. That's a good boy."

What else could I do? It's in the blood. You have to do what a lady asks you to do. Even if it should cost you your life.

Early in the morning, before the sun came up, I hurried to the docks. There was no *Tuscaloosa* to be seen. Her berth at the pier was abandoned. She had gone back home to sunny New Orleans. She had gone back home without me.

I have seen children who, at a fair or in a crowd, had lost their mothers. I have seen people whose homes had burned down, others whose whole property had been carried away by floods. I have seen deer whose companions had been shot or captured. All this is so painful to see and so very sorrowful to think of. Yet of all the woeful things there is nothing so sad as a sailor in a foreign land whose ship has just sailed off leaving him behind.

It is not the foreign country that makes him so sick at heart, that makes him feel inside like a child crying for its mother. He is used to foreign countries. Often he has stayed behind of his own free will, looking for adventure, or for something better to turn up, or out of dislike for the skipper or the mates or some fellow-sailors. In all such cases he does not feel depressed at all. He knows what he is doing and why he did it, even when it turns out different from what he expected.

But when the ship of which he considers himself still a useful part sails off without taking him with her, without waiting for him, then he feels as though he had been torn asunder. He feels like a little bird may feel when it has fallen out of its nest. He is homeless. He has lost all connection with the rest of the world, he thinks; he has lost his right to be of any use to mankind. His ship did not bother to wait for him. The ship could afford to sail without him and still be a good and seaworthy ship. A copper nail that gets loose, or a rivet that breaks off, might cause the ship to sink and never reach home again. The sailor left behind, forgotten by his ship, is of less importance to the life and the safety of the ship than a rusty nail or a steam-pipe with a weak spot. The ship gets along well without him. He might as well jump right from the pier into the water. It wouldn't do any harm to the ship that was his home, his very existence, his evidence that he had a place in this world to fill. If he should now jump into the sea and be found, nobody would care. All that would be said would be: "A stranger, by appearance a sailor." Worth less to a ship than a nail.

Pretty, isn't it? So I thought. But the depressed feeling that was looming up within me didn't grip me in full. Before it could get hold of me I knocked it cold.

Shit the bucket. There are lots of other ships in the world. The oceans are so very big and so full of ships. They have hardly room enough to sail without choking each other. How many ships are there? Surely no less than half a million. One of those half a million seagoing ships, one at least, will need, some time sooner or later, a plain sailor. My turn will come again.

As for Antwerp, well, it's a great port. All ships make this port some day or other. What I need is just patience. That's all. Who would expect that somebody, maybe the skipper himself, would turn up immediately and yell out: "Hey, sailor, what about signing on? Union pay!" I can't expect anything like that to happen.

Thinking it all over, well, what's there to worry about a faithless bucket leaving me flat in Belgium. Like all women do —leave you the first time you try it out with another dame. Anyway, I have to hand it to her, she sure had clean quarters and showers—and swell grub. No complaints about that. Right now they're having breakfast. Those guys will eat up all of my bacon, and the eggs too. The coffee will be cold again when I come into the mess. If they leave any coffee at all. Sure the cook has burned the bacon again. He'll never learn. I wonder who made him a ship's cook. Perhaps a Chinese laundry man. As for Slim, I see him already going through all my things, picking out everything he likes, before he hands the bag over to the mate. Maybe they won't even turn in my things to the mate. Those bums. Not a decent sailor among them. Just running around with dames. Using perfume and facial soap. How I hate them! Sailors? Don't make me laugh. But I'd never have expected this from Slim. Seemed to be a regular guy. You would not have believed Slim'd be that bad; no, sir. You can't trust anybody any longer. But then—he always used to steal my good toilet soap whenever he could lay his hands on it. What can you expect from a fellow who steals your soap when you're out on deck?

What's the use worrying about that bucket? Gone. It's all right with me. Go to the devil. The ship doesn't worry me at all. What worries me is something different. I haven't got a red cent in my pocket. She told me, I mean that pretty girl

I was with during the night, protecting her against burglars and kidnappers, well, she told me that her dear mother was sick in the hospital, and that she had no money to buy medicine and the right food for her, and that she might die any minute if she didn't get the medicine and the food. I didn't want to be responsible for the death of her mother. So what could I do as a regular red-blooded American except give her all the money I had left over from the gilded house? I have to say this much, though, about that pretty dame: she was grateful to me for having saved her mother from an early death. There is nothing in the whole wide world more satis-fying to your heart than making other people happy and always still happier. And to receive the thousand thanks of a pretty girl whose mother you have just saved, that is the very peak of life. Yes, sir.

3

I sat down on a box and followed in my mind the *Tuscaloosa* steaming her way home. I wished earnestly that she would spring a leak, or something, soon, and be forced to return and give me a chance to hop on again. I should have known better; she was too good a bucket to run foolishly on the rocks.

Another hope of mine went bluey. I had hoped that the crew might object to leaving me behind and make it tough for the skipper, or even engage in a mild form of mutiny. Apparently they didn't care. Anyhow, I wished that damned canoe all the shipwrecks and all the typhoons any sailor ever heard of from old salts spinning yarns that made even drunken quartermasters get the shivers.

I was just about to doze off and dream of that little peach of a girl when somebody tapped me on the shoulder.

Right away, without giving me a chance to see what was

going on, he talked to me so rapidly that my head began to buzz.

I got mad and I said: "Rats, be damned, beat it, leave me alone. I don't like your damn jibbering. And besides I don't know what you want. I don't understand a single word of your blabbering. Go to the devil."

"You are an Englishman, are you not?" he asked, speaking in English.

"Nope; Yank."

"Then you are American."

"Looks like it. And now that you know all about me, leave me in peace and go to your wifie. I've nothing to do with you, no business."

"But I have some with you. I am from the police."

"Your luck, old man. Fine job. How much do they pay the flats here? What's troubling you with a swell job like that? Something wrong?"

"Seaman, hey?" he asked.

"Aha. Any chance for me?"

"What ship?"

"*Tuscaloosa*, from New Orleans."

"Sailed at three in the morning. A long way off, I dare say." That made me mad again. "I don't need you to tell me any stale jokes."

"Your papers?" he asked.

"What papers do you mean?"

"Your passport."

"*What?*"

"That's what I said; let me have your passport."

"Haven't any."

"Then your sailor's identification card or whatever you call it in your home country." He sort of pushed me.

"My sailor's card? Yes, yes." Hell. My seaman's card. Where have I got it? I remember now, it's in a pocket of my jacket; and my jacket is in my sailor's bag; and the bag is stowed nicely away under my bunk in the foc'sle in the *Tuscaloosa;* and the *Tuscaloosa* is now—gee, where can she be right now? I wonder what they've got for breakfast today. Sure, that damned cook has burned the bacon again. I'll get him some day and tell him what I really think of him. Just let me be around, painting the galley. Guess I'm getting hungry.

"Well, well," said the flat, shaking me, "your sailor's card. You know what I mean."

"My sailor's card? If you mean mine, what I want to say, my sailor's card—I'll have to come clean about that card. The truth is, I haven't got any."

"No sailor's card?" He opened his eyes wide in sheer astonishment, as if he had seen a ghost. The tone of his voice carried the same strange amazement, as if he had said: "What is that, you don't believe there is such a thing as sea-water?"

It seems that it was incomprehensible to him that there could be a human being with neither a passport nor a sailor's card. He asked for the card for the third time, almost automatically. Then, as though receiving a shock, he recovered from his astonishment and sputtered: "No other papers either? No identification certificate? No letter from your consul? No bank-book? Or anything like that?"

"No, no, nothing." Feverishly I searched my pockets, so as to make a good impression upon him. I knew quite well I had not even an empty envelope with my name on it.

Said he: "Come with me."

"Where to?" I wanted to know. Perhaps he was sent to fish up some derelict sailors for a rum-boat. I could tell him right then that not even wild horses could drag me aboard one.

"Where? You will find out pretty soon. Just keep going." He wasn't so friendly any more.

After some hopping we landed. Where? Yes, sir, you guessed right. In a police-station. Here I was searched, and how! When they had searched all over, and had left unsearched not even the seams of my clothes, one of the searchers asked, absolutely seriously: "No arms? No weapons of any kind?" I could have socked him one right then, I was so mad. As if I could hide a machine-gun in my nostrils, and a couple of automatics under my eyelids. That's the way people are and you can't do anything about it.

The examination over, I had to stand up before a high desk, behind which sat a man who looked at me as if I had stolen his overcoat. He opened a thick book filled with photographs. The guy that had pinched me acted as the interpreter. Without him I would never have known, until the end of my days, what the man behind the desk wanted. Funny that these people understood our language pretty well when they needed our boys to fight for them, and when they wanted our money.

The high priest at the desk looked at all the photographs, and after each photograph he looked at me. He did this a hundred times. He had that way of looking upwards with his nose kept close to the thick book that people have when they look over the rims of their eye-glasses.

At last he got tired of moving his neck up and down. He shook his head and disgustedly closed the book with a bang. It seems he hadn't found my photograph. I could have told him before that he wouldn't, if he only had asked me, because I knew damn well that I had never been photographed in Antwerp. I too got tired of this lame business, and I said: "Now I am hungry. I want to eat. I haven't had any breakfast this morning."

"Right," the interpreter said. I was taken into a small room, with nothing in it that I would call furniture.

I wonder if all the Belgians call what I got a breakfast—coffee, bread, and margarine. It was the minimum in quantity and quality.

Then I was left alone to occupy myself with counting the bars at the window, a job I did rather well.

About noon I was again brought before the high priest.

"There are nine," I said right away, "exactly nine."

"What nine?" the high priest asked with the help of the interpreter.

"Nine bars at the window," I answered.

The high priest looked at the interpreter, and the interpreter looked at him, and then both of them looked at me, finally shaking their heads; and the interpreter said: "Well, they are this way, sir. You know it from the war. There is something loose in their upper stories. One cannot take them seriously."

"Do you wish to go to France?" the high priest asked me.

"No, y'honor, I don't like France. Under no circumstances do I wish to go to France. I don't like war-mothers running wild about the battlefields. No, France is no place for me."

"What do you think of Germany?" He asked.

"I don't care to go to Germany either, if you please, sir."

"Why, Germany is quite a fine country. Take Hamburg for instance. You could easily find there a good ship to take you home."

"No, I do not like the Germans. They often go out of their minds without any warning."

The high priest assumed a dictatorial attitude: "Well, then, it is all settled now, once and for all. No more objections on your side, sailor. You are going to Holland. And understand, this is final."

"But I do not like the Dutch," I said, and I was just about to tell him why, when he cut me short: "We do not care a rag if you like the Dutch or if you don't. You may fix this with the Dutch yourself, when you meet them in person. In France you would be best off. However, for a rich gentleman like you, France is not good enough. Too bad we have nothing better to offer you. You don't want to go to Germany either. The Germans also are not good enough for you. Hell, just tell me what people other than your own do you like? None apparently. So you are going to Holland, and that is that. We have no other border. We cannot, just to please you, acquire another neighbor who might find favor with you. And, just

to make clear to you what we think of you, we don't even care
to throw you into the water. That is the only border we have
besides the others already mentioned. It's all right with me
if you choose the water. We are at your service, mister. And
so you are going to Holland and like it. That's all. Be glad
you're getting off so easily. We have jails, and we have camps
for people without papers."

"But see here, gentlemen, you are all mistaken. I do not wish
to go to Holland, because the Dutch—"

"Quiet now. This question has been settled, for good. How
much money have you got?"

"Why, you searched me all over. How much money did
you find on me? That's how much money I've got."

"Which means, in other words, not a single cent. Is that
what you mean?" he asked.

"Exactly, y'honor. Right you are."

"Take him back to the cell," commanded the high priest.
"Let him have a bite to eat."

A bite. I would like to know when these people really eat.

4

Late the same afternoon I was taken to a railroad station.
Two men, one of them the interpreter, accompanied me. No
doubt they thought I had never before been on a train, for they
would not leave me alone. Not for a minute. One of them
bought the tickets while the other remained standing near me.
He took good care that no pickpocket should try to search
again where they had searched without success. I'd like to see
a smart pickpocket find a red cent in pockets that have been
searched by the police.

Very politely they escorted me aboard the train and offered
me a seat in a compartment. I thought the gentlemen would

now take leave. They did not. They sat down. Apparently afraid that I might fall out of the window when the train was moving, they seated themselves on either side of me. Belgian policemen are courteous. I could find no fault with them. They gave me cigarettes, but no matches. They were afraid I might set the train afire.

We came to a very small town and left the train. Again I was taken to a police-station. I had to sit down on a bench. The men who had brought me told a long story to the high priest in charge.

All the policemen stared at me as if they thought me a murderer who had not been properly hanged and had escaped. Suddenly I conceived the idea that I was to be hanged and that they were all only waiting for the hangman, who could not be found for the moment because he had gone off somewhere to a wedding. This idea, that I was to be hanged, impressed me more and more every minute. Had not the high priest in Antwerp said clearly that they wouldn't mind throwing me into the water? Why not hang me just as well? It's the easiest thing to do in a lonely spot.

There's nothing to laugh about; no, sir. It was a very serious matter indeed. Only consider, please: I had no papers; the high priest had not found in his thick book my photograph either. Things would have been different if he had found my photograph, because then he would immediately have known who I was, and that I was an honest sailor. Anybody could say that he had been left behind by the *Tuscaloosa*. Where are the proofs? I had signed on half an hour before the *Tuscaloosa* was leaving the port of New Orleans. The skipper had no time then to sign me on properly. I am sure he didn't even know my name. He never cared to know it. What was a plain deck-hand to him? He had other worries; he was not sure what his woman was doing when he was at sea. Therefore, even if somebody took the trouble to wire him, he would just answer: "I don't know the bum; hang him if you wish."

He was that kind. Better for him to ignore me altogether than to run up expenses for his company bringing me back home.

Y'see, sir, I had no proof of any sort as to my legal existence. I had no established home anywhere in the world. I was a member neither of a board of trade nor of a chamber of commerce. I wasn't the president of a bank. The truth is I had no bank-connections at all. I've never heard yet of a sailor with a savings-account. It's not the sailor's fault. It's the wages, which never allow him to meet all his expenses ashore.

I was just a nobody. You can't blame the Belgians if they don't want to feed a nobody. You see, the Belgians already have to feed so many nobodies who are only half Belgian, while the other half is French, English, Austrian, German, American, or Scotch, on account of the trouble they had with the war and the occupation of their country. I would have been only another reason for not paying us back the money they borrowed from us when they were in a hole.

So hanging me was the simplest thing to do, and the quickest. There was no one in the world who would worry about me. No one who cared. One bum more or less, what does it matter? There was even no necessity to put my name in the thick book in which all hanged people are written up.

Now they were waiting only for the hangman, because without the hangman it would have been plain murder, and illegal, and it would have been a blemish on as civilized a nation as the Belgians are.

I was right. They were waiting for the hangman. They made preparations. One of the flats came along and handed me two packages of cigarettes. The last gift to a condemned man. Then he gave me matches, seated himself near me, and started to talk English. He slapped me on the back, laughed, cajoled me, and tried to tell me an Irish joke, which, as he explained, he had studied in a book that was supposed to teach English in six weeks without a teacher.

"Don't take it so hard, old man," he said. "Smoke your ciga-

rettes and be happy. See, we all have to die some day. I was
spared in the war. But one day I too have to swallow dirt.
As for you, sailor, we have to wait until dark. We can't do
it in bright daylight very well."

Not take it so hard. I wonder if he ever was as close to
being hanged as I was then. Perhaps he was the kind that doesn't
take being hanged so hard. Maybe he was used to it. I was
not; no, sir.

The cigarettes had no taste at all. Straw and nothing else.
Damn it all, I don't want to be hanged. I looked around for a
chance to make a clean get-away. Nothing doing. They were
staring at me all the time. I was the first American sailor that
ever had come their way. An interesting circus animal to them.
How I hate these Belgians! I'd like to know why we ever helped
them out when they had their pants full.

When darkness had fallen, about nine, someone brought me
my last supper. Nasty people, these Belgians. So that's what
they call the last supper for a poor condemned man. I can
assure them I will never commit murder in Belgium. Potato
salad, three slices of liver-wurst, each slice as thin as paper.
Clever people, the Belgians, not cutting their fingers when
slicing liver-wurst for the last supper of a poor devil. There
were also a few slices of a bread that was neither really black
nor really white, and the inevitable margarine. Belgium has
no cows and therefore no butter. Why don't they come to
Wisconsin, where people throw butter into the fire to make
coffee boil quickly. What a supper! That's the gratitude of
these Belgians. And I was nearly wounded once when they
were down on their knees begging us for help.

The flat who had used up one hour and a half to tell me an
Irish joke now came up with a bottle.

"What are you, feller? A good American or a bad one?"
he asked.

I looked at the bottle in his hand, and I answered: "I am
a bad one, officer."

"Exactly what I thought," he laughed. "And since you are a bad one I am allowed to give you this bottle of red wine to wash down your supper with. If you had said you are a good American, I would have taken you to be a true believer in prohibition."

"Prohibition?" I said. "Shit prohibition. Let me have the bottle and I'll show you the real gargle of a real American sailor, a gargle such as, migud, you have never seen and never heard of in all your life."

"That's right, old feller. I thought so all along. Your prohibition. Don't make me laugh out loud. Fine men like you Americans letting yourselves be bossed round by hysterical church-sisters. Not us Belgians, sailor. With us Belgians it is still the man who wears the pants. And if we men like to get a good shot, we damn well drink it and care the devil about women and sin."

What a pity that a man like that is a cop! Why isn't he a sailor? And why doesn't he come to God's country? That's the kind of people we need back home. The Belgians are not so bad after all. I felt now rather glad that we loaned them our good money, even though there's no chance in the world of ever getting it back again. It pleased me a lot to see that our money helped to keep alive a spirit like this one. So our money was not altogether wasted.

About ten that night the cop who had made me feel at home with his bottle said to me: "It's time now, sailor. We have to step on it. Come along."

No use crying now: "I don't want to be hanged." It's fate. That's what it is. If the *Tuscaloosa* had waited only two hours more, this would never have happened. It seems I am not worth two hours. Well, let's go and get it over with.

Then something awakened within me. After all, I am not an animal that anybody can do with as he pleases. Where there's life there's hope. An old sailor's saying, and it has always been a good and truthful one.

I shook off the hands which were upon my shoulder, and I yelled: "I'm not going. I'll resist. I'm an American. I'm an American citizen. I'm going to complain to my ambassador and to my consul. I haven't done anything wrong."

Said the interpreter: "You are going to complain? You? And just who are you? You are no American. Prove it. Come, come, show us your passport. Or your sailor's card. We'll even be satisfied with a letter from your consul. See, we are generous. Even a letter from your skipper will do. You have no passport. In any civilized country he who has no passport is nobody. He does not exist for us or for anybody else. We can do whatever we want to. And that is exactly what we're going to do right now. If we want to, we can even hang you or shoot you or kill you like a louse. Just like that; chip, and off you are." He snipped his fingers and rubbed the nails of his thumbs one against the other. "Out with him," he commanded.

"And don't ever bring him back here," shouted the high priest from behind his desk, where he had been asleep during the past few hours. He had just been awakened by the row I made. "If any one of you," he addressed the two men taking me, "ever brings him back here, I will hang you instead of him. The least I shall do is to put you behind the bars for three years. Get him out now and execute him right in front of the station; what do I care?"

I said nothing more. The two flats were armed, and I was not.

We three left the town, and soon we arrived in open fields.

The night was pitch-black. It was a bad road we walked, rough, broken up. When we had gone about a mile and a half, we turned off the road and entered a narrow path crossing a meadow. For another mile we walked only across meadows.

Suddenly we came to a halt. I wonder if Belgian cops are mind-readers. Just when I was about to swing out and land one on the jaw, one of them grasped my right arm. "We are

here now. We will have to say good-by to each other; don't
mind the tears."

I had an ugly feeling in my throat now, when I knew the last
minute had arrived. All my life I had wanted so badly to live
in Australia and make good. Now my life was snatched away
from me. There were hundreds of things I had planned to
do some day. All over now. Too late. Terrible words: too
late.

I felt so dry that I would have liked to ask them for a bottle
of that fine stuff they used to prove that they still wore the
pants. But really, I thought, what does it matter whether my
throat's dry or not? What difference does it make whether I
go to hell with a drink or without one? I had always pictured
hangmen as morons, not the sort these two guys were. Anyway,
hanging for money and as a profession is a dirty business. I
don't know why people do it when there are so many other
jobs in the world just as interesting, as, for instance, being a
piano-player during the rehearsals of the Follies, or something
like that.

Never before in my life had I realized how beautiful life
really is.

"Oui, oui, mister. We have to say good-by," the interpreter
said again. "We have no doubt you may be a fine fellow and
a good sailor, but right now we have no use for you here in
Belgium."

For such a simple reason they hang a man in Belgium. What
people!

He raised his arm, apparently to throw the noose over my
neck and to strangle me first so as to make me entirely helpless, as I could see that they had not spent any money to erect
real gallows. I wasn't worth the gallows, because I had not
committed a murder, and so no newspaper was interested about
the way I was executed.

With his outstretched arm he pointed in a certain direction, and said: "Over there, just where my finger points, there is Holland. The Netherlands, you know. You have heard of the Netherlands, haven't you?"

"Yes, officer."

"You go right in the direction I am pointing out. See? I don't think you will meet a customs officer or patrol on the way. But if you should see someone hovering around, then take care not to be seen yourself. Keep out of his way and don't mind him at all. After going in this direction for about one hour you will come to a railroad track. Follow this track for a while in the same direction until you reach the depot. Hang around until dawn, but be careful. Avoid being seen. Early in the morning large groups of working-men will come to take the train to Rotterdam, where they work. You go then to the ticket-office and say: '*Rotterdam, derde klasse.*' Don't say one word more. There, take this money, five gulden."

He gave me five coins and then said: "Here is a bite to eat. Don't buy anything at the station. Your talk would betray you. Somebody might get suspicious and start to question you. Then everything would be lost and you'd be done for. Understand? Take this."

He handed me a couple of sandwiches wrapped up nicely, two packages of cigarettes, and a box of matches.

"You see, you don't have to buy anything. Here is everything you need. Soon you will be in Rotterdam. Don't talk to anybody. Pretend you're deaf."

I was overwhelmed with joy. Ordered to hang me, they helped me to make off and clear out. I am glad we helped them win the war. These Belgians are people who really deserved to be on our side during the war. I don't care if they never pay back the money we loaned them. I am paid in full, and whether others get their money or not certainly does not concern me any longer.

I jumped like a spring chicken and cried: "Thank you, thank

you ever so much, and if you should ever come to Cincinnati or some other place up there in Wisconsin, be sure and call me up. Thank you, boys."

"Don't make a fuss," he interrupted me; "one of those bone-heads over there might hear you yelling. And I tell you that would be no good for you, nor for us either. Now, listen carefully to what I have to tell you." He whispered, but he re-peated every word three or five times so as to impress me with the full meaning of his warning. "Don't you ever dare to come back to Belgium. I warn you, sailor. If we ever find you in our country again within the next hundred years, I swear we will lock you up for life, and ninety-nine years more. Life imprisonment. That's something, sailor, believe me. I have orders to warn you properly so that you can't say later you have not been warned. Because we don't know what to do with you. Bums and unemployed and other thieves we have aplenty. We don't need any more."

I didn't want to leave these Belgian officers with a bad im-pression about a stranded American sailor. So I said: "Maybe my consul could—"

"Hang your consul," he broke in. "Have you got a pass-port? You have not. Have you got a sailor's card? You have not. What could your consul, *your* consul, do with you with-out a sailor's card? He would kick you in the pants, and we should have you again to support at the state's expense. Don't try your consul. You have been warned properly—life impris-onment. So you'd better cut this consul business."

I shook hands with them again and again, and said: "You are right, gentlemen. I promise solemnly never again to set foot on Belgian soil."

"That's a good boy."

"Because," I added, "I am really happy to leave Belgium. I haven't got anything here. I suppose you are right, Holland is far better for me. I worked for a while in Pennsylvania. That's why I know I'll understand at least half of what the

Dutch say, while here among you Belgians I never know what's wanted of me."

"Don't talk so much nonsense," the interpreter said. "You'd better be going now. Be smart. Should you hear somebody popping up while on your way to the depot, you just lie down quietly until the danger has passed. Don't let them get you. Never forget the life imprisonment. We would make it tough for you, sailor, believe me. I mean well. Good-by."

They went like shadows.

I started off on my way to the depot.

5

Rotterdam is a beautiful city. If you have money. If you haven't any, you are better off in New Orleans. Besides, New Orleans is just as pretty, and more interesting.

I hadn't any money. So I found Rotterdam just a city like all others. To be sure, it is a great port. But there was no ship in dire need of a deck-hand or a plain sailor or an engineer. I would have taken the job of engineer at once if there had been an opening. The joke would have been on the ship as soon as she was out at sea. The skipper would not throw me overboard. That would be murder. Something in the line of painting or brass-polishing can always be found aboard, and you take it even if you have signed on as a second engineer. I would not have insisted on the pay for a second; no, sir.

I would have taken any job on any ship, from kitchen-boy to captain and everything between. As it happened, not even a skipper was missing.

In these European ports it is hard to get a ship. To get one that crosses over to the home country is impossible. Everybody wants to go across to God's own great country. I simply can't get it into my head what all these guys are looking for there.

They must have got the crazy idea that everybody lies on his back and needs only to open his mouth and in goes the roast turkey with cranberry sauce and all the trimmings; and no one has to work, everybody gets high wages just for doing nothing, sitting around watching baseball games.

What with hundreds of mugs hanging around waiting to take a job on a ship without pay, there was no chance for an honest, home-made sailor like me to get a bucket sailing home.

The Belgian cops had talked about my consul. Yes, why not? Why hadn't I thought of my consul before? My consul. The American consul. Good idea. Splendid. He, my consul, he clears scores of American ships. He makes out all kinds of papers for them. If there is any man who knows every American ship coming or going, it is he. He is asked to supply sailors when the skipper is short of hands. There are always guys who would rather stay in a wet country with low wages than live in a dry country with heaps of dollars a week. If you get the heaps of smackers, I mean.

The whole affair passed by quicker than the time it had taken me to get the idea about seeing His Holiness the American consul at all.

"You are American?"

"Yesser."

"Where is your sailor's identification card?"

"I have lost it, sir."

"Passport?"

"Nosser."

"Citizenship papers?"

"Never had any. Born in the country. Native state—"

"Never mind. Well, what do you want here?"

"I thought maybe, sir, I mean I was thinking, since you are my consul, that maybe you might—what I was going to say, you perhaps might do something to get me out, because, you see, sir, I am stranded, to make it short."

He grinned at me. Rather nasty. Strange that bureaucrats always grin at you in a nasty way when they want to thumb you down.

Still grinning, he said: "Your consul? My good man, let me tell you something: if you wish to address me as your consul, you will first of all have to prove that I am really your consul."

"I am American, sir. And you are the American consul."

"Right-o. I am the American consul. But who are you to tell me that you are American? Have you got any papers? Birth-certificate? Or passport? Or authorized sailor's identification?"

"I told you already that I lost it."

"Lost. Lost. Lost. What do you mean by lost? In times like these one does not lose such important papers. Ought to know that, my good man. You cannot even prove that you have been on the *Tuscaloosa*."

He pronounced "have" like *hauve* and "know" like *knouw*, trying to make us poor Middle West guys believe that he came from Oxford or Cambridge or I don't know what.

"Cawn you prove thawt you hauve been on the *Tuscaloosa*?"

"No."

"Then what do you want here? I might cable the *Tuscaloosa*, provided she has wireless. But who pays for the cable?"

"I thought you could do it."

"Sorry. I am not provided by the government with funds out of which I could pay for such cables. Did you sign on in New Orleans in the shipping offices of the company?"

"No, I did not. There was no time to do so, because the ship was already up and down when I came aboard, because two men had made up their minds to stay off."

The consul meditated for a few seconds. Then he said: "Suppose you could prove that you really shipped on the *Tuscaloosa;* that is no proof that you are an American citizen. Any

Hindu or even Hottentot may work on board an American merchant vessel if the mawster of the ship needs men and he is not in a position to get American sailors."

"But, sir, Mr. Consul, I am American, sure."

"That's what you say, my good man. That's what you've told me several times. But you have to prove it. With papers. That's a rule. I cawn't accept your declaration as sufficient evidence. By the way, how did you come from Antwerp to Rotterdam? And without papers? How did you cross the international lines without papers?"

"But, Mr. Consul, haven't I told you, the Belgian police—"

"Nuts. Don't try to pull my leg or I am through with you right here and now. The Belgian police! Who ever heard of such a thing—that officials, state authorities, would send a man without papers, without his consent, across the international border in the middle of the night? To whom do you think you are selling that yarn? Authorities committing unlawful smuggling of aliens into foreign countries? Pshaw! Tsey, tsey, tsey. Nonsense. Where did you pick up that story? Out of a magazine? Come clean, come, come."

While he was making this fine speech, he played with his pencil. When he had finished, he began to hum "My Old Kentucky Home," beating time with his pencil upon his elegant desk.

So I knew that no matter what he had said, his thoughts were somewhere else. Perhaps at a supper for two with a dame from Louisville.

I was extremely polite. Nevertheless, something inside me told me to take the inkstand and fire it right into the middle of his grinning plaster sponge. Yet I knew how an American has to behave in an American consul's office in a foreign country. Never forget it; as an American in a foreign country you are always representing your dignified homeland.

He looked at me with empty eyes for a long while. I was sure he was still at supper with his dame and was not quite sure if the time had now come to tell her why he had invited her to have supper with him so late at night, and in his apartment, too, and all alone.

I didn't want to wait until he had reached breakfast with that Kentucky dame, so I said: "Maybe, Mr. Consul, sir, there might be a chance to get me a ship making for home. A skipper may easily be short a man."

He came to, and snapped: "Eh? What did you—? No, no, of course not. There is no such possibility. An American ship without papers? Not from me, no, sir. Not from me."

"Then, where can I get papers, if not from you, sir?"

"Not my concern, old man. Did I take away your papers? I certainly did not. Any bum might step in here and ask me to provide him with legal papers. No, sir."

"Has it never happened, here in your office, sir, that people have come in to tell you that they have lost their papers or that their papers have been stolen?"

"Of course. Things like that do occur. But those people have money. They are not just bumming about the world like sailors, getting drunk and selling their papers to get the money to buy more booze."

"But I tell you, sir, I lost my papers. They are on the *Tuscaloosa*."

"Perhaps they are. Perhaps they are not. Even if you left them there as you say you did, how do you know a fellow-sailor of yours hasn't sold them? What do you say to that?"

"I don't think so."

"Now, of course, if you had money, we could cable to Washington. But since you have no money, I can do nothing. My salary is not so high that I can afford to pay for a cable for you worth perhaps fifty or sixty dollars."

"Won't you tell me what I can do?"

"Since you have no papers and no proof of your American citizenship, there is nothing I can do for you. I am only an official. I have to obey rules. It certainly is not my fault. I didn't make the law. By the way, have you had something to eat?"

"No, sir. I told you I have no money, and I haven't gone begging yet."

"Wait just a minute."

He rose from his chair and went into another room.

After a few minutes he came back and gave me a sort of ticket.

"With this ticket you will be provided for three full days with three meals each day and lodging. The address of the boarding-house is printed here. After this ticket has expired, if you are still without a berth, you may drop in here again for another one. You are welcome. Why don't you try some ship sailing under a different flag? There are a good many ships nowadays that are not so very particular as to papers. Some even go across to the Canadian coast. Of course, you understand I make no suggestions. Find out for yourself. My hands are bound in a case like yours. After all is said and done, I am nothing but a servant of the government. Really sorry, old man. Good-by and good luck!"

I was almost convinced that that man was right after all. Maybe he was not to blame. Why, he has no reason to be that way with me. I never saw him before. I never did him harm. Why should he harm me? He was only a servant of that soulless beast called the state. He had every answer ready for me before I spoke. They must have been part of his education, and they had to be memorized before he could pass the examinations for his diplomatic career.

However, when he asked me if I was hungry, he really forgot for a second or two that he was nothing but a servant of the state. Then he became quite human and showed that he still had some soul left. Nothing strange about that. To be hungry is human. To have papers or not to have papers is inhuman. It is against nature's laws. That's the point. There is a good reason for being the way he is. The state cannot make use of human beings. It would cease to exist. Human beings only make trouble. Men cut out of cardboard do not make trouble. Yesser. Excuse me, I mean: yes, sir.

6

Three days are not always three days. Some three days are very long, some very short. But no matter how short three days really are, the three days for which I had a meal ticket were over before I had had time to realize how short three days can be.

I had made up my mind that, regardless of how hungry I might feel, I would not go again to my consul. I thought it silly to listen to his memorized sermon once more. He would not provide me with a ship. So what was the use of giving him the pleasure of having a man sit in front of him listening with attention to his speech? There would be no change in his way of explaining how helpless he was and how sorry he felt for being unable to do something for me, except to give me another meal ticket—but this time with a sour look. No, before I would go again to see him, I would prefer to look for itching pockets.

I had another reason for not wanting to see him. His eyes, when he had asked me if I were hungry, had a look almost like my mother's used to have when she said: "Like that pie, Gerry? Have another cut."

This time he might tell me what my mother would never have said: "Sorry, but it is the last time. There are too many asking for help. You understand." No.

Oh, you forgotten goldfish, with the folks all off for a long vacation! Was I hungry? Bet your life I was. And tired. Migud, so tired from sleeping in gateways, in corners, in nooks. Always chased and hunted by policemen, striking matches or flashing their search-lights at me.

A civilized country means a country that sends to jail a man found asleep in the streets without evening clothes on. You have to have a house, or at least a room to sleep in. How you get it is of no concern to the police.

No ship in port short of hands. And if there was a ship that needed a man, fifty sailors, natives of the port, and all with excellent papers, came to apply for the job. A hundred jobless to one job. And none for a foreigner. Taking on a man whose papers were not in good shape, who was not in the country legally, was punishable with a big fine. It was punishable even with a prison sentence. It was the law that protected the jobless of their own country. If you don't belong to a country in these times, you had better jump into the sea. No other way out.

Each protects his own kind. Internationalism is just a word that sounds fine from a soap-box. Nobody ever means it; not the Bolshevists either. Stay with your own tribe. Or with your clan. The chiefs need you. If for some reason or other you cannot belong, you are an outcast. You cannot even stay with the dogs of the tribe. Any papers to identify you? No? Out you go and stay out; hell, we've got enough of your kind, get out of here. What's that? Don't let any more workers in. Keep wages up. What do I care if the workers of the other clan cannot even buy dry bread. That's why we call ourselves Christians—because we love our neighbors dearly; so let them go to hell or heaven, wherever they want to, so long as they don't try to eat their daily bread with us. We haven't got enough for ourselves; that's why we have to burn it to raise prices. When you are hungry, and chased when you want to sleep, you easily fall for the wrong religion.

So it happened.

A dame and a gent were standing in front of a shop-window. Said the lady: "Look, Fibby, how lovely these kerchiefs are!"

Fibby, apparently knowing nothing about kerchiefs and thinking about lunch, mumbled something that could be taken for an affirmation or for something concerning the stock-market.

The lady again: "No, bless me, I've never seen anything so cute and so lovely. Must be old Dutch peasant art."

"Yep. Right you are," Fibby said, entirely uninterested. "Genuine. Genuine old Dutch. But, in old English, it's probably copyright nineteen hundred and twenty-two."

"Aw," said the fine lady, "zatso? Let me tell you something."

I didn't wait to hear her tell him something, for now I was convinced that it was Forty-second or Times Square or Park Row. And it was music to me.

I went about the job rapidly and very cunningly. That's what I thought. But Fibby knew all the tricks. He must have been in the trade before he got into magazines. So we had a lively argument, and the lady, bored to death all day long, liked it immensely.

Fibby got interested in the story far more than did his wife, or his lady friend, or his—well, what do I care what she means to him—they've got their passport in fine shape and are unmolested sharing a double stateroom. As I was saying, Fibby got interested in my story far more than his wife or his lady friend—oh, hell, what do I care?—well, more than his lady could make him interested in old Dutch shawls.

He seemed to have a great time listening in to my story. He smiled, then he laughed, then he roared with laughter. People passing by thought another couple of Americans had gone crazy about nothing at all, as they usually do. He found no other expression to comment on my story with but "Zat so! Zat so? Gee, zat so? Man, zat so!"

There may be stories that have no end, but mine had one. When I had finished, he was still roaring and bellowing.

"The greatest comedy in all of this lousy Europe couldn't have made me laugh like you did. Oh, boy; oh, boy! What a story! A whale of a story. That's what I've been looking for.

What I came over for. Man, you don't know what you mean to me."

On he went, laughing and laughing.

And I, ass that I was, I had thought he would weep about my sad tale and my hopeless fate. Of course, he only had to listen to it, not live it. He saw only the humor of it; he wasn't hungry, and he had an elegant room in a swell hotel where no policeman would ever kick him in the ribs.

"Listen, Flory," he said to his lady friend. "What do you think about the story that boy just told us? Isn't that story great? A birdy dropped out of its little nest. And says he was hungry. Imagine, Flory, here in Holland, where they throw cheese and butter in the ash-cans, and where the people have so much spare time that they haven't got anything else to do but grow flowers instead of cotton or wheat. What a country!"

"Oh, his story is wonderful! It's marvelous. It's peachy. I think it's the greatest, cutest little story I have ever heard." That's what Flory, the lady friend, said. She went on: "Wonderful. Just too wonderful for words. Where are you from? From New Orleans? My, my! What a town! Still French and Blackies there? Why, isn't that interesting? It's really thrilling. Why, Fibby, did I ever tell you I still have an aunt living there, down in Dixie, in New Orleans, I mean? Have I ever told you about Aunt Sophronia of New Orleans? Haven't I? Oh, I must tell you all about her. You know, the one that starts every sentence with: 'When gran'pa, the colonel, you know—was still living in South Carolina.'"

Fibby didn't listen to Flory. He had become accustomed to putting down the phone any time she called him up and letting her talk until he was sure it was time to hang up or to say: "Yes, honey, I am listening."

He fumbled about his pockets and fished out a bill. He gave it to me and said: "Here, take this. It's not only for your story, but for your having told it so splendidly. It's a great gift, my boy, to tell a story the way you did, a story that is not true, but that sounds true. That's the point in story-telling. Making people believe the story is true. You are a great artist, you know. I feel it. A pity that you are bumming your way through the world. But some people, I think, have to do it this way. Can't help it. You know, my boy, you could make quite a pile of dough, the way you tell stories. You are an artist." He turned round to Flory: "Isn't he an artist, sugar?"

"He is a great artist," the lady friend admitted, happy that she could say something again after such a long silence. "He is a great artist. Why, I feel sure he is the greatest artist I have ever seen. Listen, Fibby, won't you ask him for dinner? Dear me, we would show those Penningtons something worth while. Calling themselves The Penningtons. Upstarts. The! I could just scream out loud. The! What were they anyway, only five years ago? The! I'm just waiting for the day when they say the word *Mayflower*. I'm only waiting for that day."

They are married. With a license, wedding march, church bells, and everything.

Fibby paid not the slightest attention to the onrush of Flory's eloquence. He kept on smiling and then again fell into heavy laughter. Once more he fished in his pocket and produced another bill.

He handed this one also to me, and now he said: "Get that, my boy; one is for having told your story so very well; the other one is for having given me a most excellent idea for my money-making machinery; I mean my paper. You see, it's like this: in your hands your story is worth just one dime. In my hands your story is worth in the neighborhood of five grand cold cash. I am paying you your dime with full interest. I am honest, you see; I do not steal plots, I pay what they are worth to the owner. Many thanks for your trouble. See me again some time. You may look me up in New York. Well, so long. Good-by and good luck. It was a real pleasure."

That was the first cash I ever received for telling a story. Yes, sir.

I went to a money exchange. I reckoned this way: for one dollar I'll get about two and a half gulden Dutch, so for two bucks I'll get five gulden. Welcome, little smackers; I haven't met you for a long time. I threw my two bills upon the counter. The man picked them up, looked at them quickly, and then began to pay me out gulden one after another. When I had five I wanted to leave, but the man said: "Wait a minute; won't you take all with you?" So I stayed and let him pay and pay as long as he liked. What did I care? When he had finished, he said: "This makes it exactly twenty Americans." Was I surprised! Fibby, may Wall Street bless his bank-account, had given me two tenners, and I had thought it was only two ones. I hope he makes a pile of money with the story I told him. He is a swell guy. Of course, he is from New York. People having New York for their home town are that way, not like the misers from Iowa.

It looked to me like quite a good bit of dough. But somehow, before I could realize what a good feeling it is to have some cash, it was gone. Only those people who have lots of money learn to appreciate the real value of money, because they have time to find out. On the other hand, how can people who have no money, or very little, ever find out what money really means? It is in their hands so short a time that they have no chance to see what it means. Certain people, however, preach that only the poor know the worth of a cent. This difference in opinion is the cause of class distinction.

7

Far sooner than I had expected came the morning which I knew to be the last one in a long time that would find me in a bed. I began already to hear the footsteps of policemen and night-watchmen.

I searched my pockets and found just enough coin to make possible a hasty breakfast. Hasty breakfasts are not at all to my liking, because they are but invitations to lunches and dinners that never come. Meeting a Fibby is not an everyday occurrence. Suppose I should have the good fortune to meet one again: I shall tell the same story, but this time I'll make it funny. It may just happen that the gent I tell the story to in a way befitting a musical comedy will receive it weeping bitterly and will get an idea contrary to Fibby's. And if this bird happens to have a magazine for railroad men and gas-station operators and girl stenos, he might easily be willing to spring another twenty bucks. Money can always be squeezed out of an idea, regardless of whether it makes some-body laugh or somebody else cry. In this world there are just as many people who like to weep and will pay two dollars for that pleasure as there are people who will pay for having lots of fun. Usually it costs more money to see a bad tragedy than to see a good comedy. People are like that, and nothing can be done about it. Anyway, I like people who prefer a good time better than—

A good time! What's the matter now? Can't a guy have his beauty nap for the last gulden he paid for a bed? I'd like to know where the next bed will come from.

"Leave me in peace, damn it all. Yes, I paid for my bed last night when I went upstairs. Yes, I paid for it all right, so let me sleep. I am tired."

The knocking and banging against my door, however, does not cease.

"Goldfish in shit, leave me alone. I want to sleep. You heard me. Get out of here. Get away from that door or I'll sock you." I wish that bum would only open the door so that I could fire my shoe into his face. So they call the Dutch a quiet people!

"Open that door"; again the voice at my door. "Open! Police. We want to speak to you for a minute."

"All right, all right. Coming." I begin to doubt that there
are some people still left on this earth who are not policemen
or who have no connection with the force. The police are
supposed to maintain quiet and order, yet nobody in the whole
world causes more trouble and is a greater nuisance than the
police. Chasing criminals, and thereby killing innocent women.
Keeping order, and throwing a whole town in the middle of
the night into an uproar. Nobody drives more people crazy
than the police. And just think, soldiers are also a police force,
only with another name. Ask me where all the trouble in the
world comes from.

"Hey you, what do you want of me? I'm not wanted anywhere."

"We only wish to ask you a few questions."

"Go ahead. I'm listening."

"You'd better open that door. We want to see you."

"Nothing interesting about my face. I've never been on the
screen."

"Come, come, or we shall have to break in the door."

Break in the door. And these are the mugs paid by the tax-
payer to protect him against burglars. Break in the door. All
right. No getting away. So I open the door. Immediately one
of the guys sticks his foot in so the door can't be closed again.
The old trick of the master. It seems to be the first trick a
cop has to learn on joining the force.

Two men. Plain-clothes men.

I am sitting on the edge of my bed and start to get dressed.

"Are you American?"

"Yip. Any objection in Holland?"

"May we see your sailor's card?"

It seems to me the sailor's card, and not the sun, is the
center of the universe. I am positive the great war was fought,
not for democracy or justice, but for no other reason than that
a cop, or an immigration officer, may have the legal right to
ask you, and be well paid for asking you, to show him your

sailor's card, or what have you. Before the war nobody asked
you for a passport. And were the people happy? Wars for
liberty and independence are to be suspected most of all,
ever since the Prussians fought their war for liberty against
Napoleon. All peoples lost their freedom when that war was
won, because all liberty went to that war and has been there
ever since. Yes, sir.

"I haven't got a sailor's card."

"Wha-a-a-t? You ha-a-a-ave no sailor's card?"

The tune of this long-drawn-out question reminded me of
the question with which I had been bothered not long before,
and exactly at the same time—when I wanted to sleep.

"No, I ha-a-a-ave no sailor's card."

"Then you have a passport."

"No service, gentlemen. Gas-pump out of commission."

"No passport?"

"No passport."

They looked at each other, nodded, and felt well satisfied
with the work they had done so far.

"I suppose you have no identification card from our police
authorities either?"

"You hit it, gentlemen. I have not."

"Do you not know, mister, that no alien is permitted to live
in Holland without proper identification papers viséd by our
authorities?"

"How should I know?"

"Do you mean to say that you have been living on a mountain on the moon?"

Both cops consider this so good a joke that they laugh and
laugh until they cough.

"Get dressed and come along with us. The chief wants to
see you."

I wonder if the Dutch hang a guy without papers or just
kick him in the buttocks and take him to the chain-gang.

"Has any of you gentlemen a cigarette?"

"You may have a cigar if you like. We don't smoke cigarettes around here. We are men, and mean to stay men. But if you wish, we'll buy you a package of cigarettes on our way to the station."

"All right with me. Shoot the cigar."

I smoke the cigar, which is rather good, while I wash and dress. The two cops sit close by the door and follow everything I do like dogs.

I am in no hurry. Anyway, regardless of how much time I take to get ready, there is finally nothing else to do but shove off.

Upon coming to the police-station I was searched. This was done with all the cunning they had. Tearing open even seams. Still thinking of spies, I thought. But later it dawned upon me that they were looking, whenever they caught a sailor, for Bolshevik ideas rather than for photographs of fortresses or warships.

They had more luck than their brethren in Antwerp. They found some twenty-eight cents in Dutch money, with which I wanted to buy a hurried breakfast.

"Is that all the money you have?"

"As you haven't found any more in my pockets, it must be all."

"What money did you live on while here in Rotterdam?"

"On the money I no longer have."

"Then you did have money when you came here?"

"Yep."

"How much?"

"I don't remember right now how much, but it must have been in the neighborhood of a couple of thousand dollars or so."

"Where did you spend it?"

"With the dames. Where else could I?"

"Where did you get the money you had when you came here?"

"I had taken it out of my savings-account."

The whole outfit roared with laughter. Somehow, they took good care to watch the high priest before they started to laugh. When they saw that he was laughing, they also laughed. As soon as he became serious again, they did exactly the same. It couldn't have been any better done if it had been commanded by a movie-director in Hollywood.

"How did you come into Holland? I mean without a passport? How did you pass the immigration and so?"

"Oh, that? Oh, well, I just came in, that's all there is to it."

"Exactly. That is what we want to know. How did you come in?"

"How can a fellow come in? I came on a ship."

"What ship?"

"Oh, you mean the ship? Well, she was—it was—sure, it was the—the—yes, it was the *George Washington*."

"So? On the *George Washington*?"

"Yes, sir."

"Sure? You are sure of that?"

"Bless my grandmother's soul."

"When?"

"Oh, you mean when? Well, I don't quite remember the exact day. Musta been six or nine weeks ago or so."

"And you came on the *George Washington*?"

"Yes, sir."

"A rather mysterious ship, your *George Washington*. As far as I know, the *George Washington* has never yet come to Rotterdam."

"That's not my fault, officer. I am not responsible for the ship."

"That's all right. And so you have no passport? No sailor's card? No sort of paper to show who you are? Nothing to identify you? Absolutely and definitely nothing? Nothing at all to show that you are an American?"

"Evidently not, sir. What can I do about it? Certainly, my consul—"

"As you have no papers and no proof, what do you expect your consul to do?"

"I don't know. That's his business, not mine. I have never been a consul, to know what a consul's duty is in a case like mine. Sure, he will furnish me with papers."

˙ "Your consul? The American consul? An American consul? To a sailor? To, maybe, a communist? Not in this century, my boy. And most likely not during the next either. Not without papers. Not unless you are, let us say, a member of the New York stock-exchange or the first president of the Missouri Railroad. Never to a bum like you."

If I had a million dollars, I would give half of it—well, one tenth of it—to know where this chief of police got such a fine understanding of God's great country. He cannot have collected his wisdom in Rotterdam.

"But I am American."

"Why not? Fine. You see, it's like this. Suppose we take you to your consul. As you have no papers he will not recognize you. So he will, officially, hand you over to us. Then we have no way ever to get rid of you. I hope you understand? Do you?"

"I think so, sir."

"So what could we do with you? The law is that anybody picked up without papers must be imprisoned for six months. When he comes out, he is deported to his native country. Your native country cannot be determined, since your consul does not accept you as a citizen. Then we have to keep you here with us, whether we like it or not. We cannot shoot you like a dog with a disease, or drown you in the sea, although I am not so sure but that sooner or later such a law will be passed in every country, above all in every civilized country. Why should we, having two hundred thousand unemployed, feed an alien who has no money? Now, listen, do you want to go to Germany?"

"I do not like the Germans."

"Neither do I. All right, then, Germany is out. Well, my man, this will be all for the morning."

What a man! He was a thinker. I wonder where the Dutch get people like that for their cops. Back home he would have the capacity of solving problems of national economy, or be dean of Princeton. That's the difference between those European countries and ours.

He called a cop to his desk and said: "Take him to his cell. Fetch him breakfast. Buy him a few English magazines and newspapers and get him cigarettes. Make him feel at home."

Feel at home with this sort of curtain at the window! All right, let's have breakfast first and do the thinking later.

8

Early in the evening I was taken in again to the chief of police. He ordered me to go with two plain-clothes men, who would take care of me.

We went to the depot, boarded a train, and left for the country. We came to a small town where I was taken to the police-station.

It was about ten o'clock when the two men in charge of my future said: "It's time now. Let's get going."

Across plowed fields and swampy meadows we went, or, rather, staggered. I was not sure that this was not another road to execution. I should have inquired, while I was still a free man, if in Holland the noose is in vogue, or the hatchet, or the guillotine, or the chair, or just choking a man to death with bare hands. Now it worried me not to know how the

Dutch would do it. Then again I thought that maybe the Dutch have the same system of doing away with sailors without passports that the Belgians have.

They have.

We came suddenly to a halt and one of the two cops said in a low voice: "You go right on in that direction there. You won't meet anybody now. It's not their time. If, however, you see somebody coming, get out of the way or lie down until he has passed. After a mile or less of walking you will come to a railroad track. Follow this track in that direction, the one I am indicating here, look. You will come to the depot. Wait until morning. Be careful you're not seen by anybody, or it will be too bad for you. As soon as you see a train ready to leave, you step up to the window where they sell tickets, and you say: '*Une troisième à Anvers.*' You can remember those words, can't you?"

"Easy as pie. I know it's Spanish."

"It isn't Spanish at all. But never mind. It's good French."

"Doesn't sound like the language we have in New Orleans."

"Quiet, now. You will do what I tell you or land in jail for six months. Don't answer any questions anybody might ask you. Just play deaf. You will get your ticket all right, and after a certain time you will come to Antwerp. Antwerp is a great port. Hundreds of ships there all the time. They are always badly in need of sailors. You will get a ship before you even have time to ask for it. Here is a mouthful to eat, and also cigarettes. Do not buy anything before you are safe in Antwerp. Understand. Here, take thirty Belgian francs. It will do for all you need."

He handed me three packages of cigarettes, a few sandwiches wrapped up, and a box of matches.

"Don't you ever dare return to Holland. You surely will get six months of hard labor, and then afterwards the workhouse for vagrancy. I will see to it that you won't miss it. Well, shove off, and good luck."

Good luck! There I was in the middle of the night, left alone in a foreign country.

The two cops disappeared.

I strolled along. After a while I stopped to think it over.

Belgium? In Belgium, I had been told by their police, I would get life if they caught me again. On the other hand, in Holland the worst that awaited me was six months, and after that the workhouse for sailors without identification cards. It may be that the workhouse in Holland would be for life. There is no reason why Holland should make it cheaper than her neighbor Belgium does.

After long thinking I made up my mind that, all circumstances considered, Holland was cheaper. Besides, the food was better. Above all, the Dutch speak a human language, most of which I can understand almost as well as the lingo on the road in Pennsylvania.

So I went, first, off the direction, and then I turned back into clean Holland.

Everything went fine.

So I was on my way to Rotterdam again. I couldn't go to the depot to take a train. The two cops who had brought me to the border might take the same train back.

I tried hitch-hiking. I don't know if any American stranded in Europe ever tried the game there. It is different from what it is on the Golden Highway or the Lincoln Highway.

The first idea I got about how it is done was when I met a milk-wagon going to town. It was drawn by two mighty horses of the kind the breweries of St. Louis used to have in the good old days.

"Hop on," the driver said. "So, you are a sailor? I have an uncle over in America. If you meet him, just tell him that four years ago we lost a cow; she fell in the canal and was drowned. He will remember the cow; she was sort of checkered. Welcome. I hope you have a pleasant trip home."

Then I met another peasant who had hogs on his wagon.

He gave me a lift and was friendly. It took me all day long to reach Rotterdam, but I saw quite a bit of the country. I told everybody who gave me a ride all about myself and all that had happened. None of them minded. No one said: "What are you doing here in our country? Why haven't you got any papers? Out with all aliens."

It was the other way round. I was invited here and I was invited there, to have a bite or a cup of coffee or a shot of gin. I got from this man two cents, from that woman three cents, and from another man one cent to help me along. They were not rich, but plain peasants. But they had a heart, every one of them. They all hated the police, and they cursed whenever I told what they had done to me.

I would give a second tenth of my million to find out who it is, in reality, that makes the laws about passports and immigration. I have not so far found an ordinary human being who would say anything in favor of that kind of messing up of people's private affairs. It seems to me governments have to mess up things to create new jobs for officials and to produce evidence of their god-given right to collect more taxes.

9

Thirty francs, no matter how you get them, don't last very long. Money always goes sooner than you expect it will. The same with really fine people.

Hanging around the docks one day, I saw two guys walking along and caught a few words of their conversation. There is something queer about languages. The English say that we can't speak English, while we say that what the English talk is a sort of ancient Scotch, because no serious-minded person can ever guess what they mean when they start talking about races or movies or, worse, politics. That's why the first English settlers couldn't get along as well with the Indians as we can, because the Indians are hundred-per-centers, and the English are not.

But whatever language the limeys talk, I am not crazy about them. They don't like us, either, and never did. It's been going on now for more than a hundred and fifty years—ever since the tea-party that had no bridge-partners. The war made things worse.

You come into a port where the limeys are thick, and they shout as though they owned the world. Maybe in Australia, or in China, or along the coast of the Indian Sea. You step into a tavern like a good and decent sailor who is ashore for a couple of hours and wants to wash down the salt from his throat.

You don't have to say who you are. You just step across to the bar and you say: "Hello, pal, gimme a shot. No, straight. Make it two."

That's all you need to say, and hell is let loose.

"Hey you, Yank. Who won the war?"

Now, as a decent sailor, what can you say to that? What has that to do with me? I didn't win the war. Of that I am sure. Those who say they won it would rather that nobody reminded them of it, true or not true.

Again: "Hey, Yank, you're a smart sailor. Tell the world who won the war!"

What do I care? I am drinking my hard washer, and ask for another, straight. Mother told me long ago not to meddle with boys who are not honest and who seek only trouble.

Now there are about two dozen of the limeys. Grinning and laughing. I am alone. I don't know where the other fellows from my can are right now. Not very likely to drop in here, anyhow.

"Make this one a doubler. Mother's son is thirsty."

"Hey, submarine admiral, Nancy of the gobs. Tell us real sailors who won the war."

I do not even look at the drunks. I punish them with my

profound disrespect. But they cannot leave a guy in peace, especially since I am all alone. I don't even know if the barman will keep neutral. I guess I shall have to say something. The honor of my country is at stake. No matter what it may cost me.

Now what can I say? If I say: "We," there will be roaring laughter and a big fight. If I say: "The Frenchies," there will be a fight. If I say: "I won it," there will be a fight, and most likely the jail afterwards and then the hospital. If I say: "The Canadians, the Australians, the Africans, and the New Zealanders," there will be a fight. If I stay on saying nothing, it will be taken to mean: "We Americans won it," which, I know, will surely result in the biggest fight. I could say: "You English, you won the war." This would be a lie, and that reminds me again of my mother, who told me a thousand times never to tell a lie, and always to think of the cherry-tree that was responsible for a president. So what else can be done about it? There is a fight on. That's the way they treat the fine guys whom they called, when they needed them badly, "our cousins across the sea." Not my cousins; no, siree.

So that's why I am not so crazy about the limeys. But whether I liked them or despised them made no difference now. I had to be friendly, for they were all I had to rely on.

"What bucket are you from, chaps?"

"Hello, Yankey, what're you doing here?"

"I was mixed up with a jane who had a sick mother. Had to take her to the hospital myself. So I was skipped, see?"

"Now it is too hot here for you, isn't it? Polishing anchor-chains, hey?"

"You said it. How about stowing with you?"

"It might be done. Always a free hand for a sailor feller."

"Where are you making for?" I asked.

"Lisbon and old Malta, and then Egypt. Can't take ye that far, but welcome to Boulogne. From there on, you have to look out for your own future."

"Boulogne will be okay with me."

"See, the bos'n we have is a bloody devil, he is. If it were not for him, we could take you round the world sightseeing. Now, tell ye what we'll do for you. You come round about eight at night. Then the bos'n will be so filled up he'll be kicking over the rim. Doesn't see anything and doesn't hear anything. Now, you just come up. We'll wait for you at the railing. Just look at me. If I tip my cap over onto my neck, everything is shipshape and you just hop on. But if anybody finds you aboard, don't ever say who heaved you up. Sailor's word."

"Understand. I'll be there at eight."

I was there. The cap was cocked onto his neck. The bos'n was so well drenched that it lasted until Boulogne. There I got off, and that's how I came to France.

I changed my money for French coin. Then I went to the depot. I bought a ticket to the first station on the way to Paris. The Paris Express. I boarded it.

The French are very polite gents. No one molested me to show my ticket.

The train pulled in at what they call a *gare*, which means their depot. So I came to Paris, which is supposed to be the paradise for Americans who have become sick of God's country.

Now the tickets were asked for.

The police are quick in Paris. Since I had no ticket for Paris, and I had ridden all the way down from Boulogne on a very soft seat unmolested by anybody, I had become a case for the Paris criminal investigation police department, or something that sounded as high-falutin' as that.

I knew a few words of French, and I hoped that this would save me, but these cops knew more about the English language than I shall ever be able to pick up. They must have had better teachers than we usually have.

Where did I come from? Boulogne. How did I come to

Boulogne? On a ship. What ship? The *Abraham Lincoln*. No *Abraham Lincoln* lately in Boulogne. Where is my sailor's card? Haven't got any.

"You mean to say you have no—"

"No, I have no sailor's card."

I had become so used to that question that I would understand it even in Hindustani, whatever that may be. The tune of the words, and the gestures, and the lifted eyebrows that always accompany the question are so unmistakably alike among all the bureaucrats and policemen of the world that there never can be any doubt about what is asked.

"And I have no passport either. Nor have I an identification card of the French authorities. No immigration stamp. No customs-house seal. I have no papers at all. Never in all my life did I ever have any papers."

I rattled off all this to spare them the work of questioning me for an hour. I could easily pass the toughest examination for immigration officers, because I have had the best schooling any guy ever can have.

The chief, who had wanted to spend an easy hour or two with me, became confused. He looked at me with dying eyes. He seemed to feel that I had taken from him all his upholstered authority. He pushed around some papers lying on his desk to find a few questions for me. After a while, trying to compose himself, he gave up for the day.

Next day there was a hearing, of which I did not grasp a single word, since everyone spoke in French. When it was all over, somebody tried his best to explain to me that I had got ten days in prison for cheating the French railroad out of the money for a ticket to Paris. I learned later that in France one might get for such an offense as much as two years, but someone in court had said that I was too dumb to understand the French law and it would be an injustice to load two years on me.

That was the welcome the French gave a good American who had been willing to help them win democracy.

I have never been in prison back home. When home I am very decent and dull, just like all the home folks. When living among baboons, do as the baboons do. Life is easier that way, and you may find a dame who thinks you are a great guy—in fact, the greatest guy on earth. But in foreign countries everything is different, and so am I. That's why travel is educating. You never get educated staying home, because you stay dumb like the rest. If you show only a bit of intelligence above the average, everybody says you must be a crank, or something else must be wrong with you, or else you would not act the way you do and upset everything. Back home in Sconsin I would never have told a good story. Everybody would have said that I was silly, and I'd better buy the gas-station Mr. Jorgson is offering for sale. So I do not know how prison life is at home.

In Paris it was this way:

First day: Registration. Bath. Health examination. Bed-clothes obtained. A book from the prison library. Cell assigned. Take possession of cell. First day gone.

Second day: The money they found on me was handed over to the treasurer of the prison. I had to make several statements as to whether it was my money, whether any of it was missing, whether the coins were exactly the same as far as I could remember. All this was written in three thick books. Also information was asked as to other valuables found on my person, of which there were none, and which I had to testify to several times, signing my name about two dozen times in as many books and on as many blanks. Afternoon: Called for by the minister of the prison. Sort of Protestant or Calvinist. He spoke good English. It must have been the English William the Conqueror spoke before he landed on the coast of old England. I did not understand one word of his English. I was in France, therefore I was more courteous than at home, where one is thought silly when courteous; so I did not let the minister feel that I did not understand what he was talking about. Whenever he mentioned God, I thought he was talking about a goat. That was the way he pronounced it. Not my fault. So the second day came to an end.

Third day: In the morning I was asked by about fifteen different officers if I had ever in my life sewn strings on aprons. I said that I had not, and that I had not the slightest idea as to how it is done. Afternoon: I am called for by eight or nine prison officials who inform me that I have been assigned to the sewing department to sew on apron-strings. I have to sign my name on dozens of blanks, which takes all the afternoon.

Fourth day: I have to appear in the store, where I receive a pair of scissors, one needle, about five yards of thread, and a thimble. The thimble did not fit any of my fingers. I complained, but I was told to be quiet; they had no other thimble to satisfy my peculiarities. I had to sign my name in books several times. Each time, before signing my name, I was asked if I had the needle, and if the needle was still good, or if I thought it looked as though it had a dull point. Afternoon: I was shown how to set up in the middle of my cell a little bench in such a way that it would be seen from the peep-hole in the door. On this bench I had to lay out in open view the scissors, the needle, the thread, and the thimble. These things were not laid out any old way. They had to be arranged in a special manner, which took me all afternoon to learn, because every time I thought it was right, the officer told me it was wrong and I had to do it all over again until he was satisfied. But he added that there was still something lacking in accuracy. Outside my door a cardboard sign was put above the peep-hole, which stated that the resident of the cell had scissors, a needle, a thread, and a thimble. When this sign had been put on my door, the fourth day was gone.

Fifth day: Sunday. Something said about good behavior, and the Lord will do all the rest.

Sixth day: In the morning I am taken to the shop in which I have to work. Afternoon: I am given a place to sit and to work. Sixth day gone.

Seventh day: In the morning a prisoner is introduced to me as the professor who is going to teach me how to sew on apron-strings. Afternoon: The prof shows me how to use the needle, and how to get in the thread without biting up too much of it. Seventh day gone.

Eighth day: The prisoner in charge of my education shows me how he himself sews on apron-strings. Afternoon: Bathing and weighing. I am asked if I have any complaints as to treatment or food. I tell them that I am used to better food and a better sort of coffee. No one takes any notice of my complaints; they only say it is all right, they cannot grow a special coffee for me. The eighth day is gone.

Ninth day: During the morning I am sent for to see the chief warden. He asks my name, and wants to know if I am the guy whose name I said was mine. I answered: "Yes, sir." Then he asks me if I have any complaints. I tell him that I am not much satisfied with the food and the coffee. He says: "The French law is the best law in the world, and there is no country more civilized than France." I have to sign my name in two books. Afternoon: I am shown how to sew on apron-strings. The ninth day gone.

Tenth day: During the morning I sew on one apron-string. The guy who teaches me how to do it examines the string it took me an hour and a half, perhaps two hours to sew on. Then he says that it is not sewn as well as he had thought I would do it, and that he feels sorry that he has no other remedy but to cut off the string and have me do it all over again. Afternoon: When I am half-way through sewing on the string again, I am called to the chief warden, who tells me that tomorrow morning my time is up. Then he says that he is sorry that I have to leave, but it is the law; he has been satisfied with my good behavior, and I have been an example to other prisoners.

After this is over, I am weighed and examined by the doctor, who asks me if I am all right. Then I am called to the receiving hall, where I have to return the prison garment. For a while I have to wait in an open cell without anything on but a towel. Then I have to go to a desk where I am handed my civilian clothes. I am asked if anything is missing. I say: "No, sir." Then I am allowed to dress in my own clothes. The tenth day is over.

I am called the next morning very early and asked if I wish to have breakfast here or if I want to get out in a hurry. I say that I would prefer to have breakfast in town. So everything is hurried up, and I don't have to wait until breakfast-time. I am taken to the treasurer, who returns my money. He asks if the amount is correct. I have to sign my name in three books. Then I am notified that I have earned fifteen centimes while working here. These fifteen centimes are paid out, and I have to sign my name again in three or four books. I am asked again if I have any complaints. I say: "No, sir, thank you, mercy beaucoup," which means the same. I am now discharged, and taken to the gate, where another warden looks me over, reads some papers, and then opens the gate and says: "Marshey," which means in French: "Scram!"

I do not think that the French government made much money out of me. And there is still a question whether the French railroad will be convinced now that my ticket was paid for by sending me up.

When I had gone hardly twenty feet, two policemen met me and said that they had waited for me only to tell me that I had to leave France within exactly fifteen days by the same road I had come in, and if I am still found in France after the fifteen days have expired, the law will take care of me and not with very soft gloves; so the best thing for me to do would be to leave even before the last of the fifteen days. They did not tell me how the law would take care of me. Perhaps by shipping me to their Devil's Island and keeping me there until death do us part. Every age has its Inquisition. Our age has the passport to make up for the tortures of mediæval times. And unemployment.

"You ought to have some papers to show who you are," the police officer advised me.

"I do not need any paper; I know who I am," I said.

"Maybe so. Other people are also interested in knowing who you are. Of course, I can get you the prison release paper. Somehow, I think it would not do you much good. I have no authority to furnish you with any other paper."

"But you have authority to put me in jail, haven't you?"

"That is my duty. That is what I am paid for. What did you say? I do not understand you. Now you may go. I have warned you officially that you have to be out of the country within fifteen days. How you manage it is not my business. You came in some way; you may go out the same way. If you are still here, then I shall find you, be sure of that. Why don't you go to Germany? A big country, and a very fine country at that. Try the Germans; they like fellows like you. Well, good luck! I hope never to see you again."

There must be something wrong somewhere, that the police of all the countries I have been in want to ship me off to Germany. The reason may be that everybody wants to help the Germans pay off the reparations, or everybody seems to think that Germany is the freest country in Europe. How can that be, with a socialist president who is more nationalistic than old man Bismarck ever was?

10

I stayed in Paris for several days. Just to see what would happen. Unexpected happenings often help you more and push you further ahead than plans worked out carefully. I now had a right to walk the streets and boulevards of Paris. My railroad ticket had been paid for, so I did not owe the French nation a cent, and I was entitled to make use of their sidewalks and their street illuminations. I have to admit that I did not see for a moment the American paradise that I had been sure I would find at every corner and in each nook.

I felt bored, and I did not know what to do, where to go, or how to entertain myself. So I hit upon the idea that the cheapest way to have fun would be to see my consul. I had a desire to find out if he had passed a different examination for his diplomatic career than had his brother in office in Rotterdam. I thought I might take up studying the representatives of our diplomatic service overseas. I had seen so many American consuls in the movies and in musical comedies like *Madame Butterfly*. Having a rare opportunity to do so, I thought it might be a good idea to learn whether the movie-makers have again lied, as they mostly, not to say always, do.

I had to wait the whole morning. Nor did my turn come in the afternoon. The class I belong to always has to wait and wait, stand long nights and days in long files to get a cup of coffee and a slice of bread. Everybody in the world, official or boss, takes it for granted that our sort of people have ages of time to waste. It is different with those who have money. They can arrange everything with money. Therefore they never have to wait. We who cannot pay with cold cash have to pay with our time instead. Suppose you get sore at the official who lets you wait and wait, and you say something about the citizen's right—it won't help you a bit. He then lets you wait ten times longer, and you never do it again. He is the king. Do not forget that. Don't ever believe that kings were done with when the fathers of the country made a revolution.

The waiting-room was crowded with people, with plain people like me. Some of them had already been sitting there four days. Others had been there scores of times. First a certain paper had been missing, then a certain certificate was not complete, then some record was not sufficient, and blanks had been filled in fifty times, and fifty times torn up and thrown into the waste-basket and done over again. The whole thing was no longer an affair of human beings; it had become an affair of papers, blanks, affidavits, certificates, photographs, stamps, seals, files, height-measuring, and quarreling about the correct color of the eyes and the hair. The human being himself was out and forgotten. A piece of merchandise would not have been treated so.

The good old flag spread all over the wall. A picture of the man who had said something about the country being created by the Lord to be the land of the free and for the hunted. Another picture of another man who had said great things about the right of human beings, even Negroes, to unrestricted freedom.

A huge map was there also. It was the map of a country great and large enough to give some space to an extra fifty million human beings eager to work and to find happiness on earth. I looked at the map and I was pleased to see that good old Sconsin was still on it.

I was still looking around when a lady came in like a clap of thunder. Short, unbelievably fat. In this room where everyone awaiting his turn had a lean and hungry figure, this lady had the effect of a loathsome insult.

The fat lady had curly, bluish-black, oily hair, done up in the manner affected by street-girls when they want to go with their men to the chauffeurs' ball. She had a pronounced hooked nose, thick lips, brightly painted, brown dreamy eyes that were larger than the holes they were set in and looked as if they might pop out any moment. The fat lady was dressed in the most elegant masterpiece of a French dressmaker. Looking at how she tried to walk like a human being on her immensely high heels, one had the impression that in a minute she would collapse under the weight of her heavy pearl necklace and the heavy platinum bracelets around her wrists. Her fingers were ridiculously short and thick. On all fingers, save on the thumb, she wore diamond rings; on some fingers she carried two and even three rings. It seemed that the finger-rings were necessary to keep her thick fingers from bursting open.

Hardly had she opened the door when she cried: "For God's sake, I have lost my passport." (She pronounced it "pace-pot".) "Where is that consul? He has to receive me immediately. I must have another pacepot. I take the Oriental Express in the evening."

I had been made to believe that only sailors can lose their papers. Now I see that even well-dressed people can be without passports. Hello, Fanny, I can tell you that Mr. Consul is going to say something very interesting to you about lost passports. I feel some sympathy for that fat lady. The sympathy of the galley-slave for his fellow.

The clerk jumped to his feet, all devotion. He bowed and said in a soft and very polite voice: "Of course, madame. I will announce you right away to the consul. It will be a pleasure. Just one moment, please."

He ran and brought a chair and begged the fat lady to be seated. He did not say: "Sit down!" Just: "Will you be seated, madame? Thank you."

He helped the lady to fill in all the blanks. The hungry and lean people who had been waiting for weeks had to do this by themselves, and when it was not satisfactorily written they had to do it over and over again. The lady perhaps could not write. So of course the clerk had to help her. Or she was so great a personage that she did not need to write. At home she probably had a social secretary who did all the writing for her and told her all the gossip.

No sooner had the clerk filled out the applications than he took up the forms, ran to one of the doors, behind which the death-sentences were passed out, knocked softly, and went in. In less than half a minute he returned, ran up to the lady, bowed, and said: "Mr. Grgrgrgrs wishes to see you, madame. I am certain you have the three photographs with you."

"Here they are," the fat lady said, and handed the photographs to the clerk. Then the clerk sprang to the door, opened it with a bow, and let her in.

The lady was not long in the holy chamber. When she came out, she closed her hand-bag with an energetic gesture which announced better than her speech ever could: "Thank heaven, we have money. And we do not mind paying for quick and good service. A consul cannot live by his salary alone. Live and let live." Then she walked across the room wagging her hips like a dog that is pleased with itself.

The clerk rose from his chair and invited her to be seated again. The fat lady sat down, using only half of the chair, thinking this would indicate best how much of a hurry she was in. She went fishing in the depths of her hand-bag, took out a powder-puff, and began to powder her thick nose. She had taken out not only her powder, but something which distinctly crinkled in her hands. She pushed the crisp affair among papers lying on the table. As she did so, she gave the clerk a glance, which he caught all right. However, he made believe he did not know what the glance meant. When the lady had whitened her nose, she shut her hand-bag with the same energetic snap she had used on coming out of the holy chamber.

The hungry men and women waiting in the room had never been in God's country before. They merely wanted to go there and partake of the riches of the world. So they were still innocent and did not understand the universal language of snapping hand-bags. Since they did not know how to use this sort of language, and since they had no means of using it in the right way, no one offered them a chair, and they had to wait until their turn came.

"If it would please you, madame, will you call for your passport in half an hour, or do you wish us to send it to your hotel?"

"Never mind, mister," the fat lady said. "I shall drop in myself in an hour on my way to the station. I have signed the passport already, in the consul's office. Good afternoon."

The fat lady returned in an hour. She received her passport with a bow from the clerk and with: "Always a great pleasure to be at your service, madame."

I was still sitting and awaiting my turn.

I apologized mentally for my unjustified bad opinion of American consuls. They are not so bad as I thought. It was nothing but national jealousy, what Belgian, Dutch, and French policemen had told me about American consuls being the worst of all bureaucrats alive. Here, at this consulate, I certainly would obtain the passport that would help me get a ship to go back home and be an honest worker ever after. I would settle down somewhere in the West, get married, and do my bit to populate my country and make the kids bigger and better citizens.

II

I was asked to "come in." All the other people waiting here had to go, when their number was called, through a different door from the one I used. I passed through the same door through which the fat lady had passed. So I was, after all, to see Mr. Grgrgrgrs, or whatever his name was. Exactly the gent I was most eager to see. A person so kind as to give a lady in need, in so short a time, a new passport would understand my troubles better than anybody else.

The gentleman I met was short, lean, and rather sad or worried about something. He was dried up to the bones. He looked as though he had been working in an office before he had reached fourteen. I had the impression that, should it ever happen that he could no longer go to an office at a certain hour in the morning and work there or sit there until a certain hour in the afternoon, he would die inside of six weeks, believing himself a failure.

"Sit down. What can I do for you?"

"I would like to have a passport."

"Lost your passport?"

"Not my passport. Only my sailor's identification card."

"Oh, then you are a sailor?"

When I said: "Yes, sir," he changed the expression on his face, and his voice took another tone. He narrowed his eyes, and from then on he looked at me with suspicion written all over his face.

"You see, sir, I missed my ship."

"Drunk, eh?"

"I never drink, sir. Not a drop. I believe in prohibition."

"But did you not tell me you are a sailor?"

"Exactly. My ship got under weigh three hours before the time we were supposed to sail. I had presumed that we would go out with high water. As we had no cargo and were going home in ballast, the skipper didn't have to wait for high water to come in, and so he ordered the ship to make off early in the night."

"Your papers were left aboard, I suppose?"

"Right, sir."

"I might have known this before. Do you remember the register number of your sailor's card?"

"No, sir. I am sorry."

"So am I. Where was the card issued? By what shipping board?"

"I don't remember where it was. You see, I have shipped in coast traffic, Boston, New York, Philly, New Orleans, Galveston, and all along the Mexican Gulf. You see, sir, a sailor does not look every day at his card. In fact, I have never looked at all at what it said. Often it is not even asked for by the skipper when he signs you on. He takes it for granted that a guy has his card. More important to the skipper is what ship you have been on before, and under which master, and what you know about the job."

"I know. You don't have to tell me."

"Yes, sir."

"Naturalized?"

"No, sir. Native-born!"

"Birth registered?"

"I do not know, sir. When this happened, I was too small to remember exactly if it was done or not."

"Then your birth has not been registered."

"I said I do not know, sir."

"But I do know."

"Well, sir, if you know everything beforehand, why do you ask me?"

"Now, don't you get excited here. No reason for that. Was your mother married to your father?"

"I never asked my mother. I thought it her own business, and that it concerns nobody else."

"Right. Excuse me. I was only thinking that the marriage license might be found somewhere. Your father was also a sailor, like you?"

"Yes, sir."

"I thought so. Never came home again I suppose?"

"I do not know, sir."

"Any relatives alive?"

"I do not know, sir. Never knew any."

"Know somebody in the States who has known you since you were a boy?"

"I think there ought to be lots of people who ought to know me."

He took up a pencil and got ready to write down names and addresses. "Will you, please, name any of these people who have known you for a long time—let us say fifteen years or so?"

"How could I recall any of them, sir? They all are people of no importance. Just plain people. Working folks. Changing places whenever their work calls for it. I would not know their full names or even their real names, only the names we knew them by or called them."

"Have you a permanent address back home?"

"No, sir. I could not pay for one. You see, I live on my ships, like most sailors do. When laid off for a while I stay in a sailors' home or just in any cheap boarding-house near the waterfront."

"Your mother still alive?"

"I think so. But I do not know for sure."

"You do not know for sure?"

"How can I know for sure, sir? While I was away, she changed her address several times. Perhaps she's married to somebody whose name I do not know. You see, sir, with us working people and sailors everything cannot be done as fine and smooth as with the rich guys that have an elegant house of their own and a swell bank-account and a telephone and a lot of servants. We have to look out first for a job, and afterwards we worry about other things. The job means eating. Without a job we are just like a farmer without a farm."

"Ever gone to the polls to vote in any state election?"

"No, sir. I never had any time to mix with politics."

"You are a pacifist?"

"A what, sir?"

"Well, I mean you are communist. You do not want to fight for the country."

"I did not say so, sir. I think that as a sailor who works hard I am fighting every day for the greatness of my country. Our country would not be a great country if there were no sailors and no working-men."

"Didn't you say you shipped in New Orleans?"

"Yes, sir, that's right."

"Then, of course, you are a member of the—now, what is the name? Yes, of the Industrial Workers of the World. Syndicalism and such things?"

"No, sir, never heard of it."

"But you said you shipped in New Orleans?"

"Yes, sir."

"Never in Los Angeles?"

"No, sir."

For a long while he looks at me with dull eyes. He does not know what more to ask. He drums the desk with his pencil. Then he says: "Well, I cannot give you a passport, and that is all there is to it. Sorry."

"But why, sir?"

"Upon what proofs? Your statement that you claim American citizenship is no proof. Personally, I believe that you are American. However, the Department of Labor in Washington, to which I am responsible for making out passports and other identifications, does not wish to know what I believe and what I do not believe. This office in Washington accepts only unquestionable evidence and no mere belief of a consul abroad. If you bring proper evidence, it will be my obligation to issue a passport to you. How can you prove that you are American, that I am obliged to spend my time on your case?"

"You can hear that, sir."

"How? By your language? That is no proof."

"Of course it is. It is the best proof."

"Here in France there live thousands of Russians who speak better French than the average Frenchman does. That does not make a Russian a Frenchman, does it? In New Orleans, on the other hand, there are several thousand people who speak only French and very little if any English. Nevertheless they are as true Americans as I am. Texas and southern California are full of people who speak Mexican and Spanish, but they are Americans in spite of their foreign language. So what proof is the language you are speaking?"

"I was born in the States."

"Prove that and I will give you a passport within two days. But even if you were born in the States, I would still have the right to question your citizenship, because it might have happened that your father, before you were of age, certified on your behalf for another citizenship. I would not go that far, of course. Just prove to me that you were born in the States. Or name me a few persons who will testify that you are native-born."

"How can I ever prove anything, then, since my birth was not registered?"

"That is not my fault, is it?"

"It looks, sir, as though you would even doubt the fact that I was born at all?"

"Right, my man. Think it silly or not. I doubt your birth as long as you have no certificate of your birth. The fact that you are sitting in front of me is no proof of your birth. Officially it is no proof. The law or the Department of Labor may or may not accept my word that I have seen you and that, as I have seen you, you must have been born. I know this is silly, it is nonsense. But I did not make the law. Do you know that I might get fired or discharged from public service for having given you a passport without any other evidence than your word and your presence in person? Frankly, in your case I do not know what to do."

He pressed a button. In came the clerk. The consul writes my name on a scrap of paper, asking me how I spell it. "Look up this name, please, Gerard Gales, last residence New Orleans, sailor, *Tuscaloosa*."

The clerk leaves the door partly open. I see him going into a small room where all the files are located. I know what he is looking for: the deported, the undesirables, the criminals, the anarchists, the communists, the pacifists and all the other trouble-makers whom the government is anxious to refuse re-entry into the country.

The clerk returned. The consul had been standing at the window in the meantime, looking out into the street, where life went on as busy as ever, papers or no papers.

The consul asked: "Well?"

"Not on file. No records."

"You gave your right name, did you?" the consul asked. "I mean the name you were living by in the home country?"

"Yes, sir. I never had any trouble back home."

The clerk left the room and I was again alone with the consul.

There was silence for a long time. I looked at the pictures on the wall. All faces familiar since I was a kid. All great men. All lovers and supporters of freedom, of the rights of human beings, builders of a great country, where men may and shall be free to pursue their happiness.

The consul rose and left the room.

After five minutes he came back. A new question had occurred to him: "You might be—I do not insinuate you are—an escaped convict. You might be wanted by the police at home, or in any other country."

"You are quite right, sir. I might. I see now that I have come in vain to my consul, who is paid to help Americans in need. I see it is hopeless. Thank you for your trouble, sir."

"I am very sorry, but in your case I simply do not see any way I could do anything for you. I am only an official. I have strict regulations by which I have to work. You should have been more careful with your papers. In times like these nobody can afford to lose his passport or similar important papers. We are no longer living in those carefree pre-war times when practically no papers were asked for."

"Would you, please, and if you do not mind, tell me one thing, sir?" I asked.

"Yes?"

"There was here, yesterday afternoon, a very fat lady, with a dozen heavy diamond rings on her fingers and a pearl necklace around her fat neck which might have cost ten thousand dollars at least. Well, that lady had lost her passport just as I have. She got a new passport here in less than an hour."

"I see, you are referring to Mrs. Sally Marcus from New York. Surely, you have heard the name before. That big banking firm of New York." This the consul said with a gesture and a modulation of his voice as though he had wanted to say: "My good man, don't you know, this was His Royal Highness the Prince of Wales and not just a drunken sailor without a ship."

He must have noticed by the expression on my face that I had not taken the information as he had expected I would. So he added hastily: "The well-known banking firm, you know, in New York."

I still did not satisfy his hope of seeing me turn pale when such a great personage was mentioned in my presence.

But Wall Street, the house of Morgan, the richness of the Rockefellers, a seat on the stock-exchange has never made any, not even the slightest, impression upon me. It all leaves me as unimpressed as a cold potato.

So I said to the consul: "I do not believe that this lady is an American. I would think her born somewhere in Bucharest."

"How did you guess?" the consul opened his eyes wide and almost lost his breath. "Sure, she was born in Bucharest, in Roumania. But she is an American citizen."

"Did she carry along her naturalization papers?"

"Of course not. Why?"

"Then how could you tell that she is an American citizen? She has not even learned to speak the American language. Her lingo is not even East Side. I bet it is not even accepted at Whitechapel."

"Now get me right. In the case of that lady I do not need any evidence. Her husband, Mr. Reuben Marcus, is one of the best-known bankers of New York. Mrs. Marcus crossed in the most expensive stateroom on the *Majestic*. I saw her name on the list."

"Yes, I understand. You said it, Mr. Consul. I crossed only as a plain deck-hand in the forecastle bunk of a freighter. That, I see, makes all the difference. Not the papers. Not the birth-certificate. A big banking firm is the only evidence needed to prove a man a citizen. Thank you, sir. That's exactly what I wanted to know. Thank you, sir."

"Now, look here, mister sailor. Let's talk this over and get it straight. I do not wish you to leave here with the wrong impression about me. I have told you that, under the circumstances, I have no power whatever to do anything for you. I am not to blame. It is the system of which I am a slave. If I had the power—let us say if I were going to leave office anyway during the year to retire—I promise you, upon my word, I would be pleased to give you any paper you need. But I cannot do it. My hands are bound. Entirely. Frankly, I believe your story. It sounds true. I have had cases similar to yours. The same result. Could do nothing. I believe you are American. I almost think you are a better American than certain bankers ever will be. You belong with us. You are the right blood. But I tell you just as frankly: should it happen that the French police bring you here before me, to recognize you, I would deny vehemently your claim to American citizenship. I might say, as a man, I would do it with a bleeding heart, but I would do it, because I have to, as a soldier in war has to kill even his friend when he meets him on the battle-field clad in the uniform of the enemy."

"Which means, in fewer words, that I may go to hell."

"I did not say that. But since we have become frank with each other, I might as well admit, yes, it means exactly that. I have no other choice. I might, of course, write to Washington and present your case. Suppose you could produce the names and addresses of people back home who know you. It would nevertheless be from four to eight months before your citizenship would be established satisfactorily. Have you got the means to stay that long in Paris to wait for the final decision of Washington?"

"How could I, sir? I am a sailor. I have to look for a ship. There are no ships in Paris. I am a high-sea sailor, not a sailor of vegetable boats on the river Seine."

"I knew that. You cannot wait here in Paris for months and months. We have no funds to provide for your staying here. By the way, would you like to have a ticket for three days' board and lodging? When it expires you may drop in again to have another one."

"No, thank you just the same. I'll get along all right."

"I suppose you would rather have a railroad ticket to a port where you might pick a ship sailing under another flag, or you may have the good luck to find a master of an American ship who knows you."

"No, many thanks. I shall find my own way."

He sighed. For a while he went to the window looking out again. Nothing new seemed to come into his mind. It would have been a rare thing anyhow for an official to come upon an idea that is not provided for in the regulations.

So there was nothing left for him to say but: "I am so sorry. Well, then, good-by and all the luck!"

After all, there is a great difference between American officials in general and European officials in general. The office hours ended at four, or even at three. When I was out in the street again I noticed that it was five. But at no time during my conversation with the consul did he show any sign of impatience or make me think that he was in a hurry and had to go home or to the golf links. Not all American officials are like that, yet there are still some. In Europe, however, I have never met any official who did not, fifteen minutes before his working hours terminated, start showing me my way out regardless of how important my business might be.

Now I had really lost my ship.

Good-by, my sunny New Orleans! Good-by and good luck to you.

Well, honey, you'd better stick up with somebody else now. Don't wait any longer on Jackson Square or at the Levee. Your boy is not coming home again any more. The sea has swallowed him. I could fight gales and waves, be it with fists or with the paint-brush. But I have lost out in my fight against the almighty papers and certificates. Get another boy, sweetheart, before it is too late, and ere all your blossoms have fallen off in the autumn winds. Don't waste the roses of your sweet youth waiting for the guy who no longer has a country, for the man who was not born.

Damn the skirt! Ship ahoy! Fresh wind coming up! All hands, hear, get all the canvas spread! Sheet home! And all of it. Up and high! A fresh wind is coming up!

12

The Paris-Toulouse Express. I am on the train and have no ticket. Just before we reach Limoges, tickets are examined. I have very urgent, and very private, business to attend to, and disappear. The conductor notices neither my presence nor my absence. I am still on the train after it pulls out of Limoges, and I still have no ticket.

I don't understand why train officials always have to examine tickets. There must really be many railroad cheaters. Well, I won't say cheaters; let us say, people who cannot afford to buy tickets. Oh, of course, there must be some kind of inspection. Who would pay dividends to the stockholders if everybody rode free?

French trains are different from ours. There is a long corridor on one side that runs the length of the car. From this corridor doors lead into small compartments in which five or six persons can be seated.

All of a sudden the conductor walked through the corridor and opened the door to the compartment in which I was sitting. I had no time to attend to my urgent private business. So I sat there and looked him straight in the face. I used mental influence, or what is called telepathy. I looked at him as if I had a ticket. He caught my stare and closed the door. I knew telepathy was a great science, and it worked fine. He was absolutely convinced that I had a ticket.

I was just about to think it over and decide how to use telepathy in other things, particularly with my consuls, when the conductor returned. He opened the door, looked at me doubtfully, made a gesture as though to close the door again, and then said: "Excuse me, sir, where did you say you wanted to get off or change trains, please?"

He said this in French. I could grasp the meaning, but not the exact words. So I had no answer ready. I tried to think up a few French words to answer him with.

The conductor, however, gave me no time to explain. He pleaded: "Will you, please, let me have your ticket again?"

He spoke very politely. Yet he could not get from me what I did not have.

Satisfaction with his own cleverness spread all over his face when he said: "I thought so."

Since I was sitting next to the door and as there were only two more passengers in the same compartment, sitting by the window, they did not notice the tragedy that was happening right under their noses.

The conductor took out a notebook, wrote something in it, and went his way. Perhaps he has a good heart and will let me slip by? I shall never forget his kindness. Maybe some day his grown-up sons will come to Cincin, and I shall treat them fine.

In Toulouse, right in front of my car, I was awaited and

received. The conductor made a slight gesture toward me, and two gentlemen said in a low voice: "Please follow us, quietly."

Nobody seemed to notice what was going on. The gentlemen put me between them exactly as though they were friends meeting another friend who had just arrived at the depot.

Outside, a motor-car is waiting. French motor-cars, as I now notice for the first time, are different from our flivvers. They are fire- and burglar-proof. There are tiny little compartments inside, just big enough so you can sit down without spreading your elbows in comfort. Each compartment has a door. I am let in and the door is locked from the outside. The car, after a while, makes off. There is one little window close to the top. I can see nothing from it but the upper floors of the houses we pass. It's an important car, because a whistle from the chauffeur gets it the right of way over all other vehicles.

I have a feeling that the car will take me to some place I do not like. I have gathered sufficient experience by now to know that whenever I run up against certain strange customs anywhere in Europe, then I am on my way to a police-station. I never had anything to do with the police back home. In Europe everything is different. I may sit quite satisfied with myself on a box by the docks, and, sure enough, a cop comes up, asks me questions, and takes me to the police-station. Or I may lie in bed, doing nobody any harm, and somebody knocks at the door, and half an hour later I am again in a police-station. There are still people who say you cannot sin while you're asleep. But the police in Rotterdam insisted that I did sin while asleep that morning. Then again I may sit in a train, speaking to nobody, looking into nobody's purse, asking no one for his paper. It doesn't help me a bit. I find myself in the police-station as soon as the train has pulled in. I think that must be the trouble Europe is suffering from. These people simply cannot attend to their own affairs. The police will not allow them to do so. Seven-eighths of their short lives have to be spent, some way or other, with the police. Whenever they move from the second floor to the third floor in the same house, they have to notify the police that they have done so, and they have to fill in three blanks, in which they specify their religion, the names of their grandfathers, and where their grandmothers were born. And that is only the brighter side of their intercourse with the police. They can do practically nothing without asking the police for their kind permission. Even closing or opening your own window in your own home is regulated by the police. And heaven knows for what reason, they are for ever acting like sergeants with liver trouble; they never act like human beings who receive their salaries from the very same people they push around day and night. You cannot even dance in your own home, or in a public dance-hall, without a special permit from the police. All Europe is a paradise for bureaucrats. Under such circumstances it is no wonder that our bankers will never collect from any European countries the debts they ran up fighting for democracy and civilization and humanity. All the money these people earn goes to building up a better bureaucracy and a bigger police force. I hope only that somebody will come up to me again to offer me liberty bonds on the installment plan.

"Where do you come from?"

A uniformed high priest is sitting behind a very high desk, in front of which I stand like a two-legged mite. They are all alike, be they in Belgium, Holland, Paris, Toulouse. Always asking questions. Always asking the same questions. Always doubting every answer given them. I cannot get away from the idea that if some day a sailor without a passport should land in hell, he would have to pass the same kind of desk before he is admitted.

Now, of course, I might just ignore their questions and say nothing. Yet who is he that could stand a hundred questions and answer none? An unanswered question flutters about you for the rest of your life. It does not let you sleep; it does not let you think. You feel that the equilibrium of the universe is at stake if you leave a question pending. A question without an answer is something so incomplete that you simply cannot bear it. You can get crazy thinking of the problems of an unbalanced solar system. The word "Why?" with a question mark behind it is the cause, I am quite certain, of all culture, civilization, progress, and science. This word "Why?" has changed and will again change every system by which mankind lives and prospers; it will end war, and it will bring war again; it will lead to communism, and it will surely destroy communism again; it will make dictators and despots, and it will dethrone them again; it will make new religions, and it will turn them into superstitions again; it will make a nebula the real and the spiritual center of the universe, and it will again make the same nebula an insignificant speck in the super-universe. The little word "Why?" with a question mark.

So what could I do, a sailor without papers, against the power of the word "Why?"

"Why are you here? Where do you come from? What's your name?"

I have given no answers as yet. But now I can no longer resist the question mark. I have to say something. I do not know what might be better, to tell him that I came from Paris or to tell him I came from Limoges. Since Limoges is nearer, the railroad hasn't got so big a claim on me as it would have if I said I came from Paris.

"I took the train at Limoges."

"That is not correct. You came from Paris."

Let's see if they are smart.

"No, officer, I was not on the train since Paris, only since Limoges."

"But you have a station ticket here from Paris, good only for the first suburb out."

With this I realize that my pockets have been searched again. I hadn't noticed it at all. I seem to have become so accustomed to being searched that I have lost my capacity to take account of it. It must be the same with married people and their kisses; divorce proceedings begin when they take account again.

"This ticket? Oh, you mean this ticket from Paris? I have had this for a long time."

"How long?"

"Six weeks or so."

"Strange ticket. Rather a great miracle. The ticket given out to you six weeks ago bears yesterday's date."

"I am sure, then, that the clerk must have postdated it by mistake."

"We have this fact clear now. You boarded the train at Paris."

"I paid from Paris to Limoges."

"Yes, you are a very good payer. You even buy two tickets. Because you would not have needed this ticket if you had bought a ticket to Limoges. Where is your ticket from Paris to Limoges? Since you did not leave the train at Limoges, the ticket must still be in your possession."

"I gave it to the conductor on reaching Limoges."

"Then where is the ticket from Limoges? How could you get into the train after you handed in the ticket at the collection gate at Limoges?"

"I do not know."

"Let us now take your name."

I could not spoil my decent American name. Some day I might belong to society. It is only a question of making money. So I gave him a name which I borrowed for this occasion from a grocer I used to know in Chic, who once threw a stick after me. For that he is now on the police blotter in Toulouse, France. A warning to all grocers never to throw sticks after little boys when they catch them with their dirty hands in the barrel of maple syrup.

"Nationality?"

What a question! It has been testified to by my consuls that I no longer have such a thing as nationality, since there is not the slightest proof that I was born. I might tell here that I am French. My consul told me there are lots of people who speak excellent French but are not Frenchmen, so there must also be lots of people who do not speak any more French than I do, but who are nevertheless French citizens. I should like to know for whom it would be cheaper to ride on a French railroad without a ticket—for a Frenchman, or for an American, or for—?

There's an idea! A German! A Boche! Right now, only a few years after the war. All France is still filled to the brim with the most terrific hatred against the Heinies. Might be a new experience. One should never cease to learn. If you cannot go to college because you have no money and you have to sell papers to make your own living, you should nevertheless not miss any means by which you can get educated. Traveling, and having lots of experiences in life, are the best education for any man. Profs are as dull as last week's morning paper. I wonder what they'll do to a German caught riding on their express trains so soon after the war.

"I am only a German, sir."

"A German? What do you know about that! A German! I suppose from Potsdam, too?"

"Not, not from Potsdam, officer. Only from Vienna."

"That is in Austria. Anyway, it is all the same. They are all alike. Why have you no passport?"

"I had one. But I lost it."

"You do not speak the hacky French of a German. What district are you from?"

"The district I was raised in is situated in a region where Germans still speak an old English tongue."

"That is right. I know the district well. It is where English kings had a great influence up to the middle of the last century."

"Yes, sir, you are right. It is called Saxony."

For the first time I learned that it is a good thing not to have a passport. If you haven't any, nobody can find one in your pockets; so nobody can look up your record. Had they known that I had already robbed the French national railroad, it might have cost me two years, or even Devil's Island. I got only two weeks.

When the first day in prison was over, taken up with registration, signing my name in dozens of books, bathing, weighing, medical examinations, I felt as though I had done a long and hard day's work.

Kings and presidents don't rule the world; the brass button is the real ruler.

Next morning, right after a poor breakfast which did no justice to the overestimated French cuisine, I was taken to the workshop.

In front of me was a pile of very peculiar-looking nameless things stamped out of bright tinned sheet iron. I wanted to know what they were. Nobody could tell me, neither my fellow-prisoners nor the wardens. One said that he was sure they were parts of a dirigible manufactured in different sections throughout the country. The day after the declaration of the new European war all these parts would be gathered together, and within less than a week about five thousand dirigibles would be ready for service. Others denied this and insisted that the little things had nothing to do with dirigibles, but were parts of secretly manufactured submarines. Again, others said they were parts of a new machine-gun, one as effective as the best in existence, but so light that a soldier could carry it like a rifle. Others, that they were parts of a tank that would have a speed of about seventy miles an hour. Another fellow told me that they were parts of a new type of airplane, each carrying no less than two hundred gas-bombs, fifty heavy nitroglycerin bombs, and three machine-guns, and having a speed of six hundred kilometers per hour, and a service-time of eighteen hours without refueling. Not one person, warden or prisoner, ever suggested that they might be parts of machinery or something else useful to mankind. Such an idea occurred to no one. It was the same everywhere in France. Whenever something was made that nobody knew anything about, everyone concluded that it was to be used in the next war to end war.

I myself could form no idea as to what these little things might be good for.

The warden in charge of the shop came up and said: "You count off this pile one hundred and forty-four pieces. Then you make a new little pile of a hundred and forty-four pieces. Then again you count off one hundred and forty-four pieces, pile them up neatly, and put them aside. That is your work."

After I had counted the first pile, the warden returned. He looked at the little pile and said: "Are you sure there are exactly one hundred and forty-four pieces, not one more or less?"

"Yes, officer."

"Better count them again. I trust you fully. But, please, I beg of you, count them with the greatest care. That's why I gave you this special work. You look intelligent. I think you are the only man here who has the intelligence to do work with his brain and not with his hands."

"You may be assured, officer, I shall do my best."

"Please do. That's a good boy. You see, suppose my superior checks up and finds one piece above or below the hundred and forty-four I have to deliver; I might get a terrible rebuke. I might even lose my job here. I would not know what to do, with a wife sick at home and three little kids; and my mother and the mother of my wife also depend upon me. I could not afford to lose the job. Please be careful when counting."

I counted them first in one heap; then I made twelve dozens, counting carefully each dozen, then all the dozens twelve times. After that I counted them all over in heaps of ten each, making fourteen heaps of ten, and adding at the end four single pieces. Having done that, I counted them in piles of twenty, making seven piles all together, and again four extra.

The warden came up, looked at what I was doing, and said: "That's the way to do it. You are the first one that ever could do it right. I knew that you had brains, and that you know how to use them. I can depend upon you. Thank you."

When finally I had decided that I had one pile of one hundred and forty-four pieces, I laid them aside and reached out to count off a second pile of one hundred and forty-four. No sooner had I started than the warden, who had been watching me all the time from a seat in the corner, came up and said: "Better count them once or twice more. There might easily be a mistake. I would commit suicide if I lost my job for such a grave error."

I took the pile and began to count the pieces again, one by one. The warden stood for a while watching me, and said: "That's exactly the way it has to be done. Just use a little brain, that's all. I will see to it that you get some cigarettes for good behavior."

After two hours I decided once more to start counting off another pile. The warden came. He looked with a worried face at the pile I had shoved off to make room for the new one. I took profound pity on him. I thought he would break out crying any minute. I could not stand it. So I took back the first pile and began to count it all over again. His face immediately began to brighten up, and I noted even a faint smile around his lips. So pleased was he that he tapped me on my shoulder and said: "You have brightened up my whole life as nobody else ever did around here. I wish you could stay here for a few years."

When at last my time was up, I had counted the grand total of three piles, of one hundred and forty-four pieces each. For months afterwards I still wondered whether perhaps one

of the three piles was not counted incorrectly. I trust, however, that the warden gave my piles to a newcomer to count
over.

I received fourteen centimes in wages. I didn't want to
ride on a French railroad again without a ticket. It was not
that I was afraid of being caught once more. No, it was just
that I could not burden my conscience with the thought that
on my account the French railroad or the French nation would
go bankrupt. It might come to a point where the French government would say that I was responsible for their failure
to pay their debts. (By the way, these are the same people
that make such a fuss about the Russians not paying their
debts.)

To tell the truth, I must say that it was not my concern for
the welfare of the French nation that made me decide to
leave France and go elsewhere. It was that when I found
myself outside the prison there were again two gentlemen
waiting for me to warn me seriously to leave the country
within fifteen days or go back to jail for six months and after
that be deported to Germany. I did not like to see the Germans go to war with France again, this time on my behalf.
I do not wish to be responsible for another war. It will come
anyway.

13

Going south, following the sun. I wandered along roads
as old as the history of Europe. Perhaps older.

I stuck now to my new nationality, merely to see what
would happen so soon after the war to a vagabond in France
who said openly: "I am a Boche." It appeared that everybody
took it good-naturedly, sometimes entirely indifferently.
Wherever I asked I got food; and the peasants were always

willing to put me up for the night in their barns, often even in their spare rooms inside the house.

Instinctively, it seemed, I had hit upon the right nail. Nobody liked Americans. The French peasants cursed us. We were the robbers. We coined our dollars out of the blood of the glorious French youth. We were the Shylocks and the usurers. We cut their throats; we made money out of the tears of the French orphans and widows. We took away from them their last cow and goat. We could not swallow all the gold we already had, but we wanted the last French gold coin found in the stocking of the poor grandmother.

No matter where I met those small-town folk and village people, it was always the same: "If we only had one of those damned Americans here, we would beat him up as we do all swindlers. They don't deserve anything better than to be treated like a filthy dog. Did they fight for us? The hell they did. They only ran after our women. They sold us ammunition. But what sort? We couldn't kill a single German soldier with their ammunition. Their shells killed our own soldiers, because they always came out backwards. Fought for us? Don't make me laugh. They sent their men over not to fight for us, but only to look after their money.

"Where do you intend to go now, boy? To Spain? That's right. A good idea, a splendid idea. Spain is pretty. And warm. They have more than we have to feed you. Just look what those Americans have done to Spain. They cannot leave any country alone. They must put their fingers into every country on earth and make all the people in the world slave for their bankers. What have they done to Spain? I mention only Cuba, and the Philippines, and Puerto Rico, and Florida, and California. Always robbing us poor European countries. Now go on and eat, just help yourself. We have still a few potatoes left and a stale bread crust.

"And when a poor fellow saves up a little money, and wants to go to America to earn a few dollars and send them home

to his poor parents, do they let him in? They do not. First
they steal all the land from the defenseless Indians, and then
they want to keep it all for themselves.

"Say, Boche, do you know what? Look here, you stay here
with us for a couple of weeks and work. Spain is still far, far
off. *Mon dieu,* far off. Of course, we cannot pay you very
much for your work, because the Americans haven't left us
anything. Let's say thirty francs a month. Eight a week. Before
the war we paid only three francs to our farm-hands. Then,
of course, our franc was worth a lot more than now. For a
franc you could buy five times what you can buy now,
or even ten times. We had a Boche here working with us
during the war. He was a prisoner of war. I have to say this
much about him, he was an industrious laborer. We were all
very sad when the war was over and he had to go back to
his country. Say, Antoine, wasn't that Boche a hard worker?
I should say he was. Wil'em was his name. But he said he
wasn't related to the emperor. Just his name. We all liked him
a lot. People told us we were treating him too well, since he
was only a prisoner who had killed perhaps a thousand of
our boys. Anyway, he didn't look that way. He was tame
and he knew how to work on a farm. He worked like three
oxen, didn't he, Antoine? I should say he did."

I stayed and worked there. Soon I learned that Wil'em must
indeed have been a worker such as none other under the sun.
Half a dozen times every day I had to listen to some remark
like this: "I don't understand, but Wil'em must have come
from another part of the country than you. You cannot work
as Wil'em could. Am I right, Antoine?"

Antoine answered: "You are right, mother. He is surely not
from the same province. He cannot work like Wil'em. I suppose even among you Boches there are differences, just as
with us; some are good workers, some are so bad they don't
even earn the salt they put in their soup."

This soon got on my nerves. Wil'em must have understood

more about farming than I. One doesn't learn agriculture in Lincoln Avenue in Chic. At least I didn't. I am sure Wil'em worked so hard, not because he liked to work hard, but because he preferred to stay with these peasants rather than work on Algerian roads, as tens of thousands of other German prisoners did. No matter how hard I worked, no matter how early I rose in the morning and how late at night I turned in, Wil'em had done better. But the peasant I was working for will never get a farm-hand as cheap as he got me. Other peasants in the same village had to pay their hands as much as twenty, twenty-five, and even thirty francs. I received eight. Of course, I was that poor Boche who had been found and picked up on the roadside half starved and nearly dying. They had saved my life, they told everybody. It was only fair that I worked for them for eight francs.

When finally Wil'em appeared in my dreams, I thought it time to leave. I explained I had to see relatives in Spain whom I had not seen since the Goths had left Germany for Spain.

"They sure will be pleased to see you looking so fine," Antoine said.

Instead of eight francs a week, they made it eight francs for six weeks of work. Mother said: "It's easier to count a round number, so we'll make it even."

I said: "It's all right with me, mother."

"Of course, you understand," Antoine said, "we cannot pay you your wages now. You will have to wait until after the New Year. Then we get our money for the crop. But the good food you got here has done wonders for you. You haven't overworked yourself. See, that Wil'em, he—"

"Yes," I interrupted him, "Wil'em came from Westphalia. I am from Southphalia. We don't work so hard. Everything grows there of its own accord. We only have to pray once in a while. We are not used to working hard. Everything is thrown into our laps."

"You certainly are clever people. I must say that much of you," the peasant said. "We won the war, of course, as was expected. But we take it like good sports. The war is over now, so why should we be angry at each other? We all must live, mustn't we? Well, here, take a franc. The rest, after New Year. I hope you have a good time in Spain."

14

The longer I wandered on, the more mountainous became the country, until I found myself in surroundings so desolate and dreary that I longed to see a human face. I would have been contented even with a bandit or a smuggler, in whom, I had been told the day before, this region was richer than in goats. And I saw plenty of goats.

"The border is not far off now," the shepherd with whom I had stayed last night told me in the morning when I left. This shepherd, poor as he was, had shared with me his bread, onions, goat-cheese, and watery red wine.

Walking along a winding path, I saw something near by that looked partly like walls covered with mud, partly like the ruins of an ancient castle. I thought I might find a treasure left hidden there by the old Romans, so I went closer.

Suddenly two soldiers sprang up right in front of me, pointed their rifles at my stomach, and said: "Vollevoo, where are you going?"

"To Spain," I answered. "It must be right over there, right behind this mountain."

"It is," they said. "There is Spain. But first you will have to come to our officer in command. Don't you know where you are?"

"How should I know, messieurs, I am here for the first time in my life, and I wish I were in Spain."

"You are within the French fortifications," one of the soldiers said, "and I might just as well tell you that if your story is not good, or if the old man has got a letter that he does not like from his lady, then there is a good chance of your being shot at sunrise, whether you like it or not."

They gave me cigarettes and brought me to a gate that was so well hidden in the mud wall that I almost got a shock when it appeared before us as if it had risen out of the ground at the word of Aladdin.

I was led in, searched, and ordered to wait until called for.

Two hours passed. Then I was taken across a big yard where I saw a dozen heavy guns and soldiers lined up for drill.

Again I had to wait in a small room, always with the two soldiers at my side, with bayonets fixed.

A door opened and an orderly told my soldiers to bring me in.

Behind a desk sat an officer. Rather young.

My soldiers made some report that I only partly understood, because they spoke in military language—which in all countries is different from the language of the people who pay taxes so that soldiers may live.

"You are Dutch?" the officer asked.

"No, I am Boche."

"You look more like a Dutchman."

I am sure he wanted only to know whether I was lying or not, because the soldiers certainly had told him that I said I was a Boche.

"What are you doing in a French fortress?" the officer asked.

"I did not know that this is a French fortress. It does not look like one."

"What did you think it was?" he asked.

"To me it looked like ruins left by the old Romans."

"Can you sketch?" he wanted to know.

"No, sir, I cannot."

"Know how to make photographs?"

"I never spent any money buying a camera. Really, I am not much interested in photography. I think it rather silly, because you can get photographs made anywhere for little money."

"Did you find anything on him?" the officer asked the soldiers.

"No," they said.

Then he said: "Shershey!" which is French, and which means: "Search him again."

One really gets sick of so much searching.

"So during the war you were a German officer, weren't you?" he asked when the searching was done and nothing was found save a comb and a piece of soap, which they cut open to see whether I had hidden a machine-gun or something inside of it.

"No, sir. I wasn't even a common soldier."

"Why not?"

"I am a C.O. I mean I was one of those birds who had to remain in prison while the war was on."

"For spying?"

"No, sir. Only, the Germans thought that I would not allow them to make war if they let me go free, so they put me in jail, and then they felt safe to do as they pleased."

"You mean to tell me that you and a dozen more who were also in jail would have been able to prevent the war?"

"That's what the Germans believed. Before they put me away I never knew how important a person I was."

"Which prison were you in?"

"In—yes—in—in Southphalen."

"What town?"

"In Deutschenburg."

"Never heard of such a place."

"Nor have I. I mean not before I was in prison there. It is a very secret place, about which even the Germans themselves don't know anything."

The officer took a book, opened it, looked for certain chapters, read them, and said, when he was through: "You will be shot at sunrise. Sorry. On account of being in a fortification near the Spanish border. Since the Spaniards and we ourselves are still at war with the African colonies, the war regulations have not been canceled. Nothing else for me to do but shoot you."

"Thank you, officer."

He stared. Then he asked: "What are you thanking me for?"

"For the good meal you have to give me before you shoot me. Y'see, officer, I am hungry, very hungry; in fact, I am nearly dying. What do I care about being shot so long as I am sure of getting a good farewell dinner?"

At this the officer roared with laughter. He gave an order to one of the soldiers, and I was taken out and given coffee and cigarettes.

About six in the evening I was taken to still another room and ordered to sit at a table. I was hardly seated when two soldiers started bringing in plates, glasses, knives, spoons, forks. As soon as the table was laid, the two soldiers began to bring in the eats.

The officer who had sentenced me to be shot came in. He said: "Don't ever think that we French are stingy, not even to a Boche. For your farewell dinner you will get the officers' Sunday dinner, in double portions. We don't want you to go— All right, I don't know where you will go, and I don't care either. What I mean to say is, we do not send anybody away, no matter where to, without giving him a good meal."

I think the French are far more polite to the fellows they want to execute than the Belgians, who gave me only a bite of potato-salad and three slices of liver-wurst.

The French are really poets when it comes to cooking dinners. "*Mon dieu,* officer, sir, for a dinner like that I wouldn't mind being shot twice every day in the year. I am sorry that I have only one life to be shot; I wish I had a thousand."

"I like to hear that, my boy," he said; "I take it as praise of my nation. Have two cigars and make yourself comfortable until sunrise. Good night."

Funny, I couldn't feel like a condemned man who has only seven or eight hours to live. The dinner had been too good to let me have any foolish sentiments. I think the horror one has of being shot, hanged, electrocuted, strangled, beheaded, drowned, or killed by whatever other means people use to kill the condemned—I think that horror is not of the execution in itself, but of the stingy last dinner that one gets the night before. In China they get nothing; just kneel down, and off goes the head. Everything looks different when your belly is full of an elegant dinner. Of course, a hamburger and a cup of coffee won't do the trick. Nor hash.

15

Reveille awakened me. The sun was already out. I thought they had forgotten me and had shot somebody else instead. Or maybe the French have another notion as to what sunrise is than we have. But they'll let me know on time. Why worry?

A soldier opened the door.

"Breakfast," he said. "Washed up already? Fine. The officer wants to see you right after you have your coffee. Come along."

After breakfast, which was a short affair, I was taken to the officer.

Said he: "Still alive? How do you like it? We have delayed execution because I got a telephone call from headquarters concerning you. I shall have to ask you some more questions. All you have to do is just tell the truth regardless of the consequences."

"All right, shoot, sir."

"Suppose we let you go. Where would you go?"

"To Spain, and if I cannot go to Spain, I want to be shot—of course, with the understanding that I get another last dinner."

He broke out into a terrific gale of laughter. Still giggling, he said: "If I were not convinced that you are a Boche, I would think you an American. Only Boches and Yankees think of nothing but: When do we eat? So you are going to Spain?"

"Yes, colonel."

"Captain to you."

"Yes, captain colonel."

"We would rather that you go back to Germany. Free railroad fare."

"Not even in an aeroplane, colonel," I said. "Germany is entirely out. Not for the kisses of two French girls. Note me."

"But then you would be at home."

"Who wants to be home, colonel? I am happy that I am so far away from home."

"What do you want to go to Spain for? There is no job waiting for you."

"I don't mind the job, captain. You see, colonel, it's like this. Winter is coming on. I have not stored away any fuel. I thought it might be a swell idea to go to Spain, where there is always sunshine. And no worry about where the food will come from either. It's warm there all the time. One just sits in the sun and eats grapes and oranges and chestnuts and such things. Fruits grow wild there. You just pick them up wherever you see them."

"I think," the officer said after some meditation, "we cannot let you go to Spain. Will you promise to go back to Germany if we let you go free?"

"I won't promise, and I won't do it either. Spain or death. I hate to help the Germans pay the reparations. And I don't want to go there. You are really nice people, you French people. But I shouldn't like to stay here in France either. You also have to pay too many debts. I don't feel like paying those debts, because I did not make them. I never like to pay the debts of other people. I am going to Spain. And if I cannot go to Spain, you may shoot me; it's okay with me."

Another young officer, who was sitting in a corner of the room and had listened to our conversation, stood up and came over to the desk.

The two officers talked in the French soldier's lingo, which I could not understand.

When they had talked for a while, laughing most of the time, the officer in charge said: "Now listen here, fellow, we shall do as you wish. We are not barbarians, and I think I can take the responsibility for what I am about to do. You are going to Spain. We shall bring you under guard to the border, and if the Spaniards have no objection to letting you into their country, you will be handed over to them. The Spaniards are fine people. They won't hurt you a bit. They are better off than we are. They like the Boches. Of course, if you were an American, you couldn't live in Spain for twenty-four hours. But a Boche—that's different. Dismissed, until we call you."

I did not heed his order. I shifted from one foot to the other.

"Anything else?" he asked.

"Yes, colonel, captain."

"Well, what is it?"

"May I—I mean, can I—or rather, would I get another Sunday officers' dinner, double portions, before I leave? What I mean is, since this is the last dinner I'll get on French soil, may I have the Sunday officers' dinner, double portions, colonel, captain?"

Did the officers and the soldiers in the room laugh? I should say they did.

I could not see why they were laughing. What is there to laugh about if a guy is hungry and tries to get as much out of the army kitchen as he can? I stood amazed, and so they laughed all the harder.

Finally the captain said: "That's out, my good fellow, no Sunday dinner today, because it is Monday. But you'll get the officers' dinner, and double portions. I sincerely hope that it will be the last meal you ever eat in France. If I ever catch you eating another, I will see to it that you are shot, spy or no spy."

They started laughing again.

16

Two soldiers, with bayonets fixed to their rifles, accompanied me to the border. With all military honors I marched into sunny Spain.

It was the turning-point of my life. I did not know it then, but I know it now; yes, sir.

"He has no papers," the corporal said to the Spanish customs officers, who appeared to be glad to get something to worry about, because the post was a quiet one.

"*Es alemán?*" the Spaniard asked.

"*Si, señor,*" I answered, "*soy alemán con mucho hambre.*" Which is Spanish and which means: "I am a Boche and I am plenty hungry."

"*Bienvenido,*" he said, which is the same as our "Be welcome." We, of course, seldom mean it, but the Spaniards really mean it and they act accordingly.

The soldiers presented a paper which the Spanish officer in charge signed. Then the soldiers, their duty done, sat down and talked with the Spaniards. They got wine and cheese, and they made merry, because after a while Spanish girls came along to pep up the lonely post. They played guitarras and accordions and danced. The wives of the customs officers were in the village and could not see what was going on here, where, they thought, their husbands sweated about the collection of customs and the writing of reports.

As soon as I was handed over to the Spaniards they pulled me, almost triumphantly, into the customs house. They shook hands and embraced me. Some kissed me on my cheeks.

War against the Americans, and you will find no better friends on earth than the Spaniards. If they had only known who I really was, that I had robbed them of Cuba and the Philippines, and that I had cracked up some of their battleships! I still wonder what they would have done to me if they had known my nationality. I was a victim of circumstances, and I hope the Spaniards will forgive me, and besides I personally had nothing to do with Cuba and the battle-ships, because all this happened before my time.

My outward appearance was exactly what a Spaniard had imagined a German would look like. Since the *Tuscaloosa* had sailed, I had changed neither suit, cap, nor shoes, for there was nothing to change them for. My linen looked like linen when it has been washed in brooks, creeks, and rivers, sometimes with soap, mostly without. Yet my appearance was, to them, the best proof that I had come directly from Germany.

They were sure that I must be as hungry as only a man who has been blockaded by the English can be. Consequently they gave me enough food to last a week. Whenever I tried to stop eating, they used all kinds of tricks to make me go through the whole course again.

While I was eating, two of the officers went to the little town near by. When I was stuffed to the limit, the two officers came back with bundles. I got a shirt, a hat, shoes, half a dozen socks, handkers, collars, ties, a pair of pants, a jacket. I had to throw away everything I had about me, and I had to dress. When this was finished, I looked so much like a Spaniard that anyone who had known me back home would have thought I had turned bullfighter.

It was late. The French soldiers said they had to go home. So they left, saying good-by to me. I told them to give my regards to their colonel, and thank the whole of France for what they had done to me. They won't pay their debts anyhow, so why shouldn't I send them my regards?

Now the customs officers started playing cards. They invited me to play with them. I did not know how to play with those funny-looking Spanish cards, but I was taught. Soon I played so well that I won quite a stack of Spanish pesetas, which pleased them immensely, and they urged me to go on playing. I felt like a robber. Whatever I did, when a play was over, they said I had won.

Oh, you sunny, wonderful Spain! May you prosper and live long! No one calls you God's country. It was the first country I met in which I was not asked for a sailor's card or for a passport. The first country in which people did not care to know my name, my age, my beliefs, my height. For the first time my pockets were not searched. I was not pushed at midnight across the border and kicked out of the country like a leper. Nobody wanted to know how much money I had, or what I had lived on for the last three months.

The Spaniards did not fight for liberty, and that's why they still have it.

I spent my first night in Spain in the customs house, because it was late when we had finished playing cards, and I was not yet used to the gallons of wine I had drunk.

From then on I had to pass every night in another house in the little town. Every family considered it partly the greatest honor, partly the highest duty, to have me. Each family wanted to keep me for a whole week. Most evenings there were fights going on over me. The family I was staying with did not want to give me up to the family whose turn it was next to have me. When all turns were up, the whole round started over again. Each family tried to do better than the former. I felt myself getting fat. Worse than that, I got sick. These people were all well-to-do. Smuggling is still a great business, and it is a very honorable business. The king of the smugglers was honored by being made mayor of the town, and the vice-king was made chief of police. No wonder these jolly folks treated me like a bishop on a vacation.

I escaped one night. Like a thief. I am sure these good people think ill of me. They think me ungrateful for having left them without saying good-by and many thanks. Anyway, only an imbecile or a feeble-minded individual could have stood it for long. Those folks would never understand it, good-natured as they are. They think a man treated as I was treated should feel as though he's in heaven. But even in heaven I should feel sick if I just had to sit around and eat and eat. Slavery results from such treatment. You forget how to work and how to look after yourself. I should feel unhappy in a communistic state where the community takes all the risks I want to take myself. In that Spanish town I could not even go into the back-yard without having some one yell after me if I were sure I had soft paper. Yes, sir. I mean, no, sir.

If I had not escaped, there might have come a day when I would have started to kill them, one by one, for having made me utterly useless and for making me hate myself.

17

When I got tired of Seville, I made for Cadiz. As soon as I began to dislike the climate of Cadiz, I returned to Seville. And when the hailing of a new-born torero was too much for me, I was again on my way to Cadiz. By doing so frequently enough, the winter passed. A winter balmier than most winters are in New Orleans. About good old New Orleans—I could have sold that ole town now for a quarter without feeling conscience-stricken. There were lots of other sunny places in the world! Why, of all places, should it be just New Orleans?

My pockets were exactly as empty as they were when I arrived at the border. And still no flat ever asked me about papers or about the means I lived by. The cops had other worries. What did they care about a penniless foreigner?

When I had no money to buy me a bed for the night, I slept anywhere I found to stretch my bones. The morning found me lying there peacefully. The cop on the beat had passed by a hundred times, but he respected my slumber and he took good care that nobody should kidnap me. Here homelessness and poverty aren't crimes like at home, where they put a man in jail if he hasn't got a place to sleep. That is why at home a man who is expert at robbing is considered a respectable citizen whose property must be protected by the police.

Once I was awakened by a cop while asleep on a bench. He said that he was very sorry to disturb me, but he wanted to warn me that a heavy rain was on its way and that I had better go over to that shed yonder, where I would find straw and a tight roof, and where I would sleep a lot better.

I was hungry and I stepped into a bakery and told the man behind the counter that I had no money, but was hungry. I got all the bread I needed. No one ever bored me with the silly question: "Why don't you work? A strong and healthy fellow like you!"

They would have considered such a question unbecoming. They had no job to offer—they knew that jobs were scarce—but they knew that men must eat to keep the world going.

Many ships sailed from here. Some days half a dozen at a time. Certainly there were ships among them that were short a sailor or two. That, however, did not worry me in the least. Why, there were other fellows who wanted the job. Why should I rob them of their chance? Besides, spring was here.

Life was beautiful. The sun was so golden and so warm. The

country was lovely. People were friendly, always smiling, singing; and there was music in the streets, in the gardens, on the shore. The people who sang and made music and made love were mostly in rags, but they were smiling and friendly and lovely. Above all, there was so much freedom. Do as you like, dress as you can afford, don't molest me, and to hell with everything. And don't you forget: Spain has no Statue of Liberty.

In Spain no one speaks of liberty, because people have it. Perhaps their political liberty is not much compared with that of other nations; but no one butts into the private lives of the people; no one tries to tell them what they must drink or eat, or with whom they have to spend the night.

When I was in Barcelona, one day I passed a huge, sinister-looking building, out of which came horrible shrieks.

"What's going on in there?" I asked a man who happened along.

"That's the military prison," he said.

"But why do the people inside cry so heart-breakingly?"

"People? They are not people. They are only communists."

"They don't have to cry because they are communists," I said.

"Oh yes, they do. They are beaten up by the sergeants, and they are tortured. See?"

"Why are they beaten?"

"Didn't I tell you they are communists?"

"No reason to beat them up. Lots of them in Russia."

"We don't want them here. That's why they are beaten until they die. Beaten and whipped to death. At night they are taken out and buried secretly."

"Then they must be criminals?"

"No, they are not criminals. They haven't stolen anything. Some killed the minister. But those have been dead a long time. They are beaten and tortured just because they are communists."

"I tell you again, amigo, I still cannot understand why they are killed in such a horrible way."

"Can't you see? Those men are communists. They want to change everything in the whole world. They want to make slaves of everybody, so that nobody can do what he pleases. Those silly people want the state to do everything, regulate everything, so we should be only slaves of the state. We don't want this. We honest people want to work when and how we wish to. And if we don't wish to work and we prefer to go hungry, then we don't work and we go hungry. We want to be free and to stay free. If we starve to death, that is nobody's business but our own. But the communists want to interfere with everything, with our private lives, with our occupations, with our marriages, and they say the state should command and order everything and leave nothing for us to worry about. That is why these communists are beaten to death, and it serves them right."

There seemed to be a cloud over sunny Spain, but soon the cloud went away. Why should I condemn Spain because of what I had heard? I do not want to judge. Each age and each country tortures its Christians. That which was tortured yesterday is the powerful church today and a religion in decay tomorrow. The deplorable thing, the most deplorable thing, is that the people who were tortured yesterday, torture today. The communists in Russia are no less despotic than the Fascists in Italy or the textile-mill magnates in America. The Irish who came five years ago to the States and who took out citizenship papers yesterday are today the most ardent supporters of all the narrow-minded God's-country-praisers who want to bar from these United States everyone who did not ask his parents to be hundred-per-centers. Whose fault is it that a Jew was born a Jew? Had he a chance to ask to be born a Chinese? Did the Negro ask the English or the Puritans to bring him to the only country worth living in? Since the great George was not an Indian, he must have been an offspring of one of those god-damned immigrants, and to hell with them.

So why should I feel a furrener in Spain, where shines the same sun that shines in Sconsin. The moon is just the same, too; Honey may see it in New Orleans, when she thinks of me. If she does. The *Tuscaloosa* is back by now. I shall look into the matter later. Let us have Spain first. It's closer, anyway.

There is no reason why I should run after a job. I'd have to stand up before the manager like a beggar, cap in hand, as sheepishly as if I were asking him to let me shine his shoes with my spit. In fact, usually it is less humiliating to beg for a meal than to ask for work. Can the skipper sail his bucket without sailors? Or can the engineer, no matter how clever he is, build a locomotive without workers? Nevertheless, the worker has to stand with his cap in hand and beg for a job. He has to stand there like a dog about to be beaten.

Thinking of all the humiliation made it easy for me to go to a restaurant or hotel to ask for the left-overs. The cook doesn't treat me as degradingly as foremen and bosses do.

After all, why chase jobs when the sun is so golden and clear and the skies are so blue, so wonderfully blue, tinged with flares of white gold? Why hang around factory gates when people are so friendly and so polite even to me. As long as I don't commit murder or burglary, I am a decent citizen, and everybody respects me as such. No cop comes up and wants to search my pockets to see if he can find a lost formula for the manufacture of unbreakable wineglasses.

One day I smelled fried fish. When I came up to ask for the left-overs, the people begged my pardon for not having anything to give me.

I concluded that the best way to eat fried fish is to catch'm and fry'm. I was used to asking for a meal, yet I thought it rather unusual to go begging for hooks and a line to fish with. I waited at the pier until a passenger boat came in, and then I waited outside of the customs house. Somebody handed me a bag and told me to follow him to his hotel. He gave me three pesetas and his thanks.

I went to a hardware store and bought a line and a couple of hooks. It amounted to about a peseta. Just to make friends, I told the salesman that I was a stranded sailor in Spain, waiting for a ship to pick me up. He wrapped up the goods for me, and when I handed him my peseta he said: "It's all paid for, sailor. Thank you very much for your patronage. Good luck in fishing. *Adios.*"

Such a country I should leave? Such people I should spoil by chasing jobs and looking busy and hustling? Not for the world.

Spain backward? Don't make me laugh, sir. Those folks know more about the values of life and the destinies of the human race than any prof of phil at the State U of Sconsin.

18

I was sitting on the quay with my hook and line in the water. The fish wouldn't bite. I did my best to feed them with black sausage, which I had got from a Dutch that had come in the day before. She was going to Java or thereabouts.

I had gone cooking to the Dutch. "To go cooking" is another way of saying "to make friends with the crew" of a bucket that's in port—to get the meals so necessary for the health of a stranded sailor who is in Spain just to study the land and the people. To go cooking is not always a pleasure, sir. No, it is not.

The worker who has a job feels superior to a worker who is without one. Workers are not at all as chummy toward each other as some people think when they see them marching with red flags to Union Square and getting noisy about a paradise in Russia. Workers might have a big word in all affairs were it not for the middle-class ideas they can't shake off. The one who makes the delicate parts of an engine feels superior to the man who stands before a lathe making bolts by the ten thousand. And the man at the lathe feels superior to the poor Czech who gathers up the scraps from the floor and carries them in a wheelbarrow to the back-yard.

Sometimes, while standing on the quay, looking up at the fore of a tub where the hands sit at lunch, I hear one of them yell out: "Hey, you bums, you stinking beachcombers, nothing to swallow, hey? I suppose you want to come up here and lick spit, hey? All right, but only two of you, so we can keep an eye on you thieves."

There were others who enjoyed throwing all the food— soup, meat, bread, beans, prunes, coffee—into one pot together with all their half-chewed left-overs, and then handing us this mess and saying: "Well, if you are really hungry, eat that, and say thanks, buddy." We were hungry and we had to eat it.

Or they gave us a huge bowl full of good soup, and then threw into it all the spoons they had, and we had to fish the spoons out with our dirty fingers, to the merriment of the comrades. They did not mean it, they just wanted to be funny. And funny, too, were those who saw us standing hungrily on the quay and yet would throw, before our eyes, half a dozen loaves of white bread into the sea, and potfuls of meat.

Since no working-man can ever be sure of his job and of his superior standing, it happened often that one of those friendly fellow-proletarians was left behind when the ship sailed. He then had to go cooking with us to the buckets coming in, and he learned how it felt to be on the shore and to be treated that way by members of his own class.

They were not all of this sort. Most of them were really true fellow-workers who parted easily with a peseta or a pair of pants and with the best meals they could offer. There were some who even went to the cabins of the officers and stole soap and towels for us, and dozens of cans of meat from the galley. Once I got twelve roasted chickens for lunch—and I couldn't keep the left-overs for a rainy day because I had no refrigerator in my pocket.

The crews of the French and the American ships were the best of all. When there happened to be exceptions, they were foreigners to the flag under which they sailed. The German ships were, with very rare exceptions, the worst of all. It was not the crew that was nasty, although sometimes they were too. It was the officers who acted like little gods. The German ships, long before they put in, fastened at the railings huge wooden posters with gigantic letters: "No Admittance"; and to be sure, they never forgot to hang out the same poster in Spanish. I still wonder what the Germans do with their left-overs. I suppose they can them and store them away for the next war. Yes, sir.

The fish would still not bite, and the black sausage from the Dutch got smaller and smaller. Perhaps that part of the ocean hasn't got any fish left.

While I was hanging around in Barcelona, one day sailors told me that there were many American ships in Marseille that were short of hands, because lots of them had jumped to stay in France and study the French girls. The crew of a freighter stowed me away, and I landed in Marseille all right. Like all tales about fine jobs that were just waiting for somebody to take them—and make your own price—it was the bunk. Nothing in it. Not a single Yank in, not even a rummer with a faked flag.

I didn't have a centime. Late in the evening I stepped into a saloon in which there were many sailors. I thought I might meet somebody willing to spring a supper.

A waitress, a pretty young girl, came up and gave me a menu. She asked me what I wanted to have. I said I had no money and I was just looking around to find a friend. She asked me who I was and I said: "Boche sailor."

She asked me to sit down, and she added: "I'll bring you something to eat."

Again I told her about my not having any cash.

"That's all right," she answered. "Don't you worry, you will have plenty of money soon."

Now I got seriously worried. I felt sure that there was a trap somewhere or that they needed a guy to frame for someone else. I tried to wind myself out. Before I could do it, however, the waitress was back at the table with soup, fish, meat, and a bottle of wine. Seeing this in front of me, I forgot all about traps and frame-ups.

After having eaten, and drunk the red wine, and a second bottle was put on the table for me, the girl, all at once, cried out: "Messieurs, here is a stranded German sailor who cannot pay for his supper; won't you help him out?"

I felt lousy hearing this. But it was too late now to skip. I expected that very second to be beaten up and my bones broken into bits.

I was wrong. Nothing of the sort happened.

All the men in the saloon, sailors and longshoremen, turned around to look me over. One of them stood up, came over to my table, clinked glasses, and said: "Here's to your luck, sailor." He did not say Boche.

The girl passed a plate around, and when she brought it to my table, there was enough on it to pay for my supper and the two bottles of wine, and something was still left for breakfast the next morning.

When closing-time came, the girl asked me if I had a place to sleep. I said I had not. Then she said: "You may come with me for the night; I will put you up."

She had only one bed in her little room. I wanted to lie down on the floor, the way they do it in the movies, to show the girl that I was a gentleman. The girl, however, did not seem to like it very much. She said: "Don't make me ashamed

of you. What do you think I brought you here for? You will
have to pay for the night. And pay rather well or I shall be
sorry in the morning that I believed you to be a good sailor."

What else could I do? I had to do what she ordered.

"Do you think," she said when the light was switched off,
"that I got you a good supper just for your belly's sake? No,
my boy. You will have to pay for the supper also. I don't
want you to catch cold on the floor, and, besides, I am afraid
of burglars, and of mice, too."

In the morning she said: "Leave quietly. If the landlady
sees you, she's liable to raise my rent, thinking that I make
a little money on the side. Come again whenever you can,
sailor. Always pleased to meet you, and supper will always
be ready for you."

I would have liked to tell her right then that she was wrong
in thinking that a Boche was a good payer. Anyway, I am sure
some fine day she will find out, because quite a few American
buckets put in at Marseille port, and there are lots of guys
on them who like to pay well.

The same day I hopped another freighter and went back
to Barcelona.

19

Have I sailed many ships, sir? I should say I have. And I
have seen thousands of ships. Even the great unbeliever Saint
Tom would believe that. But, migud, I have never seen a ship
like that one.

The whole thing was a huge joke. Looking at it, one wouldn't
believe that it could ever keep above the water. One would
readily believe, though, that it might be an excellent means of
transportation over the Sahara Desert. Yes, sir. A team of camels
could pull her fine along the sand.

Her shape was neither modern nor pre-Roman. To try to place her in any period of shipbuilding was futile. She did not fit in any age I could think of. In no marine-museum anywhere in the world had I ever seen a model like that one.

On her hull was her name: *Yorikke.* The letters were so thin and so washed-off that I got the impression that she was ashamed to let anybody know her true name. *Yorikke.* Now, what language could that be? Almost any language. It sounded Nordic. Perhaps she was a hang-over from the old Vikings, hidden for centuries in a lonely bay somewhere in Iceland.

I don't know why, but that ship got me like a spell. I couldn't get away from it; no, sir. I stopped fishing, and I went over to look at the stern. According to international agreements, the name of her home port should have been painted there clearly. Apparently she did not want to betray her birthplace. So you're like me, I thought, without a proper birth-certificate. Bedfellows, hey? Of course, there was something painted on the stern. But, I am sure, only a well-trained archæologist could have deciphered what those spots meant.

There was a flag, of course, flying above the stern. The flag, however, was so pale, so flimsy, so shredded, that it might have represented any flag of any country in the world. It looked as if it had been flown from the battle-ships of all the fleets that had partaken in sea-battles for the last five thousand years.

I was interested in the color of the hull. I couldn't make it out. It looked as if it had been snow-white when the ship was still in her baby-shoes. That, however, must have been some time before old man Abraham left Ur of the Chaldees with his wife Sarah. I could see that at least two hundred new layers of paint had been put on top of the original white. As a result there were as many different colors painted on her hull as are known to exist. Those layers of paint made her appear twice her true size.

No owner of the *Yorikke* had ever permitted all her paint

to be taken off and an entirely new coat put on. Every patch of paint that was still good had been preserved so as to make the painting as inexpensive as possible. So there were a hundred square feet of sky-blue next to a hundred square feet of canary-yellow.

When I saw her first, I almost dropped my fishing-line in my excitement at seeing that monstrosity of the sea.

Often an individual may be recognized as insane by his outward appearance. The more deranged his mind is, the more awkward or strange his way of dressing will be, provided he is left to do as he likes.

There was something wrong with the *Yorikke*. To call her a sane ship or a normal vessel would have been an insult to all the other ships that sailed the seven seas. Her appearance agreed perfectly with her mind, her soul, her spirit, and her behavior. Only an insane ship could look like that. It was not alone her coat that made her look crazy. Everything on and about the bucket harmonized with her appearance.

Her masts were like branches reaching out from a fantastic tree in North Dakota in November. Her funnel was crooked and bent like a corkscrew. I couldn't figure out exactly how her bridge was connected with the rest of her.

As I sat on the pier, looking at this old maiden *Yorikke*, I laughed and laughed. I let loose such thundering laughter that *Yorikke* became frightened. She trembled all over and began to glide backwards along the bulks. She didn't want to go out into the open water. She was, obviously, afraid, knowing perhaps that she might never come back. She grazed and scratched along the heavy timbers of the pier, making a squeaking, piercing noise. Seeing her struggling so hard against the orders of her skipper, I began to pity her. It was like dragging old Aunt Lucinda, who had never been away from her native town, Jetmore, Kansas, into a bathing-suit and out upon a diving-board thirty feet above the level of the ocean. I felt real sympathy for the frightened *Yorikke*, who had to leave the calm, smooth water of the sheltered port and be driven out into the merciless world to fight against gales and typhoons and all the grim elements under heaven.

None of her men had mercy on her. They were working like hell to get her going on her way, indifferent to her unwillingness and her shrieking. I heard the crew running about. I heard their shouting and their hustling. The windlasses were rattling and clanging. I knew they were giving that old girl the works and were beating her up to get her to do her best before the eyes of so many seafaring people staring from other ships.

What could an old defenseless jane like her do against the rough fists of so many rum-soaked guys? Scratch and squeal and squeak she might, and bite, but it won't do her any good. She simply has to snap out of it and get it over and make off.

She was always that way. Once safe in the open sea, she would start running like a young devil let loose for the first time from her grandmother's apron-strings. I found out later that she ran so fast only to get back that much quicker to a snug port, in which she could rest and dream of the days long ago when no one had to hustle to make as many trips as possible for the sake of the company's turnover.

She couldn't be blamed for her behavior. She had begun to get heavy feet; she was no longer as young and springy as she was when she stood by to guard Cleopatra's banquets for Antony. Were it not for the many thick coats of paint on her hull, she would have frozen to death in the cold ocean, for her blood was no longer as hot as it was five thousand years ago.

20

There are people who seriously believe that they know something about ships, sailors, and oceans, simply because they've crossed on passenger ships a couple of dozen times. But a passenger really learns nothing and sees nothing about ships, salt water, or the crew. I might just as well include among the ignorant the ship's officers and stewards. Ships' officers are merely bureaucrats with a claim for an old-age pension, and the stewards are just waiters.

The skipper is in command of the ship. All right. But he does not know the ship. No, sir, believe me. The guy that sits on the dromedary and tells the driver where to go doesn't know the dromedary. The driver alone knows the animal and he alone understands it. It is he to whom the animal speaks and it is he who speaks to the poor beast. Only he knows the worries, the pains, and the joys of the dromedary.

The same holds true of a ship. The skipper in command always wants to do something the ship can't do and doesn't want to do. The ship hates him, just as all commanders are hated by those they kick around. When a commander is loved, or thinks he is, it is only because everybody under his command is clever enough to know that they can get along with the old man best by complying with his whims and caprices. Always consider your boss crazy, and you will always be right and stand in good with him.

The ship loves the crew. The crew are the only true comrades a ship has at sea. They polish the ship, they wash it, they stroke it, they caress it, they kiss it—and they mean it, because they are not hypocrites where their ship is concerned. The skipper has a home, sometimes a country home or an estate, and he has a family, a pretty wife, and lots of worries about his family. Some sailors too have wives and kids. They seldom make good sailors. They look at the ship just as a factory-worker looks at the plant he works in to make a living. The good sailors, the true sailors, the born sailors, have no other home in the world than their ship. It may be this ship or that one, but home is always a ship.

And the ship knows perfectly well that she couldn't move an inch without the crew. A ship can run without a skipper and officers. I have seen ships do it. But I have not yet heard of a ship that went along with only a skipper aboard.

The ship speaks to the crew, never to the skipper or to the officers. To the crew the ship tells wonderful stories and spins yarns of all sorts. The ship in turn likes to listen to the tales told by the crew. When old salts start to spin, all the rattling and crackling of a windjammer ceases. The ship gets quiet so as not to lose a single word of the story. All the sea-stories I know have been told to me by ships, not by people, and the stories written by pensioned skippers are the bunk. I have seen ships chuckling on Sunday afternoons, when the crew was sitting on deck telling stories of the seven seas and cracking jokes about skippers and mates and chiefs. I have seen ships cry and weep when stories were told of brave sailors who had gone to the bottom after having saved a child or another fellow. And I once heard a ship sob bitterly when it knew it would go down to its last place on the next trip. It was that ship that sobbed so heart-breakingly and that never came home again that was listed four months later at Lloyd's as "lost in unknown waters."

The ship is always on the side of the crew and never takes the part of the skipper. Why? The skipper doesn't work for the ship, nor does he care for it; he works and cares for the company that pays him. Often the men don't even know which company the ship they are on belongs to; no, sir. They don't bother with such details. They are interested in the ship, and in the food the ship gives them.

Suppose the crew mutinies—the ship immediately joins them, and the skipper does not know what to do with the bucket. It's a fact; strange perhaps, but so it is. I knew a ship that went out with a crew of strike-breakers. She was still in sight of the coast, less than twelve miles off, when she went down, just to drown that gang. She did it so unexpectedly that not a single man was saved. Yes, sir.

Looking again at that old dame *Yorikke*, I could not understand how she could have a complete crew going out of sunny Spain, the land of the free and the happy. To go with that ship rather than stay behind in such a great country was beyond my comprehension. There was a secret hidden somewhere. Perhaps she was—but it could not be. Not here, so close to civilization. A death ship leaving a civilized port with clean papers? Well, it's out now. A death ship.

Why didn't I notice it at the first glance? But, still, there is something about her that makes it not altogether definite that she's that sort of tramp. The bucket begins to interest me. I simply can't stop looking at her, if only to find out what the mystery is in back of her.

Finally she seemed to give in and make up her mind to go voluntarily. Thus I learned that she had personality. Her skipper didn't know it. He was a fool. *Yorikke* was more intelligent by far than her captain. She was, I could see now, like an excellent and experienced thoroughbred horse, the kind that has to be left alone if it is to show its best qualities. A skipper has only to present a stamped certificate, indicating that he has passed an examination, and there he is in command of a ship as delicate and as individualistic in character as the *Yorikke*! Another proof of the fact that a skipper doesn't know his ship; no, sir. Anyway, what does a skipper do all day long? Only worry where and how he can cut down expenses for the company—usually by cutting down the rations for the crew, which puts something in his own pocket, too.

The skipper tried to force *Yorikke* against the tide and wind. An old lady, with the experience of five thousand years, should not be forced. If you try it, she is likely to go off her track and bust right into a heavy flood-breaker. If she goes wrong, the pilot isn't to blame. The pilot is only supposed to know the waters of the port in which he is commissioned. He is not supposed to know the ship. That's the skipper's business I could tell now what sort the skipper was who chased that dame around.

She scratched off hard against the quay. I had to draw up my legs or she would have taken them along. I had no intention of shipping my legs to Morocco while the rest of me remained in Spain.

She kicked at her stern like an old hussy trying to dance the rhumba. A whirlpool of muddy foam was stirred up by her propeller From her side she spat and fiffed and pished and sissed like an old farm-mule with bladder trouble. Then she began swaying like a drunken society lion trying to avoid the lamp-posts, and never able to do so.

The skipper tried his hand again and succeeded in steering her clear of the wharf. Seeing her now only about two feet away, and noticing that her hull looked pock-scarred, I said to myself that even if I had a chance to escape the hangman by signing on for this bucket, I would prefer the hanging. For I could not remember ever having seen anything in the world, ship or no ship, that looked so dreadful and hopeless, and so utterly lost, as did the *Yorikke*. I shivered. It was better to be a stranded sailor and hungry than to be a deck-hand on this ship.

21

While the bucket was still struggling asthmatically to come clear, I glanced up to the fore-deck, where a dozen men were standing—obviously part of the crew off duty.

I have seen in my time ragged men, filthy men, wretched, lousy, stinking, dirty, broken, drunken, besmeared, sticky, unwashed, uncombed, unshaven, pishy and pashy, slimy, dreggy, and smutty men, but, so help me God, never before in all my life, not anywhere in the world, not even excluded Asiatic and South American ports, had I seen men like that crew hanging on the railing of that ship and staring down at the pier. A crew shipwrecked and marooned on a god-forsaken island for two years might look—but probably not—like that. How was it possible for a crew on an outgoing ship to be so? It was inconceivable that a ship could sail with such a crew.

I certainly did not look elegant. Far from it. Oh, very far! A Scotchman seeing me might have thrown me a penny. Yet compared with these men I looked like the sheik of the most sumptuous chorus baby on Broadway.

This was no death ship. May the Lord forgive me for the sin of mistaking the *Yorikke* for a death ship! They were pirates hunted for a year by all the battle-ships of all nations, buccaneers sunk so low that they had come to the point of looting Chinese vegetable junks.

One of them wore neither cap nor hat; no, he had wrapped around his head, turban-like, a rag from a woman's petticoat. Another—well, sir, you may not believe me, but may I be signed on as a stoker on an outrigger-canoe if I lie—well, he wore a high black silk hat. Figure that out, a sailor with a top-hat aboard an outgoing freighter. Perhaps there was a

special regulation on the *Yorikke* that the funnel-sweeper had
to wear a top-hat. There was another guy there who had on
full evening dress, and very elegant too. Since he was only
half the size of the clothes he wore, and since the man with
the top-hat looked more like the former owner of the evening
dress, I knew the whole story. The man with the top-hat had
been to a ball at the French embassy, where he had picked
up—let's presume "picked" up—a pearl necklace belonging
to the wife of a Chicago packer, and he had had to make his
get-away quickly when the woman yelled. Or perhaps he
had been to his own wedding, and when he saw, for the first
time, his mother-in-law, he ran like hell and reached the
Yorikke just in time to be signed on as a coal-drag. Others
were clothed, or, better, bedecked, with ragged pieces of
sacks. One wore instead of a man's shirt a kind of woman's
blouse which was probably missing somewhere in the upper
room of a tavern in a North African port. I would not have
been surprised to see one of them wearing a mantilla. But maybe
that one was right now in the stoke-hold firing the boilers.

Had I been sure that they were pirates I would have begged
them to take me along to fame and riches. But piracy, nowadays, doesn't pay if you haven't got at least one submarine.

Somehow, I felt they weren't pirates. Therefore I preferred
the hangman to sailing on the *Yorikke*. The ship that can take
me away from sunny Spain has to be a hell of a lot more elegant than the *Tuscaloosa*. And I don't want to say anything
against the *Tuscaloosa*. She was fine. Yes, siree.

I wonder where the *Tuscaloosa* is now? Panama? Or home
again to New Orleans? New Orleans. Jackson Square. Levee.
Honey. Oh, shit. Well, let's put on another piece of black
sausage. Maybe we'll yet get fried fish for supper tonight. Just
one moment, until that old rusty bathtub has gone. If it isn't
fried fish, maybe we'll get some paste soup in a restaurant or
a good Hollandish supper on the Dutch yonder.

The *Yorikke* passed along like a snail that had overeaten.

When the faces of the crew on the fore-deck were right above me, one of them yelled down: "Hey, you, ain't ye a sailor?"

"Yessir."

"Want a dshop?" Not bad English he used.

Do I want what?

Chips and dancing grizzly bears, I hope he doesn't mean it! A job. If he should be serious! Gods and heathen in dark Africa, save my soul.

A job. Exactly the question I have been afraid of for months and months. The trumpets of the archangel Mike on Judgment Day wouldn't have put as much fear of God into me as that question. It is the eternal law that a jobless man has to chase around for a job. When since the days of Cain was it ever heard of that a job is offered to you without your asking for it?

I am superstitious, like all sailors. On the seas and on ships, dependent always on good luck, and on the weather, and on fair sailing ways between hidden rocks, cliffs, sand-banks, and oncoming ships in thick fog, one cannot help getting superstitious. Without some superstition to rely on in time of trouble, one would go mad, because praying doesn't do a sailor any good. Ask the skipper when he orders the life-boats down. He just shouts: "Don't waste time, hurry up or the tub'll kick over."

It is this superstitious character that makes me answer yes when I am asked if I want a job. Suppose I should say no—all my luck, for the rest of my life, would be lost. I might never again get a ship to sail on back home to New Orleans.

Besides, a day might come when I really needed cash. It may be that the girl says: "Well, the doc figgers it will be about the middle of next week, if it's late." Then you need a job and need it badly. And then you feel sorry that once in your life you refused to take a job that was offered to you.

This damned superstition of mine has already played me

plenty of tricks and put me in conditions that were not at all pleasant or interesting. It was pure superstition and nothing else that led me once to become a grave-digger's assistant in Guayaquil, Ecuador. It was superstition that led me to help sell splinters from the cross of Our Savior at country fairs in Ireland, splinters from the very cross on which Our Lord breathed his last sigh. Each splinter was sold for a half-crown, and the magnifying glass with which to see the splinter set the believer back another half-crown. Since I played the Irish that nasty trick I have given up all hope of ever being saved and getting a chance to learn how to play the harp.

22

So, on account of my superstition, it was only natural for me to answer yes when asked if I wanted a job. I couldn't see my face, but I was sure that I was pale, pale from the horrible thought that I might have to sail on that bucket.

"A.B.?" the man asked.

Now, here was my chance. They were short an A.B. and I was not an A.B. I was careful not to say "Plain." In cases of emergency even a "plain" can take the wheel, if it's a quiet watch.

Joyfully I answered: "No, mister. No A.B. Black gang."

"Splendid!" the man cried out. "Splendid! Exactly what we need. Make it snappy. Hop on. We're off."

Everything was clear now. They would take on anything and anybody they could get. I was sure they were short half the crew. I might as well have said cook, or carpenter, or bos'n, or chief, or even captain; they would have answered: "Just what we need. Hop on."

I had still a few cards to play. "Where ye bound?" I asked. A sailor has the right to refuse to sign on if he doesn't like the trip or if he knows he is wanted by the police or by a deserted jane with a child in the country the ship is bound for.

"Where ye want to go?" they shot back.

Smart folk. No getting away from them. Whether I say the South Pole or Mount Everest, the answer will be: "That's exactly where we're going. Hop on."

I knew one country where that bucket wouldn't dare to go. So I said: "England."

"Man, you're lucky," yelled the guy. "We have cargo for Liverpool. Small goods. You can be paid off there if you want."

Here I had them. I knew that the one country in the world where a sailor could not be paid off if he wasn't English was England at that time. He had to be sick, or the ship had to lay off for repairs. But—how could I prove they were lying?

It seemed utterly ridiculous. No one in the whole world could force me to sign on with that ship, and yet— Guess it is always like that. If you are happy and contented, you want to be still happier. You want a change. I am convinced that ever since old man Adam was bored in Paradise—and, by the way, it was the only human virtue he ever showed—it has been man's curse never to feel perfectly satisfied.

Fate was again playing one of her many dirty tricks. I had said yes. Kings may break their word, but a good sailor cannot. This ship I had laughed at so heartily and so loudly now took her revenge. Didn't I say that the *Yorikke* had personality?

The trouble was that I had gone to look at outgoing ships. A sailor who feels satisfied at being stranded should keep his nose away from ships with the blue flag up. A ship putting out should concern a sailor only if it's his own ship.

Another thing: a sailor shouldn't dream of fish or fishing. It's a bad dream for a sailor. It's unlucky for a sailor. A sailor shouldn't even think about fish. Even when he's eating fish, he should eat it in the belief it is something else. I had neglected to obey that good old rule that has come down to us from seafaring people much wiser than we are.

I tried my last resort: "What is the pay?"

"English money," the guy yelled.

"How is the grub?"

"Rich and plenty. And listen, you sailor, hop on and get busy, or you won't make it. We're off."

They threw me a rope. I caught it. With outstretched legs I swung over, bumping against the hull. They quickly hauled me up, and I mounted steadily until at last I swung over the bulwarks.

And there I was on the *Yorikke*.

And that very moment, as if the *Yorikke* had been waiting for me, the engine took a deep breath, and the ship got up full speed. With caressing eyes I looked back upon wonderful Spain, now vanishing from my sight, disappearing in a mist with such rapidity that I had a feeling she was punishing me for having betrayed her. Well, Spain, I am sorry, but a sailor has to play fair, and he has to keep his word better than a king.

When the last glimpse of Spain had been veiled from my eyes, I felt that I had entered that big gate over which are written the solemn words:

He who enters here will no longer have existence!

DECEMBER

2

FRIDAY

candy canes

did not originally have stripes.

Pictures on cards before the 1900s show completely white canes.

COOKIES

LOVIN' FROM THE OVEN

THE SECOND BOOK

Inscription
over the crew's quarters
of the death ship

He
Who enters here
Will no longer have existence;
His name and soul have vanished
And are gone for ever.
Of him there is not left a breath
In all the vast world.
He can never return,
Nor can he ever go onward;
For where he stands there he must stay.
No God knows him;
And unknown will he be in hell.
He is not day; he is not night.
He is Nothing and Never.
He is too great for infinity,
Too small for a grain of sand,
Which, however small,
Has its place in the universe.
He is what has never been
And never thought.

THE SECOND BOOK

23

Now I could look closer at the shark-hunters. The impression I had got when I was still sitting on the quay was not bettered. Nor did it become worse. It simply became smashing and absolutely destructive. I had thought some of them Arabians or Nubians or a new kind of Negro. But now I realized that they were whites and looked like Swahili men only on account of the coal-dust and filth that covered them.

Nowhere on earth except in Bolshevik Russia are deck-hands considered members of the same social class as the skipper. Should that ever happen somewhere else, it would lead to complications; yes, sir. One fine day somebody might mistake the deck-hand for the skipper and thereby find out that a deck-hand can be just as intelligent as most skippers are. Which, by the way, would be no evidence that the deck-hand in question is intelligent at all.

Here, on the *Yorikke*, there were, obviously, several ranks of deck-hands. I got the impression there were deck-hands of the first grade, of the second grade, and more. I noticed two men who, doubtless, belonged to the class of deck-hands of the sixth grade, which may be considered the lowest class of deck-hands. I don't think these sixth-graders would have enough intelligence to help the savages of New Guinea break open coconuts with a stone ax.

"Good day!" the gang-leader of the pickpockets said to me. "I aim de shecond enjuneer. Dat man here wat is mine nabor, now dat ish our donkey-man." Some English, I thought; henceforth I shall have to translate their lingo if I want to understand what they mean. He wanted to inform me solemnly that he was the second engineer and that the horse-thief at his side was the donkey-man, or, as we used to call him, the donk. He gets his name, not from an ass, but from the donkey-engines which are used on ships to drive the windlasses, the winches, the cranes, and such machinery.

"Thank you, gentlemen, and I," I introduced myself, "I am the first president of the company that runs this tub here, and I have come aboard to hustle you guys stiff."

They must not think that they can put one over on me— telling me that one is the second and the other the donk. Not me, no siree. I had already sailed as a kitchen-boy when birds like these were still being chased by truant-officers. I know cinnamon when I get it in chocolate.

He didn't understand me, for he went right on: "Go to the quarters afore, and get you a bunk."

Shit! Does he speak seriously? This escaped convict, is he really to be the second engineer, and the other pickpocket the donk? I tottered to the foc'sle as though I'd been clubbed over the head.

On coming to the quarters I found a few men lazily stirring about in their bunks. They looked at me with sleepy eyes, showing not the slightest interest in me. I figured that a new sailor was looked at with less interest than a new can of paint.

I am positive that the *Yorikke* had seldom, if ever, left a port with a complete crew. A nasty story was told about her always being short of men. It was rumored, and I am sure the rumor was well founded, that the skipper had several times gone out of town to the gallows, where, in the silence of night, with the help of the bos'n, he carefully examined the hanged to find one in whom there was enough life left to let him say: "Yes, cap'n, sure I'll sign on." I don't see any damn reason why I shouldn't believe this rumor. Other things have happened on the *Yorikke* that were a hundred times worse.

I asked for a vacant bunk. With a movement of his head, crooking the corner of his upper lip, a man indicated lazily an upper bunk.

"Did someone kick off in it?" I asked.

The man nodded, crooked his upper lip again, and said: "The lower bunk is also for sale."

So I took the lower. The man was no longer looking at me. I felt sure that if I asked him another question he would throw a knife at me, or at least his shoes.

The bunk was not only vacant, but also entirely free from any mattress, straw, sheet, blanket, or pillow. There was only dust and splinters and broken-off pieces of worm-eaten wood inside. The bunk was an example of how far an economical shipbuilder can go to save space without coming to the point where a labor-inspector would say: "Not enough space left for the crew." Labor-inspectors are very lenient as regards the builder and the company. In this bunk there was hardly space enough to lay two tightly folded umbrellas close to each other. A sailor, provided he was very lean, could lie in it only sideways. To sleep on his back was out of the question. The *Yorikke* took good care never to let a sailor get so fat around his hips that he would find it impossible to lie sideways in his bunk. Since every sailor coming from his watch was so tired that he couldn't even think of gin, it didn't matter, anyhow.

The aisle or, better, the gangway between the bunks was so narrow that you could sit way back in your bunk and you would still have your knees pressed against the opposite bunk. It was impossible to dress, but as a matter of fact there was little dressing ever done by this crew, for they had nothing to dress with. Everybody kept the few rags he was clothed in on his body, working or sleeping. Whoever would undress on lying down would never find again what he used to call his pants or shirt or shoes.

Besides, there were no blankets, and your clothes served to keep you at least a little warm when you slept.

In each of the bunks opposite the one I had taken there were a few pieces of ragged sackcloth and shredded scraps of old canvas and such remains of pants, jackets, and shirts as, regardless of how hard one might try, could no longer be used as clothes. These rags served as the mattresses. For pillows some guys used pieces of wood; others had old discarded cordage and junk. Now I knew it was possible to sleep on cordage, and soon I learned to envy those who had it.

Whenever a man skipped in port and was left behind or whenever one fell overboard or died, the survivors fought for those rags and cordage harder than hungry vultures fight with hyenas over a carcass.

24

The *Yorikke* had no electric light, and no machinery for it. In her immaculate innocence she evidently did not know that such a thing as electric light even existed. By many means I could discover the exact age of the *Yorikke*. One of those means was the light used to illuminate the quarters of the crew.

This apparatus we called the kerosene lamp. Newcomers, not yet initiated, called it more crudely the petroleum lamp. It was a kind of small tin kettle, pretty well shattered. The burner, which could be screwed off, had had, at the time it was bought, the appearance of brass, perhaps even bronze. Even a four-year-old girl, however, knows that brass cannot rust, but iron can and does.

The rust that had accumulated during the last five hundred years had destroyed the burner. Yet out of a habit acquired in long service, the burner still kept its original form, like a ghost. Each newcomer was warned not to touch the burner too hard when filling up the lamp, because the ghost might dematerialize, and no burner would be left.

The glass chimney of the lamp was only a short stump, always thickly blackened by smoke. By order of the bos'n the lamp had to be cleaned every day. So every morning the question was fired: "Whose turn is it, damn, to clean the lamp?" I never heard anyone yell: "It's me," nor anyone say: "Your turn, Spainy." The "you," whoever it might have been, would have fought with words and fists to win a decision that it was not his turn. The lamp was never cleaned.

It was the same lamp, as could be seen from its antique shape, that had been used by the seven virgins when they went out into the night to guard their virtue. The wick had not been changed since the time it was made, by cutting off a piece of the woolen underwear of one of the virgins. One could not expect that a lamp used by virgins to guard their virginity would light up the quarters of the crew of the *Yorikke* sufficiently so that we could see each other.

The kerosene used in the lamp was called diamond oil. It was called so in the books which the skipper presented to the company when collecting his expenses. But I had seen the skipper's cabin-boy go into the engine-hold when the engineer was called out by the skipper. The boy scratched up all the dropped oil and grease from the engine, brought it to the skipper, and the skipper mixed it with gas to make the diamond used in our lamp.

I asked upon arriving on the *Yorikke:* "Where is the mattress for my bunk?"

"Not supplied here. Must have your own."

"Pillows?"

"Not supplied."

"Blankets?"

"Not supplied."

"What is supplied here, then?" I finally asked.

"Work," a man answered calmly.

I was really surprised to see that the company supplied at least the ship; and by no means would I have been perplexed if the company had demanded that the sailor bring his own ship along.

When I hopped on the ship, I had on me a pair of still decent-looking pants, a hat, a jacket, and one pair of shoes. I was considered the richest guy aboard, for the bird that owned the evening dress wasn't so well off as I had thought when I first saw him. The pants were cut short right under his knees, and the elegant-looking coat with its long forked tail was busted in the back. Yet the front had looked grand.

After being on the *Yorikke* for a couple of weeks, I learned that those guys who had the least to call their own were liked best by the skipper and the mate. The skipper always looked with grim eyes at a man returning from shore leave with some-thing new on his back. On the other hand, he never minded a bit seeing a man return so drunk that he had to be carried aboard. He tipped mugs who had helped the sailor find his ship; and many times he willingly paid the tavern debts for one of his own men. Yet never would he have paid a dollar in advance to a man if he knew that the man was going to buy himself a new shirt.

The quarter I was in had two compartments, which were separated by a thick wooden wall against which, on either side, were fixed two bunks. Two bunks, the upper and the lower, of my compartment were fixed against the gangway wall; the other two were fastened on that same wooden wall. The other compartment had two bunks on the wall and two on the hull of the ship. Thus what was built for four men served for eight.

Regulations demand that the crew must not eat their meals in the room in which they bunk. They must eat in the crew's mess. There was no such mess for the crew on the *Yorikke*, for the simple reason that when the *Yorikke* was built, all labor in Egypt, Greece, and Persia was still done by slaves, and to demand a special dining-room for them would have meant, in the Persian language, criminal syndicalism—for which being thrown to the lions was considered a very lenient punishment. Now, there are a few ports in the world where, occasionally, labor-inspectors come aboard to see if communists, who are always yelling that crews are treated like animals, are liars or racketeers. These labor-inspectors are mild-mannered with the shipping companies; they have a very sympathetic understanding of the companies' worries. These inspectors usually feel delighted to have the skipper throw sand in their eyes. The company that owned the *Yorikke* used for sand the strange fixing of a mess-room for the crew.

The wooden wall which divided the sleeping-quarter into two did not reach from one end of the place to the other. It ended two feet beyond the bunks, where it was fixed against an iron post. From this post on, in the direction of the bow, there was a little space left. Into this space a long rough table and two benches were set up. So there you had the required mess-room. To be sure, it was still in the same room as the bunks, but it gave the impression that the mess-room was apart. You had only to use your imagination a little. Of course, there was no wall dividing the two bunk-spaces from the mess-space, and since there was no wall, there could be no doors. But since a sailor with a head could imagine a wall with a door in it, any labor-inspector with a head could also imagine it. So everybody was satisfied, and the report for the *Yorikke* was always okay.

In a corner, right by the crude dining-table, there stood an old bucket, which was always leaking. This weather-beaten bucket was the wash-basin, bathing-tub, shower-bath, and scrubbing-pail, all in one. It served, moreover, for lots of other purposes, one of which was to catch a couple of pounds of the insides of drunken sailors returning from shore leave, provided it was reached in time.

Crowded into the space called the mess-room were four

closets. These closets were supposed to serve as wardrobes for the crew. Had it not been for the filthy rags and torn-up sacks that hung inside, these closets might have been called empty. Eight men lived in this quarter, yet there were only four closets. Still the shipbuilder had overestimated the chances of the crew owning something. Because at present there was nothing worth guarding in any of the closets.

By special order of the skipper the quarters had to be swept every day. Usually it was done by one who had remained stuck in the mud unable to get his foot out, or by one who had lost a needle or a button that he could not spare. Once a week the quarters were flooded with salt water. This we called scrubbing the foc'sle. No soap, no brushes were supplied. The skipper probably sent in bills for soap and brooms and brushes, but we never saw them.

The crew did not even have soap with which to wash their shirts. Soap was a rare and precious thing on the *Yorikke*, which was additional evidence that the *Yorikke* had not yet entered the stage where civilization begins. Happy the man who carried in his pocket a little piece of soap with which to wash his face when he became ashamed of himself. Nobody ever dared let even the smallest piece of soap lie around. It could be as tiny as a pinhead, yet someone would find it and hide it like a diamond. This appreciation of soap indicated that the crew were not savages and that they still kept slightly in touch with civilization.

The filth on the floor and the walls was so thick and so hardened that only an ax could break it off. I would have liked to try it—not out of any sentiment about cleanliness, which was wholly lost on the *Yorikke*, but for scientific reasons. I felt sure—and to this very day I still feel the same way—that if I had broken open the crusted filth and mud, layer by layer, I would have found Phœnician coins and medals near the bottom. I still feel excited when I speculate on what I might have found if I had gone still deeper. There is a great possibility that I might have found the bitten-off finger-nails of the great-grandfather of the Java man, so very essential to science for determining whether the cave-man had heard of Henry Ford and if early bank mathematicians had had sufficient intelligence to figure out exactly how much money old Rockefeller makes while he cleans his dark goggles.

Leaving the quarters, one had to pass a very dark and unbelievably narrow corridor or gangway. In the opposite wall was a door leading to quarters similar to ours in shape and arrangement, but ten times worse as regards filth and dirt. I would have sworn away my soul that nothing on earth could be filthier than the quarter I was in, but when I saw the opposite quarter I said: "This is the worst."

One end of the gangway led to the deck, the other to a kind of pitfall. Near the end of the gangway, not quite at the pitfall, there were two very small rooms, one at each side. These small rooms served as quarters for the petty officers, the bos'n, the carpenter, the donkey-man, and another man who had something to say aboard ship. There was a mystery about his position. Sometimes he helped the donkey, another time he lent the carpenter a hand, and sometimes he acted like a second bos'n, chasing the deck-hands about the aft while the bos'n was chasing them about the fore. Had we still lived in the days before the revolution, I would have thought him the whipper, the chainer, the hangman. He looked like a bos'n escaped from a captured pirate-ship.

The pitfall led down into two small holds. One was the chain-hold, or the chain-chamber, in which there were all kinds of chains, emergency anchors, and such objects as might be useful for repairs at sea.

The other room, to starboard, was called the hold of horrors, or, more often, the chamber of horrors. There was nobody on the *Yorikke* who could claim that he had ever been inside it. We tried several times to find a peep-hole or a crack through which we might see what was inside. But there was no peep-hole and no crack to be found, and when, once during the night, Spainy drilled a hole through the door, we discovered that the door was protected with armor-plate.

Once when for some reason or other somebody asked for the key to this hold of horrors, it came to light that no one on the whole bucket knew where the key was. The mates claimed the skipper must have it. The skipper, on the other hand, swore by his soul and by the safety of his unborn children that he knew nothing about the whereabouts of the key to that forehold. And immediately he gave strict orders against opening the door, adding that should anyone dare force this hold open, he would shoot him like a sick dog and sink his carcass in the sea without a prayer. We got scared stiff and avoided going even near it save when we were ordered to get something out of the hold toward port.

I have never met a skipper who had no whims. This one had them wholesale. One of his many whims was never to inspect the quarters of the crew, which, according to regulations, he has to do at least once a week. He always had some excuse for not doing it, saying he would do it the next day, because at the moment he didn't want to spoil his appetite, and, besides, he had to hurry to take the position of the ship.

25

There is a rumor along the coasts of the Mediterranean and the western African coast that two men were actually in this hold of horrors and saw with their own eyes everything inside. These men, of course, were no longer on the *Yorikke.* They had been fired the moment the skipper discovered that they had broken in. He was not the same skipper who was now in command and who had sworn to shoot any man who dared look into this hold.

Nevertheless, fired or not fired, their stories remained on the *Yorikke*. The crew may leave a ship, their stories never leave. A story penetrates the whole ship and every part of it, the iron, the steel, the wood, all the holds, the coal-bunkers, the engine-hall, the stoke-hold, even the bilge. Out of these parts, full of hundreds and thousands of stories, tales, and yarns, the ship tells the stories over again, with all the details and minor twists. She tells the stories to her best comrades—that is, to the members of the crew. She tells the stories better and more exactly than they could ever be told in print. One has only to listen with an understanding heart and with love for the ship. Of course, those people who sign on for a trip the same way as they would take a job in an automobile plant never hear any of the stories told by the ship, and they sign off as dumb as they were when they came aboard. There's no use telling those guys that ships tell stories; they simply think themselves too smart to believe it; yes, sir.

This story about the two men having been in the hold of horrors remained on the *Yorikke* like all the others. The two men driven by an unquenchable curiosity had seen a number of skeletons in that hold. Frightened as they were, they could not count how many there actually were. To count them would have been, anyway, rather difficult since the skeletons had fallen apart and had mingled with each other. There was no doubt, though, that there were a lot of them. But these invaders of the hold were able to make out to whose bodies the skeletons had originally belonged.

They were the last remains of former members of the crew who had been eaten up by rats. These rats, huge as big cats, were often seen by us when they ran out of this hold through some hole which we could never find. The rats ran about the quarters trying to pick up food and old shoes; and they disappeared as quickly and strangely as they had shown up. We were all afraid of the big, savage animals, but we could never catch or kill one. They were too quick and too smart for us.

Why and for what reasons the unfortunate sailors had been thrown into the hold of horrors and given over to these terrible rats we, for a long time, could not see. But from the stories told about the *Yorikke* in the ports where we put in, we picked up here a word and there a word, and eventually we put the whole story together.

These sailors, of whom only the scattered skeletons told that they had ever been alive, had been sacrificed to cut down the running-expenses of the *Yorikke* and to keep high the dividends of the stockholders of the company.

Regulations require that a sailor must be paid overtime if he makes any by order of the skipper, because unions have had some bad influence even on the shipping business. Now, when a sailor signed off from the *Yorikke*, he naturally asked to be paid for his hundreds of hours of overtime. He relied on this pay, for his regular wages were always paid out long before in advance money.

So whenever he dropped the word: "Sir, how about my hundred and sixty hours' overtime?" he was led right away to the hold of horrors and thrown in it before he had a chance to realize what was happening. The skipper had no other means to dispose of the sailor, because the skipper was under strict orders to keep the expenses for the *Yorikke* far below the possible minimum, or he would lose his job. Skippers have a tougher time to land a job than a plain sailor has, for everybody wants to be a skipper, and very few like to be deckhands. On account of the difference in wages.

It always happened, of course, in port. No sailor has yet been found who asked to sign off in mid-ocean, without another ship standing by. Being in port, the skipper could not throw the man overboard. The port authorities would not permit such a thing to be done, because it would pollute the harbor, for which crime the skipper would have to pay a heavy fine. The port authorities were not interested a bit in what a skipper might do to his men so long as the port was kept clean. Suppose the skipper had let his man go without paying for overtime; the sailor (sailors are that mean) would have gone straight to the seamen's union, or, worse, to the Wobbly firemen's syndicate, or, in a mild case, to the consul. In any case the skipper would have been forced to pay the overtime, or the whole *Yorikke* would have been put under an embargo. The Wobblies in particular and the communists would have held the ship for half a dollar if the skipper had refused to pay it to a sailor when due.

So what else could the skipper, no matter how human he was, do? He simply had no other way out than to throw the sailor into the chamber of horrors.

He did not mean to do the sailor harm; he just wanted not to be troubled by the union or by the authorities, for he might miss his proper sailing-time and have to pay twenty-four hours more in anchorage taxes. When the ship was on the high seas again, the skipper went to the hold of horrors to release his man, whom he needed badly, because two or three men had, as usually happened on the *Yorikke*, skipped the bucket, or else they were somewhere in jail for being drunk or for a row or on account of some trouble about a dame with a baby.

But in the meantime something had happened in the hold of horrors that the skipper could not have foreseen. Certain rats in the hold had taken out marriage licenses upon seeing a sailor come in to provide them with an excellent wedding feast. So the rats had every reason not to let that sailor go, once he came within their reach. No matter how elegantly and nobly the skipper gave battle to the rats, he always lost out, and if he had fought to exhaustion, there was every possibility that he might have had to share the lot of his sacrificed sailor. The skipper dared not shoot or call for help, for then his secret would have been revealed and he would have lost for all time his chance to get away with not paying his men for overtime. There was nothing else for him to do but leave the sailor to the wedding guests.

You could never make a man who had sailed the *Yorikke* believe those dreadful stories about slaves and slave-ships; no sir. Never had slaves been packed as closely as we were. Slaves could never have worked as hard as we had to. Never could slaves have been as hungry and as tired and as down and out as we always were. Slaves had their festivals, their singing, their dances, their weddings, their beloved women, their children, their joy, their religious merriment, and hope. We had nothing. Senseless drunks and a ten-minute girl for half a peseta were all the recreation we ever had. We were as cheerless as a busted five-cent balloon in an ash-can.

Slaves were valuable goods, paid for in real money, goods that were expected to bring even higher prices if kept in good shape. They were goods handled like rare vases. Nobody would have paid even the cost of transportation of slaves that were starved to death, that were bruised from too many whippings, that were so overworked that they could hardly move a toe. Slaves were treated better than good horses, because they had a greater commercial value.

Sailors, on the other hand, are slaves that are not bought and that cannot be sold. Nobody is interested in their wellbeing, because if one of them falls overboard, or dies in the dung, no one loses any money on him. Besides, there are thousands eagerly waiting to take the place of him who is thrown into the ditch along the road to the progress and prosperity of the shipping business.

Sailors are certainly not slaves. They are free citizens, and if they have established residences, they are even entitled to vote for the election of a new sheriff; yes, sir. Sailors are free laborers, they are free, starved, jobless, tired, all their limbs broken, their ribs smashed, their feet and arms and backs burned. Since they are not slaves, they are forced to take any job on any ship, even if they know beforehand that the bucket has been ordered down to the bottom to get the insurance money for the owners. There are still ships sailing the seven seas under the flags of civilized nations on which sailors may be whipped and lashed mercilessly if they refuse to ship double watches and half of the third watch thrown in.

Slaves had to be fed well, like good horses. The free sailor has to eat whatever is placed before him, regardless of whether the cook was yesterday still a tailor. The company cannot pay wages for a real cook, because the stockholders of the company want their dividends. Suppose a good cook comes aboard and wants to do something for the hard-working crew; he cannot do it, because the skipper has to economize on the expenses for the crew's fare.

There are wonderful regulations all over the world as to the treatment of sailors aboard ship. They look fine on paper, these regulations. There are also the most wonderful regulations as to the purity of food, especially in packing-plants. And just open a can in which you are supposed to find the pork and beans that the elegant label tells you about. Instead of pork and beans you find only the effective results of the pure-food regulations. Precisely the same is true of the five thousand regulations concerning the welfare of sailors aboard seagoing buckets. Whenever new regulations are made, I think of the *Yorikke*, and right then, without the help of a communist meeting or a peace conference, I know exactly what the regulations will be good for and in whose favor they are enacted.

There are sea-stories and sea-stories, millions of them. Every week an output of at least seven hundred and fifty. If you look closely, however, at those interesting sea-stories, you notice that they tell of sailors who are opera-singers in disguise, who manicure their finger-nails, and who have no other worries than their goddamned silly love-affairs. Even that heavenly, that highly praised, that greatest sea-story writer of all time knew how to write well only about brave skippers, dishonored lords, unearthly gentlemen of the sea, and of the ports, the islands, and the sea-coasts; but the crew is always cowardly, always near mutiny, lazy, rotten, stinking, without any higher ideals or fine ambitions. Of course the crew is that way. Why? What ambition shall the crew have? For whom? The skipper has ambition, because higher wages and promotion and orders await him. His names flares over the front pages of the papers and is set perhaps in golden letters on tablets on the walls of the Board of Trade. The crew have nothing in the world but their wages, their food, their health, their lives. They have no promotion in sight and no share in the dividends of the company. So what earthly reason have they to be ambitious about anything? To save the lives of passengers in a shipwreck no crew have ever failed in their duty as human beings; but skippers have, to save the company's money. Sailors know that, and therefore they are the only people who know how to read a sea-story the right way, and how to read about the bravery of skippers in newspaper reports. Not the skipper, but the sailor is the one who is the first to risk his life, because he is always nearest the real danger, while the skipper on his bridge, like the general at headquarters, is farthest away from where he could lose something; yes, sir.

26

I hardly exchanged more than ten words with those sleepy men groaning in their bunks. When I had been told that there were no blankets, pillows, or mattresses for the crew on this bucket, there seemed to be nothing left to talk about.

Above me, on the fore-deck, I heard the rattling and banging of the chains, the clanging and scratching of the anchor against the hull, the screeching of the winches, the hustling and trampling of heavy feet, the commanding and swearing and cursing of the mates and the bos'n and of whoever thought he had somebody to chase around.

Noise like that always makes me sick at my soul. I feel best when the ship is out on the high sea. A ship in port is no longer a ship. It is merely a box to be loaded or to be unloaded. Nor is a sailor aboard a ship in port a sailor; he is just a hired man. Nothing better. The dirtiest work a sailor ever has to do is done while the ship is in port; the sailor works there exactly like a worker in a factory. No watches, only a full day's work. Cleaning, scrubbing, wiping, painting the hull, polishing, sweeping, washing, repairing. You get sick only thinking of it.

I didn't leave the quarter while I still heard the noise overhead. It isn't a good policy to go near where work is being done. No hurry for me. I don't get paid for it, anyhow. Work always comes your way, don't you worry. A long life of work is still ahead of you.

I have read a hundred times in the magazines stories of men who succeeded in life, who were never such horrible sinners as to be failures, with pictures and photographs taken from life, in which you saw the great gun first as a dirty baby, then as a farm-boy, then shining shoes, running errands, selling newspapers and uxtras in the streets, then working as an office-boy for three bucks a week, and soon afterwards becoming the president of the bank and owning all the savings-account deposits of the customers, and marrying Margaret Wackersford and in doing so becoming the son-in-law of the president of the First National and the brother-in-law of the vice-president of Bethlehem Steel and the nephew-in-law of the Secretary of the Navy, and everything is fine now, and all he does from now on is just collect money and more money. All this is in the success stories, with pictures, and therefore it is the whole truth and nothing but the truth, so help me. I have done exactly the same. When I was not yet seven, I was up at four

in the morning working for a milkman until six thirty for
forty cents a week; from six thirty to nine I worked for a
news-agent, who paid me sixty cents a week for running like
the devil from residence to residence with an armful of papers;
from nine to twelve I shined boots; then there were the afternoon papers; then chopping wood and running to the laundry
for ladies; then came the evening papers, and so on until I
fell like a stone on the bare floor of a room in Lincoln Avenue,
Chic, in which I was allowed to sleep free of charge for
washing dishes at night for a German clergyman who had
fled from his country on account of having, like a true gentleman, sworn falsely to save the reputation, if any, of a married jane. Before I was ten I shipped as a kitchen-boy on a
Spanish tramp, making all the Pacific ports from Mexico down
to Chile, after having had a hurried career as a dumb boy in
a circus assisting a clown who couldn't be funny without
pushing and fighting a half-starved boy. I certainly have always known how to work, and I have always worked four
times more than I was paid for. But I am still far from being
the first president of the California Railroad and Steamship
and Fruit Corporation. Suppose I should really work for thirty
long years in a steel mill, always doing more and more in
the hope that I might at least become cashier. Then, one day,
thinking that the time has come to cash in the promised reward, I would go to the office and ask: "How about the job
as assistant vice-president to begin with?" The answer is:
"Sorry, nothing doing right now, but just go on the same way
as you have been during the last thirty years. We are watching you all right and taking proper notice of all you do. As
soon as we need another president, we will think it over. Don't
forget to punch the time-clock." Meanwhile I have become
forty, and soon out I go with the short but plain notice: "We
have to take in younger men; you will find something else."

I don't know where jobs as presidents and as millionaires
could be found for all the readers of success stories if they

should try to cash in on the promises. A hundred and twenty years ago there was a saying: "Every one of my soldiers carries a marshal's baton in his bag." Today it is: "Every one of our employees may become president of our company; look at Mr. Flowerpot, he did it." I think all these successful men must have shined boots of another sort than I, and the newspapers they sold must have been different from the papers I carried.

I waited until the noise on deck had ceased and I was sure that there was no more extra work left. When everything seemed quiet and the *Yorikke* went softly on her way, I left the quarters and went to look about the deck. The moment I stepped out, the pickpocket who had introduced himself as the second engineer hopped me and said: "Just looking for you, guy; the old man wants to see ye and sign ye on. Just follow me."

Rich experience has taught me that whenever somebody says: "Just follow me," or: "Come along," it means always: "We shall take good care of you, and keep you here for quite a while. Take it easy and don't resist."

The *Yorikke* was running like a devil flitting into hell. The pilot had left the ship long ago, and the first mate had taken the bridge.

The skipper was still a young man, hardly more than thirty-five. About five seven in height. Slightly fat without looking it. He certainly never overate, though what he ate was good. His face was healthy and red; he must have had freckles when a boy. His hair was brownish yellow; it might have been nearly red when he was ten. His eyes were light waterish blue, without a definite expression, and with the look of a man with very little energy. Later I learned that his eyes did not indicate his character. Very well dressed, one might say really elegant. The color of his suit, his tie, his socks, and his smart shoes all matched well and showed him to be a man of good taste.

If one did not know his profession, one would never think him the captain of a tramp. He would have been the glory and essence of an ocean liner in which women between thirty and forty were sailing to get away from their rich and boresome husbands. But any person who was in a hurry to reach Europe safely would never have trusted a liner on which he was the skipper, looking as he did. From his looks one would not have guessed that he could ever bring even a three-hundred-ton bucket from one port to another in calm weather. Here again he betrayed his looks. I learned soon that he was one of the ablest skippers and the most daring and enterprising I have ever met. In war-time he would make a skipper of a torpedo-boat chaser such as there are very few of in the whole world.

He spoke a refined English, the kind one may learn in a good school in a foreign country. It was grammatically too correct for anybody American or English to think him a native of an English-speaking country. When speaking he selected his words with great care and good taste, giving the impression of a cultured individual, but at the same time an English-speaking person would feel that he was not trying to give that impression, but that he talked that way because he wanted to use only words of which he was absolutely sure of the proper meaning and of the correct pronunciation. Once when I was alone in his cabin I had a look at his library. There were only four or five books of such trash as detective or mystery stories. The rest of his books were so carefully selected that ever afterwards I wondered how that man came to be the skipper of a tramp. There must have been something back of it. Perhaps his wife was found in bed with another man, and a shooting resulted. Lost honor for abandoning a ship or crew, or something like that, it could not have been. He was not the kind to do that. Later, knowing more about human beings, I think I came pretty close to understanding him through and through. He was the type that refuses an offer to be the captain of a liner, for if he had taken it he would have been bored to death and would have resigned after two trips—after being chased by American women from the East and Middle West who stepped up behind him at three o'clock in the morning or at midnight and asked questions, already twenty-five million times correctly answered, about why a ship carries green lights at star and red lights at port, and why the propellers are at the stern instead of at the bow since an airplane has the prop at its bow, and why a liner is tugged out of port instead of going out under its own power—questions never asked to learn the facts, but to brag: "Oh, my dear, I've just come from the master of the ship. I had a long talk with him about navigation. He told me all about it, and just think, oh, dear me, he's had that sort of job for fourteen years!"

The contrast between the skipper and his second engineer, who also ranks as a ship's-officer, was not striking, but simply destructive in every way. If I had still been in doubt as to what kind of ship I was on, this contrast alone would have told me and convinced me without any other evidence.

"So you are the new drag?" the skipper greeted me when I stepped into his cabin.

"The what, sir?"

"The coal-drag, the coal-shoveler; you know, the man who hauls the coal from the bunkers to the fireman, to the stoker, if you understand that expression better."

"I, sir? You mean me? I the drag, the shoveler? You are mistaken, sir, excuse me. I am no drag, I am a fireman." The truth began to dawn upon me.

"I didn't say a single word to you about being fireman," the horse-thief broke in. "I said the black gang, the fire gang, didn't I? That's what I said."

"Right," I admitted. "That is what you asked, and I answered yes. But in all my life I have never been a coal-drag."

The skipper's face showed that he was beginning to be

bored. He said to the pickpocket: "That is your business, Mr. Dils. This does not concern me. I thought everything was in shape."

"I wish to be put ashore right away, sir," I said to the skipper. "It was never my intention to sign on as coal-shoveler. Not me, sir. I shall protest, and I sure shall complain to the harbor authorities of attempted shanghaiing."

"Who shanghaied you?" the horse-thief yelled. "Did I? It's a stinking, funking lie, it is. I haven't to shanghai anybody."

"Dils!" the skipper fell in again with a warning tone in his voice. "I will have nothing to do with this, you understand, Mr. Dils." He laid, this time, particular stress upon the "Mister." "I am not responsible for anything of this sort, I want to make this as clear as sunlight, Mr. Dils. You will have to stand for what you are doing. Straighten this out between you. Outside. Not here in my cabin."

The pickpocket seemed not to mind what the skipper said. He asked me again: "What did I say to you? Didn't I say black gang?"

"Yes, you said that. But you didn't say—"

"So what? Does the drag belong to the black gang or does he not? Just tell me your opinion," the louse questioned.

"Of course, the coaler belongs to the boiler gang," I answered, "but, see here, mister, this does not mean—"

"All right then, this will do, this surely settles the issue," the skipper said. "If you really meant fireman, you should have said so. Then our Mr. Dils would have told you that we are not short a fireman. Well, now we may write."

He opened the book with the crew's register and asked my name.

My honest name in the register of a death ship? Not me. I have not come down so far yet. Never again in all my life would I have a chance to sign on for a decent ship. I sure would rather prefer a release paper from San Quentin or Leavenworth or some other honest mansion than the pay-book of a death ship. Every honorable skipper would shun me more than if I were coming full of syph ole Phillis.

So I abandoned my good name. I think it was anyway only my mother's name, since it had never been clear if my father had really his name added or not. I severed all family connections. I no longer had a name that was by right my own.

"When and where were you born?"

My name gone, I still had my country.

"In—in—in—" I began to stammer.

"Where did you say?"

"Alexandria."

"Alexandria what? In the United States?"

"No, Egypt."

With this my country was also gone. For the rest of my life I would have for identification only the pay-book of the *Yorikke*.

"Nationality? British, I presume."

"No, sir, without nationality."

Can there be anybody in the world who would expect me to register on this ship my name and my nationality? On the *Yorikke*? It would give the *Yorikke* a chance to say: "American? Shit. Bullshit. An American even came *here*, to shovel coal within my very hull, a dirty assistant to a Portuguese fireman who was an escaped convict from an Arabian pen." No, sir. I couldn't do that. It was not patriotism. It was simply —well, I could not. It would have been like betraying my country to the enemy. Sell out my country to the *Yorikke*? Whatever the consuls or all the other authorities in all the world may say, it is still my country; and it is still my country with all her gangsters, bandits, corruption, red tape, unlimited mediocrity and hypocrisy, and with her political mandarins; it is still the country which nobody can ever take away from me. It's just love, like the love for a mother whether she likes it or not. And it is so far, so very far away from all the loud jazz-patriotism and flag-waving. It is love. And against love there is no medicine and no death-penalty of any use. So for this love, and for her honor, I had to renounce my country, as if I had never heard of it.

So I repeated: "No, sir. No nationality. Without a country. League of Nations, Geneva."

He did not ask for a passport or for my sailor's card or for any paper or envelope with my name on it. He knew that men aboard the *Yorikke* must not be asked for papers. They might say: "Sorry, sir, I have no papers." Then what? In that case he would not be permitted to sign the man on, and the *Yorikke* would never have a crew. A man with any paper, whether his own or not, never shipped on the *Yorikke*. In the next port the list of the crew has to be verified by the consul of the country under whose flag the ship claims to sail. Since the man has made a trip already, the consul cannot refuse to acknowledge him a proper member of the crew. He has to accept him, paper or no paper. The man is now actually considered a resident of the country under whose flag the ship sails. But it does not give the man a country, or a nationality, or the right to claim a passport.

The consul does not know death ships, officially; and unofficially he does not believe in their existence. It requires certain talents to be a useful consul. Nor do consuls believe a person was ever born if said person cannot produce a birth-certificate.

Every skipper of the *Yorikke* knew how to get his men. He could never sign on a new man as long as the ship was still in port. In that case he had to take the man to the consul. The consul was obliged to ask for the passport or sailor's card. If he had none, the consul was not permitted to let the man sign on. Then the skipper would have been one man or many men short. The skipper always waited until the blue flag was up, the signal that the ship was sailing within two hours. The blue flag up, the ship is considered already out of port and on her way. From that moment on, the port authorities no longer have any jurisdiction over the ship, with certain cases excepted. Any man coming aboard now is regarded as having signed on under the emergency rules—a ship under weigh with crew incomplete. The skipper now has the right to sign on as many men as he wishes without being compelled to take them to the consul. After the man has made one trip, short or long, the consul must sign him on or the port authorities will report him. This, by the way, settles once and for all the question of how the skunk survived the flood. He hopped on when the ark was already under sail, leaving Noah no time to sign him on properly with the American consul, and, owing to international regulations, the skunk could not be thrown overboard, but had to be signed on under the emergency rules. That's why. Because these regulations are so old that long before Adam came to life, sailors who had sold their sailor's cards signed on that way to get away from a hot spot.

The skipper was still writing in his book.

After I had given up my name and my country, only my right to work was left. My work was the only thing the *Yorikke* wanted me for. Therefore I was going to sell my man-power as high as I could.

"The pay for coalers is forty-five pesetas," the skipper said without looking up from his book.

"Hey! What's this? Forty-five pesetas?" I yelled.

"Yes, didn't you know that?" the skipper asked with a tired look at me.

"I signed on for English pay." I defended my wages.

"Mr. Dils?" the skipper asked sharply, throwing a stern glance at the second engineer.

"Did I—I mean me, myself—ever promise you English wages? Say it. Did I?" the horse-thief asked grinningly.

Right then I could have socked that son of a beachcomber, never mind, I could have socked him so that his own mother would have said: "That is not my son, that must be the left-over of a twisted alligator." But I came to in time. I would not have liked to be in chains on the *Yorikke*, eaten by the rats that had just taken out marriage licenses. Just keep cool, my boy. I felt like ice dropped by the kitchen door at the back porch. And with an icy voice I said: "Yes, you have. You have promised me English money."

"Exactly, my man," the pickpocket said, "I have promised you English money. Exactly. But I haven't said a single word about English wages, have I?"

"Now what is this, Mr. Dils?" the skipper interrupted. "If you mean to hire men, I should suppose everything is straight."

"It is straight, sir. I have promised this man English money, but not English wages. Have I or have I not?" He was addressing me again.

"Yes," I answered, "that is right, but I was of the opinion that you meant English wages, which would be about ten pounds a month."

"We cannot take into consideration here what your opinion was," the skipper said to me. "We can only consider what was said and what was not said. If Mr. Dils has said English money, then he was right. We pay the forty-five pesetas of your monthly wages, of course, in English currency. No mistake in that. In English pounds and shillings, at the rate of the day on which the payment is due. All overtime is paid at fourpence."

Weeks later it came to me that I had not asked for how much overtime these fourpence are to be paid, for the hour, for the day, for the week, or for the year. When I found out it was meant for the week, it was too late to make any objections. Objections would have been overruled anyway, since overtime was never paid, and asking for it meant the hold of horrors.

"Where do you wish to sign off again?" the skipper asked without looking at me, keeping his eyes on the book and writing letters and figures.

"Next port of call," I said quickly.

"You cannot do that," the horse-thief said.

"Oh, yes, I can do that and I shall."

"You have it all wrong, brother, you cannot sign off at the next port of call," the pickpocket said again. "You signed on until we make Liverpool, didn't you?"

"That's what I meant," I said. "Liverpool is the next port we are putting in."

"Not on your life," the skipper said. "We cleared papers for Saloniki, Greece, you see. But in the meantime I have changed my mind. We are making North Africa. That's what I am going to do."

Cleared for Greece and making North Africa. Aye, aye, sir. Now I get the whole course straight. Morocco and Syria right now are paying well for—for— All right, skipper, I get you. As soon as you have pocketed the money you are after, we make for the grand port, or, let's say, for the ground port. From now on, you cannot hide anything from me, an old salt. Nosser. Not from me. This is not the first smuggler and armer I have shipped in. But for the sake of fighting and for another chance to look behind the curtain, I did not give in.

"You have told me Liverpool, haven't you?" I said to the horse-thief.

"Not true, sir." The horse-thief addressed the skipper with lips drawn wide, trying to grin like a hyena. "I said, when offering this man a job, that we had a light cargo for Liverpool, and that he may sign off at Liverpool as soon as we make it."

"I see," answered the skipper, "I see everything is in fine shape. We have eight cases of Spanish sardines for Liverpool. Low freight rate. Time to deliver not over eighteen months. I cannot make Liverpool on account of eight cases of Spanish sardines at the rate of seven and six each. The fresh water I have to take in for this trip would cost me more than the freight these cases pay. But, of course, as soon as there is a chance to get a full cargo for Liverpool, I shall not hesitate to make that port."

Since I am out of my baby-shoes for quite some time, I know damn well what those eight cases are for. Blindfolding for papers and clearances. Always good to have on hand for an excuse to change the course when it is necessary for some hot reason. I was sure he had small cargoes for Italian ports, French ports, Albanian ports, Turkish ports, Egyptian ports, Syrian ports. He may put in any port he wishes, without any chance for anyone to accuse him of having incorrect clearing papers. I do not know why, but I begin to like this man. I begin to understand why he, a man of culture, is running a ship like the *Yorikke*. At heart he is a vagabond, a pirate. Perhaps it is in his blood. He cannot help it. The times for pirates are gone. It doesn't pay any longer. In these times the career is too short. But there is still in modern times a sort of dangerous trading and shipping that the right man with the true pirate spirit can find far more adventurous than any pirate of old could ever have thought of. Pirates of old were brutes. They were never in need of intelligence. Sheer brutality did the job in those times. Modern pirates must have intelligence and quickness of mind, and more of it than the admiral of a fleet of battle-ships. For a man with brains and an adventurous spirit it is, by far, more thrilling to outwit clever customs officials and captains of gunboats who chase ships that run arms to Syrian and Moroccan rebels than it was for crude pirates to capture a defenseless merchant ship.

I see clearer every minute what kind of tub I am in. There is no escape. The company wants to get fat. It can't be done in decent business with ships like this one. But it can be done in a business that pays better than any decent business can ever do. Money must be made. That's religion. Because expenses must be met. The greatest disgrace is to fail to pay your debts and to go into bankruptcy. A decent citizen pays his debts. And ships cannot run without sailors. What's the use anyway?

"Sign your name here," the skipper said to me, breaking into my thoughts about economic problems.

He handed me his pen.

"Here? My name? Me? Never!" I protested.

"As you wish," the skipper cut short. "Mr. Dils, will you, please, sign here as witness for a man who cannot write?"

I felt myself going wild. That pickpocket sign for me? Such a lousy leper sign on my behalf, as a sort of representative of a red-blooded American? Not he. And nobody else, as long as I have a hand to write with.

"All right, skipper, I shall sign myself. I see there is no way out. I am caught. My just punishment for betraying sweet sunny Spain."

"Do not talk so much nonsense. Write your name and have done with it. I have got lots of other things to do than to taddle around with a stubborn coaler. Put it down and beat it. We cannot spare a coal-shoveler much time."

I wrote with clear letters that will last until the trumpets of the Last Day are calling, and somebody then will be confused as to how to call me.

"Helmond Rigby, Alexandria, Egypt."

There it now stands for ever. Black on white. I can't get away from it. Ahoy, *Yorikke*, ahoy, hoy, ho! Go to hell now if you wish. What do I care? It's all the same now to me. I am part of you now. Where you go I go, where you leave I leave, when you go to the devil I go. Married. Vanished from the living. Damned and doomed. Of me there is not left a breath in all the vast world.

> Ahoy, *Yorikke*! Ahoy, hoy, ho!
> I am not buried in the sea,
> The death ship is now part of me
> So far from sunny New Orleans
> So far from lovely Louisiana.

Hello, over there, beyond. Yes, I mean you there, you beyond. We are comrades now, gladiators. What was it you said? Yes. *Morituri te salutamus!* The modern gladiators are greeting you, O great Cæsar, Cæsar Augustus Capitalismus. *Morituri te salutamus!* The moribund are greeting you, O Cæsar, great Imperator Cæsar Augustus. We are ready to die for you; for you and for the glorious and most holy insurance. Send us to the grand port, to the ground port; you are welcome, thank you.

Oh times, oh morals! How things have changed, boys, you there from beyond! The gladiators marched martially into the arena in an array brilliant and glittering and shining against which a circus-parade in Kansas City would look like the funeral of an inmate of a poorhouse. Gee, how they marched in! With the blaring of fanfares and trumpets and the beating of great drums and the playing of marches such as Sousa would have liked to compose, if only he had had the right feeling for the tunes of true martial music. And the women! Those beautiful dames hailing the marching gladiators from their balconies, covered with carpets representing all the riches of Persia, those beautiful perfumed janes hailing and cheering the gladiators as if they were boxers in Madison Square Garden. Smiles and kisses were thrown from the ladies down to the victorious fighters. Amidst the rousing cries and hails and applause of the most excited crowds any world has ever seen, while the trumpets blared and the drums roared and the finest bands of the Roman Empire played emotional war-tunes, these gladiators breathed their last sighs, dying as no modern soldier ever has a chance to die.

We, the gladiators of today, we must perish in dirt and filth. We are too tired even to wash our faces. We starve because we fall asleep at the table with a rotten meal before us. We are always hungry because a shipping company cannot compete with the freight rates of other companies if the sailors get food fit for human beings. The ship must go to the ground port, because the company would be bankrupt if the insurance money would not save her. We do not die in shining armor, we the gladiators of today. We die in rags, without mattresses or blankets. We die worse than hogs in Chic. We die in silence, in the stoke-hold. We see the sea breaking in through the cracked hull. We can no longer go up and out. We are caught. The steam hisses down upon us out of cracked pipes. Furnace doors have opened and the live coal is on us, scorching what is still left of us. We hope and pray that the boiler will explode to make it short and sure. "Oh, down there, those men," says the stateroom passenger who is allowed a look through a hole, "those filthy sweating devils, oh, never mind, they do not feel it, they are accustomed to the heat and to such things as a ship going down; it's their business. Let's have another cock well iced."

Of course, we are used to all that may happen. We are the black gang. If you are hungry and you need a job, take it. It's yours. Others are waiting to take it for less.

We go to hell without martial music and without the prayers of the Episcopalian. We die without the smiles of the beautiful ladies, without holding their perfumed handkerchiefs in our hands. We die without the cheering of the excited crowd. We die in deep silence, in utter darkness, and in rags. We die in rags for you, O Cæsar Augustus! Hail to you, Imperator Capitalism! We have no names, we have no souls, we have no country, we have no nationality. We are nobody, we are nothing.

Hail to you, Imperator Augustus! You don't have to pay pensions to widows and orphans. Not even as little as a coffin. We do not even ask for six square feet of the cheapest ground. We, O Cæsar, are the most faithful and the most loyal of all the servants you have. The moribund are greeting you: Hail, Cæsar!

27

At half past six a Negro brought in the supper. It was brought in two good-sized tin kettles, more or less of the kind used at camp-fires. These kettles were battered as if they had seen hundreds of battles. They were dirty and greasy, and they looked as if at least a full month had passed since they had last been cleaned.

The supper was a watery meager vegetable soup with an ugly-looking layer of rancid fat on the surface. In the other kettle there were potatoes in their skins, the cheapest sort which could be found in a poor market. Then there was another tin can in which I saw hot brownish water. The Negro noted my look, and, as if he had heard of finger-bowls, he thought perhaps I might use this water for the wrong purpose. To avoid any misuse of it he said: "That's the tea." The tea smelled like the hot water Mother used in the kitchen when rinsing the dishes in the sink.

"Where is the meat?" I asked the Negro.

"No meat today," he said.

I looked up and saw that he was no Negro, but a white man. He was, as I learned right afterwards, the coaler.

"Getting supper to the foc'sle is your business," he told me in a sleepy voice, and in a way as if I had offended him.

"I am not the mess-boy on this tub; you may as well know that right from the begin."

"No mess-boys on this box, no mozos, no moises," he informed me.

"And so?"

"Well, here the drags have to do it, the coal-drags."

With this I received the first blow. The blows were now

falling so quickly and so hard, one after the other, that I ceased to count them. Fate was on. Let's have it.

"Supper is brought in by the drag of the rat-watch," he went on.

On decent ships this would be the dog-watch. Here, I assumed, the dog-watch is the watch which on honest buckets would be the palace-watch. All right with me. Go on. I am caught fine. Let the blows rain thick and mercilessly.

Rat-watch for me. The watch from twelve to four. Bells were not known here. All terms were confused. Here one might even hear such terms as downstairs and upstairs. Because high-class sailors were rare on the *Yorikke*. And if there was one, he could not use the proper terms; he would have been taken for a high-brow and ridiculed. Most of the men would not have understood him at all.

Rat-watch. The most horrible watch that was ever invented to punish rebellious sailors. You come to the foc'sle at four, tired. You wash your face as well as you can. Then you have to get the supper for the whole outfit. After having had supper you wash the dishes, since there is no mess-boy to do it for you. The cook does not care how dirty the kettles are; he throws in your grub, dirty or not dirty. Now you lie down in your bunk to get some sleep. You have to eat all that your belly will take, because there is no other meal until eight in the morning. On this full belly, full of potatoes and a thin greasy soup, you cannot sleep right away. You just turn round and round. The other guys off duty are sitting there playing cards and telling stories to each other. You cannot yell at them to be quiet because you want to sleep. They might lose their ability to talk. Knowing that you need sleep, they are already only whispering. But whispering is more annoying than talking in a loud voice. Close to eleven you fall asleep. All the other boys have turned in meanwhile. Precisel at the minute you take the first deep breath in a profound sleep, it is twenty to twelve and the drag of the other watch is waking you up as roughly as he is able. Out of your bunk, down below into the stoke-hold. At four in the morning you return from your watch. You wash your face. Maybe you don't. You are too tired. Like a stone you fall into your bunk. At about a quarter past six the noise starts on deck; the day-hands are chased around, here hammering, there sawing, yonder shouting and commanding, rattling of chains and squeaking of winches. At eight somebody shakes you out of your sleep. "Breakfast is ready," he yells into your ear. All during the forenoon there is not one minute without that hard noise of work on deck. It beats into your brain without pity. Twenty to twelve nobody comes to call you, because no one on a ship would expect anyone to be asleep at that time. The little sleep you might be favored with is also taken away from you because you have to be on time for your watch, and you must not oversleep or you will start your watch with such a row from the second engineer that anger eats you up, and your work will be twice as hard. You stagger drowsily below, and you almost fall against the furnace doors. No pity. The ship must go on, because a ship is under control only when under steam, just as an airplane is out of control when it has lost its minimum flying speed. So you go to your watch and work worse and harder than a Negro slave until four. And so it goes, on and on.

"Who washes the dishes?"

"The coal-drag."

"Who cleans the shit-hold?"

"The drag."

Cleaning privies and such things is, absolutely, an honorable work. Provided one hasn't got anything else to do. In this case it was what a Mexican would call: *la porquería y la cochinera mas grande del mundo entero.* Or something which cannot be explained well in good English with dames listening in. Anyone who would have come close to see would have said: "This is the filthiest and dirtiest cave I have ever seen in all my life." From my experience on a decent farm, and from experiences in tropical countries, I know that pigs are cleaner in fact than hundreds of thousands of human beings ever try to be. So it would do pigs, when left alone and not interfered with by miserable small farmers, an injustice if I had said this here looked like a pig-sty. I could not blame the skipper for never wishing to inspect the foc'sle, as was his duty. He sure would not have been fit for two full weeks afterwards to eat a single meal. We had to look at it every day, and we had to eat also. No excuse for anything when there are only two points around which you revolve: Live or die. Yesser.

My punishment for having left sunny Spain is hard.

On ships like the *Yorikke* it is the coal-drag who has to do any work that comes along that no one else will undertake. No matter if the work is the lousiest, the filthiest, the most dangerous, the drag is called upon to do it. He has to do it. He has no right to refuse. Suppose there are three drags, one for each watch, when the crew is complete; the lowest of these three drags is the drag of the rat-watch. And suppose the two other drags refuse to do a certain job, the last called upon to do it is—yes, sir, you guessed right—is the drag of the rat-watch. He has to do it. If he prefers rather to go overboard or knife himself, he doesn't get any chance to do so until he has completed the job to the full satisfaction of the skipper or the chief; I mean the chief engineer.

As to dangerous jobs, it went like this: The chief told the second engineer, the second told the donkey, the donkey told the greaser, the greaser told the fireman, or the stoker if you want.

Said the fireman: "Blast me somewhere, but that's not a fireman's job, I don't care a bitch who does it, but I am the one who of all the cracked nuts plumb sure won't do it, and not for twenty bucks either."

Goes the second to the drag of the noblemen-watch, that is

the watch from eight to twelve, where only stranded princes and dukes are on watch. Says the drag of this palace-watch: "Not me, sir, and never mind the double pay and fourfold ration of rum. My great-grandmother is still alive and she is dependent on me."

Goes the second to the drag of the golden middle watch; that is the watch from four to eight. "Me?" he answers. "Don't come to me that way, sweety, I don't want to be the father of a never-born child. No, sir, my dame is still expecting something from me which I have to furnish and not leave her in the cold. Thank you just the same."

Goes the second to the drag of the rat: "Hey, you guy, hop on it and make it snappy. Steam is dropping like hell. No, you cannot leave now, no going out from here until it is fixed. Get at it and hell if you don't. Stinking son of a filthy beachcomber."

After half an hour or so the drag of the rat-watch comes out bleeding all over, knuckles broken, bones freed of skin and flesh, body scorched and burned and scalded in fifty places, and he drops like dead.

Goes the fireman to the greaser and says: "I have fixed it." Goes the greaser to the donkey and says: "I have done it." Goes the donkey to the second and says: "Sir, I did it, it is working fine now." Goes the second to the chief and says: "Well, sir, I wish to report I have done it, all is shipshape." Goes the chief to the skipper and says: "Sir, I wish to have the following reported in the ship's journal, please: Chief engineer risked his life in repairing bursted steam-pipe, while boilers were overheated and the ship was falling off schedule; and by doing so saved ship from serious disaster. Yes, sir, that is right. Will you please sign it? Thank you, sir."

One day, when the board of directors of the company are reading the ship's journal, the president will say: "Gentlemen, I think we ought to give this chief engineer from the *Yorikke* a more responsible position. He deserves it." The chief gets it.

As a matter of fact, it is less responsible than the position he had on the *Yorikke*, because these engines are almost new. But the higher responsibility means a higher salary, and that is the point which counts.

The drag has the report on his body and in his body; he is crippled for life, and the twenty or more burns will leave their marks in his face, on his hands and arms, on his breast and on his back. Now, of course, one should not take it so hard, because why did he do it? He could have said: "Hell and devil alive, I won't do it." But the answer is ever ready: "Why, you man, you do not mean you are going to let the ship go to the bottom and have all your mates drowned and fed to the fish? You wouldn't do such a thing, would you? A brave and courageous man like you? You are not yellow, are you? Could you bear it on your conscience to have a ship with its men aboard go to the bottom and never come up again? There's a fine fellow, brave and smart, the true sailor."

The chief would have to do it. It's his business to know something about boilers, and about repairing broken steam-pipes on the high sea. He has to know them and he has to know how to fix them; that's why he was made chief engineer and why he gets the pay for it. But he cannot throw his life away, can he? The life of a filthy coal-drag is no life at all. What does such a man know about life and responsibility and the welfare of the country and of economic competition? Don't let us speak about it. Oh, honey, fish him out, that dear little fly in the milk-pot; he might get drowned; please save his little life. A coal-drag? He is not like a fly who has fallen into the milk-pot. He is a filthy, dirty, lousy fellow, no soul, hardly human. He is just good enough for shoveling coal on a ship. He ought to do it just for the fun of it and for three square meals a day.

Yells the chief: "Hey, coal-drag, come up here for a minute. Like a shot of rum?"

"Yes, sir, thank you."

But he cannot have it, because the glass falls out of his hand, and the rum is over the floor. The hand is burned and cannot hold anything; yes, sir.

Supper was on the table. Right in front of me. I felt hungry. So I thought I might just as well eat the supper.

I looked around for the mess-gear; I mean for spoons, forks, knives, plates.

"Hey, you bird," somebody cried at me, "leave that plate alone, it's mine."

"All right, all right. Where do I get a plate and a spoon?"

"If you haven't brought any, you will have to do without, son."

"Ain't they supplied here on this tub?"

"All the supplies here have to be your own."

"How, then, can I eat not having a plate or a spoon?"

"That's your business, not mine. Invent something new."

"Listen here, you newcomer," somebody cried out from his bunk. "You can have my things to eat with, also my coffee-cup. Of course, you will have to wash them and keep them always clean for me in return for me being so kind to you."

One man had a cracked plate, but no cup; another had a fork, but no spoon. When the grub was brought in, there usually started a fight about who might have the plate and spoon first. Whoever had them was the lucky bird who fished the best pieces out of the kettles, leaving to the others the meager remains.

Whenever the *Yorikke* left a port, there were always spoons, forks, knives, plates, cups missing in taverns. Nothing mysterious about the disappearing of such things when the *Yorikke* was in port.

The liquid called tea was brown water. Usually it was not hot, but lukewarm. And then it tasted like—like—yes, sir, right you are, it tasted exactly like that. Another liquid, which was called the coffee, was served at breakfast and about three in the afternoon. This afternoon coffee I seldom saw, because

I was at that time busy at the boilers. When I returned from my watch, there was nothing left of the coffee. Sometimes there was some hot water found in the galley to make your own tea or coffee. But if you have no coffee-beans it is rather tough to make coffee, no matter how good you are at it.

The more your coffee and tea are free from real coffee and tea, the more you wish to improve these wonderful drinks with milk and sugar, so as to liven up your imagination. Every three weeks each man received as his ration one six-ounce can of sweetened condensed milk, and every week one pound of sugar. Coffee and tea came from the galley without sugar or milk, just plain.

Upon receiving your can of milk you opened it, took out one teaspoonful, and with it you made a beautiful-looking cloud in your tea. After having done so, being an economical fellow, you carefully stowed away your can of milk to use for your next cup of coffee, because you knew that during the next twenty-one days you would not see another can of milk.

While I was at my watch, my can of milk was not stolen. Nobody stole anything aboard the *Yorikke*. But my can of milk was used up to the last drop by my fellow-sailors, who had used up their milk long before, and they were hungry. No hiding-place was so secret that it could not be detected, and since there were no doors in the wardrobes, you could lock nothing in, even if you had a padlock. Only once did my milk disappear without my assistance. The next time I received my ration of milk I ate it up at one sitting. I did not mind having a sour stomach. I had found out that the only sure and safe hiding-place for all such things was your own belly. Only what was inside your stomach was safe. After I had hidden my milk in this hiding-place I learned that every member of the crew did exactly the same. No one had ever been told to do so. No one had ever lost more than his first can of milk.

We did the same with the sugar. No sooner had you received your pound of sugar than you sat down and ate it up. Once we came to a gentleman's agreement. The sugar of the whole quarter was to be put together in one box. Whenever tea or coffee came in, each man was allowed to take one teaspoonful of sugar out of the box and sweeten his coffee. The agreement was all right, only the gentlemen were missing. Because it turned out that on the second day after the agreement was signed the entire ration of sugar had disappeared. All that was left was an empty box which I found on coming from my watch with the idea of sweetening my coffee; yes, sir.

Each day fresh bread was made by the cook. Something was always wrong with it. Sometimes it was badly kneaded, usually only half baked, often burned black. Each week every man got a cake of margarine. It was sufficient to last for a week. Yet nobody could eat it, no matter how hungry he might be. For it tasted like bad soap.

There were quite a few days when the skipper made his pocket-money, and then we had to close our eyes and shut out swear-holds and keep mum. On such days each man received a ration of two good-sized glasses of fairly good rum and half a cup of marmalade. Those were the days when some mysterious business was going on.

For breakfast we had a thick barley soup cooked with prunes. Sometimes the breakfast consisted of black sausage with rice. Then again it was potatoes in their skins with salted herring; another course was beans with smoked fish. Every four days the same dish appeared again, beginning with thick barley soup cooked with prunes.

Never before had I known that all such things could be eaten by human beings, and that such strange mixtures could exist anywhere on this earth where ships with steam-engines had been seen.

The dinner on Sunday consisted of boiled beef with mustard sauce, or corned beef and a slimy gravy, and sometimes cabbage, but mostly potatoes. Monday dinner was salt meat which no one ever ate, for it was only a sort of meat-crust soaked in salt. Tuesday we had dried salt fish, which was always stinking. Wednesday it was vegetables, and prunes swimming in a paste of potato-starch. This paste was called the pudding. Thursday the dinner was again salted meat which nobody could eat.

Supper was either one of the dinners or one of the breakfasts. Potatoes came with each meal. Potatoes were the backbone of all our eats. Half of the potatoes, however, were so bad that we could not eat them. Sometimes we had a cargo of fresh young potatoes, so-called spring potatoes. The cook stored up well from this cargo, and we had really excellent potatoes. But when we didn't have such cargoes, the cheapest potatoes the skipper could buy were served for our food.

For blinds not only potatoes were taken in, but also bananas, pineapples (real pineapples of course, not moonshine), tomatoes, dates, figs, coconuts, sweet chestnuts. Only on account of such cargoes was it possible at all for us to survive the food which was served to us. Men who had been for five years soldiers in the last war can well imagine how much a human being can endure before breaking down in health and spirit. Yet a man who has sailed on the *Yorikke* will know for sure what and how much an individual can bear and still not go overboard.

Supper over, I had to wash the kettles in which the food had been brought in. Also I had to clean the dishes that had been used on the table, at least those which I had used in common with the fellows who had been kind enough to lend them to me.

I looked around and I began to feel sick. I could not live in this dirt. It seemed impossible. I made up my mind to clean the quarter.

After the men had eaten, they let themselves drop into their bunks as if they were dead. While they had been eating, hardly one word had been said. One could easily get the impression that hogs were eating from their trough. But this impression I lost entirely before I was one full week on the *Yorikke*. Then I could no longer make any comparison. The capacity to make comparisons or to recall my former existence had been killed. I was positive that any newcomer on the *Yorikke* who still had a light cover of civilization would have thought precisely the same of me when seeing me eating as I had thought of my fellow-sailors when I saw them for the first time.

"No soap supplied," somebody yelled from his bunk. "And no scrubbers and brushes either. And for devil's sake keep quiet now and leave the quarter as you found it. Hell, I want to sleep, bigud, I need it. Shut your grub-hold."

I rushed to the chief's cabin and knocked at the door.

"I want soap and something to scrub with. I want to clean up that shit in the foc's'le."

"What do you think I am? You do not mean to suggest that I have to buy soap and scrubbers for the crew, do you? Nothing doing here. Go to the captain."

"All right, sir. But now what about me? I haven't got any soap to wash even my face. And I have to work in the stoke-hold, haven't I?"

"You are not a kid-sailor, are you? Don't look like it to me. You are an old salt. Ought to know better—any decent sailor provides his own soap. Part of his outfit."

"Maybe. News to me, sir. Fine soap of course. But not ordinary soap. Soap for the black gang has to be supplied by the company. It's regulation. Also sweat towels. What sort of a bucket is this anyway? Every decent ship supplies mattresses, pillows, blankets, ordinary towels. And above all things plates, cups, spoons, knives, forks. We are no pigs."

"Every man knows best what he is."

"All these things are part of the equipment of the ship and are no part of the sailor's outfit."

"Not here. Not with us. And besides, if you don't like it here, why the hell don't you go where you came from?"

"You dirty chunk."

"Out of my cabin and stay out. I shall report you to the skipper."

"In iron, hey?"

"Not us. We are not that crazy. I need the drags badly. And I need you even more badly. No, not iron. It will cost you two months' pay for subordination. We cannot afford iron or chains, see. And whipping neither. You cannot heave coal with a sore back."

"You are a fine bunch," I said. "So low you even steal the poor sailor's pay."

The chief grinned and said: "How come stealing your pay? I didn't invite you to come here into my cabin and insult me."

I could have socked him fine. But it would have cost me another two months' wages, and I could never sign off as long as I would not have money coming.

"I just wanted to see clear," I said. "I wanted to hear from you, from the chief, that we cannot have a cake of ordinary soap, and that we have to live here like hogs."

"Tell all this to your grandmother," he said; "maybe she'll listen to that nonsense. But I do not like it at all. And now get out of here; and do not dare step in again until you are called. Out! You had better turn in. Your watch starts at eleven."

"My watch starts at twelve. From twelve to four."

"Who said so? Not here with us. And most certainly not with the coal-shovelers. You start at eleven and you heave ashes first until twelve. Understand?"

"Heaving ashes is overtime, of course?"

"Of course not. No overtime paid for clearing ashes. Not with us. It's part of your regular work. That's what you have signed on for."

Which age was I living in? Among what sort of people

had I fallen by accident? In ancient Rome and Greece even the slaves had certain rights.

My mind befogged, I staggered to the fore.

I leaned against the railing, trying to find myself back where I really was in the world.

There was the sea. That blue glorious sea which I loved better than I ever could think of loving a jane. That wonder of a sea, in which to be drowned as an honorable sailor when doing my duty I would have felt to be the greatest honor that could be bestowed upon me. That sea, that capricious woman whom alone I felt truly married to, that wonderful woman who can smile so charmingly, can sing such bewitching cradle-songs, that can rage so furiously, that can show such a savage and alluring temperament, and then fall asleep so sweetly and so dreamily that one could do nothing better than just kiss her and kiss her over and over again.

It was that same sea on which thousands and thousands of decent and honest ships were sailing at this very time. And I, of all sane persons on earth and on sea, I had to ship on this can that was suffering from leprosy. A bucket that was sailing for no other reason but that the sea might have pity on her. Somehow, I felt that the sea would not take this tub, which had all the diseases known under heaven, for the simple reason that the sea did not wish to be infected with leprosy and pus. Not yet at least. She, the sea, still waited for the day when the *Yorikke* would have to be in some port far out of the way and when this old maid, for some reason or other, would then burst or explode or fall apart and so save the sea from being used as cemetery for this pest of the oceans.

So standing against the railing and looking up to the star-loaded sky above me, before me the whitish glimmering waves of the sea that lullingly splashed against the ship's hull as the *Yorikke* furrowed her way, and thinking of my lost New Orleans and of my dear sunny Spain, a feeling I had never had before tried to get hold of me. I thought: What's the use?

Make a clean short cut, old boy from Sconsin, chuck the coal-drag, and hop over; have done with that filth and dung. Make the hop and enter the good old sea while you're still a clean Yank sailor, and before you get soiled all over and make the sea ashamed of you when you come to kiss her good-by. But then where is the salvation? It cannot be done that easily. Because there would be only another poor, overtired, ragged, starved, and tortured coal-drag who would have to go on double watch on account of your having kicked off. This fellow-drag of mine, left behind with a double watch, would make my last trip so unbearable that I could not stay below, and it might happen that I would have to come up again just to say: "Hey, brother-sailor, I am sorry, please forgive me. Won't you forgive me, so that I may stay below?" Suppose he doesn't. What then?

Damn it, damn it all, and devil and hell. Now, listen here, boy from Sconsin, that pest *Yorikke* cannot get you. Not you. And all the consuls neither. Chin up and get at it. Swallow the filth and digest it. Quickest way to get rid of it. Some day there will be soap and brushes again, and plenty of them. Be it New Orleans or Galveston or Los An. All the filth is only outside. Don't let it go to your soul and spirit and your heart. Take the plunge head-first. That way you'll feel the cold less. And now away from the railing and away from that beast that is after you. Kick him right in the pants. Sock it right in the swear-hold. Spit it out, and do it well. Spitting out the filth you feel in your throat is all you can do now. But make a good job of it. Now back into your bunk.

When I was back in the quarters, which were filled with thick kerosene smoke, I knew, and this time for certain, that I was on a death ship. But I also knew for certain that it would not be my death ship, no matter what might happen to her. I shall not help the *Yorikke* make insurance. I shall not be a gladiator on her. I spit right into your face, Imperator Cæsar Augustus. You have lost one of the slaves who greet you:

"The moribund salute you, hail!" Save your soap and crash it down your wind-pipe. I do not need it any longer. But you shall not hear me whine again. I spit into your face. I spit at you and at your whole damn breed. Swallow that. I am ready now for battle.

28

I could not sleep. The smoke from the kerosene lamp of the seven virgins became thicker every minute, and it filled the quarter with a heavy cloud. Breathing became difficult and I felt a piercing pain in my lungs. I had no blanket, and, since the nights at sea can be very cold, I was freezing.

Just when I had fallen into a light sleep, I was shaken up and somebody dragged me by force more than half-way out of my bunk.

"Up now. Eleven. Don't fall asleep again. I can't come again. At ten to twelve you go get up your fireman and bring him his coffee."

"Don't know him. Don't know where he bunks."

"Get going. I'll show you."

I sprang up, and I was shown the bunk of my fireman, which was in the opposite quarter, at the port side.

"Hop on it. Go right away to the winch at the ash-pipe. We've got a hell of a load of ashes to heave."

The man that had called me had come like a phantom, and like a phantom he disappeared. I had not seen his face.

The quarter was dark, for the virgins' lamp gave no light. It just glimmered along.

When I came to the gangway at port side, where the ash-tube led down into the stoke-hold, Stanislav was waiting. He held an open wick-lamp which he hung up on some hook near the ash-tube.

Stanislav was the coal-drag of the watch now on duty. He tried to explain to me how to handle the winch, a sort of a windlass, which was used to heave up the heavy ash-cans from the stoke-hold.

"Now look here, Stanislav, I don't understand anything at all here," I said to him. "I thought I was an old salt. Yet never have I seen a bucket like this one here on which the coal-drags have to work extra watches. Why and what for?"

"You tell me. What do I know?" he said. "I am not a baby myself. Believe me, I have shipped on a good many wash-basins. On any decent tub the fireman has to help his drag clear the ashes, so that every watch is just for itself. But here the fireman never gets a rest for a minute. The drag even has to help him stoke. Or the steam comes down to a hundred twenty just like that. Everything is busted and broken. Steam doesn't stay. See? Pipes are leaking. Furnaces rotten, see? On other ships of this size there are two firemen and a drag, or at least one fireman and a half besides the drag. Here the fireman cannot leave the fire alone for one minute. Anyway, I think by now you know where you are, my angel sailor."

"Bet your sweet little sailor life, I am not going to become an angel on this kettle."

"Going to skip next port, hey?" he asked. "Doesn't work well. You will learn this pretty soon. Just make yourself comfortable, feel at home, you know. Get acquainted with the boats, I mean the life-boats. Take a good look at the one you would like to choose on a proper occasion. Talk it over with the cook. He is the grandfather on this bucket here. Warm up with him. He can be of great help to you, if you know how to take him. He doesn't know anything about cooking. But a swell guy. He has two life-jackets stowed away."

"Why? Are there no jackets or vests for us?"

"Seen any?"

"Didn't look."

"Better don't take anything for granted here. There isn't

even a life-ring aboard. Of course, against the mid-castle you see four gilded rings, pretty to look at. Take my advice, don't touch any of them. If you stick your head through one of them you would be by far safer with your head stuck through the hole of a millstone. With a millstone you have a chance that a miracle might happen. But with these gilded rings around you, even your mother would say, it serves you right, boy, you ought to know better."

"How can that lousy dog do such a thing, leave us without life-vests or jackets? So used to see them in the quarter that I didn't notice that there were none."

Stanislav laughed: "You never shipped a box like this one. That's why. *Yorikke* is already my fourth death tub. In these days, I mean since the war is over, you can pick tubs like this one here at random. Never before seen that many."

"Hey Lavski!" the fireman yelled from below.

"What's up, fireman?" Stanislav cried through the ash-tube.

"Are you devils heaving ashes or are you not or you want me to come up and sock you in the grub-hold, hey?" the fireman answered.

"Shut up, down there. I have to teach the new drag how to work the ash-winch. Has never seen one in his life," Stanislav explained.

"All right, get going and come below here. A bar fell out," the fireman cried angrily.

"Let's heave the ashes first, the bar can wait. I have to teach the new one," Stanislav cried back.

"What's your name?" he asked.

"Mine? Pippip."

"Pretty name. Are you a Turk?"

"Egyptian."

"Good to hear it. An Egyptian, eh? That's exactly what we were missing to be complete. You see, we have all nationalities here on this can."

"All, you say? Yanks also?"

"I guess you are still asleep to ask such a silly question. The only two representatives of foreign nations that never ship on a death can are the Yanks and the Comms."

"Comms?"

"Don't try that old trick on me, making me think you a baby. Playing the innocent kid. Not me, buddy. You know quite well what I mean. Comms, you ass. I mean Bolshes. Communists, you bonehead. Yanks do not hop on such a bucket, because they would die in that filth within twenty-four hours. Apart from that, Yanks are always well tipped off by their consuls. They have got the finest consuls on earth. Almost as good as are the British."

"And the Comms?" I asked.

"Those guys are too smart, by far too clever. Cannot catch them. I tell you they have got a smeller that knows right away what's the matter. If they see only the mast-head of a can, they can tell you offhand every meal that is served on that ship, and they guess the pay so close to the fact that you can bet six shillings on their being correct. Whenever there is a Comm on a bucket, no insurance money can ever be cashed in. They bury every insurance policy regardless of how well it is sugar-coated. And if they smell something about the can, they right away start making a mess. No port inspector can get away with five dollars for closing his eyes. I tell you whenever you see a regular bucket on which are shipping not alone Yanks, but, what is more, Yanks that are Commses, why, man, then you may say to yourself that you are sitting now fine and deep in real sugar. Right now I am sailing for no other reason than to get some day a chance to sign on for such a can. I certainly shall never leave it again, and I wouldn't even go ashore to have a shot, because I'd be afraid I might lose that can. I would be the lowest drag in the lowest rat-watch to be on such a bucket. And of all the ships in the whole world the best of all are those Yanks from New Orleans. That's the fortification of the Wobblies, and they sure know what they want. It would be paradise to have such a ship to sail on."

"I have never seen a ship from New Orleans," I said.

"A Yank from New Orleans would never take you on. Not even when you wait a hundred years for it. Not you. Not an Egyptian. They are particular. They don't look at you even if you have got a sailor's card like sweet honey, clean and honest. Well, now of course this dream, like so many others, is also gone. Any guy on earth that ever shipped on the *Yorikke* can never again get an honest tub. It's after you, all the rest of your life, like the stinky pestilence. Oh, shit, let's get at it."

He yelled down the ash-tunnel: "Got it hooked, fire'm?"

"Fire'm" meant fireman, in the *Yorikke* lingo.

"Heave up!" the fireman cried.

Stanislav moved the lever, and the ash-can came up, rattling against the tunnel-walls. As soon as it appeared at the mouth of the tunnel, Stanislav moved back the lever, and the can swung out.

"Now take the can off the hook and carry it to the railing, and there you dump the ashes into the sea. I warn you, do it carefully or the whole can'll go overboard. Then we sit here and have to do the whole shit with only one can."

The can was so hot that only with pain could I get a good grip on it. Stanislav saw it and said: "Hot, is it? You'll get used to that after your hands have been scorched enough, don't you worry. It won't be long."

The can was heavy. Eighty or ninety pounds when full. I carried it, holding it against my chest, across the gangway, which was about twelve feet. At the railing there was a short wooden shoot through which the ashes were dumped into the sea. This wooden shoot prevented the outside hull from being soiled by the ashes. The ashes were swallowed up by the sea with a loud, angry, whistling hiss. I carried the can back to the opening, hung it on the chain, and Stanislav pushed forward the lever. The can went down the tunnel like thunder.

"Naturally," Stanislav said, "it's clear why the life-jackets and the rings are gone. They say the old man sold them to make some extra coin. I know better. It wasn't just for making that side-money. You see the whole thing is like this: if there are no life-jackets, then there can be no witnesses. And if there are no witnesses, there can be no proper hearing in the court of the shipping board, see? Guess you get me. Old trick. They never can depend on witnesses. Witnesses might have seen something· or heard something, and then the insurance would get pretty sour with all the presidents and vice-presidents. You shouldn't miss looking at the boats some time. What was your name? Yes, what I said, Pippip, look at the boats. You can throw both your shoes straight through the cracks the boats have. No survivors. Sorry, no witnesses."

"Don't tell me tales, young man. Doesn't the skipper want to get out safely?"

"Now don't you worry about the old man. Look after your own skin first," Stanislav said ironically. "The skipper will get out all right. Never mind him. Would to the devil that you knew everything as well as that. He will make it fine. Ought to see how he is fixed."

"But didn't you come home safely from three death tubs already?" I asked.

"Yip. That's true. The last one that shuffled down I forgot, at the last port, to board, and so I let her go without me. You just have to figure out when and where is the best time to stay behind. As to the other two, well, you have to have a bit of good luck. If you haven't got luck, not any, you better stay away from the water by all means, or else you might get drowned even in a wash-basin when bathing your feet. They haven't invented yet any kind of useful water in which you can find hooks hanging around wherever you grasp."

"Lavski! What for thousand devils are you doing up there?" the fireman yelled up through the tunnel.

"Oh chucks," Stanislav cried, "the chains have gone off the drum. I'll have them fixed in a minute."

"Now, you try the winch," said Stanislav to me. "Take care. It kicks and hammers and jams worse than an overfed horse. It knocks your head off just like that if you don't look out."

I pushed the lever forward and the can was shot up right against the top of the tunnel. It sounded as if the whole tunnel would go to pieces. Before I could snatch the lever to pull it back, the winch set in reverse by itself, and the can shot down into the stoke-hold, hitting the bottom with such a bang that I thought the whole can must be smashed. The fireman bellowed that if I had any intention to kill him I should come down and do it like a brave sailor. I had not yet caught his words in full when the winch again reversed itself and the can, now half empty, thundered up the tunnel and again crashed with a bang against the top. When the can was just about to shoot down again into the tunnel, Stanislav grasped the lever. The can stood still as death the same instant.

"You see," he said, "it isn't quite as easy as kissing the bride. You will learn that all right. Just get all your knuckles peeled off and then you will know how it is done. Tomorrow at daylight I will show you the trick. You better go now, shovel the ash into the cans, hang them on the hooks, and I will serve the winch up here. You might smash the winch. Should that happen, my boy—well, I would not wish it to you nor to me. Then we would have to carry all the cans up here on our backs. Don't you ever wish it, man. After we are through just with the ash of one watch, you would no longer know if the sky is above you or below. We would not walk, we would crawl instead. We sure would just roll from one place to the other. So better treat the windlass with love and kisses."

"Let me try once more, Lavski," I asked him. "I will say Gracious Lady to her. Maybe if I consider that winch a person, then she will do it and work with papa."

I yelled down: "Hook on!"

"Heave up!" came the call.

"Hello, Duchess, come, let's do it together. Come, come, come, up with the shirt."

Mohammed is my witness, she did it, and fine she came along. Like oil and soft flesh. Gentle like a lambkin. Papa is not without experience. I guess I know the *Yorikke* better than her skipper or her grandfather, the wise cook. That winch was still the same that was used by old man Noah. And the *Yorikke* had been built after blueprints left over by the Ark-builder. This windlass, therefore, belonged to pre-Flood times. All the little goblins of those far-off times which were to be destroyed by the Flood had found refuge in the *Yorikke*, where they lived in all the corners and nooks. The worst of these little evil spirits had taken up quarters in this winch. Consequently the winch had to be respected and the goblins hidden within her had to be treated well. Stanislav had won over these ghosts by long practice. I tried to make them friendly with noble speeches.

"Hey, Your Highness, once more, get your legs going, please."

And how she came, that winch! Smoothly and with a decent shame. The can stood like a soldier exactly where I wanted it to make my embrace more powerful and carry the ash to sleep in the sea.

Of course, the winch was not all the time good-humored. More than a hundred times she played me nasty tricks. What else can you expect from women? If the lever was not pushed or pulled exactly at the right fraction of the right second at the right distance, the can shot with rattling thunder up against the top of the tunnel so that the whole ship seemed to shake in her bones. Pushing the lever in or pushing it out one thirty-second of an inch too far made all the difference in whether the can stopped exactly in the right position.

Stanislav had gone below to shovel the ash and the slags into the cans. After I had heaved about fifty cans, Stanislav cried up that we would leave the rest to take out during the next watch.

I felt like breaking down at my knees after having carried so many heavy cans across the gangway. Hardly could I catch my breath. But before I had time to get acquainted with my feeling of collapse, Stanislav bellowed: "Hey, get ready, you, twenty to twelve."

Partly crawling, partly staggering, I dragged my carcass to the foc'sle. There was no light on deck. Kerosene costs money. The company could not afford it on account of hard competition with other companies who offered still lower rates.

Several times I struck my knees and shins against something hard before I reached the quarters. Not easy to describe in detail everything that was lying about the deck. To make the description short I would say: everything possible under heaven was lying on deck. Even a ship's carpenter was lying there, drunk like a helpless gun with all its ammunition shot off. Later I learned that this carpenter got drunk in every port we put in, and that, for this reason, during the first two days after the ship was out he could not be used even to scrub the deck. The skipper always felt lucky when the A.B.'s did not join the carpenter in his happiness, and when at least one A.B. was left sound enough to hold the wheel fairly by the course. The carpenter and the three A.B.'s were, by the way, so thoroughly drenched in body and brain that the skipper could give them life-jackets without any fear of making them bad witnesses when riding out the insurance. They had lost every ability to gather and to assort their ideas of what they had seen and what they had not seen. All they knew about the economic welfare of civilized nations was the exact price of whisky in the various taverns of the different ports the *Yorikke* usually put in. The skipper mentioned frequently that he considered these four men real pearls of first-class sailors.

In the quarter I fetched the coffee-can, went with it to the galley, and filled it with hot coffee which stood on the stove. With this coffee-can in hand I again had to make my way across the dark deck to the quarters. By now my shins and knees were bleeding, so often had I knocked them against boxes, hold-shafts, beams, chains, anchors. There was no such thing aboard as first-aid. The first mate played doctor. The medicine and other helpful material were stowed away well, so as not to make any extra expenses. With trifles like these— bleeding shins and knees and knuckles, anyway—one could not have gone to the first mate.

He would have laughed and said: "Where is it you are hurt? Don't be silly, I can't find anything wrong. Rub in coal-dust— bleeding will cease then. Out of here."

I had to get up my fireman. He wanted to break my neck for waking him up so early. He said he had missed two full minutes of sound sleep on account of me being such a sap. But when the bell rang out and the watch from the bridge was singing down the "Ship all right!" my fireman wanted to smash in my head because I had called him too late and he sure would start his watch right away with a row with the second engineer, with whom he was not on good terms, he added. He gulped down his black unsweetened coffee, tore off a chunk from the loaf of bread that was lying on the table, pushed it into his swear-hold, and with a full mouth, while his eyes were swimming in red ink, he yelled at me: "Go below. I'll come right after you. Get water ready for the slags." His movements were heavy and tired. He did not sit upright at the table, but half lay on the bench. With his arms spread out on the table he pushed one hand forward as if in a dream to reach a knife he saw. He could not reach it with this movement. He gave it up. The knife was too expensive for him. So he grasped only the loaf of bread and tore off another chunk of it. Again he swallowed a gulp of coffee, and the bread in his mouth swelled up, compelling him to chew with his mouth wide open.

I drank half a cup of coffee. Before I could grasp the bread
to cut off a slice, he said gargling to me: "You better go now.
I come right after you."

Passing the galley, I saw Stanislav moving about inside. It was
dark in the galley. Only the glimmering live coal of the stove
gave an uncertain light. Stanislav tried to find and steal soap
hidden by the cook. The cook in turn stole the soap from the
steward. The steward took the soap out of the skipper's chest.
Each of these persons was always surprised on finding his soap
missing again. The rats were accused of being responsible for
the disappearance of so much soap.

"Won't you show me off to the stoke-hold?" I asked
Stanislav.

He came out of the galley.

We climbed up to the upper aft deck of mid-castle. He indicated a black shaft and said: "There you see an iron ladder
leading below. You can't go wrong. I have not finished yet in
the galley. Don't know where grandfather has hidden the
soap this time."

All around me was the clear night, deep black blue. Out
of this surrounding beautiful night, resting upon the lulling
sea, I looked down that black shaft.

The depth appeared to have no limit. At the bottom below
I saw the underworld. It was a smoke-filled hell, brightened up
by darting spears of reddish light which seemed to dash out
of different holes and disappear as suddenly as they had come.
Every other second this underworld was wrapped in bright
fire, which broke out somewhere and swept this hell below
all over and went off again, leaving behind thick clouds of
smoke. This smoke stayed solidly in that hole, and the underworld could now be recognized only by a very dim yellowish
light.

As if he had been born out of this thick smoke, the naked
shape of a human being stepped into the center of the hall. He
was black from a thick layer of coal-dust which covered all

of his body, and the sweat ran down him in streams, leaving glittering traces in the soot on his body. The man stood there for a while with arms folded. He stared motionless in the direction from which the reddish lights came flaring out. Now he moved heavily about and seized a long iron poker. He stepped a pace forward, bent over, and suddenly it looked as if he were swallowed up by the sea of flames which enwrapped him. He sprang forward with his poker, pushed and pulled with it as if were fighting an escaped dragon. Then, with a swift move, he jumped back, straightened up his body, and put the poker against the wall. The flames had been quieted, and the hold was black and smoky more than ever, lightened up only with that ghostlike yellowish glimmer.

I tried to go below. No sooner had I set my foot on the fourth rung of the ladder than I felt myself being smothered by a blast of heat, by a choking oilish smoke, by thick clouds of coal-dust, and by heavy fumes of a mixture of steam, kerosene, and burning rags. I coughed and I jumped up to get fresh air into my lungs, which seemed to have become paralyzed.

There was no hope of getting away from this job. I had to try it again. No matter what happens. Below there was a human being. A living soul could breathe there in that hell. Wherever any other human being can live and work, I can. I am no exception. I am no sissy either. I have to do it. The watch has to be relieved.

Hurriedly, so as to overcome the uncomfortable effects of a plunge, I stepped down again, and right away I took six rungs. There I stopped. I could go no farther. My lungs were bursting again. I had to take in once more fresh air to survive.

I made a third attack. This time I reached a landing about four feet long and two wide. From this stage another ladder led farther below. But I could not reach it. Because through a crack in the steam-pipe, shooting up right where you had to pass, a fierce blast of overheated steam hissed across the stage near the first rung of the second ladder. I tried to make it. But my face and my arms were caught in this hot gust and I was sure I should be scalded beyond recognition, and my eyes lost, if I went on.

I knew then that I had gone the wrong way and that there must be some other way to reach the stoke-hold.

Stanislav was still in the galley and still looking for the hidden soap of the grandfather.

"I shall go below with you," he said willingly.

On our way he asked: "You have never been part of the black crew, have you? Don't tell me. I knew it when I had the first look at you. How come you say Gracious Lady to the winch? If she does not work and go with you as you wish, just sock her. Most dames like it. And those who don't like it, let them go. Lots more in the world."

I wanted to tell him that many things apparently lifeless have really souls like humans and that you have to treat them accordingly. Yet I thought there would be time enough to tell him my ideas of a sound philosophy.

So I answered only: "Right you are, Lavski. Never been before a boiler. Can hardly remember that I have ever even looked down below into the stoke-hold. Have been cabin-boy, steward, deck-hand, A.B., carpenter even. Never liked the smell of the black gang. Listen, comrade, won't you lend me a hand for my first watch before the boilers?"

"Don't talk nonsense. Of course I will. Know your trouble better than you do, baby blacker. It's your first death-mobile. I know these wagons all right. Believe me. But I tell you there are times when you will thank heaven and hell for a *Yorikke* putting in port. And you hop on with all the joyful feelings you have in store, making faces at the one or the ones that are hot after you. Just call on me, sweet innocent, whenever anything goes queer. I get you out of the dirt. I even break jail for a regular guy to get him out of a jam. You see, it's like this, old Egypt, even if we are all dead ones, all of us, it is not worth the trouble to lose heart. Don't get down on

your knees. Blare them all in their stinking faces even when
sighing your last. You cannot live beyond for a thousand years
or a hundred thousand with the feeling eating at you that you
gave in during your last hour. Don't lose heart. Stick it, and
stick it hard. It can't come worse. I ought to know."

These, surely, were words to pep me up when I was so near
to go bitch and ditch. However, it came worse. Much worse.
One may ship on a death ship. One may be a carcass among the
dead. One may be all wiped out of all that lives, one may
have vanished from earth and sea, and yet there can happen
horrors and tortures which you cannot escape no matter how
dead you are. For when all means of escape are cut off, there
is nothing left to do but to bear it.

29

Stanislav went to the shaft I had just left, which I thought
was the wrong way below. He climbed down the ladder and
I followed him. We came to the stage on which the steam had
halted me.

I called to Stanislav: "We cannot make this. Your hide will
be scalded off all your bones."

"Don't be funny, sailor son. I make this every twenty-four
hours two dozen times. Course you have to know the trick.
Tricks is the only assistance here on this pest-basin that you
have to keep away from the bottom. There is no other way
for us to reach the stoke-hold. The god-damned engineers,
devil may have them for nothing, they don't allow us to go
through the engine-hold. They say we are too filthy and
stinking and leave in the hold a smell like skunks for a week.
Some day in hell we'll all stink together and I shall call them
up then."

I watched him throw his arms about his head to protect his

face and neck against the steam sword. Then, more agile and swift than a young snake, he twisted his body through this labyrinth of hissing steam-pipes and darts of shooting steam rays, so that, before I had caught my breath on seeing his elegant acrobatics, he was across to where the ladder went below.

All paddings of those pipes were rotten and in pieces, fittings burst, pipes cracked all over. Since the company had decided where to send the ship, it would have been a foolish expense to have properly repaired the steam-pipes, boilers, grates, or anything else aboard that was rotten, broken, burst, cracked, leaking. Repairs were done with the cheapest material, and done only when there was danger that the ship might go too early to the ground port. The ship had first to make some good money, by making excellent use of certain quarrels among peoples in rebellion against their protectors, who protected by mandate of sheer conquest or by mandate of the friendly acts of the noble League of Nations.

When I saw Stanislav doing the snake-dance, I thought highly of his ability, and I felt that no one else could do it so elegantly. I learned soon that every member of the black gang could do the same. He had to. Because only the best snake-dancers survived the black gang. All others who had tried and failed were no longer alive.

I now understood also why we never got food enough to feel satisfied, why we had to be undernourished. Suppose we had been fed like on a regular decent ship; we could not have done the snake-dance. Only men lean and without indigestion could reach the stoke-hold. There was a strict regulation aboard that we never must throw overboard anything which could not be eaten, but that, instead, all left-overs, even bones and crusts and rinds, had to be returned to the galley for the grandfather to make Irish stew, hash, goulash, and mock fricassee out of.

"That's the way you have to do it, brother," Stanislav said.

"Don't hesitate. If you do, you are finished. You would not be the first one either. If you ever have seen a scalded guy, you won't fail to be good."

I did not think at all. I imitated what I had seen. And there I was, through, caught only by a few hot shots.

"Don't feel sorry learning this elegant slip," Stanislav said. "Acrobatics like those may be of great help some day in your life. In particular if somebody finds your hand in a pocket which is not yours. Having been an excellent snake-dancer on the *Yorikke*, believe me, the iron bars have to be damned close together or they won't hold you for long."

From the other side of that landing a long iron ladder, or, if you wish, gangway, led below, to the base of the under-world. This ladder, like the one I had passed already, had the rail not at the side, from which you could fall twenty feet and break your neck and bones; no, the rail was close to the brick wall of the boilers. So close, indeed, that you could hardly squeeze your hand between rail and wall. The boilers were covered with a thick brick wall in front and on all sides and on top, to keep the heat better inside. There was a reason why the rail was not outside the ladder, but against the boiler-wall. Suppose the winch that was used for heaving the ashes cracked up or otherwise went out of commission; the ash-cans had to be carried on one's back up the ladders. This would have been rather difficult, not to say almost impossible, if the rail had been outside, for the ladder was just wide enough to be used by a single man. If this man were to carry the ash-can on his back, he could not go straight up the ladder, but had to go sideways with his face against the boiler-wall, and the ash-can hanging outside the ladder.

When I touched the rail to get a hold on it, I found it was so hot that I had to let go. It was heated partly by the immense heat of the wall and partly by the heat of the streams of steam pouring out of the many cracks.

Stanislav had a way of using that rail that was really amazing. He touched it more lightly than he would have touched eggs. He did not *go* down, but he *flew* down, playing on the rail with his finger-tips just enough to keep his equilibrium. Only when for some reason or other he seemed to sway did he grasp the rail for the fraction of a second longer and more firmly, to balance himself. A piano-player could not do better on the keys than he did on that rail.

Everything would have been easier if the shaft had had proper light. But all the light there was came from the smoky yellowish glimmer which filled the stoke-hold below.

Not being used to this ladder, I had to feel my way step by step. The rail became so hot that I felt my hands getting scorched. The lower I came, the thicker, hotter, and more choking became the smoke. The fumes from burned oil and the coal-gas from the slags pierced my lungs like poison gas. I was sure that this could not be the hell I had been condemned to go to after my death. In hell devils have to live. Yet I could not imagine for a second how it would have been possible for the most savage devil to live here and do his work of torturing poor sinners.

I looked up, and there stood a man. Naked and covered with streaming sweat and soot. He was the fireman of the watch I was to relieve now. Human beings could not live here, since devils could not. But this fireman, he could, he had to. So had all the others of the black gang. They were dead. Without a country. Without nationality. Without birth-certificates with which to prove that they had been born of a mother belonging to the human race. Men without passports by which to prove that they were citizens of the earth, given by the Lord to all animals and insects and all human beings. They could not prove their existence to the satisfaction of consuls and immigration officials and passport-printers.

Devils could not live here, for some culture and civilization are left even among devils. Just ask old man Faust. He knew them personally. But men with no papers had to work here. They were not asked, they were ordered. They had to work so hard, they were chased about so mercilessly, that they forgot everything that can be forgotten. They even forgot more than that. Long ago they had forgotten their own selves; they had abandoned their souls. Whoever took the trouble to pick up their abandoned souls could have them for the taking. It would have been a feast in hell. But the devil is not hot after souls that he can have for the picking. Such souls are worthless. These humans here on the *Yorikke* forgot more than that; they went so far as to forget to think that it might be impossible to work in this hell.

Have I any right to despise the company which runs this ship and which degrades her crew to the lowest kind of treatment in order to keep down expenses and make competition possible? I have no right to hatred. If I had jumped over the railing, nobody could have made me work in this hell. I did not jump, and by not doing it I forsook my prime right to be my own master and my own lord. Since I did not take my fate into my own hands, I had no right to refuse to be used as a slave. Why do I permit myself to be tortured? Because I have hope, which is the blessing, the sin, and the curse of mankind. I hope to have a chance to come back to life again. Sooner or later. I hope to see New Orleans again and Baby waiting there, perhaps. I hope. I'd rather eat all that filth than throw my sweet and adored hope into that stinking mire.

Imperator Cæsar Augustus: don't you ever worry! You will always have gladiators. And you will have more than you will ever need. The strongest, the finest, the bravest men will be your gladiators; they will fight for you, and dying they will hail you: *Morituri te salutamus!* Hail, Cæsar Augustus! The moribund are greeting you. Happy? I am the happiest man on earth to have the honor to fight and to die for you, you god Imperator.

30

Of course, sir, I can work here all right. Others are working here. Why can't I do the same? Man's aptness for imitation makes slaves and heroes. If that man yonder is not killed by the whip, then I won't be either. So let him whip. "Look at that fellow there. My, what a brave guy! He goes straight into the machine-gun fire just like that. There is a great man. You are not yellow, are you?" Others do it, so I can do it. That's the way wars are fought and death ships run. All after the same idea. No invention of new ideas or new models is necessary. The old ones are still working smoothly.

"Hey, what are you brooding about? What's your name, anyway?"

My fireman had come below. He seemed to be in very bad humor.

"My name is Pippip."

He brightened up a bit and said: "Looks to me you are a Persian."

"Guessed wrong. I am an Abyssinian. My mother was a Parsee. Those are the people that throw their dead to the vultures instead of burying them in the ground."

"We throw them to the fish. It appears from this that your mother was a rather decent woman. Mine was an old whore doing it for half a peseta. But if you ever say to me son of a bitch, or, worse, *cabrón*, I sock you so that even your vultures won't find you. I respect my mother, don't you ever forget that."

Now I knew he was a Spaniard.

The fireman of the other watch, now off duty, pulled out of the furnace a thick glowing iron bolt and stuck it into a bucket of fresh water to heat it. He began to wash himself with sand and ashes, because he had no soap.

The stoke-hold was lighted by two lamps. I call them lamps, but the word "lamps" was all they had in common with a lamp. One of the lamps hung against the boiler near the water- and steam-gauges. The other hung in a corner to be of use to the coal-drag.

In the world to which the *Yorikke* belonged, little was known of modern things. The only modern object the *Yorikke* ever saw was the suit the skipper wore. Nobody seemed to know that there existed on earth things like gas lamps, acet- ylene lamps, to say nothing of electricity.

The lamps used in the stoke-hold and in the engine-hold were the same the *Yorikke* carried when she was making old Carthage on regular trips from Tyre on the coast of ancient Phœnicia. In the British Museum one still can see such ancient lamps. They were iron vessels big enough to hold a pint. From the bottom of this vessel, going outside and upwards, a funnel was stuck in. Inside of this funnel there was a wick. The wick was as far from a real wick as this lamp was from being a lamp. The company did not supply wicks. We had to get them somewhere. When we knew the engineer was not in the engine- hold, we sneaked in and searched the box where the engineers kept the rags with which they tightened up leaks in the fit- tings. To explain it more clearly, the wicks were of the same kind that were used in the quarters and which had their origin in the woolen petticoats of the seven virgins who kept their candles burning all night to guard their worthless virtues. Suppose they had not had candles lighted at night; some guy might have mistaken them for pretty girls and gone off with their virtue.

The fuel for these lamps was the same famous diamond oil. But while the fuel for the lamps in the foc'sle still, sometimes, had a slight touch of real kerosene, the fuel we got for these stoke-hold lamps was pure burned-out and scratched-up oil and grease from the bottom of the engine-hold and from the catchers beneath the bearings and cushions of the engine.

Four times during one hour the wick had to be pulled out of the funnel because it burned off so quickly. You had to pull out the wick with bare fingers; no other instrument was at hand to do it with. After your first watch you left the hold with your nails half burned off and your finger-tips scorched.

Stanislav had already worked a double watch that day. Later it will be understood what a double watch on the *Yorikke* really meant, and then only will it be fully understood what kind of a guy Stanislav was when he decided to help me during my first watch before the boilers. He could hardly crawl by himself. None the less he stayed with me a full hour helping me shovel coal into the stoke-hold.

The fireman had to wait upon nine fires, three for each boiler. Two boilers would have been sufficient to produce the necessary steam for the *Yorikke*. One boiler was meant to be the reserve boiler, to rely upon in case something happened to one of the other boilers. But since all pipes were leaking, too much steam was lost, and therefore the reserve boiler, which should be used only in port to feed the winches and windlasses, had to be used permanently, otherwise the *Yorikke* would never have had steam enough to weather off a rough sea and gales.

It was the duty of the drag to haul into the stoke-room all the coal needed to feed these nine fires.

Before the coal could be hauled in, there was a heap of other work to do. The fires, of course, did not take into consideration any other job save swallowing fuel.

So to complete all the work that was already waiting, quite a huge load of ready coal had to be held in reserve before the boilers. This heap of coal had to be furnished by the watch that was leaving now; that is to say, when the watch went off duty, it had to leave an amount of fuel ready large enough so that the new watch could work before the boilers one full hour without having to haul in more coal. When the present watch was relieved, it also had to leave behind a similar amount of ready coal, to be used by the next watch.

Only during the two middle hours of one's watch could this great extra supply be hauled in—in my case, from one to three. At three o'clock the drag of the relief watch came, and with his help the ashes that had accumulated in the stoke-hold were cleared out. For this reason at three o'clock there had to be in the stoke-hold sufficient fuel ready to serve the nine fires during the hour while the ashes were cleared, plus the fuel which had to be left over for the relieving watch. Naturally, during the two hours in which the hauling of the fuel went on, the fires of the ship under full steam were incessantly fed, eating and eating away from the heaps of coal you were hauling in. Whoever had not superhuman strength, a heart like a sledge-hammer, and lungs which worked like the sails of a racing yacht could not make it, regardless of how willing he might be. He collapsed for sure. In one case which I remember he never stood up again and died in less than six hours.

The back of the stoke-hold was toward the bow, and the boilers, lying parallel to the keel, were located in such a way that the doors of the furnaces looked toward the bow. The engine-hold was situated behind the boilers in the direction of the stern.

At the back of the stoke-hold there were two huge coal-bunkers. When they were well filled, only the gates had to be heaved and the coal would fall right in front of the boilers. This was honey to the drag. There was practically no work for him to do—just shovel the coal still nearer to the furnaces to make it easier for the fireman.

The *Yorikke*, though, was obviously cursed, because whatever sort of work was to be done on her was the hardest work one can think of. Nothing was easy on her. If for some reason you had a sunny day, then you could be sure that the next fifty days would be only that much harder for you. So it is not to be wondered at that in those coal-bunkers, at the back of the stoke-hold, only very seldom was there any coal at all. And if there was, the second engineer, that devil of a pickpocket, locked the gates. He did not open them until all other coal on the ship, no matter where it was housed away, had been taken out first. In the meanwhile the *Yorikke* coaled afresh in some port, and the hard job of hauling in fuel from the farthest holds of the *Yorikke* began again. To be honest, hard as it was for us to haul fuel all the time from the far bunkers, there was some sense in keeping the gates to the stoke-hold bunkers locked. In the heavy gales which might break upon us at any time, it would mean the safety of the ship to have fuel in reserve so close at hand. For in a very heavy sea it might have been near impossible to haul sufficient coal from the other bunkers.

The regular work on the *Yorikke* for the fireman and the drag would have been considered on any decent ship the work of four healthy well-fed men. Since even galley-slaves develop pride, why shouldn't we? There are galley-slaves who are proud of being good galley-slaves. When the overseer who sings out the strokes walks up and down the plank with his whip in his hand, lashing here and there, and he looks with approving eyes on a husky fellow who is hauling out with long sweeping strokes, then that husky feels like a soldier called for at an honor parade to be decorated with a bronze medal by Mr. Pershing. "That's nothing," says the worker close to a collapse, "I can still do better; just watch me and see what a real guy can do." All right, the medal is yours, keep it and be happy; some day you will tell your grandson how smart a slave you were. Honors are so cheap, you can pick them like fallen leaves in November.

The fireman stirred open three fires, skipping two of each

boiler and going from one boiler to the next. After having worked boiler number three, he returned to boiler number one, breaking up fire number two, then going to boiler number two, breaking up fire number two, and so on. On each furnace door the numbers of the fires were written with chalk, beginning with number one and finishing with number nine.

Breaking up the fire was done with a long heavy poker. The slags and cinders were broken off the grate-bars to clean the fire and let it have all the draft it needed to keep it going with full force. Artificial fans were not known on the *Yorikke.* All the draft was provided by nature.

When the furnace doors were opened, a tremendous heat flared into the stoke-hold. The glowing cinders were broken off the bars and pulled out of the furnace. The fire inside the channel roared like an angry beast ready to jump at the trouble-maker. The more cinder was broken off and cleared away, the wilder the fire seemed to act. In front of the furnace the glowing slags mounted until the fireman had to jump back, lest he be scorched. He yelled: "*Agua,* water, cool'm off." I had to spray water over the cinders to kill them. With each spray a cloud of hot steam sprang up and filled the stoke-hold with a hot fog, making it difficult to see what was going on.

As soon as the fireman heard the hissing of the water on the slags, he hurriedly began to shovel coal into the furnace. He did it so quickly that one hardly could follow his movements. Before the steam cloud had disappeared, he was done with the job, and with a bang he closed the furnace door. He wiped his forehead with one stroke, jumped to furnace door number four, opened it, poked off the cinder, yelled: "Get the water, hell and devil!" and began at the same time throwing up coal by the shovelfuls, wiped off the sweat, swore, and jumped to furnace door number seven, jerked it open, crashed off the slags from the grate-bars, howled: "*Agua!*" and threw in the fuel. Like a black tiger he jumped to boiler one, pulled open furnace door number two, and so the work went on: Jumping tiger-like, yelling for water, throwing up fresh fuel, closing the doors with a bang, swearing, spitting, wiping off the sweat, jumping again.

We wore only pants. On his feet the fireman wore a sort of cloth slipper. I had shoes. Now and then the fireman jumped back with a curse and shook off the cinders that leaped upon his bare arms and naked chest. There were no hairy apes around with lurking strains of philosophy for stage purposes. No time for thinking and looking under dames' skirts. Five seconds lost thinking of anything else but your stoke-hold might cause twenty square inches of your sound flesh to be burned away. A stoke-hold in a stage-play or in a movie is something different, at least more pleasant. People in evening dress would not like to see the thing as it is and still pay for it.

More often than upon his breast and arms the embers sputtered upon his feet. Then he danced and swore and howled like a savage. The embers slipped inside of his footwear, where they scorched his flesh before he could even find them and get them out.

After three fires had been broken up, the poker became so hot that the fireman could handle it only by wrapping thick rags around his hands.

The cinders taken out from the furnaces and accumulated in front of the fires gave forth such heat that it became impossible for the fireman to go near the furnaces. That bowl of water shed upon the cinders and ashes when the fireman working at the furnaces sang out: "*Agua*, for devil's sake!" did not suffice to kill the cinders thoroughly. Only the surface got slightly cooled off for a few seconds, giving the fireman just a breathing-space to hurry up to finish this particular fire. When he was through with all nine fires, and the heat had become unbearable, the cinders had to be cooled more completely. The stoke-hold had almost to be flooded to accomplish this. They never could be cooled entirely until they were thrown overboard. For, underneath, the embers kept glowing and they spread the fire to any bit of coal among the ashes not fully burned.

This flooding of the stoke-hold brought up thick clouds of scalding steam, from which we could protect ourselves only by jumping into the farthest corners of the hold.

The stoke-hold was ridiculously small. The space between the boilers and the back of the stoke-hold was considerably shorter than the length of the fire-channels beneath the boilers. Pulling out the poker from the furnace could not be done straightway, because the end of the poker would hit the back of the stoke-hold long before the whole poker was out of the fire. Therefore the fireman had to go sideways and jerk the poker up and down to get it out. He had to do a real dance about the stoke-hold to handle the poker properly. In heavy weather, when the ship rolled hard and fell off big breakers, the dances the fireman had to do looked funny enough to anyone watching it. But there was anything but fun about it. The fireman was then thrown about; he fell with his face upon the red-hot poker, with his bare breast or back upon the heaps of white-hot slags, tumbled over the mounds of fuel against the open furnace, lost his clogs and stepped right into a hill of embers. Incidents like that happen on any ship and in any stoke-hold when there's a rough sea. But in a good-sized stoke-hold the horrible consequences of such incidents can be avoided to a great extent. On the *Yorikke*, however, these dreadful burnings, scaldings, and scorchings could not be shunned, regardless of how hard one might try. Here they were part of the job. Working before the boilers meant getting burned, scalded, and scorched, all over.

Death ship; yes, sir. There are several kinds of death ships. In some the carcasses are made inside the hull; in others dead sailors are made outside. And then there are death ships that make fish-fodder everywhere. *Yorikke* made carcasses inside, outside, and everywhere. She was a model of a death ship.

While we were cleaning up the fires, the fireman of the former watch finished his bath. All the time he was washing himself in the bucket, entirely stripped, he was in danger of being burned or scorched either by the poker or by sputtering embers. He did not mind. He felt sure that since he was dead nothing could happen to him. From his face, after he had washed himself, one could see that he was really dead.

His face and body had been washed fairly well with the help of white ashes and sand. But he could not rub the ashes into his eyes, and consequently his face was white while his eyes had big black rings around them. Perhaps this was the reason why he looked like a man with a death skull instead of a face. His cheeks were hollow, his cheek-bones stood out, and they were white and polished like billiard-balls. There seemed to be no flesh in his face.

He put on his pants and his torn shirt. He groaned a deep "Ough," which he meant perhaps as a good-night. Tired and heavily he climbed up the ladder. When he had reached the landing, I just caught a glimpse of him doing the snake-dance.

Stanislav had meanwhile been busy dragging coal into the stoke-hold to build up a pile for me to have on hand until I had found myself.

When we were breaking up fire number six again, Stanislav came to me and said: "Well, brother, I am sinking now. I can't do it any longer. I am finished. Guess I have to shuffle off. It's about half past one. I am on the spot now for almost sixteen hours. At five I have to hop on again and heave ashes with you. It's a great thing that we have you with us now. I could not have done it any longer. I have to make a confession which I should have made earlier. But you see, bad news is always told too early. It is like this, we are only two coal-drags on this bucket, if I count you in. That means that each of us has two watches with six hours each; and taking in each watch one hour extra for clearing ashes, it makes seven hours, or, to make it quite clear to you, fourteen hours' tough work within every twenty-four hours, as long as twenty-four will last. Tomorrow we will have still more extra work. We have to clear the whole deck of the mountains of ashes left there while the can was in port. You know, in port no ashes must be cleared into the water. That's all left on deck until the can is in the open again. It will cost us another four hours' extra work."

"Of course, all these hours more than the regular watch of four hours are overtime, aren't they?" I asked.

"Yes, buddy," Stanislav said, "you are right, all this is overtime. But it won't make you any happier. You may write it down on paper, all the hours you call overtime. Only you mustn't expect anybody to pay for it."

"Oh, I settled that with the old man when I signed on," I said.

"Now look here. Don't be a sucker. Whatever you settled here when you signed on or after has no value. Only what you have got in your pocket, that's what you may rely on, as long as it isn't pinched by somebody in the foc'sle. And don't you ever think that you get paid here. Not in your life-time. What you get is advances and advances. Just enough to get drunk and get a dame under your legs. Sometimes there is just a bit left to buy a shirt, a pair of pants, or new clogs. You never get enough to buy you a complete outfit. You see, if you look like a respectable citizen, you might get some ideas into your head and walk off and become alive again. Nothing doing. Get the trick now? As long as you haven't got money, and as long as you are in rags, you cannot get away here. You stay dead. If you try, he orders you arrested for desertion and they keep you in jail until the very minute the *Yorikke* is putting out. Then they bring you aboard, and all the costs for jailing you are cut off your pay. And the old man fines you two or three months' pay extra for desertion. That's in the regulations. He can do it. And he does it. Then you go to the old man on your knees and beg for a peseta and you apologize. Because you must have likker. You can't do without. Or you go all nuts. You need the shots and the dames. Without, you can't stand it. Believe me, buddy, it's a lie that the dead has no feeling. You will learn how much a dead one still can suffer before he has become accustomed to it. I won't wash myself. I cannot lift my hands any more. Good night. All the luck, and I wish that no grate-bars fall out. That costs life-blood, Pippip. Good night."

I could not answer him. I had no words. My head was humming. I saw him dragging his tired body up to the landing at the middle of the gangway. As in a dream, I saw him doing the snake-dance. For a second it looked as if he had lost his hold and was about to fall below. Then he climbed farther up and disappeared in the dark hole through which I could see a few stars sparkling in the black sky.

"Holy Virgin, *Santísima Madre, Purísima en el cielo.* Thousand holy sons of skunks. Damn the whole—"

The fireman was howling as though bitten by a mad dog. He took a breath, and then he began again to curse whatever came into his mind, which for a long while seemed to be the meeting-place of degenerate individuals and animals with over-animated sex deviations. Nothing was left of the purity of the Heavenly Virgin, or of the holiness of the saints. They all were dragged by him into the gutter. If ever hell had held any horror for him, he now did not care any more. He smashed hell, with a few good words, into an insignificant dung-hole, and he cursed the devils to useless mongrels disrespecting their mothers. He was no longer afraid of anything on earth or in hell. He was in a state where he could not be punished by anybody or by anything. For when I asked: "Hey, fire'm, what is up?" he beat his chest like a jealous gorilla and, with blood shooting into his eyes, he roared savagely: "Hell is upon me, six grate-bars have dropped. Holy alligator-tail and ogress-mouse."

31

The last word of Stanislav on leaving me had been that it would cost life-blood if grate-bars fell out. He had meant one bar. Now six had dropped.

I soon learned that to put them back into their berth not only cost blood, not alone flesh torn off, large pieces of skin scorched, but cost bleeding sperm, shredded tendons, and painfully twisted entrails. The joints of all limbs cracked like broken wood. The marrow in one's bones appeared to flow out like hot lava. While we worked like Egyptian slaves to bring the bars in again, the steam was falling and falling. Ahead of this hard work we saw already, crawling upon us, the hard work that was to follow to bring the steam up again to its full pressure. The longer we had to work with the bars, the lower fell the steam. I may justly say, though, that since that night, my first night with grate-bars in the ash-pit, I feel myself standing above the gods. I am free. Unbound. I may do now whatever I wish. I may curse the gods. They cannot punish me any more. No human law, no divine commandments, can any longer influence my doings, because no longer can I be damned. Hell is now paradise. However horrible hell may be, it cannot frighten me any more. There is nothing under heaven or in hell that can be compared with putting back fallen-out grate-bars on the *Yorikke*.

To know what it meant makes anyone understand that the swearing of my fireman was not swearing at all, but in fact only a sweet love-song. His language, rich as it was, could not meet the situation. No language, not even the Chinese, could possibly express in words the feeling any sane person simply had to have when confronted with a problem like setting in dropped grate-bars in the stoke-hold of the *Yorikke*.

Paradise, whatever it may mean, was for the black gang of the *Yorikke* not the opposite of hell, but was simply freedom from the obligation to set in their place dropped grate-bars.

The skipper never came into the stoke-hold; neither did the two mates. I have never heard that one of them ever even went below to the engine-hold. They even avoided passing too closely to the hatchway that led below to the stoke-hold.

The engineers dared enter the stoke-hold only when the *Yorikke* was snugly lying in port and the black gang was wiping and greasing and doing odd jobs about the boilers and the engine. Even then the engineers were soft-footed with the blacks. The firemen and the drags on the *Yorikke* were always, even in port, in a state of exaggerated anger, ready any second to throw at the engineer a hammer or a wrench. Prison, hangman, or the like did not mean a thing to any of the blacks. It would have been only liberation from the grate-bars of the *Yorikke*.

The engine was set up in a hold which was so small that the engineer on watch had to move about carefully to avoid being caught by the engine. Towards starboard there was in the engine-hold a heavy work-bench with tools for emergency work on the engine, the boilers, or the pipes. This bench could not be set up anywhere else. So it had to be in the engine-hold. Between the bench and the engine there was a space hardly two feet wide. On the other side of the engine, toward port, there was a space of only one foot, which had to be sufficient for the engineers when they wanted to go round the engine to look after the greasing. The slightest slip at either side would have been the last of the engineer. He would have fallen into the running engine. Both engineers were hard drinkers. They could get drunk like a Dane at the funeral of his mother-in-law. And they got soaked whenever the *Yorikke* was in port. But I have never seen either of them drunk, at least not in full, the same day or the same night the *Yorikke* was putting out. They knew that being drunk in the engine-hold of the *Yorikke* on high sea meant death surer than by the noose of a lynching party in Kentucky.

There was a good reason why the engine-hold was so narrow. On either side of the engine-hold coal-bunkers had been built in. Coal-bunkers must be. But since they do not carry any payload, they are built in any space that cannot be used for any other thing. At least so it was on the *Yorikke*.

From the stoke-hold, along starboard and along port side, a very low and narrow gangway led to these bunkers alongside the engine-hold. At the back of the boilers, toward starboard, an iron door led into the engine-hold. This door was supposed to be sea-tight to shut off the engine-hold from the stoke-hold in case water should break in. Since nothing was sea-tight on the *Yorikke*, no one expected this door to be tight. And it wasn't. It was this door that was used by the engineers when they wanted to enter the stoke-hold. When they wanted to go from deck to the engine-hold they had, of course, a separate hatchway.

This gangway was about four feet wide and so low that if you forgot about it you hit your head severely against the iron beams which strengthened the boiler-walls against the ship's hull. Like everything else aboard the *Yorikke* these gangways were dark like a coal-mine, day and night alike. Since they ran alongside the boilers they were so hot that a Turkish steam-bath seemed to be at freezing-point compared with their permanent heat.

We, the drags, could find our way in these two gangways just as easy as a drunken mole coming home at midnight. Because these gangways played a great part in the tortures that the coal-drags had to undergo on the *Yorikke*. Through these gangways we had to shovel and to haul and to squeeze numberless tons of coal toward the front of the boilers. So it will be understood why these gangways, and the labyrinths of the bunkers next to the engine-hold, held no secrets for us. Other people, among them our two engineers, did not know these gangways so well.

Suppose the steam, for one reason or other, began to fall. Then the engineer had to do something about it, because that was what he was paid for. Now, the first engineer never entered the stoke-hold when the *Yorikke* was on high sea. A broken shoulder would always remind him that the boiler-gang must not be molested when the ship is in the open. But since he had to do something about the falling steam, he went to the hatchway on deck leading to the stoke-hold, and from here he cried: "Steam goes down!" No sooner had he spoken than he fled away from the hatchway like the devil from an open church. From below a yell sprang up: "Damned greaser, go to hell and stay there. Just hop below, reception service is ready." And right after this a mighty piece of coal was flung upwards toward where his face had been for a second.

No use to preach to the working-man courtesy and politeness when at the same time the working-man is not given working conditions under which he can always stay polite and soft-mannered. One must not expect clean speech from a man compelled to live in filth and always overtired and usually hungry. Well fed, and sitting in a deep soft seat in an Episcopalian church, it is a godly pleasure to listen to a high-powered sermon about the wickedness of an ever unsatisfied working-class. Make all the wicked sailors and restless workers, after a good meal, sit in the same soft church seats, and they will listen with the same joy as do the others to the sermon about the lost proletarians who won't believe in God or heaven.

The second engineer, the one I thought a pickpocket and a horse-thief, was still rather young. Perhaps thirty-five. He was very ambitious and hoped to be, some day, first engineer on the *Yorikke*. His idea was that he could show his ability to make a good first engineer no better than by chasing the black gang, especially when the *Yorikke* was in port, for then he was in full command of the black gang. I, for one, did not think he had a chance ever to make a good first engineer—a chief, as we would express it properly. He learned very slowly. In fact, he could not learn at all how to get along with the black gang. At least not with a black gang like the one the *Yorikke* had. Maybe most of us were wanted, somewhere or everywhere, for murder, more or less, or the like, or pretty near the like. Who knows? But no matter what we had been before, and no matter for what reason we had come to sign on for the *Yorikke*, the firemen and the drags on the *Yorikke* were workers such as hundreds of decent ships would like to have and would pay real gold to have.

There are chiefs by whom the black gang swears. I knew a skipper once who was worshipped by the boiler gang as no god would ever be adored by them. That skipper every day went in person to the galley: "Cook, I wish to see and taste the food my firemen and coalers are to have today. Well, cook, this goes overboard. My blacks are no pigs. Understand. They have to get food. Real food. And when I say real food I mean it, or you and me are through. This steam-bucket is run by my firemen and by nobody else." And when he met a fireman or a coal-drag occasionally on deck, he would halt him and ask: "Fireman, how was the grub today? Enough to eat? Well, tonight you are to get an extra ration of bacon and eggs. By the way, does the boy bring you below regularly the iced tea I ordered for you? Just tell the truth. I cut his ears off if he doesn't do as he has been told to." The natural result was that you could go a long way through trouble in the stoke-hold before you would hear the fireman or the drag yell a couple of sons of bitches or something to that effect. You could have invited the whole black gang to a Rotarian's luncheon, and the Rotarians would have thought that these boys had come straight from the reception given in honor of the ambassador of Wortisdansikan in Washington. Yes, sir. A worker only blares back what he is blared at. In his face you see the face of those who make him the way he is.

While the grate-bars were worked into the frame the steam was falling and falling. The second engineer, then on duty, crawled through the gangway and came into the stoke-hold. Or, to make it clearer, he stopped where he just could let us see his head. From there he said: "Hell, what's the matter with the damn steam? The bucket will stop now any minute."

At this moment the fireman happened to have in his hands the red-hot poker with which he was just about to lift the bars. When he saw the second peeping in, hearing him talk utter nonsense, blood shot into his sweat-covered eyes, and his mouth became frothy. He yelled some inarticulate row of sounds, straightened up, and then, with superhuman force, he ran the poker toward the second with the intention of running him through and pinning him against the boiler-wall. The engineer, having seen the move in time, and the fireman, on account of the heavy weight of the poker, missed each other. The engineer fled, with all the speed he had, through the gangway back to the engine-hold. Since he was not so accustomed to this gangway as we were, he smashed his head several times against the iron bars.

The poker of the fireman went into that corner of the wall from which at that instant the engineer had disappeared. With so much power was the poker shot against the wall that a thick piece of that wall was broken off like so much pie. The fireman was not yet satisfied. He dropped the poker and ran after the engineer into the gangway. If he had caught him, not a pound of the engineer's body would have kept together. The second engineer, knowing that his life was forfeited if he failed to reach the door to the engine-hold, was by far quicker than I had ever expected him to be. He made the low door all right, though bleeding all over, and had just bolted the door behind him when the fireman bounced against it with a heavy bolt in his hand.

The second engineer did not report the attack. Perhaps he knew he would lose the case. As he, or anybody else on earth, would have lost the case against any member of the boiler gang of the *Yorikke* as long as one member of this gang was the only witness. What I would have done, any other of the gang would have done. If I had been asked to testify, I would have sworn, on any amount of Bibles, that the second engineer had come into the stoke-hold with a wrench in his hand to kill the fireman, because the steam had come down, and because the second was stink-full drunk. And why should I not testify against the trouble-maker? Right or wrong, my country. All right. Justified. Agreed. But then I am also entitled to say: Right or wrong, my fellow-worker; we work together, we suffer together, we laugh together, we die together. Now come on, who wants to blame me? My closest countryman is the one who burns his skin at the same furnace I do. After we have settled this relationship, then let's talk about nationality.

Next day the chief asked the second when and how he had received so many holes and bruises on his block. The second said that he had obtained them in the low gangway when making his get-away from the savages in the stoke-hold.

The chief, cleverer and with a better understanding of the worries of the blacks, did not report the case to the old man either. He ignored the case entirely, for he also knew it would be useless. For what could the skipper do? Lay us in irons? The *Yorikke* could not afford such a luxury. Every man was needed. In the trenches, when an attack is expected any minute, the soldier is at liberty to beat or to insult his officers as much as he likes. If you shoot him you may lose the trench. Here it was the same. If you laid a fireman in irons, the *Yorikke* in turn might never weather off a gale.

Said the chief in answer to the complaints of the second: "Man, you are lucky. Don't ever try that again, if you want to live. When grate-bars have dropped, then don't go near the stoke-hold. Let the steam go down. They will bring it up all right as soon as they have a chance. But if you go in to bother them, or even to let them see your face, then I haven't to be a crystal-gazer to foretell your fate. You cannot get away if they catch you. They eat you up alive, they tear you to little pieces, and they put you into the furnace, and when the relief comes they throw you overboard with the slags. No one ever will know what has become of you. That's what you ought to blame, not the black gang, but the grates we have on this can. Try it once yourself. Ought to. And if I drop in and ask you why the steam is dropping, you will do exactly the same and throw me into the furnace without mercy. Better leave them alone. Well, I warned you. Keep out of their way when they are hard at it. That's all I can say."

The second never again entered the stoke-hold when grate-bars were out. At times he would come in when the steam did not rise. He then just looked around without saying a single word. He would look at the steam-gauge, would hang around for a little while, offer the fireman and the drag each a cigarette, and then would say: "A rotten cheap coal we have bunkered this time. There is no fireman on all the seven seas who is apt to keep up steam with stinking fuel like that."

The fireman, of course, understood quite well what the second meant. He did his best to bring up the steam. He worked his whole body into rags to get the right pressure. Not alone the swell guys with money, but also working-men, no matter how low they may seem, have got the true spirit for sport. They feel as proud of a job well done as the Harvard guys feel when they have won a football game. Only no one cheers up the black gang with Rah-Rahs when in a heavy sea, with all the dead-wind that can blow, they have to keep the steam up with a fuel which would not be good enough for Mother to cook a proper meal of corned beef and cabbage. Our quarter-backs in the stoke-hold of the *Yorikke* sure were filthy and dirty; but that does not mean that they were not quarter-backs as noble in spirit and as brave in work as any fine quarter-back of Princeton. There would be no dukes if we all were princes.

No man could have a better college than the college represented by the *Yorikke*. Six months shipping before the mast on the *Yorikke*, and you no longer have any idols left to worship. Help yourself and do not depend so much upon others, not even upon your union officials. Kick off the authorities who want to wisecrack at you and mold you to a uniform opinion of what is good for you. If you do not know yourself, nobody can tell you, no matter how much you pay to be a member of something.

Of all the schooling the *Yorikke* had to offer, there was nothing which could yield better results than fishing dropped grate-bars and setting them back into the grate-frame.

Each of the three boilers had three furnaces. Two of these furnaces were side by side, with a space of about two feet between them. The third furnace was squeezed in between these two, but above them. All three furnaces were actually located inside the boiler. The furnaces were not square, but cylindrical. The fuel rested upon a grate. This grate was a heavy iron frame along the length of which were lying nine bars which could be removed from the frame one by one. Each bar was about five feet long, about an inch and a half thick, and four inches wide. In front and at the back the frame had a rim upon which the bars rested. This rim was less than a half-inch deep. Hence the bars rested rather uncertainly. Neither in front nor at the back was there a higher rim against which the bars would have found a brace. It was only this three-eighths of an inch against which the bars could be fixed. Each bar weighed between eighty and a hundred pounds.

The grates were really simple affairs. Only the use of these grates made them such a horror. When the boilers and the grates had been new, which, as I figure, must have been about the time when the good old British Queen married, even then it must already have been quite a job to hold these bars in the frame, or to put them back after they had dropped. In the course of so many thousands of trips the *Yorikke* had accomplished to make money for her owners these rims had burned away.

The slightest disrespect of the fireman toward the grate when knocking off the slags was inevitably punished by a bar dropping into the ash-hole. As soon as this happened the fire had to be left alone, and the combined efforts of the fireman and his drag had to be exerted to set the bar back into its berth.

First thing to do was to fish the bar out of the ash-hole. This was done with the help of a pair of tongs which weighed about forty pounds. These tongs did not work the way the tongs a blacksmith uses work. They were, like all things on the *Yorikke*, the other way round. That is to say, if you pushed the handles together the mouth opened, and vice versa. It would have been too easy for us had it been otherwise.

The bar was red-hot, and the furnace was white-hot. One of us held the bar up with the tongs, the other steered the bar into the furnace and then steered it alongside of those bars still quietly resting in their berth, until the opposite end of the bar reached the rim at the back. There, with the help of the poker from beneath—that is, from the ash-hole—the bar was slowly and carefully moved into the rim at the back. Then we worked to get the bar into the front rim too. One push too much toward the back rim, or one very slight pull too much toward the front rim, and the bar said good-by and dropped off again into the ash-hole. One of us lay flat on the ground to use the poker while the one that held the tongs tried once more to move, with tenderness, the bar back onto the rim. All this was done while the bar was red-hot, and while the open furnace roared into our faces, scorching face, hands, chest.

Now, of course, to set in one bar, hard and cruel as this job could be, was considered merely an interruption of the regular work. The real torture began when, on trying to set in one bar, other bars were stirred and pushed so that they also dropped, until five, six, or even seven bars had dropped into one fire alone. If this happened—and it happened so often that we forgot how often—then the whole fire went out of commission, because all the fuel broke through into the ash-pit. The furnace had to stay open, for otherwise the bars could not be set in again. So after a while the whole boiler cooled off so much that the two remaining fires could not keep it working at even half its capacity. Consequently the boiler became practically worthless. The more time we had to spend at the bars, the less time we could afford for the two boilers which alone had to furnish the steam necessary to keep the engine running. No wonder these two boilers also began to slack and we had to leave the dropped bars for a long while and bring up the remaining boilers to a point where they were ready to explode any minute. As soon as we had them going far above their power, we again started to work at the dropped bars. Seldom did we get a bar in right at the first attempt. It dropped in again and again, often ten times, until we, finally, had them all in—to last only until they were ready to drop once more during the same hour or the next.

When, after long slaving, the bars were now in again, we had to build up the fires anew. Having accomplished this also, both of us dropped as if we were lifeless into a pile of coal or wherever there was any space free from embers and red-hot cinders. For ten minutes we could not stir a toe. Our hands, our arms, our faces were bleeding. Our skin was scorched; whole patches and strips had been torn off or burned off. We did not feel pain any more, we only felt exhausted beyond description.

Then a glimpse at the steam-gauge whipped us into action. The steam would not stay. The fires had to be stirred, broken up, and filled.

When bars were out I had to assist the fireman. One man alone could not put them back. While I helped the fireman with the bars I could not haul in coal. But whether I could carry in coal or not was of no concern to the fires. They ate and ate, and if they did not get enough to eat, the steam came down. So whatever huge piles had been in the stoke-hold just before the bars began to drop were all gone by now. To drag in the coal needed during one watch took all the hard work the coaler could give. There was hardly a free minute left to step up to the galley and bring below a drink of coffee or cold water to the fireman. The oftener bars dropped, the harder the drag had to work afterwards to pile up coal in the stoke-hold, which always, no matter what happened, had to be a certain load, of which not ten pounds could be cut off. Within four hours the fires of the *Yorikke* swallowed about sixteen hundred well-filled large shovelfuls of fuel. The fuel was in many instances so far away from the boilers that these sixteen hundred shovelfuls had to be thrown in four shifts before they reached the fireman, so that the real hauling for the drag was not sixteen hundred shovels, but sometimes close to seventy hundred shovels. Some of the bunkers were located close to the foc'sle, others close to the stern.

This work, unbelievable any place on earth outside of the *Yorikke*, had to be done by only one man, by the drag. It had to be done by the filthiest and dirtiest member of the crew, by one who had no mattress to sleep on, no pillow to rest his tired head upon, no blanket, no coffee-cup, no fork, no spoon. It had to be done by a man whom the company could not afford to feed properly on account of the competition with other companies. But the company had to stand competition, because it was very patriotic, and every company had to go the limit to keep a good record in shipping in favor of its country. The country had to be first in all things, exportation, importation, production, shipping, railroad mileage. All was done for the good and for the glory and for the greatness of the country. A company cannot take care of two things that are contrary each to the other. If the company wants to beat competition, the drag and the fireman have to pay for it. Some way or other. Both the company and the crew cannot win. One has to be the loser in this battle, as in all other battles. Here on the *Yorikke* the biggest losers were Stanislav and I.

The *Yorikke* has taught me another big thing for which I am grateful. She taught me to see the soul in apparently life-less objects. Before I shipped on the *Yorikke* I never thought that a thing like a burned match, or a scrap of paper in the mud, or a fallen leaf, or a rusty worthless nail might have a soul. The *Yorikke* taught me otherwise. Since then life for me has become a thousand times richer, even without a motor-car or a radio. No more can I ever feel alone. I feel I am a tiny part of the universe, always surrounded by other tiny parts of the universe; and if one is missing, the universe is not com-plete—in fact does not exist.

The winch used for heaving ashes had personality, and it had to be treated accordingly. Everything and every part of the *Yorikke* had individuality and soul. The *Yorikke* as a whole had the greatest personality of all of us.

When once on a trip from Santander making for Lisbon we were caught in one of those terrible cross-gales in the Bay of Biscay, the *Yorikke* was thrown about so that we all thought she would never weather it out. When we—my fireman and I—came below to relieve the former watch, and I saw how the pile of fuel was thrown from port side to starboard unceas-ingly, I had only one thought: what will happen to us or to the *Yorikke* if six bars should drop in one fire. If the steam in such a heavy sea is too low, the ship will easily get out of control, and it may be smashed against cliffs or helplessly driven ashore or upon sand-banks.

Any sailor who is not superstitious—which would be the rarest thing under heaven—would certainly become so after being on the *Yorikke* hardly a week. My fireman was no ex-ception. So that night, when we came below, the fireman knocked his head three times against the boiler-wall, then spat out, and said: "*Yorikke* dear, please, don't drop any bar this night, please, just this night." He said it almost like a prayer. Since the *Yorikke* was not something dead, but a ship with a soul, she understood what Spainy had said. You may believe it or not, but the truth is that for thirty hours, while the heavy weather lasted, not one single bar fell off. When we were near Lisbon and the sea had become fine again, the *Yorikke* joyfully dropped nine bars in our watch, four in fire number two, one in fire six, three in fire seven, and one in fire number nine, just to keep us from getting haughty. We did not mind the nine bars, hard as it always was to bring them in, and Spainy swore only fifteen times, while usually he never ceased to swear, nor did I, for a full hour after the bars were in.

My fireman was relieved at four. My watch did not end until six. I went to call Stanislav at twenty to five. We had to clear ashes for an hour. I could not get him out of the bunk. He was like a stone. He had already been a good long time on the *Yorikke*. He had still not got used to it. People who do not know what hard work really means and do nothing but just figure out new laws against criminal syndicalism and against communist propaganda usually say, when they see a man at hard work: "Oh, these guys are used to it, they don't feel it at all. They have no refined thinking-capacity, as we have. The chain-gang means nothing to them; it's just like a vacation."

They use that speech as a dope to calm their consciences, which, underneath, hurt them when they see human beings treated worse than mules. But there is no such thing in the world as getting used to pain and suffering. With that "Oh, they are used to that!" people justify even the beating of defenseless police-prisoners. Better kill them; it is truly more merciful. Stanislav, a very robust fellow, never got used to the dropped bars or to all the rest of the hard work on the *Yorikke*. I never became used to it. And I do not know of anybody that ever became accustomed to it. Whenever a fireman with fairly good papers, or on reaching his country, had a chance, he skipped off; if he could do no better he skipped without waiting for his pay. There is no getting used to pain and suffering. You become only hard-boiled, and you lose a certain capacity to be impressed by feelings. Yet no human being will ever become used to sufferings to such an extent that his heart will cease to cry out that eternal prayer of all human beings: "I hope that my liberator comes!" He is the master of the world, he who can make his coins out of the hope of slaves.

"You don't mean? Is it five already?" asked Stanislav. "I just lay down. It cannot be five." He was still as dirty as when he had left the fire-hold. He had no ambition now to wash up. He was too tired.

"I tell you, Stanislav," I said, "I cannot stand it. We had six bars out in one fire, and two in another. I cannot come at eleven to help you clear the ashes and then start dragging again at twelve. I am going over the railing, I tell you."

Stanislav was sitting on his bunk. His face black. In the thick kerosene smoke of the quarter I could not distinguish his face well. He turned his head to me and he said with a swollen sleepy voice: "Nope, don't you do it, Pippip. Don't leave me. I cannot do your watch also. I will have to make the railing also. No. Hell, I won't. I would rather bury two cans of plum marmalade in the furnaces and let the whole thing go to blazes, so that they could no longer catch lost souls to get their insurance with. I still feel something in my breast here for the poor guys who might come after us. Geecries, that game with the plum marmalade might be a pretty come-off. I have to think it over some time."

Plum marmalade? Poor Stanislav, he was still dreaming. So I thought.

32

My watch ended at six in the morning with an hour's work clearing ashes with Stanislav. I could not leave any reserve fuel for him. The shovel dropped out of my hands. "It's okay, Pippip, don't mind. We'll get even some day when I am down."

I did not miss mattress, pillow, blanket, soap. I understood now why such things were not supplied on the *Yorikke*. They really were not needed. Covered with soot, dirt, oil, grease, as I was, I fell into my bunk. What meaning inborn cleanliness? All culture and civilization depend on leisure. My pants were torn, burned, and stiff from oily water and soot. My shoes and my shirt looked no better. Now, when we put in the next port and I stand at the railing and look down upon the pier, side by side with my fellow-sailors, I shall not look any longer different from those who I thought were the worst of pirates when first I saw them. I, like the rest, was now clothed in striped garments, in prison clothes, in death-sheets, in which I no longer could escape without falling into the hands of the guards of the world of bureaucrats, who would pinch me and bring me back to where I now properly belonged. I had become part of the *Yorikke*. Where she was, I had to be; where she went, I had to go. There was no longer any escape to the living.

Somebody yelled into my ear: "Breakfast ready." Not even an ambassador's breakfast would get me up and out of my bunk. What was food to me? A saying goes: "I am so tired I can hardly move a finger." He who can say that does not know what it means to be tired. I could not even move an eyelid. My eyelids did not close fully. So tired they were. The daylight could not make my eyelids close. No power was left within me even to desire that the daylight go away and give my eyes a rest.

And at that very instant when I had the feeling: "Why worry about daylight?" the huge iron mouth of a gigantic crane gripped me, then tossed me violently up into the air, high up, where I hung for a second. The man who tended the crane had a quarrel with something or somebody; and, being a bit careless, the brake slipped off his hand and down I fell from a height of five thousand feet, and I dropped squashing upon a pier. A mob gathered around me and cried: "Get up, you, come, come, snap out of it, twenty to eleven, heave ashes."

After I had heaved ashes with Stanislav, there were just about ten minutes left. I had to hurry to the galley to carry dinner for the black gang to the foc'sle. I swallowed a few prunes swimming in the watery starch. I could not eat one bite more. The jaws would not work. Somebody bellowed: "Hey, drag, where is my dinner? Hop at it." It was the donkey-man, who had to be served separately in his own quarter. For the drags were the stewards of the donkey-man, who was their petty officer. He could have done all this alone, because he had practically no work to do. Yet he would have lost his dignity if he had to go to the galley and get his dinner himself. Hardly had I set the dishes on his table when the bell rang and the watch on the bridge sang out the watch-relief. I went below to help the fireman break up the fires and haul in the fuel from the bunkers.

At six in the evening I was relieved. Supper was on the table in the quarters. It had come in at five. It was now cold and everything edible had been picked by the other hungry men. I did not care to see what was left. I was too tired to eat anyway. I did not wash myself. Not for all civilizations present and gone did I care to have a clean face. I fell into my bunk like a log.

That lasted three days and three nights. No other thought entered my mind and my feelings but: "Eleven to six, eleven to six, eleven to six." The whole universe, all religions, all creeds, and my entire consciousness became concentrated in this idea: eleven to six. I had vanished from existence. Two painful yells cut into what had once been my flesh, my brain, my soul, my heart. These yells caused a piercing pain, as the feeling might be when the bared brain is tickled with a needle. The yells came, apparently, always from far away, falling upon me like avalanches of rocks and timber, thundering into my shattered body like the onrush of a hundred express trains gone wild. "Up, twenty to eleven!" was one of the yells. And the other: "Holy sons of fallen saints, three bars have dropped! Turn to it."

When four days and four nights had passed, I felt hungry. I ate heartily. Now I was initiated and a true member of the *Yorikke*. And I began to get accustomed to it. I had lost the last tiny little connection which up to this hour had bound me to the living. I had become so dead that no feeling in mind, soul, or body was left. There were times when I felt that my hands were steam-shovels, that my legs and arms moved on ball-bearings, and that all the insides of my body were but running wheels.

"It is not so bad after all, Stanislav," I said ironically to him when I came below to relieve his watch. "The hash tastes all right. The grandfather is not so bad a cook. If, the hell of it, we could get only more milk. I say, brother, the pile of coal you are leaving me here in reserve isn't very much to brag about. We stoke it off in three fires without even saying so much as pem-pem. Listen, how do you think I can loosen the chief from a good shot of rum? Haven't you got a good tip?"

"Nothing easier than that, Pippip. You are looking sour enough. You will make it. Go right up and tell him your stomach won't hold, you spill it all at the fuel, and if you won't get a stomach-cleaner you cannot stand the watch through. Tell him you are spilling all green. You will get a good full-sized swinger from him. You can ride this same horse twice a week. Only make sure not to come too often. Then he gets wise and he may fill your glass with castor. Being used to good clean drainings, you won't notice it until you have shot it all in. Then it is too late. You cannot spit it into his cabin. You have to finish up and get it all down. It won't do you any good if, after having sipped the castor, you drop six or eight bars in your watch. Believe me, it sure would not be a sweet watch. Keep that prescription for yourself. If you spill it, it will be

ineffective. The firemen have got one of their own invention.
They don't give it away, those sinners. They often make as
many as four, even five shots a week. But they don't know
genuine comradeship, those knights in shining armor."

The time came, though slowly, when I began to get my
own ideas again, and this was when the two piercing yells
ceased to have any corrupt effect upon me. No longer did I
stagger about the bucket in a dazed and unconscious state. I
began to see and to understand. Rebirth had taken place. I
could now, without the slightest feeling of remorse, bark at the
second that I would allow him to throw me overboard for
bragging if I would not smash his head with a hammer and
drill his back with the poker if he ever came into the stoke-
hold again when we were on high sea, and bars were out, and
the steam was falling to a hundred twenty. I swore to his face
that this time he would not get away through the gangway
safely like he did the other night. He could not have done it
anyhow. Maybe he knew it. We had placed in the gangway a
heavy poker, hung up in such manner that when, from a certain spot in the stoke-hold, one of us pulled a string, the poker
fell down, making impossible the get-away of anybody in
that gangway. Whether he, once trapped, got off with his
life or only with a bleeding head and shins depended in the
last decision not on what he had said to us but only on how
many bars had dropped into the various ash-pits.

There were no regulations and rules for the fire-hold.
Articles, of course, were signed when signing on, but the
articles were never read to anybody as is required by law. Yet
we had proof that people can live without laws and do well.
The fire gang had built up among themselves rules which were
never mentioned, but, nevertheless, kept religiously. No one
was there to command, no one to obey. It was done to keep
the engine, and so the ship, going, and at the same time give
each member of the fire gang exactly the same amount of work
and worry. Since there were nine fires to serve, each fireman

left to his relief three fires elegantly cleaned of all slags and cinders. The first watch cleaned fires number one, four, and seven; second watch fires number two, five, eight; third watch fires number three, six, nine. The relief could depend on these fires being left clean by the former watch. Therefore, no matter how much trouble the new watch had with their bars, they were sure to have at least three fires going at full blast. The relief, furthermore, found a certain amount of fuel ready in front of the fires. The former watch did not leave the stokehold until the ash-pits were drawn clear. Without this unwritten agreement in the black gang, work would have been nearly impossible.

Another important agreement was that the outgoing watch did not leave one single bar dropped. All bars were in when the watch was relieved. Sometimes a watch worked half an hour into the new watch just to bring in the bars which had fallen out ten minutes before the relief came.

Now let us have a heavy sea with all the trimmings. Such as we had once when sailing along the Gold Coast of western Africa.

The pleasure began with the heaving of ashes. I released the heavy ash-can from the hooks, and, hot as the can was, I carried it against my chest across the gangway toward the railing. Long before I reached the railing, the *Yorikke* swung out on a swell roller, and I with my hot can rolled some thirty feet toward the bow. I had not yet got up on my feet when the *Yorikke* fell off to the stern, and I, still with my can, had, of course, to follow the command of the *Yorikke*. After two of these rollers there was nothing left in the can, and the first mate cried from the bridge: "Hey, drag, if you want to go overboard it's all right with me. But you'd better leave the ash-can with us, you really won't need it when you go fishing."

In such a heavy sea it is considered a good job if you can get half of the ashes over the rail. The other half is strewn over all the decks. And since they are ashes, it is the job of the drags to clear the decks of this useless cargo.

Below, in the fire-hold, things are just as interesting as they are up on deck. The fireman is about to swing a beautiful shovelful into the furnace when the roller meets him square. He is thrown, and the whole shovelful of coal goes splashing right into the face of the drag. When the roller comes over from astern, the fireman, with his shovel, disappears into a pile of coal, out of which he emerges again when the *Yorikke* falls off from afore.

Jolly dances take place in the bunkers. I have a huge pile of fuel, one hundred and fifty shovels, right near the hatchway to the fire-hold when a breaker throws the *Yorikke* over to port and my pile of coal goes the same way, back to where I had just taken it from. So this swell job has to be repeated. After a while one learns to time the rollers, and as soon as a certain amount of fuel is near the chute, one shovels it down into the stoke-hold so quickly that, before the bucket falls off to the other side, nothing is left that can go with her. A coal-drag has to know how to time the rollers correctly in heavy weather. He must therefore understand the principles of navigation just as well as the skipper does. If he could not time the moves of a ship, he might never get a single shovelful of coal in front of the boilers. But by the time a good coal-drag is through with his studies in navigation, he comes from his watch in a heavy sea brown and blue all over, with bruises and with bleeding knuckles and shins. What a merry adventurous life a sailor has! Just read the sea-stories. They can tell you all about it.

A merry life. Hundreds of *Yorikkes*, hundreds of death ships are sailing the seven seas. All nations have their death ships. Proud companies with fine names and beautiful flags are not ashamed to sail death ships. There have never been so many of them as since the war for liberty and democracy that gave the world passports and immigration restrictions, and that manufactured men without nationalities and without papers by the ten thousand.

A good capitalist system does not know waste. This system cannot allow these tens of thousands of men without papers to roam about the world. Why are insurance premiums paid? For pleasure? Everything must produce its profit. Why not make premiums produce profit?

Why passports? Why immigration restriction? Why not let human beings go where they wish to go, North Pole or South Pole, Russia or Turkey, the States or Bolivia? Human beings must be kept under control. They cannot fly like insects about the world into which they were born without being asked. Human beings must be brought under control, under passports, under finger-print registrations. For what reason? Only to show the omnipotence of the state, and of the holy servant of the state, the bureaucrat. Bureaucracy has come to stay. It has become the great and almighty ruler of the world. It has come to stay to whip human beings into discipline and make them numbers within the state. With foot-printings of babies it has begun; the next stage will be the branding of registration numbers upon the back, properly filed, so that no mistake can be made as to the true nationality of the insect. A wall has made China what she is today. The walls all nations have built up since the war for democracy will have the same effect. Expanding markets and making large profits are a religion. It is the oldest religion perhaps, for it has the best-trained priests, and it has the most beautiful churches; yes, sir.

33

Overworked and overtired men do not care what goes on about them. There may be corruption, robbery, banditry, gangsterism, piracy, all at wholesale, right in their neighborhood. What do they care? They are the best people to govern. They never criticize, they never argue, they do not read papers, and they feel sure that everything in the world is just fine and could not be any better. They are satisfied and they hail the ruler if sometimes they get an extra ration of pudding or rum. They only sleep, and sleep, and sleep. Nothing else interests them. That was the reason why I had been a good long time on the *Yorikke* before I got even a dim idea what the *Yorikke* was really doing and how she was doing what she did.

I was standing against the rail, rather sleepy. There were near us quite a number of feluccas, with their strange sails. They were around us as if they were about to attack us. This aroused my attention. They came and went, returned and sailed off again. Perhaps they were fishermen or smugglers. Great crowds of them often came in certain ports. There was a crowd that day when I looked at them with more interest than usual.

Suddenly I was wide awake. I could not understand at the moment what it was that had made me so. It had been like a shock. Fixing my mind upon this strange feeling, I noticed a great quietness. The engine had ceased to work. Day and night there is the noise of the engine; its stamping, rocking, and shaking make the whole ship quiver. It makes the ship a live thing. This noise creeps into your flesh and brain. The whole body falls into the same rhythm. One speaks, eats, hears, sees, sleeps, awakes, thinks, feels, and lives in this rhythm. And then quite unexpectedly the engine stops. One feels a real pain in body and mind. One feels empty, as if dropped in an elevator down the shaft at a giddy speed. You feel the earth sinking away beneath you; and on a ship you have the stark sensation that the bottom of the ship has broken off, and the whole affair, with you inside, is going right through to the opposite end of the globe. It was this sudden silence of the engine that was the cause of my awakening.

The *Yorikke* drifted swanlike upon a smooth, peaceful, glittering sea. The chains were rattling, and the anchor dropped with a splash into the water.

At this very moment Stanislav passed by, the coffee-can in his hand.

"Pippip," he whispered to me, "now we have to step on the gas. God damn it, below we have to raise the steam up to a hundred ninety-five."

"Are you mad, Lavski?" I said. "Why, we would fly up straight to Sirius without a single stop-over if you raise the steam to a hundred eighty-five. At a hundred seventy we are already twisting our bowels."

"Precisely, that's the reason why I try to be up on deck as often as I get a chance," Stanislav grinned. "Here, when the bucket goes up, you may have a chance to fly off and save your hide by getting a good swim. Below you are finished, there is no getting out. Trapped in for good until the police of the Last Judgment snatch you out of it. You see, Pippip, you have to be smart to go round the world in slippers. I mean, when I peeped so many feluccas hanging about us, then I knew the skipper is going to cash in. So below I worked like the devil to pile up a good heap of reserve fuel and so get my chance to be on deck as much as I can. I told my fireman I had got the colic, and that's why I had to beat it every four minutes. Next time you are in this mess you will have to find some other excuse. Or he gets wise to what is going on, and he won't stay below alone."

"Now, spring it, damn, what is the trouble?" I asked.

"Don't make me sick with your innocence. The skipper is collecting the dividends. I have never in all my life seen such a silly fool like you. What do you think you are sailing? A mail-boat under the flag of the lime-juicers? Your head is dumber than the clogs on my feet."

"I know well enough that I am shipping on a death bus," I said, defending my intelligence.

"At least something you have got clear," Stanislav answered. "But don't you ever believe that they are running down to ground port a bucket without music. Don't you misjudge them. The funeral of the *Yorikke* is well advertised and registered. The death ticket is all written up; they have only to fill in the exact date. You see, any man playing on his last string, and knowing it, may do as he pleases. Because it cannot come worse. The *Yorikke* may risk whatever she wants to. If taken in by a French chaser, before she reaches port for investigation, she sinks off, plugs out. The insurance is safe. No evidence found. Just send up a glance to the topmast head. What do you see? Yep, siree. The bos'n with the skipper's prisma-squeezer overhauling the horizon. Suppose he finds the air getting thick. Then, O boy of my dreams, then you will see the *Yorikke* hobbling off. Tell ye, you will be surprised to see how this old maid can raise a fuss when forced to and when willing to help her master across the lazy river. For the first fifteen minutes with that steam-pressure pepped up she makes twenty-two knots, and I bet you my black girl in Tunis free of charge that she makes even twenty-five when whipped into it. French chasers afraid to take such a risk with safety-valves under screws cannot come up with this old dame. Not during the first fifteen minutes. Of course, after fifteen minutes the old jane puffs and pants through all piss-ports and buttonholes, and as long as twenty-four hours you think she is going to fall apart at all her seams. For weeks afterwards she has got the acute asthma. But she made it. She wasn't pinched. And that's the only important thing, not to get pinched. Well, Innocent, I have to hop below, or my fireman'll smell a deceased monkey."

When caught in heavy weather we carried a hundred fifty-five pounds steam, while the ordinary pressure was a hundred and thirty. A hundred and sixty pounds meant *Attention;* a hundred sixty-five *Warning;* at a hundred seventy-five there was the thick red line *Danger* which meant: one pound more

and the boilers will most likely go straight up to heaven,
taking the *Yorikke* with them. Such a hasty leave from her
earthly existence, though, was prevented by the proper functioning of the safety-valve, which opened automatically when
the steam had reached that high pressure, and by doing so relieved the boilers of their dangerous fevers. At the same time
when the safety-valve opened, the steam blew the warning
whistle, and so the boilers howled out their mistreatment to
the whole world. Then the ship would get in an uproar from
the skipper to the last deck-hand, and the ship would become
like a stirred-up beehive.

Now, of course, everything was different. The skipper
wanted to make his collections. Therefore he had given orders
to the donkey to prevent the *Yorikke* from crying by screwing
tight her tear-ducts, so making it impossible for her to open
her safety-valves when the stream-pressure threatened her life.

The feluccas swarmed closer. Two approached the *Yorikke*
and made fast alongside. The gangway was lowered away.

The feluccas had fishermen of the Moroccan type aboard.
These men climbed up the *Yorikke* like cats, swift and oily.
On deck they moved about as freely and lightly as if the
whole ship was theirs.

Three Moroccans, intelligent and distinguished-looking gentlemen, though garbed like ordinary fishermen, after very cere-
monial salutations toward the second mate, were led by him
to the skipper's cabin. Then the second mate came out again
and directed the unloading. The first mate was on the bridge.
Every once in a while he would look up at the topmast head
and cry: "Orl korrect, bos'n? No nasty weather in sight?"

"All shipshape, aye, aye, sir!" answered the bos'n from the
look-out.

Boxes and crates appeared from the holds like magic, and
like magic they disappeared into the feluccas. Ants could not
work better. No sooner was one felucca loaded and the cargo
well covered with fish, than it pushed away from the ship and

sailed lustily off. The second it was off, another one came alongside to take in cargo. Before you would have thought it fastened, it was already loaded and off on its way. Each sailed off in a different direction. Some even went seemingly toward parts where land could not be found. It would have been almost impossible for any chaser to catch more than three, at best, so widely did they stray.

The second mate had a pencil and pad. He counted the boxes. One of the Moroccans who had an air as if he were the supercargo of the outfit repeated the numbers the second mate sang out. All the numbers were called in English.

When the last felucca was loaded, the first were out of sight. They had sunk beneath the horizon or had been veiled by curtains of mist. The others had become tiny bits of white paper floating upon the calm sea.

One felucca which all the time had hovered about now came close and made fast. This one took no load on. It carried only the usual cargo of fresh fish.

The three Moroccan gentlemen who had been with the skipper came out on deck, accompanied by the old man. They all laughed and talked merrily. Then, with their beautiful courteous gestures, they took leave of the skipper and climbed down the gangway. They boarded their felucca, put the sail into the wind, and the gangway was taken in. The anchor chains began to clank, and soon the *Yorikke* was running wild as if chased by the hells of all religions.

The skipper had gone to his cabin. After about fifteen minutes the skipper came out and cried up to the bridge: "Where is she?"

"Six off the coast, sir," the first mate answered.

"Then we are out of the limit, mate?"

"Aye, aye, sir."

"Give the course to the A.B. and come below to my cabin; let's have breakfast," the skipper said, smiling.

Thus the finale of this strange comedy.

The skipper, however, was no miser. Eat and let eat, he thought. We all had the so-called after-weather dinner: fried sausages, bacon, cocoa, French potatoes; and each got his coffee-cup filled with rum. Besides this everyone received ten pesetas in cash paid out the same day at five o'clock.

No one had to tell us. We knew the after-weather dinner, the extra rum, and the cash were mum-pay—that is, offered us to keep our swear-hatches shut up. The skipper's and the mate's breakfast sure was rich. The richest part of which, naturally, was not to eat; it was to be put into a pocket-book and not into a belly.

We had no complaints whatever. With that skipper we would have sailed straight to hell if he had wished us to. No thumb-screw would ever squeeze out of us what we had seen.

Yes, of course, we had seen something. Our engine, on account of being overheated, had become defective, and the ship had come to a stop, until the damage had been repaired. While we stood by for repairs, several feluccas had come alongside, offering us for sale fruit, fresh fish, and vegetables. The cook bought fish and vegetables, and the officers had bought bananas, pineapples, and oranges.

Swear to that? Of course, quite simple, because it is the truth and nothing but, so help me, lordy. Yes, sir.

You don't suppose a decent sailor gives his skipper away, do you? No, sir, certainly not. If pirates have got their honor, how much more so do decent sailors have theirs, if the skipper treats them like decent sailors.

34

Any man who is not overworked and not overtired begins to worry about things which ought to be of no concern to him. Right away he has ideas and an imagination which, when nursed and pepped up, might easily start to nibble at the very foundations of the state and of its sacred institutions and constitutions. Therefore a very good piece of advice to a sailor who wishes to stay an honest sailor runs thus: "Remain where you are, at your wheel, and at your paint; do not think about how the world is run; then you will always be a good sailor, beloved by everyone. Trouble-makers are hated everywhere."

The chief ordered open a coal-bunker which was right at the back of the fire-hold. More, the *Yorikke* coaled in the next port, and we had all the fuel so close at hand that we almost fell over it when at work before the boilers. This rare pleasure lasted three days and three nights. There were watches beautiful as holidays with money. Hardly any work at all. Just heaving ashes, and occasionally one bar to be set in.

While we were coaling through lighters, a mile and a half or so out of port, I noticed that, besides coal, other cargo was taken in. It must have been somewhere off the coast of Portugal, for the men bringing on the cargo spoke Portuguese. The loading was not so much different from the unloading that had taken place some time before.

Two men, clothed like simple fishermen, but who otherwise did not look like it, came aboard from one of the lighters. They went to the skipper's cabin. While they were talking things over with the old man, boxes were unloaded from the lighters. The boxes had been hidden under the coal. Smaller boats came alongside the *Yorikke*, and, taken out from under loads of fish and vegetables, more cargo was heaved in. Cargo in boxes, in barrels, in crates, in bales. It was loaded from starboard, while the port side was toward the coast. Therefore from the harbor nobody could have seen what was going on at the opposite side of the *Yorikke*.

As soon as all the coaling was done, the two gentlemen left the ship. The gangway was still lowered and the two gentlemen were barely in their boat when the anchor came up and the *Yorikke* went under full steam.

This time no after-weather dinner was served. We had only cocoa and raisin cake. Because there was nothing yet to swear about and tell the truth and nothing but.

Said Stanislav: "And why should you have to swear, anyway? Suppose somebody comes aboard and starts looking around. Let him open the hatchway. What is he to find? Boxes and crates and barrels. Naturally, you cannot deny that. You cannot swear that there are no boxes aboard when the reeker has got his hands upon them. Only the skipper will have to swear what is inside and what he means to do with the contents. None of your business, Pippip. Never worry about the old man, he sure will know all right what he is going to swear about, bet your life and my black girl free of charge."

Did we have elegant watches then? I should say we had. The ash-cans heaved and dumped off, the fires stirred, the slags broken off, and then you went just to the bunkers at the back, opened the gate, and the stoke-hold was filled with fuel. No dragging, no hauling, no shoveling, no pushing the wheelbarrow and knocking off your knuckles.

During one of these blissful watches I started to examine the holds so as to see if there was some loot loose. Sometimes there is genuine money in that game if you have a soft hand. Oranges, nuts, tobacco leaves, and lots of other things which any decent tavern-keeper likes to take for cash. At times one has to open a few boxes to see if there are shirts, or silk hose, or shoes, or soap. Man has to live. Morals are taught and preached not for the sake of heaven, but to assist those people on earth who have everything they need and more to retain their possessions and to help them to accumulate still more. Morals is the butter for those who have no bread.

The important thing is to close the boxes well after you have looked into them. It is not wise to put on the shirt and the shoes right after you have found them. You might make a bad impression on somebody, and you might even lead innocent youngsters to follow in your footsteps, which is a real sin. The best thing is not to use anything you should find for yourself, but to sell it honestly when you're in the next port. Any fine citizen will buy from you, because everybody knows the sailor always sells cheap, for he is not greedy for a big profit. He has no taxes to pay, no store rent, no light and telephone bills to bother about, so he can sell well below factory prices. If you need something good and really cheap, always try a sailor first. After this has failed, you may still go to the Jew.

Of course, it is not so that a sailor has no expenses at all. It is not always easy to go through the boxes and bales. One has to be a sort of snake. I had learned the snake-dances and I kept in good shape because I trained several times every day. If you made just one wrong step in your daily snake-dances, you felt it right away in the scorches and burns on your skin. What better training can anybody have? Going about the holds and looking intelligently for the most salable goods has some difficulties too. It is not at all easy to make money, no matter where you try it and how. Here a box falls upon you, there a barrel comes down and squeezes you in and peels off your hide a strap of useful leather. There is no light in the holds at night. You may, if you are very careful, light a match for a moment. But suppose the mate on the bridge sees the flicker; it would not be so good for you. Better leave the matches altogether and rely upon your soft hands and your true feelings.

The *Yorikke* carried rarely goods of real importance. Highly valued merchandise was not trusted to her. These frequent loadings and unloadings, though, did not let me sleep. I knew the Moroccans and the Riffs. Furthermore, I had examined the life-boats, and I had found that only one boat was in a seaworthy condition. It was the boat the skipper was supposed to man, with the chief, the carpenter, and two A.B.'s. All the other boats were hopeless decorations. Since the skipper's boat was still dry and without water and provisions changed, I was convinced that the *Yorikke* had something in the hold too expensive yet to touch ground.

One quiet night I went exploring again, and I came upon little barrels which, as I could see by the light of a match, were labeled thus: *Garantiert reines unverfalschtes Schwabisches Pflaumenmus. Keine Kriegsware. Garantiert reine Früchte und Bester Zucker. Kein künstlicher Farbstoff verwendet. Erste und älteste Schwabische Pflaumenmusfabrik Oberndorf am Neckar.* Which when explained in a human language would mean: Guaranteed Genuine Plum Marmalade. No War Substitute. Pure Fruit and Sugar. No Artificial Dyes. First and Oldest Plum Sauce Packing Plant Oberndorf on the Neckar.

Now, what sort of boneheads are we? was my first thought. There we are pushing down with our bread some ordinary laundry soap which somebody calls margarine, while here the holds are overflowing with the finest and purest marmalade the German people can produce for the customers abroad. "My, my, Stanislav, I always had figured you a smart guy with a lot of good intelligence; but now I see I was mistaken; you are the biggest ass I have ever known."

What a feast this will be in the morning—to smear this wonderful marmalade thick and soft on the warm bread! The Moroccans sure knew what was good for them. They preferred pure and guaranteed German marmalade to their dates and figs—of which they surely sometimes became as sick as we back home were of cabbage and potatoes.

I heaved two of these small barrels and took them to the upper coal-bunker, where I could use the lamp without any suspicion from the bridge. No one could enter this bunker without my permission. Because a plank led from the bunker to the hatchway of the stoke-hold. None of the engineers ever ventured across this plank, for one roller of the ship or one false step would have thrown them twenty feet below. It took nerve to use this plank as a gangway when the ship was under weigh. What was more, the plank was not very strong, nor was it new; it might break any moment. When Stanislav or I crossed this plank, we did it flying. To be absolutely safe from any intruders, anyway, I drew the plank back into the bunker. I was now ready to get the barrel open and go at the marmalade.

The barrel was open. I must state that I felt a shock, because I was astonished really to find plum marmalade in the barrel. To tell the truth, I had expected something different; I had thought that the label was misleading as to the contents. But sure as daylight at noon, there was plum marmalade inside the barrel. One should not do such a nasty thing as be suspicious all the time of good old *Yorikke*. Why, she is as honest and decent a tub as any other—as any other—as any— now, wait a minute. What is that? The marmalade tastes like— Let me get this straight, hell. It tastes like—well, I should say it tastes rather good. Good? I don't know for sure. Now, I'll be damned, there is a taste of green copper in that marmalade. Haven't they put pennies in the sauce? Sure, they must have. Like Mother did back home when she was cooking preserves for the long winter; when she wanted to keep the string beans in good color, she put in a penny. Old Norse custom I guess, invented by the good old Vikings who put into their preserves old copper nails left over from building boats. And here the label lies: No artificial dyes. I will try it again. Perhaps it is only imagination, while thinking of Mother's string beans. No, no getting away from that taste. It really tastes like brass, really all verdigris. I can't eat that on bread. Impossible. Rather prefer the laundry soap. I cannot get rid of this taste once it's on the tongue. It sticks against the gums.

The Moroccans must like this taste. They have got strange tastes anyway in lots of their eats, I know. Or maybe only the upper layer has got this brass taste. All right, boy, let's go deeper with your finger into the sauce. Hello, good morning, now, what of all the fallen angels is that? These Germans or Swabes were in a hurry when cooking this marmalade. They sure have left all the stones inside. It was too much trouble for them to stone the plums. I wonder what kind of people these Germans are, eating the marmalade with all the stones in. There sure are still some savages left among them in the Black Forest and in Swabia. Let's have a look at these stones. Funny shape. Let's take one and look closer at it. Oh, well, of course, that's why the strange taste. The stones are made of lead, covered with nickel lining, and put into an elegant little brass bottle. And inside the little brass bottle? Now, let's get this straight. Yes, that must be the pure sugar. Swabian sugar. Fine little black glittering leaves. Pretty sugar they have in Oberndorf on the Neckar. That must be the plum stones and the pure sugar the Moroccans and the Riffs like; for which they sell all their dates and figs and horses. Swabian plum marmalade. The Moroccans like this taste.

Yorikke, you have won back my respect. I was seriously afraid you had cheated me. It would have broken my heart. I don't like women that cheat. If you want to go astray, all right, go ahead, but don't be lousy and cheat with dirt. And just to see how loyal good old *Yorikke* really was, I crawled back into the holds to look at other barrels and boxes. Label: Mousetraps. What do Moroccans care about a couple of mice, having all the harems full of them? And, sure enough, there were, in those boxes, as many real mousetraps as there was real plum marmalade in the barrels. But when I looked for the stones left in the marmalade, I found no mouse, but Mausers, named after the great man who invented them.

I found other boxes. Label: Toy Automobiles with Mechanism for Self-Running. When I saw where these toy automobiles were made, which was Suhl in Thuringia, I did not open them. Suhl in Thuringia is known as a town in which all the inhabitants live by making hunting guns and ammunition. I could have saved myself the trouble of opening the barrels of plum sauce had I known, what I learned a few years later, that in Oberndorf on the Neckar is not a single marmalade plant, but one of the greatest rifle and munition factories in Germany. To know something about geography is always a good thing, because then labels won't catch you so dumb. On a label you may print anything you like, the label does not object. On the other hand, it is rather unlikely that a well-established munition and arms factory will be converted overnight into a plum-marmalade packing plant. Therefore, if some grocer wants to sell you canned pork and beans made in Chic, better be careful, you might find anything inside, even Scotch or an automatic. Nothing strange about that. Who ever saw in Chic somebody raising pigs or beans?

It was not alone Germany that was well represented in the holds. Stepmother England also was there, partly with Sheffield, partly with Manchester. Belgium, not minding her neutrality in the boxing match between the Moroccans and the French government, had contributed sugar-coated fruits. The English merchandise was labeled: Tinned Sheet Iron, Galvanized Corrugated Iron, Frying-pans. On seeing the sugar-coated fruits of Belgium, shipped from Liége, you became sure that those fruits were so indigestible that if you were to swallow only one you would never need any castor oil until all graves open again and the real name of the Unknown Soldier is headlined in the New York papers.

The Moroccans are quite right. They have my sympathy. Spain to the Spaniards, France to the French, China to the Chinese, Poland to the Poles. What did Wilson chase the American boys into the European war for? Wasn't it for the simple reason that the Czechs should have the right to call their sausages in Czech instead of in the uncivilized Austrian lingo? We don't want any Chinese in our God's country, or other furreners either, to help us eat up our surplus wheat. Let them stay at home, where they belong. So I don't see any reason why I should get sore at the Moroccans. And, just for Wilson, as a good Yank I have to ship on the *Yorikke* and get things cleared up for democracy and for the liberty of small nations.

I feel as though I am going to fall in love with that hussy *Yorikke.*

35

"I say, Stanislav, haven't you got any pride left? I simply cannot understand how you can swallow all the time that marge. Ain't you ashamed a bit?"

"What else could I do, Pippip?" Stanislav said. "Above all things I am sure hungry. You don't suppose I should boil my rags and thicken the juice that comes out to have something on the bread, do you? I have nothing on the bread save that stinking margarine. You just get cracked up eating all the time that stale bread without something on it. I feel like concrete in my stomach sometimes."

"Now, aren't you just as dumb as I imagined? Man, don't you know that we are shipping right now the finest German plum marmalade?"

"Yep, I know."

"If you know, why don't you loot a barrel or two?"

"That marmalade is no good for us."

"Why not?" I asked innocently.

"Good only for the Moroccans and the Syrians, and, of course, for those who make it and those who sell it. The Frenchmen get all the time belly cramps whenever they eat it. Or let's say when it is fired into them. Then they run so fast that they can catch up with their grandfather and overtake him at his funeral."

This answer made me wonder: "Then you know what is inside?"

"What sort of an ass do you believe me?" He laughed. "The two gentlemen of Portugal were still in the skipper's cabin when I was already through with my exploration. It would not be me, an old honest sailor, if seeing labels of Danish butter, or sardines, or corned beef, or chocolate, I didn't right away investigate the possibilities of a bargain sale at the next port."

"This time you are mistaken," I said; "there is really marmalade inside."

"There is always something inside. But this marmalade you cannot eat. Has got a horrible brass taste and a smell after black sulphur sugar. If you eat too much you may get belly poisoning. You may get green all over the face like the statue of a general. Last trip, before you were on, we had corned beef. It was genuine. Nothing inside. The finest stuff you can think of. Sometimes you are lucky. The skipper had to ship honest goods for a trip or two. He was sure he'd be brought up by French chasers. See? It was a thick layer. Going to Damascus. The Syrians were in dire need. They had some misunderstanding with the French governor as to the people they wished to trade with."

"How were the stones beneath the thick layer?"

"The stones? You mean what was the true inside of the corned beef? Well, as I said, the layer was fine. For days I did not have to touch the galley vomit. Of course, if you went sufficiently deep into the corned beef you found excellent carbines. Made in U.S.A. Late model, had come out during the last weeks of the war and could not be sold, because the armistice came too soon before they could cash in on them. They had to sell them. You cannot have them wait until the next war and then be stuck with them. Next war they have got a better model. Tell you, when we had landed those corned-beef cans without any trouble and the skipper had got all the syrup he had expected, we got two cups with real cognac, roast beef, chicken, fresh vegetables, and canned English pudding. Yes, siree. Because. Well, because, you see, it was like that. A French chaser got us up. The officers came aboard. Spying about, asking the crew, spreading francs and cigarettes just like old junk, expecting some guy to spring a word or two. But they had to leave with a sour face, and they had to bow and salute to the skipper as though he was their admiral."

"And no one gave the skipper away for the francs and the cigarettes?" I asked.

"We? On the *Yorikke?* We took the francs and the cigarettes all right. But give away somebody? We are filthy. And we are dead. Gone beyond hell. We would take in a little purse or a pocket-book of somebody who is careless about it and might lose it anyway when going along the street. We loot the holds and sell out at bargain prices. We would throw a hot bolt at the head of that second engineer when he comes bothering us about the steam and the bars. That's all honest and clean. But squeal to the police and the customs guards and the arms-chasers? Not for a thousand pounds in cold cash, fine as it would be to have them. But, you see, what good would these thousand pounds or francs do to you? No good at all. What's the use of having a thousand pounds in your pocket and lose all the honesty of a decent sailor? You cannot look at your own face any more for the rest of your life."

We were lying before anchor off the coast of a small port

in Portugal. The skipper felt that the *Yorikke* was suspected. He was sure that as soon as he should be in French waters he would be stopped and searched. So he took in honest cargo for the next two trips. The cargo was not worth much. But anyway it was cargo, and he could get hold of the most elegant clearance papers. The French would have to pay good money for having molested him and for making him reach his port twenty-four hours late. After two such searches, and after having made so much trouble for the French government and getting a payment of some ten or fifteen thousand francs in damages, he then could afford again a half a dozen trips that really paid, without any fear of being molested.

On such occasions, when the *Yorikke* lay about, waiting to take in cargo, we knocked off work at five in the afternoon and were free until seven in the morning. Since we were at anchor off the coast, we could not get ashore. The boatmen charged too much, and the skipper refused to give any advance, being afraid that we might not be aboard when the *Yorikke* was ready to go under weigh.

So we now had time to sit together quietly and peacefully and just tell our stories and exchange our opinions of life and the world.

There were as many nationalities represented on the *Yorikke* as there were men aboard. I have not found a single nation as yet which has no dead citizens somewhere on this earth— I mean such dead as still breathe the air, but that are dead for all eternity to their nation. Some nations have their death ships openly. These nations call their death ships the foreign legion. If he survives this death ship the legionnaire may have a new name and a new and legally established nationality with all the chances to come back to life again. Certain nations give citizenship to men who sail under their flags for three consecutive years. It was different with the *Yorikke*. The longer you shipped on the *Yorikke*, the farther away you sailed from any possibility of winning or regaining any citizenship. Even the Chinese or the Swahilians would not have taken you in, regardless of how many applications you might make and how many truckloads of papers you might fill in.

The *Yorikke* was a nation all by herself. She had her own language, her own established morals and customs, her own tradition.

In Algiers I once met a man who claimed to be a hundred and sixty years old. He was a Syrian, from Beirut. He looked like forty, and at the same time like two hundred. He told me that he had so far been on the *Yorikke* twenty-three times. The skipper knew him; and he admitted that he could vouch for the fact that this Syrian had shipped on the *Yorikke* at least four times. The Syrian, having invited me to a cup of coffee in a Turkish coffee-house, told me that he had shipped first on the *Yorikke* when he was rather young, as a kitchen-boy. I asked him what the *Yorikke* shipped in those times. He said that while he was kitchen-boy she was used as a transport ship for Napoleon, to transport his soldiers to Egypt. It was before he made himself emperor. Then, of course, as the Syrian told me, the *Yorikke* carried only sails and had no steam-engine. Which, by the way, proved that the Syrian was entirely correct in his story. He could not have known what the *Yorikke* looked like in those days if he had not been on her.

I asked him how come he had shipped so often on the *Yorikke*. He told me that the *Yorikke* had always been his guardian angel, and that he would never forget the good service she had often rendered him. For, poor man, he was always in trouble with his wives. Each time, of course, it was another wife. He had consumed about nineteen, which accounts for the times he shipped on the *Yorikke*, taking into consideration that during the first trips he was still too young to be able to consume a healthy wife. It so happened that whenever he had a wife who was a real nag, he had no money to get rid of her. So he just waited for the *Yorikke* to come in port and off he went. When he returned he found his wife otherwise provided for, and he was free again for the next issue. The next issue, after the proper time had passed, proved a worse nag than the former. So he again had to make use of the *Yorikke* as an effective divorce lawyer.

I thought that now, since he had become rather old, he would no longer be in need of consuming wives, and that might be the reason why he had not been seen on the *Yorikke* for quite a while. But he said that this was only my mistake, not his, because he now had a new wife oftener than before. I said to him that very likely the women of Algiers were not the nagging type. He answered that in this I was mistaken again, and that he suspected that I had had no experience with women at all. He said he had to admit that the women of Algiers were a lot worse even than those of Damascus and Beirut. But the case is simpler dealt with in Algiers than in Syria. In Algiers, whenever he thinks that his wife is nagging too much, he has her put in jail, because these fine people of Algiers are of the opinion that a nagging wife cannot be considered sane, and besides it is a law with these people that the nagging of a wife is a criminal offense. So my Syrian said: "Now you will understand why I no longer need the *Yorikke*. Algiers is heaven for me. And if I had ever been in Algiers during my early youth I would never have been on the *Yorikke* when she was in the midst of the battle of Abukir. There it happened that the middle finger of my left hand was shot off by some silly English gunner." This finger was really missing. Therefore I do not see any reason why I should not believe his story. He finished his story by saying that if, and may Allah prevent it, the people of Algiers should ever change their humane law in regard to nags, he would see no other way out than to start again shipping on the *Yorikke*, even as drag.

I made up my mind that if I could get away from the *Yorikke* I would live in Algiers, where there are people who have their hearts in the right spot. And no alimony either. Gee, what a man with the true working spirit could achieve in such a place!

With so many different nationalities aboard, it would have been impossible to sail the *Yorikke* unless a language had been found that was understood by the whole crew. From that Syrian, who of all living people I have ever met knew the *Yorikke* longest and best, I had learned that the universal language used on the *Yorikke* had been usually the language most widely known at the time on the seven seas. When the *Yorikke* was still a virgin maiden the language spoken by her crew was Babylonian; later it changed to Persian, then to Phœnician. Then came a time when the Yorikkian language was a mixture of Phœnician, Egyptian, Nubian, Latin, and Gaul. After the Roman Empire was destroyed by the Jews, through the means of a renegade puffed-up religious movement, with Bolshevik ideas in it, the language on the *Yorikke* was a mixture of Italian, Spanish, Portuguese, Arabian, and Hebrew. This lasted until after the Spanish Armada was knocked out. Then French influence became more dominant in the lingo of the *Yorikke*. At Abukir the *Yorikke* was on the side of the French, and old man Nelson took her as a prize. He sold her to a cotton-dealer and shipping agent in Liverpool, who in turn sold her to English pirates who worked the Spanish Main, then already in its declining glory. Anyway, from that time on until today the lingo of the *Yorikke* was English. At least that was the name the language was given, to distinguish it from any other language known under the moon.

Only the skipper spoke English that was without flaws. A prof of Oxford could not have spoken it any better. But the lingo spoken by the rest was such that Chinese pidgin English would be considered elegant compared with the Yorikkian English. A newcomer, even a limey, a cockney, or a Pat, would have quite a lot of trouble during the first two weeks before he could pick up sufficient Yorikkian to make himself understood and to understand what was told him.

Every sailor of any nationality knows some thirty English words, which he pronounces in such a way that after half an hour you may get a rough idea of what he wishes to say. Each sailor, though, does not have the same vocabulary as the others, and hardly two have the same pronunciation of the same word. Living together and working together, each sailor picks up the words of his companions, until, after two months or so, all men aboard have acquired a working knowledge of about three hundred words common to all the crew and understood by all. To this vocabulary are added all the commands, which are given without exception in English, but in a degenerated cockney flavored with Irish and Scotch, the r's and ch's mostly out of place. This lingo, of course, is enlarged by words which are brought in by sailors who, owing to their lack of the right words, have to use occasionally words of their own home-made language. These words, used over and over again, are, after a while, picked up by others and used at the proper place. Since usually one fireman at least was a Spaniard, it had become proper to use for water and for fuel never any other words but *agua* and *carbón*. Even the engineers used these words.

We found ourselves able to tell each other any story we wanted to. Our stories did not need more than three hundred and fifty different words, more or less. And when a good story, born in the heart and raised in the soul and fattened on one's own bitter or sweet experiences, had been told, there was nothing left unexplained or misunderstood. They all could have been printed, but, of course, it must be added that no bookstore would have sold two copies and bookstore-keeper, printer, and publisher would have been in the pen for thirty years.

Regardless of how far from the academic the Yorikkian English strayed, the fundamentals remained English; and whenever a newcomer hopped on who spoke English as his mother tongue, the Yorikkian lingo once more was purified and enriched with new words or with a better pronunciation of words which by long misuse had lost their adherence to their family.

A sailor is never lost where language is concerned. He always can make himself fairly well understood, no matter which coast he is thrown upon. He surely will find his way to an answer to the old question: when do we eat? Yet whoever survived the *Yorikke* could never be frightened any more during his lifetime by anything. For him nothing had become impossible as long as it was within reach of a courageous man.

36

Stanislav was called Stanislav, or, usually, Lavski, only by me and by the firemen. Everyone else aboard, including the engineers and the mates, called him Pole or Polack.

The majority of the crew were called after their nationalities. Hey, Spaniard, or Spainy. Portes or Portuguese. Russ. Dutch. Germy. Dansky. Taley the Italian. Finsky the Finn, who, by the way, when he joined the *Yorikke*, understood only a few commands, but otherwise knew no word of English; and since there was nobody aboard who understood Finnish, he was for months unable to say to anybody even so much as: "May I have your spoon?"

That everybody was called according to his nationality was one of the great ironies of which there existed so many aboard the *Yorikke*. Their native lands and the authorities of their native countries had denied all of them citizenship, and therefore passports, for some reason or other. But on the *Yorikke* their nationality was the only thing they possessed to distinguish them from anybody else. Whether, however, the nationality they agreed to have was their true nationality was never proved. When a newcomer joined the crew and was asked what nationality he had, he gave one in answer; and hence he was called as he had answered and was believed by everybody.

Rarely if ever did anybody on the *Yorikke* reveal his real name. No one, not even the skipper himself, knew for sure if the name and the nationality given by a man when signing on were correct. The skipper was very discreet about what he wrote in the crew's record-book concerning a man. He was the kind of master who stuck to his men; and most likely he would never have given away a man of his to the authorities as long as he could avoid it. The true facts about a man came out only from the man himself, who told frankly all about his person and his past. Few ever did such a thoughtless thing. When a newcomer, after having signed on, left the skipper's cabin and stepped on deck and was met by the mate or the bos'n or the chief and asked his name, he usually answered: "I am a Dane." With this he had answered already two questions, his name and his nationality. Henceforth he was called: Dane! Nobody, officer or man, ever asked him again. The officers were sure that Dane was already a lie. Anyway, they never went deeper into the matter, because they did not want to be told more lies. It is an old rule, only not sufficiently obeyed, but a good rule: If you do not wish to be lied to, do not ask questions! The only real defense civilized man has against anybody who bothers him is to lie. There would be no lies if there were no questions.

One evening, while the *Yorikke* was at anchor off an African port, waiting for cargo and orders, Stanislav told me his story, and I told him mine. The story I told him was not my true story; it was just a good story, which he accepted. Of course, I do not know if the story he told me was true. How can anybody know if any story told or heard is true? Does even a girl tell her own mother always a true story about what she did last night between nine and twelve? She would be a fool and would have endless trouble if she did. And as to true stories in general: I do not even know if the grass is green;

it may just happen that the grass causes within my brain an illusion which reminds me instantly that I was told, when I had no judgment of my own yet, that whatever looks like grass must be green. Besides, green is not something by itself, but green is everything which I can compare with the color of fresh grass. So how do I know whether the story Stanislav told me was the story of what he had experienced in fact, or whether it was the reflection in his mind of what he believed he had experienced? Another man than Moses, who was trained in an Egyptian priests' college, would have told the story of the creation of the world and the history of the Israelites in a way entirely different from what we now believe to be the only true story of the misleading of the human race.

But there were many reasons that made me feel that the story Stanislav told me was true, for the story did not differ much from all the other stories of men who sail death ships.

His true name, which, together with his story, I never betrayed to anybody on the *Yorikke*, was Stanislav Koslovski. He was born in Poznan, which then was the capital of the Prussian province of Poznan, or, as it was called by the Prussians, Posen.

In Poznan he went to school until he was fourteen. All instruction was given in German, but he knew a little Polish from his parents, who spoke it occasionally, mainly at church service. The German Poles, it seemed, had the idea that the Lord would not understand them if they addressed him in German.

When he was about to leave grammar school, his parents wanted to give Stanislav as an apprentice for four years to a master tailor. A couple of hundred stories in imitation of Cooper's *Last of the Mohicans*, sold at a dime apiece, and another couple of hundred sea-stories and pirate-yarns, had ambushed his spirit, and he ran away from home, landing in Stettin, one of the greatest German ports in the Baltic Sea. Here he stowed away in a Danish fishing schooner and came to the Danish island of Fünen. The fishermen found him here half frozen and nearly starved to death.

He told them that he came from Danzig. He assumed the name of the bookshop-keeper where he had bought all the dime novels that he had consumed during his schooldays. He said (rather intelligent) that he was an orphan and that he was so mistreated and so cruelly beaten every day by his foster-parents that he had jumped into the sea to end his life. Since he was a good swimmer he could not die in the sea, however, and he swam for his life and reached the fishing schooner, where, not seeing anybody aboard, he stowed away to escape from his martyrdom. He finished his story, his eyes filled with tears, and said: "If I am brought back to Germany I will tie my hands and feet and jump again into the sea and this time make a good job of it. I prefer rather to go to hell than to return to my foster-parents."

He told his story so excellently that all the fisherwomen were bathed in tears over the terrible fate of a fine good German boy. So they kept him there.

Not only the German, but also the Danish and Swedish newspapers were full of stories about the tailor-apprentice who had mysteriously disappeared from Poznan, probably kidnapped by Jews who needed, for a religious ceremony, the blood of a Christian boy. A similar affair had happened not so many years before in Konitz, another town of the same province, where, according to police records, Jews had kidnapped and butchered a Christian college boy. All Germany, then already in the grip of anti-Semitism, believed this horrible story true.

The boy was sought all over Germany, and the most gruesome stories as to his possible fate were published in the papers. The Danish fishermen, having other troubles to worry about, did not read newspapers. And if they did, as the story was in all the Danish papers also, they never for a moment thought their boy from Danzig to be the tailor-apprentice from Poznan. Stanislav had to work hard with the fisher-folk on Fünen.

He ate nothing which he had not earned honestly. He liked it, nevertheless, a hundred times better than sitting on a tailor's table. If he seriously meant to become a good sailor, he could have had no better schooling than he had with those fishermen. The Baltic Sea, looking often so calm and so smooth, is in reality one of the most capricious of waters. Four miles off the coast you think you can make it whistling and singing, and before you have got time to think what has happened, a squall has got your craft so hard that, with the coast at arm's reach, you have to struggle for your life. If you can sail a plain fishing schooner from Svendborg on Fünen to Nykjöbing on Falster in any weather, and you bring the ship home again and no sail lost, you have got every right to call yourself a great sailor. Compared with this it means absolutely nothing to bring a transatlantic liner from Cherbourg to Hoboken. Any fool can do that and be thought a great captain.

No matter how hard the work was, when Stanislav thought of being a tailor-apprentice he lost all and every desire to send word home that he was still alive and not sacrificed in Jewish rites. His fear of being made a tailor was greater than the love for his parents, whom in fact he hated profoundly for their attempt to make an honest tailor of one who wanted to detect new straits and unmapped islands in the South Sea.

At seventeen he had become an A.B., a real able-bodied seaman. With the good wishes of the fisher-folk he left for Hamburg to look for long trips and so satisfy his craving for the great seafaring world.

He could not find the right ship going out on a big voyage. For a few months he took up work with a sail-maker. Having in mind to sail on real big ships under his true name, he went to obtain a legitimate sailor's identification book, or what they called a seaman's book, with which he could ship in the finest of German ships. German shipping was then at the peak of its glory. By working at this sail-maker's he had established his residence in Hamburg, and so it was easy to obtain true papers. He shipped for a few trips on honest great German merchants.

For a change he shipped on good Dutch vessels, with which he made several trips to the East Indies.

While on a Dutch the bloody dance about the golden calf started. His ship happened to be in the Black Sea. When it passed the Bosporus on its return to Holland it was searched by German officers in the service of the Turks. He and another German were taken off the ship and put into the Turkish navy under assumed names, because when arrested he did not, for some reason, give his true name. A Belgian sailor on the Dutch ship had betrayed these two Germans to the officers, but the Dutch master of the ship said he had nothing to do with this and added that he did not know their names and was not sure if they were Germans at all.

Two German war-ships, which had been in an Italian port and had evaded the English, reached Constantinople, and by order of the German government they joined the Turkish navy. So Stanislav served under the Turkish flag for a while.

Smart as he was, he quit the Turks as soon as he had an opportunity. He shipped on a Danish merchant. The ship was brought up in the North Sea by a German submarine. Stanislav, whom everybody on the Danish ship believed a Dane, had made the gross mistake of telling a Swede, also on the ship, that he was a German. So when the Germans examined the Dane, the Swede gave Stanislav away. Stanislav came to Kiel, the most important port of the German navy. He was put into the navy, again under an assumed name. Artillery service.

In Kiel he met, by chance, another coolie, as a gob was called in the German navy, with whom he had once shipped on a German merchant. By sheer carelessness, and not through betrayal by this fellow-sailor, Stanislav's real name became known. Now he was in the German navy under his right name. Had he given his right name before, when in the Turkish navy, he could have been court-martialed for desertion.

Stanislav was at the sea-battle of Skagen, where two nations who were at war against each other came out victors at the same time and where the English lost more ships than the Germans, and the Germans more than the English. It depended on the papers you read.

The ship on which Stanislav was a gunner was blown up by a torpedo. Since the battle was off the Danish coast it happened that Stanislav was picked up by Danish fishermen after having been in the water for about thirty hours. They took him to their village. He knew how to get along with Danish fisherfolk, and so they did not hand him over to the Danish authorities, but helped him to hide. By his good luck Stanislav met a fisherman who happened to be the brother of that fisherwoman of Fünen who had picked him up first. With the help of this brother he was roaded to Esbjerg, where he was put as a Dane on a Danish ship, with which he again sailed for the great voyage. He had learned his lesson, and so he never told anybody his true nationality any more. He could laugh at all English, German, and French submarines whenever they searched the Dane. He never was caught again, and he kept himself out of the struggle for supremacy of the big banking firms.

The governments thought it wiser, finally, to make up again. Time had come when all governments were convinced it would be cheaper and more profitable to talk peace and wait for a better chance. The burglars and gangsters sat down to an elegant peace-banquet. The workers, and the little plain people of all countries, had to pay the damages—that is, the hospital bills, the funeral expenses, the tombs for unknown soldiers, and the bills for all the banquets and conferences which left everybody in the world, save the hotel-owners, exactly where they had been before. And all those little people, who had, not profits, but all the losses and all the deaths, were now allowed to wave flags and handkerchiefs at the victorious armies coming back covered with glory and everlasting fame.

The others, who could greet only an army which had not been victorious on the battle-field, but which never had been defeated on the battle-field, did not wave flags and handkerchiefs, but cried instead at the tops of their voices: "Doesn't matter at all. Next time it will be our turn. Hurrah! Hail!" The workers and the plain people became dizzy when presented with the bills they had to pay. If they tried to rebel they were led to the tomb of the unknown soldier, where they were lectured so long and with such deafening jazz that they could do nothing but admit their solemn duty to pay the bills and believe in the existence of the unknown soldier. In those countries where there was no unknown soldier to offer, a whole army was stabbed right in the back, and all the workers and plain people were kept busy smashing each other's heads to find the man who had stabbed the army in its back.

This was the time when in Germany one match cost fifty-two billion marks, while the expenses for making these fifty-two billion marks were higher than a whole truck-load of Kreuger matches. For this reason the Danish shipping company thought it most profitable to send her ships to the dry-docks of Hamburg to be overhauled. For twenty Danish kroner five hundred German shipyard workers would work six weeks under the whip of a Socialist president who had ordered his Socialist secretary of war to break the bones of every German worker who dared strike for better wages. The German labor leaders, having sold every sound principle to satisfy their personal ambition, and having handed over the fate of a new-born republic to unscrupulous financiers like Sklarz and Barnat, had taken already their first successful steps in paving the way for the powerful foes of modern civilization.

The future, which lately had looked so very rosy for Stanislav, was darkened once more for him. He came with his Danish ship to Hamburg; and when it was docked he was laid off.

Thus he found himself again without a berth.

37

The more the Americans advertised all over the earth that the world had now been saved for democracy, the more narrow-minded became all nations, including the American. Only true Englishmen could hope to land a job in England if there was any. If you had not been English for ten centuries, you had to look elsewhere. Italy did the same; only good Italians were allowed to work for the profit of Italian exporters. The States, feeling as nationalistic as the other nations, closed all the doors against immigrants, with the exception of the Russian grand-dukes, and only Americans were sure to get a well-paid union job. If the great-great-grand-uncle of your great-grand-uncle had not come over on the *Mayflower*, there was little chance for you to be employed as a street-cleaner in an American city.

Since this fine spirit of human fellowship was enforced all over the world, it was not strange to see Stanislav, with his Danish sailor's pay-book, go in Hamburg from ship to ship and from agency to agency without the slightest chance of getting a job. All and everything was reserved for their own nationals. Even Danish ships did not want him any longer. Their shipping business had gone from bad to worse and was actually on bed-rock.

When he, then, came again to German skippers he was told: "No Danes for us. To hell with the Danes, who have taken our Slesvig and who now want Holstein also. No Danes, off you go."

While the pay for German sailors went down more each day, it was still the only hope he had, as Danish ships without a complete crew hardly ever put in port.

Stanislav had to look for a good German sailor's book.

Asking at the office of the seafaring bureaus where such papers were issued, he was ordered to go first to police headquarters and take out a certificate of good behavior.

"I have got here my old sailor's book."

"Let's see. That is Danish. We are not in Denmark, we are in Germany. We do not recognize what those people up there write or say."

His Danish book had his assumed, not his true name. So he could not very well present it to the police authorities.

At police headquarters he gave his right name and asked for a certificate with which he could secure the sailor's book.

"Registered in Hamburg?" he was asked.

"No. I arrived here only yesterday, coming in with a Dane that went to dry-dock and was laid off."

"Then you will have to send first for your birth-certificate; without it we cannot certify you anything," the police inspector said.

Stanislav wrote a letter to Poznan, asking for his birth-certificate. He waited one week. No certificate came. He waited two weeks. No answer. He waited another week. The certificate still did not come. He had sent a registered letter and put in two hundred and fifty billion marks to cover the expenses. All this was of no avail. No certificate was sent and no answer either.

He should have known better. What does anybody care about a jobless worker? It would have been different if he had been a banker or a railroad president. But just a bum sailor without money and without a job. Why doesn't he die or emigrate? And, besides, what did people care in Poland about the birth-certificate of a jobless man living in Germany? If he were a good Pole, why didn't he live in Poland and be decent and join the army? The Poles had other worries right then. There was for instance Upper Silesia, about which Poland was rather patriotic, because it had rich coalfields and well-developed industries. Then there was Danzig, another worry of the patriots who wished to own all Germany up to sixty miles west of the River Elbe, which part of the world had been in possession of the Slavs two thousand years ago. And why not also take all Saxony, which had been ruled two hundred years ago by a Polish king, the strong man August? Once granted the right to be an independent nation, make use of it and take in all the world. Who knows anything about that god-damned birth-certificate of that drunken sailor? Let's go out and see the parade of the army in their new uniforms.

The money which Stanislav had brought from his Danish ship was long since gone. It was spent all over St. Pauli. There they knew, especially in those times, the exact value of genuine Danish kroner. Danish kroner were almost as good as dollars, and sometimes even more welcome. No one in St. Pauli better knew the kroner, carried in the pockets of a fine-looking sailor, and appreciated them more than the janes. Didn't the gals of St. Pauli do everything to get just one Danish krone from that swell-looking swanker Stanislav? I should say they did. And of course that's the way of all money in the world. It always goes so easily and friendly. After it's all gone and not a cent left, then you know how hard it comes in.

"Anyway, only dumb-heads and oxen heave coal and take any job," Stanislav said. "An honest trade will always keep a good man above the mud. Just take it up and stick to it."

So it happened that occasionally a box or a crate would drop out of a freight-car of which the door opened too easily. "All you have to do," Stanislav said, "is be close to the spot at the time when boxes or crates are tumbling out of a freight-car. That's all there is to it. Easy, isn't it?"

"Looks like," I said.

"What else could I do? Hell, how I wished to work honestly! Heaven knows, bigud. But simply you could not land a job even when you tried to hire out as a dumbwaiter. Other times, if you had a bit of good luck, a couple of bags of sugar or green coffee would open almost by themselves, and right in front of you. Now, if you happen along at the right moment with an empty knapsack and you hold the knapsack right under the spot where the bags ripped open, then, of course, the goods would drop into your empty knapsack. If you don't put something under the rippings, then the whole thing would go right to the ground to feed only rats and mice. Well, it surely is not my intention to fatten up rats. And if the sugar and the coffee, so useful for human beings, fall into the street-mud, man, it would mean an insult to God, who gave the goods that humans might enjoy themselves. And suppose the coffee or the sugar or whatever it may be has dropped, by chance, into your empty knapsack and you were fool enough to pour it out again, somebody might see you doing it and might think you stole it and call the cops to have you arrested for pilfering from freight-cars. You may get into such trouble quite innocently, see."

There was also cocaine and salvarsan and such things. "You must have a feeling for the poor, suffering beings badly in need. You can't help it. It is your heart that commands you. You don't realize what it means to be in need of salvarsan and then not have it. You mustn't be that kind, always thinking only about your own welfare. If you wish to be good, you have to think of other people who suffer."

"You see, Pippip," Stanislav explained, "there is a certain time for everything. Then a time will come where you will say to yourself it's better now to think about something else for a change. You see, the big mistake most people make is that they do not say at the right time: 'Now you'd better hop down from the baby because the old lady is about to make a surprise visit with all the trimmings, before you can get out of the window.' So I said to myself: now you have to get a bucket even if you have to steal one or you will find yourself in a tough spot."

When Stanislav came to that decision he again went to the

police and told them that his birth-certificate had not arrived yet.

"There you are," the police inspector said; "those damned Polacks, they do this just to make us mad. But don't you worry, we sure will make it hot for them when the great day comes. Let only the English in China and India, and the French in Africa, and the Italians in Albania, have their hands full of mud one pretty day, and then we will show these stinking Polish pigs where they get off."

Stanislav was not interested in the political opinions of the police inspector, but he had listened and nodded his head to make himself amiable to the authority that had the power to issue passports and sailors' books. After he had fully agreed with the killing of all the Poles he said: "Where do I get my sailor's book, Mr. Inspector?"

"Ever lived in Hamburg before?"

"I have."

"Before the war?"

"Yes, Inspector."

"Long?"

"More than half a year."

"Properly registered with the police?"

"Yes, sir."

"Which ward?"

"This one here. In this same precinct."

"Everything fine," the inspector said. "Now you go to the head office of the police registration and let them hand you an application paper. You bring it with you and three photographs so that I may stamp it all."

Stanislav obtained the application paper from the head office, and he came back to the station.

The inspector said: "Application is all right. Yet how do I know that you are the person named in this certificate of registration?"

"I can easily prove that. You see, I may bring up here Mr.

Andresen, the sail-maker, with whom I worked when I lived in Hamburg. But no need to do that. There is a sergeant who knows me, right behind you, sitting on the bench."

"I? Know you?" the sergeant said sourly.

"Yes, sergeant, you know me rather too well," Stanislav explained. "I have still to thank you for a nine marks' fine which I received on account of your reporting me for disturbing the peace when I was in a row. That time, of course, you carried a little-fly-brush on your lower lip; you have shaved it off since then, I see."

"Yeap, yep. Now I remember you. So you are that guy. Well, how do you do? Grown up since that time. You were working with old man Andresen all right." The sergeant came closer, and he smiled as though he were thinking of the good old soft times before the war. "Yea, I remember all of you. We had lots of trouble with you. Poznan was looking for you. You had left home, and the whole world thought you butchered. We did not send you back to Poznan, because we had no right to. You were working here and there were no bad records on file. So Poznan lost all interest in you."

"So I see," the inspector said, "all is in shape. Now of course I have no longer any objection to give you all the police identification stamps on your sailor's book application and on your photographs. As many as you wish."

Happily Stanislav went next day with his application to the seaman's registration office.

The officer in charge said: "Application and police registration are in perfect order. The inspector confirms personally that he identifies you, the applicant. So everything seems to be correct."

Stanislav was smiling. He knew he would have his sailor's book inside of two hours.

"B-u-u-u-t," the officer drew out to start a long bureaucratic explanation.

Stanislav lost his smile and looked anxiously up.

"But," the officer said again, "the nationality, the citizenship, does not seem very clear in your case, as I see here, Koslovski. We doubt your citizenship as written here in your application. You say here: German nationality. You will have to prove this before I can give you a German sailor's identification book. We do not issue sailor's identifications to other nationals but our own."

He had been told already at the police station that he might have to prove before the seaboard authorities his genuine citizenship.

Very politely Stanislav answered: "But, officer, I have served the K.M., the Kaiserliche Marine, the Imperial Navy, and I have been severely wounded at the battle of Skagerrack and picked up and interned by the Danes."

The clerk lifted his eyebrows high up. He felt himself growing to the size of a god. Before he spoke he made a gesture with his hands and with his head as though he wished to impress on a mortal in distress that the continued existence of the universe depended upon what he was to utter. From the attitude he assumed it could easily be expected that he might cry out: "Be there no earth before me!" and the earth would disappear into a fluttering fog.

The great gesture finally materialized: "That time, when you were serving the Imperial Navy—Hurrah for our poor great Kaiser!—then, of course, without the slightest doubt, you were a German citizen. Because we never allowed an alien to set foot on our Imperial battle-ships. And that glorious day when you were wounded at Skagerrack you were still a German citizen; it was then that we gave these perfidious sons of that even more perfidious Albion the licking of their lifetime. Those glorious times! I pray to the old God of the Germans that they may come soon again to finish those stinking dogs for good. In those times you surely were a German citizen of whom the country could be proud. But, understand this, my man, if you are still a German citizen you will have to prove it, and there's no way of getting out of it. As long as you cannot prove you're still a German citizen, sorry, my man, I can do nothing for you, and there will be no sailor's identification book for you. That's all, good-by."

"Pardon me, sir, where do I have to go to prove my German citizenship?"

"Police headquarters, Resident's Registration, Citizenship Department."

38

Stanislav had to eat. He could not have a ship without proper papers. So he had to take up once more what he used to call his honorable profession. If all people had a decent job to occupy their minds, and regular meals to satisfy their hunger, most crimes would not be committed. Sitting in an easy chair, the belly filled with an excellent supper topped off with a pint of good Scotch, it is a pretty entertainment to talk about crime waves and the vanishing morality of the jobless. Standing in the shoes of Stanislav, the world and its morals look entirely different. Stanislav could not help it. It was not his fault that the world was as it was presented to him. No job was to be had at this time, not even as third assistant to a ragpicker. Everybody lay upon the dole. Stanislav had an aversion to live on unemployment relief funds. He preferred his honorable trade.

"You feel so terribly depressed," he said, "standing all the time among the unemployed to get your few cents. The whole world looks then as if only unemployed were still alive and as if every hope for any better time had vanished for ever. I'd rather look around to see if somebody's pocket-book is annoyed with its owner than stand in file with those jobless talking of nothing but their misery. Matter of fact, I respect everybody's property. But I assure you I didn't make this world. And I have to eat. Had these god-damned bureaucrats only given me a sailor's book, I would have been off on the great voyage long ago."

He went to police headquarters, Department of Citizenship. He was asked: "Where were you born?"

"In Posen, or what is now Poznan."

"Birth-certificate?"

"Here is the postal receipt of the registered letter I mailed them weeks ago to send the certificate. They don't even answer. And the money I put in for expenses they have kept."

"The identification stamps of the inspector of your district will do. I accept them. It is only the citizenship which is in question. Have you adopted for Germany?" the clerk asked him.

"Have I done what?"

"Have you adopted for Germany? I mean have you officially chosen German citizenship? Did you, within the proper time given, declare before a German authority, especially assigned to take such declarations, declare that you wish to retain German citizenship after the Polish provinces according to the provisions of the Treaty of Versailles were returned to Poland?"

"I did not," Stanislav answered. "I did not know that it had to be done. I always thought that if I was once a German I should always be a German as long as I did not take out citizenship for any other country. Why, I was in the K.M. I have fought for Germany at Skagerrack."

"Then you were a German," the clerk admitted. "Because then Poznan belonged to Germany. Where were you when all the people born in the Polish provinces but living in Germany were officially ordered to adopt either country as their native land?"

"I was shipping on a Dane. I was likely then somewhere off the Chinese coast."

"It was your duty to go to a German consul at the nearest port and make there your proper declaration."

"But I did not know that such a thing had to be done. You see, when sailing, and working hard, out on the sea, you have no time or even thoughts to think of such things."

"Didn't your captain tell you that you had to go see the German consul?"

"But I shipped on a Dane. It was a Danish master I was with. He sure was not interested in any orders issued by German authorities."

"Very bad for you, Koslovski." The clerk sat back and seemed to work his mind for a solution. When, after long meditation, he had found one, he said: "Bad for you, I say again. I think that is all. I can do nothing for you in this case. Are you rich? I mean do you hold any property?"

"No, mister, I am a sailor."

"That settles it, then. Nothing I can do for you. Even the periods of grace for proper adoption have expired. Sorry, but you cannot even rely on the fact that a higher power prevented you from making the declaration when there was time. You were not shipwrecked. You called at many ports in which there were German consuls, or at least consuls of other nations who were authorized to represent German interests. The call for adoption was published profusely and repeatedly all over the civilized world. At all consulates there were the bulletins on the blackboards."

"Sailors never read newspapers. When in port, one has other things to do than to go to the consulate and look at bulletins. Where could I get a German newspaper? Papers in other languages I do not understand well. Sometimes, by good chance, one may pick up a German newspaper. But I never saw any notice about this adoption thing."

"I am not responsible for this, Koslovski. Sorry. Sure I would like to help you. Yet I have not the power to do so. I am just a clerk here, an official to do what I am ordered to do.

Now, of course, it is not quite as bad as you imagine. There is still a way for you—make an application to the Secretary of State. He can do it. But this takes time. Probably two years or three. Since the war, citizenship has become a more definite matter than it used to be. Besides, the Poles do not show any consideration toward our nationals. Why should we be more generous? In a certain way you are a Pole. You were born on soil that is now Polish territory. I tell you, my good man, it sure will come to the point where the Poles, those stinking godless dirty pigs, will drive out of Poland all those Germans who have adopted for German citizenship. I assure you, Koslovski, we will do the same. The only way to deal with those bandits."

Every official assured him that he would like so very much to help him, if only he had the power to do so. Yet, suppose Stanislav had talked loudly or without proper respect to any clerk, high or low in office, or he had dared to look sternly at the face of an official, he would have been thrown into prison without mercy for having insulted an official and for having committed a criminal assault upon the state. Then the official would become automatically the almighty state in person, endowed with all the powers, forces, responsibilities, and privileges of the state. The brother of the insulted official would pass sentence, another brother of the official would beat him up with a club, and still another brother in office would lock him up in jail and guard him there for as long a time as another brother of the official thought suitable for such a horrible offense. But none of all these brothers in office have the power to help a poor individual in distress. "What, then, is the state and all its great apparatus good for if it cannot help a being in need?" Stanislav questioned.

"I can give you only one piece of good advice," the clerk said, swinging leisurely in his chair: "You'd better go to the Polish consulate general. The Polish consul, believe me, is simply under obligation to give you a Polish passport, with which you may easily obtain a sailor's book. If you bring us a Polish passport we will make an exception of you, having served the German navy, and having lived in Hamburg now and before the war. I will see to it, personally, that you get a German sailor's book upon presenting a Polish passport. That is the only advice I have in your case."

Next day Stanislav was at the Polish consulate.

"Born in Poznan?"

"Yes, my parents still live in Poznan."

"Speaking Polish?"

"Not very much; practically none."

"Did you live in Poznan, or in West Prussia, or in any of the Polish provinces then under the rule of Germany, Russia, or Austria at the time when Poland was declared an independent and sovereign country?"

"No."

"You did not live in any territory considered Polish territory between 1912 and the day of the armistice?"

"No. I was on high sea, mostly with Danish or German merchants."

"What you were doing, where you were sailing, and on what ships you were at that time, I have not asked you. Answer only my questions."

"Stanislav," I broke in while he was saying this, "here was the right moment to grasp this nuisance by the collar, drag him across the desk, and land him the best you have in store."

"I know, Pippip. I felt that way. But I was smart. I kept on smiling like a gal at her first dancing party. You see, first I wanted my passport. Then, one hour before my ship would sail, I would come back to this guy and sock him until he went shreddy. And then out and off with the can."

The Polish consul continued: "You said that your parents are still living in Poznan."

"Yes."

"Since you are of age, we, of course, could not consider any

258 THE DEATH SHIP

adoption made by your parents on your behalf, even supposing they had done so. What concerns us is the correct answer to my question: Have you in person registered your serious intention to remain a Polish citizen before a Polish consul or any other person authorized by the Polish government to accept such declarations?"

"No. I did not know that I had to do this."

"What you did know and what you did not know is of no importance to me. What I wish you to answer is: Did you register your declaration?"

"No."

"Then what do you want in this office? You are a German and no Pole. Go to your own officials and do not molest us here any more. That's all. Good afternoon."

Stanislav narrated this experience not in an angry tone, rather sadly and almost pitifully. He would have liked to express his ideas as to bureaucracy in true sailor's fashion. Yet it was too late for this now. The consul was not at hand.

I said: "Now look how quickly those new-born countries have acquired Prussian officialdom. Some of those countries did not even have a complete civilized language of their own yesterday, and today they are doing even better than the big powers. You may be sure that these new countries that, so far, are not even sure of their own names, will go a long way to make bureaucracy their one and only state religion. You ought to know what America has achieved in the hundred and fifty years of her existence. How fast she works to surpass even Imperial Russia with passports, visés, restrictions of free movements. Limitations and moldiness everywhere. All the world over, in consequence of the war for democracy, and for fear of communistic ideas, the bureaucrat has become the new czar who rules with more omnipotence than God the Almighty ever had, denying the birth of a living person if the birth-certificate cannot be produced, and making it impossible for a human being to move freely without a permit properly stamped and signed."

"They are all talking high-hat at conferences about the progress of culture and civilization and the welfare of mankind," Stanislav said. "It looks fine on the front page of the papers. But it is all talk, with nothing back of it save hypocrisy, egoism, and an insane nationalism. There is hardly any chance to become alive again, once on the *Yorikke*. Not under conditions as they are today. The only hope you have to be free again in this world is that the can goes down to ground and doesn't take you along, but spits you out like a leper. And suppose you find yourself after such an affair at some shore again; where do you get off? Only on another *Yorikke*."

Stanislav went again to police headquarters, Citizenship Department.

"The Polish consul does not recognize me as a Pole," he said.

"You might have known this before," the inspector explained. "These stinking Polish pigs need a licking, that's what they need. The old German God in heaven is our witness, they will get it soon enough, and after that they will never come for more." The inspector banged the desk with his fist.

When he was calm again, he said: "Now, Koslovski, what can we do for you? You must have some papers. Otherwise you will never get a ship. Not in these days."

"Certainly, Mr. Inspector, I must have papers."

"Right, right, Koslovski. Tell you what I will do. I shall give you a police certificate. Tomorrow morning you go with this certificate to the passport department. It is room—wait a minute—yes, it is room 334, here in the same building. You shall have your passport all right. With this passport you go to the sea board, seamen's registration, and there you will get your sailor's book. With a good sailor's book you will get the best liner the Hapag can afford."

"Thank you, Mr. Inspector."

"That's all right. We do what we can for an old man of the K.M."

Stanislav felt so happy that he wanted to embrace the whole world.

The Germans proved that, after all, they were less bureaucratic than all the other nations.

He went to the passport department, presented the police certificate and the photographs, stamped by the inspector as evidence that he was the person whose face the photographs showed, signed his beautiful new passport with the German republican eagle printed on it, paid seventy-five thousand billion marks as fee, and left the department with the most elegant passport he had ever possessed in all his life. With such a passport in hand he could even emigrate to God's own beloved country, and he would be received at Ellis Island with a brass band, and all the sirens singing. Yes, sir.

He could hardly believe he had in his possession such a fine passport. Everything in it was fine and perfect. Name, birthday, birthplace, occupation: Able-bodied seaman, honorably discharged from the Imperial Navy. Everything like a hymn. Now, let's see, what is this? Wha-a-a-t? "Without country?" All right. It won't matter. He will get a sailor's book like a whiff. Well, well? What does this mean? "Good only for the interior." Maybe the clerk thinks that ships sail on the sands of Brandenburg, or on the moors of Lüneburg, or only on the river Elbe. Doesn't matter. The passport is a peach.

Next day Stanislav went with his beautiful passport to the sea board to take out a sailor's voyage book.

"You want a sailor's book?"

"Yes, please."

"We cannot give you a sailor's book on this passport. You are without nationality. To have a citizenship, properly established, is the most important thing for a sailor's identification book. Your passport is all right for Germany, but not for any foreign country. It gives you no right to a German sailor's book."

"How, then, can I get a ship? Won't you, please, tell me this?"

"You have got a good passport. You will get any decent foreign ship with that passport. Only not a German ship. The passport says that you are living here in Hamburg, it tells who you are, where you come from, and all that. You are an old sailor with experience. Easy for you to get any ship. Any foreign ship. You make more money on a foreign ship than on a German, since our money is without any value."

Stanislav found a ship. Two days later. A Dutch. An elegant merchant. Almost new. Was still reeking of fresh paint. Fine Dutch pay.

When the skipper saw the passport he smiled with lips lifted high and said: "Good paper. That's what I like, men with fine papers. Let's go straight to the consul, read the articles, sign on, and you get your advance. We sail with high water early in the morning."

The Dutch consul registered his name in full: Stanislav Koslovski. A.B. Age, height, weight.

Then he asked: "Sailor's book, please?"

Stanislav said: "Passport."

"Just as good," the consul said.

"Passport is brand-new. Ink still fresh. Only two days old. All shipshape. I know the officer personally who signed this passport," the skipper said, and lighted a cigar.

The consul held the passport, satisfied to have in his hand such a wonderful piece of bureaucratic fine art. He turned the leaves and nodded approvingly. He was pleased.

Suddenly he stared. He stopped, and his satisfied smile froze on his lips. He turned the pages back and on again.

He took a breath and said shortly: "You cannot sign on."

"What?" Stanislav cried.

And "What?" cried the skipper. He was so surprised that he dropped the match-box.

"That man cannot sign on," the consul repeated.

"Why not?" the skipper asked. "As I said, I know the officer who has signed the passport. The passport is correct."

"No objection to the passport," the consul said. "But I won't sign on this man. He is without a country."

"What do I care?" said the skipper. "I want this man. My first mate knows him to be a first-class man at the helm. I know the ships he has been on, and I know their masters. Therefore I know what he is worth. So that's why I want to have him. I need men like him."

The consul clasped his palms together and said: "Listen, captain, since you say you like that man so very much, are you willing to adopt him?"

"Nonsense," the skipper said.

"Do you take all the responsibility for this man after he signs off your ship again?"

"I don't quite understand you, Mr. Consul."

"I'll explain it. This man, no matter how good a sailor he is, may not go ashore in any country he wishes; he cannot stay in any country he would like. He may go ashore, of course, as long as the ship is in port. But if he is found ashore after your ship has put out, the company of your ship is made responsible for him. Your company has to get him out of this country again. Where are you, or your company, going to take him?"

The skipper was quick with an answer: "He can always go back to Hamburg, where he comes from."

"Can. Can. The truth is he cannot." The consul began to talk like a judge sitting at his bench and pouring out stale moralities. "He has got a German passport good only for Germany. Germany has no obligation to let him in again once he has left it. Now, of course, he might obtain a special certificate, independent of this passport, which would permit him to enter Germany and to live there whenever he wants to. Such a certificate, though, can only be issued by the German secretary of state. I do not believe that this German authority will give him such a paper, because it would equal a paper of citizenship, and that is exactly what was denied him, or else he would have obtained a passport without any restriction. Fact is, and so far a well-established fact, that he was born in Poznan, and that neither Germany nor Poland, for some reason or other, has acknowledged his citizenship. He may go to the League of Nations. But the League of Nations has no country to give him. So, whatever paper the League of Nations may issue on his behalf, the fact that he has no country to call his own would still be unsettled. Only if you are willing to make out an affidavit here that you take the responsibility for him after he leaves your ship—"

"I cannot do such a thing. I am only an employee of my company," the skipper said.

"Then, of course, no other road for me. I do not sign him on." Saying this, the consul, with a heavy double stroke, crossed out the name of Stanislav, already written in the registers, so indicating that for him the case was at end.

"Listen." The skipper leaned over on the desk. "Couldn't you make an exception here? I would like to have him. I cannot find a better man at the helm than he is. I can go to sleep and leave the whole ship to him and nothing would go wrong. He got the right sailing instinct with the first bottle of milk he drank. I know this. We have talked together for a couple of hours."

"Sorry, captain. Very sorry indeed that I cannot be at your service." The consul rose from his chair. "My powers are extremely limited. I must obey my regulations. I am not the government. I am only her faithful servant."

When he had finished he drew his mouth wide into his cheeks, as if he wanted to give a smile studied before a mirror. At the same time he lifted up his shoulders so that they almost reached his ears. His arms hung down flabbily, and they swung slightly at the elbows. He looked like a plucked bird with both wings broken. He made a sad picture, but it was a true picture of an excellent bureaucrat, who knows that by his word men may live or die.

"Damn it all, and to hell with it," bellowed the skipper. With a powerful gesture he threw his cigar upon the floor, and crushed it with half a dozen steps, dancing like a savage Negro. He sent the consul a look as if this shrimp had been a deck-hand and been caught kicking a full pail of black paint over a washed deck. He stormed with two long steps to the door, jerked it open, went out, and banged the door so that the whole building seemed to shake.

Stanislav, having already left, waited outside in the corridor.

The skipper came up to him and said: "What can I do now with you, Lavski? Nothing. Devil knows how much I would like to have you with me. I cannot get you now, not even under the emergency. That guy knows your name, and if he finds out, then I will find myself not in good shipshape. These god-damned scribblers, how I hate them! More than squalls on the Zuider. Well, here, take five gulden. Have a good time tonight. Now I have to run around to find another A.B. Good ones are rarer than sunshine on the North Sea. Good luck."

The skipper was gone. And so was the elegant Dutch with milk and honey.

39

A ship. Stanislav needed it badly. "Honorable trade," he said, "is all right for a certain length of time, provided this length is not too long. You see, here a box, there a crate, then yonder a bag with crude coffee or sugar—all this doesn't hurt anybody. This goes for overhead expenses and inevitable losses of the big merchants. They don't feel it, while it will help me well over water. The boxes and crates and bags may just as well have been broken or busted while being loaded. Anyway, this is not the point. The point simply is, one gets tired of the honorable trade."

I said nothing and let him go on spreading out the inner part of his soul.

"Yep, believe me, Pippip, you get awfully tired and bored of this kind of business. There is something which is not true about the whole thing. And you feel it, see? You are just like lying all the time upon somebody's pocket. Almost like living on a woman. So you feel dirty, see? For a certain time, well, you cannot help it. You do your very best to land a job, but you cannot get one, not even by selling your soul to the devil. You see, you want to do something. You wish to be useful. I do not mean that silly stuff about man's duty. That's bunk. There is in yourself that which is driving you on to do something worth while. Not all the time hanging on like a bum beggar. It is like this—hell, I can't explain what I mean. It is that you want to create something, to help things going. You—you—I mean, some day when you know it is all over, you wish to have the true satisfaction of having done at least something while you were alive on this crazy earth. What I mean is, to stand by the wheel, say, in the dirtiest weather hell and devils can think of and then, in such weather, keep the course straight. That is something which nothing in the whole world can be compared with. No honorable trade, no matter how thick and honey it may be, is like that. Damn my soul. There you stand by the wheel, and the old bucket kicks around and around and wants to get off the course by all means and by all forces under the thickest sky you can imagine. But no matter how hard she may kick, you hold the wheel by the course just like that, see?"

Stanislav grabbed me by the belt and with a powerful twist tried to throw me off my feet and around, just as if he had his hands clenched to the wheel.

"Let go," I cried, "I am no rudder."

"Don't get sore. I only wanted to show you what I mean. See, when you get her through and out of that sour weather without losing so much as half a point off the course, I can tell you, your heart jumps like a fish in a frying-pan. Then you could just bellow loud, out of joy and satisfaction. Just think how powerful you feel—you, such a little mite of a human thing, you can hold a fifteen-thousand-ton bucket in the heaviest gale straight on, as if it were a baby coming straight from mother, innocent like new-fallen snow. And then the old man comes along, or the first, and he glances at the rose, and he says: 'Fine work, Koski. Man, you are some sailor, as I haven't seen many the last twenty years. Damned fine accurate work, my boy. Hold her on this way and we'll still back her through and we won't lose even fifteen minutes off the schedule.' Tell you, Pippip, then your heart knocks right in your throat, you can feel it. And you just could cry out aloud how happy you are and all the world around you. Believe me, the finest honorable trade, no matter how much you may get out of it, cannot beat such a feeling as holding old Caroline straight by the course."

"I never stood by the wheel of a big can," I broke in, "but I had the rudder of five-hundred-tonners all right. I suppose what you say is positively correct. Painting is just as pleasing often as standing by the wheel. If you can draw a green edge without breaking over into the brown layer, it sure makes you feel that you have done a great job. Because it takes a good time before you can accomplish this when the ship is in the open, and before you learn not to spit and splash the paint all over like a puppy does on mother's fresh-washed floor."

Stanislav did not speak for a while. He was meditating. After a few minutes he spat in good fashion over the railing. He bit off a cigar he had bought an hour ago from a dealer who had come alongside with his boat and had sold tobacco, matches, postal-cards of acting couples, fruits, chocolate, chewing-gum, buttons, thread and needles, writing-paper, stamps, and all such things as are offered to crews by these small traders in rowboats.

Stanislav lighted his cigar, spat out again, and said: "Perhaps you are going to laugh at what I am going to tell you. Anyway it is the truth. Now I am here on this can to shovel coal, to cart coal, to heave ashes, and to do the dirtiest and most miserable kind of work any rotten landlubber can do aboard a ship, while actually I am an A.B., and for sure a ten times better one than any of these three brazen drunkards here that think themselves such great guys. Maybe it is a shame, a real disgrace for me, a good sailor, to shovel coal here and all that goes with it. But maybe it is not. It has to be done to keep a can going, and somebody has to do it. I tell you, Pippip, even this has got its fun. You see, to throw into the tunnel, down to the stoke-hold, some six hundred shovels of coal and do it fine even in heavy weather, and then look at this mountain of fuel you have shoveled in, right in front of the furnaces, so that the fire'm stares at you in admiration, you feel so happy that you just could go and kiss that mountain of coal. Because it all looks so funny and so useful at the same time. That mountain also stares at you, and rather bewildered, for only a half hour ago it was still in the farthest corner of the upper bunker and now, without giving it any time to think things over, it is down here, ready to go into the furnaces and make steam for the bucket. Doesn't that make you happy and feel as if you had done something important? Sure it does. And even here, believe me, the best honorable trade cannot be compared with what you feel having this mountain of coal down in the stoke-hold. You feel so healthy and so sane that I think the skipper can't feel any better after having brought the ship home through a nasty sea."

"Sometimes I feel that way also," I said.

"And why is it that you have to do the honorable trade? Is it your fault? I should say not. You haven't got anything better to do. You can't lie in bed all day long or bum about and hang at the curb-stones day in, day out. You get plumb crazy in your head if you do."

"Well, and you forgot to tell me. What happened when the Dutch was gone?" I asked him.

"I could not stand it any longer. I had to have a ship and go out again. Or I would have gone nuts. That excellent passport I had, which was no good for me, I sold to a stranded American for twelve dollars. Then, one night near the freight depot, a sack of coffee burst open again and in that way I got some sugar; I mean, of course, dough. Coffee was high then in Germany. Occasionally I went with Danish fishermen, helping them getting brandy into Denmark. Denmark had extremely high duty on foreign brandy. This business paid well. When I, finally, had shoveled on enough money, I took the train to Emmerich, which is the border station on the German-Holland international line. I got across fine at night. Yet when I bought a ticket to Rotterdam I was caught, and in the dark of night pushed across the border back into Germany again."

Surprised at such a yarn, I asked: "You don't mean to say the Dutch secretly smuggle people at night across the German border?"

I was anxious to hear Stanislav's opinion of a case about which I thought I was an expert.

"They?" he said. "They? Don't make me laugh. They do other things. Worse than such a trifle. Every night there is going on, at all European borders, a lively exchange of unwelcome travelers. Men and women and children. The Germans kick their Jews, and their undesirable foreigners, and Bolshevists and communists and pacifists, across the Dutch, the Belgian, the French, the Polish, the Swiss, the Danish border just like nothing. And, of course, the Czechs, the Poles, and all the others do exactly the same in exchange. They simply cannot do it openly. It would cost them milliards of money. Who is going to pay for that? It's being done on such a great scale that it has become almost a legitimate procedure. Everybody knows it, yet nobody admits it."

Shaking my head I said: "Stanislav, now don't you try to pull my leg over the table. I can't believe it."

"They do it just the same, whether you believe it or not. That doesn't matter a bit. I have met scores of men along the Dutch line who have had experiences you sure would get the kick of your life out of if I told you about them. What else can the officials do? It seems still the most human thing to do under the circumstances. They can't murder them or throw them into the ocean. Those people haven't committed any crime or anything bad. Only they haven't got a passport. Some can't pay for it. Most of them have had trouble with their voting for adoption. Lots have lost their country altogether. Their country has been split and divided up between five or six different nations. Every country tries to get rid of all such people who have no passport and no established nationality, for these people are for ever causing trouble to any nation that harbors them. Now, of course, if all the nations would cut out passports and all such things and do as it was before the war, this trade in human souls and this kicking out and pushing about of people—often very decent people—all that would cease immediately and everything would stop that goes with it."

"I have said this before," I interrupted him.

"I know you did. But don't you put into your head the idea you invented it. Thousands of people have said this before you. Whom do passports do any good? No one but the bureaucrats. As long as there are not at least five hundred million sane and decent persons found on earth who admit the same you say and I say, there will be no change. That's all I can say."

Stanislav had been warned by the Dutch border officials that if he should ever try again to come into their country he would get the workhouse, or the chain-gang, or at least the prison camp. He did not mind. He wanted to have a ship, as a banker wants depositors. He was afraid of nothing. So the same night he crossed over into Holland again. He had learned how to avoid border patrols. So he worked more cleverly and with more intelligence. He reached Amsterdam. Four days afterwards he got an Italian, a real rotter. A death ship with all the trimmings. She was all set to make sailor angels or sailor devils as the case might be. He went on his first trip out on the reefs with her. He and a couple of fellow-sailors survived and landed on some shore. In rags he bummed and begged along the shore until he came to a port where after a few weeks he got another ship. Again it was a death can. When he found it out he skipped her in a North African port. He had reached the end of his possibilities for surviving when the *Yorikke* put in. He knew what she was and what she was after. But he had not eaten for days. And having tried his honorable trade several times again, the planks of the pier had become too hot for him, and he had to look for a hole to get out. The only hole was the *Yorikke*, just hauling in anchor. He hopped on and was welcomed. Safely on deck, he made faces over the rail at the police.

Now where is he? A man fine at heart and body, for ever willing to work true and honestly. Where am I? Where are all the deads to be some day? On a desolate reef. Or on a shore with another death ship the only future ahead of them. Nobody can sail death ships for ever and get away with it. Some day, no matter how far off it may be, everybody has to pay for his voyage. And the payment is always made on and with a death ship.

One day I said to Stanislav: "I have been told that in the bunk on top of mine somebody was killed. Did you know him, Lavski?"

"Of course I knew him. We were almost like brothers. Was a German. Home in Mülhausen, in Alsace. I don't know his right name. Said name was Paul. He was called Frenchy aboard.

Coal-drag. Once, in a night, when we were sitting in a coal-bunker, he told me all about himself. He was crying like a schoolboy.

"He learned the trade of a coppersmith in Strasbourg or in Metz. Don't remember which of those two towns. When he had finished his apprenticeship he went traveling, as most young German artisans do, so as to get an all-round experience of their trade. He went to France, worked there for a few months, then he went to Italy, where he also worked for a time at his trade.

"When that bloody trouble started, he found himself in Switzerland. He had no money and no job. Was caught as a vagrant and deported to Germany. There he was put in the army. Fighting on the Italian front, he was taken prisoner by the Italians. He escaped from the prison camp, stole civilian clothes, and bummed about in Italy. It was southern Italy, where he had worked before the war. So he knew that part well enough. Somehow he was caught. Nobody knew that he was an escaped prisoner of war; they accepted his story that he had bummed in Italy all the time. He was taken to a camp for civilian aliens.

"From there he escaped before the armistice and fled to Switzerland. The Swiss again deported him to Germany. Here he found well-paid work in a brewery. It was the time when they had some kind of communistic trouble there, which after a short success was quelled by the socialists. He was thrown into prison, and later deported as a Frenchman. The French, however, did not accept him, probably because he was thought a communist. All people today are afraid of communists, as in the time of the Roman emperors everybody was afraid of the Christians. Officially, of course, the French refused him recognition on account of the fact that he had been away too long from Alsace, which was now French territory again, and that he had not declared his adoption to either country. What does a worker care about such nonsense? He has to worry and to think about other troubles when out of a job and when running around like a hungry rabbit to find something to eat.

"The funny thing was, while the French, without saying so, did not accept him, because of his communistic ideas, truth is he did not know even the elements of communism. He had no idea at all what it was all about. What he talked was pure insane nonsense. Nothing behind. That's the trouble with nine hundred ninety-nine out of every thousand people—that they think they know something and really they don't know anything. If the capitalists would know the truth about communism I feel sure they would adopt this system overnight to meet their fear of depressions. Of course, it is by far better they do not accept it; they sure would spoil the whole thing just as much as the original Christian ideas were spoiled the very moment an emperor made them his state religion.

"The Germans, now, ordered him to leave Germany within forty-eight hours or he would be put at hard labor for six months with exactly the same deportation order meeting him at the prison gate after he had served this term. And so on until his death.

"What else could he do facing such a dilemma? He had to make France. Half a dozen times he had been at the French consulate without any success. When he came there for the eighth time, the consul did not receive him, but forbade him to set foot in his office ever after. He had lost his job long ago. At the French border he was held and sent back into Germany, where again he got six months' hard labor. The Germans warned him once more to beat it. He went to Luxemburg. From there he made France. He could not speak much French. It was not long before the French caught him. He swore he was a French citizen. Official investigation was made, with the result that it was established clearly that he had tried to acquire fraudulently a citizenship to which he had no legal right. Such doing is today considered a greater crime than a bank hold-up or taking a jane behind a bush without her full consent. He was to get five years or so for this crime. To punish such a crime with five years is only the beginning. The next stage will be, without question, the electric chair. God the Almighty can no longer bestow on human beings citizenship; any bureaucrat may set it aside if he wants to.

"The French left him a hole through which he could escape a couple of years of prison. So he went to the recruiting office of the Foreign Legion and came out a legionnaire. If he could stand it for nine years, the French would grant him a little pension and about one tenth of French citizenship.

"He could not stand it and to keep alive he had to run away. He told me it is not quite so easy as one may see it often in the pictures. Where can he go? If lucky, to Spanish territory. But the distance is too far. Then there are certain Moroccans who are greedy enough to get the money that is paid for capturing a deserter. He said that he would have rather killed himself than return to the legion a captured deserter. It is not so pleasant, what awaits them when they come back.

"Then there is another type of Moroccan, who does not return a deserter, regardless of how high the reward may be. He catches the deserter, strips him entirely, and then lets him lie on the sand in the boiling sun. If he happens to meet such a fate it would be still better to be brought back to the regiment. There are still others who take a legionnaire and torture him slowly to death with a refinement that takes a week or so before it is fully accomplished. With them nobody on earth is more hated than a legionnaire. Again, there are tribes who take the captured man and sell him for a good price to the farthest interior, far south of the Sahara Desert, to be used as a slave for the treadmills. Also very pleasant. There are so many reasons why the Foreign Legion has so astoundingly few deserters. The real legion, the comradeship and the honor of its soldiers, are not quite as pictured in the movies made for salesladies and for the profit of the film companies.

"This fellow, though, he had all the luck. He met Moroccans that first wanted to tie him to the tail of a horse and skin him. Yet he could make them understand that he was German. Now, the Germans are Christian dogs as well as the French. Not much difference. Nevertheless, the Germans had fought the cursed French, which was something to their credit. Exactly as the Germans are liked in Cuba, Nicaragua, Spain and all over Spanish America for having killed some fifty-five thousand gringos. To all the Mohammedans, including the Moroccans, the Germans have got one more point to their credit. They have fought side by side with the Turks, also Mohammedans. All prisoners of war of Mohammedan faith captured by the Germans were treated as they treated no other prisoners, because these prisoners were considered rather friends than enemies. This is known all over the Moslem world.

"Only it is so very difficult to make a Mohammedan who is not a Turk grasp the idea that somebody can be a German and then fight on the side of the French in their legion. An Arabian believes a German looks different from an Englishman or a Frenchman. Seeing that a German looks almost exactly like a French, the Moroccan gets sort of suspicious against his captured legionnaire, and thinks he is being fooled.

"What happened to pass in the minds of those Moroccans who had captured Paul no one will ever know. They believed his word, however, that he had never fought against any Moroccans, and that he had joined the legion only because he had been facing years of prison in France, for some conduct of which he really was not responsible.

"So they clothed him, fed him, doctored his sores, and then handed him over from tribe to tribe and clan to clan until he reached the coast of Spanish Morocco. Here he was brought to the *Yorikke*, then right off the coast with special cargo for the Moroccans.

"Now, the old man was overjoyed to have him. Because we were badly in need of a coal-drag. Paul was happy to be with us. He did not know and had no idea that his situation had not changed at all since he had enlisted for the legion.

"It took him anyway only about two days to learn where he was, and that it was more difficult to escape from the *Yorikke* than from the legion. After he had passed a watch with three bars out in one furnace and five out in another, despite the fact that during this time all the fuel was rather close at hand, he said to me: 'I wish I had not skipped the legion. This here, I tell you the truth, is ten times worse than our sweat company and the penal company combined. Compared to this, believe it, comrade, we lived like princes in fairy-tales. We had at least decent food, clean quarters, and soap and washed shirts and some leisure. I feel I'll go to the rats here in no time.'

" 'Now, don't talk like an old woman, Paul,' I consoled him. 'You get used to it. And there is still some fun, sometimes, when in port with some cash. Don't hang your head. Up the chin.'

"It was likely that Paul had already caught something on account of his wanderings and hardships during his flight. Because it all happened rather rapidly," Stanislav went on with his tale. "He began to spit thick blood. Every day more and more. Then he vomited blood, pails of it. One night, when I came to relieve him, I found him in the upper bunker, lying upon a pile of coal, his face bathed in thick blood.

"He was not dead. I carried him to the quarters and put him into his bunk. I took his watch on, so that he could rest.

"In the morning, when I went to see him, he was dead. At eight he went overboard on a greasy plank. The skipper did not even take off his cap and say a prayer for him. He only touched his cap and said: 'Lower away.' The boy was not clothed. He only had his rags on him, stuck on his body by his blood. A big lump of coal was tied on one of his legs to hold him down in the sea. I had the feeling that the skipper

would have liked to save even that piece of coal. He looked
that way.

"Paul had never been registered in the pay-book of the ship.
He left the world like so much useless dust. Nobody ever knew
his name. He was just Frenchy. A member of a civilized nation which had denied him legal existence."

40

While Stanislav was on the *Yorikke*, more than one coal-
drag had been taken, eaten, and digested by that can.

There was Kurt. He was from Memel territory, which was
a part of Germany that had been taken away from the Germans after the war, without any other justification than to
bite away from Germany as much as possible. Nobody had
any idea what to do with or to whom to give this territory.
So it stayed independent.

When the residents and the natives of Memel had to make
up their minds what nationality they wished to adopt, Kurt
was in Australia. During the war he had not been molested
very much by the Australians. The war over, he got homesick and wanted to return to Germany.

He had been mixed up with a strike. In a battle with strike-
breakers one of those rats had been beaten up until he was
left dead in the street. Kurt was supposed to have had a hand
in this, and he was sought by the police. He could not go to
the German consul. If he had done some damage to the
Australian army, the consul would have done all in his power
to help him out of the country. But being mixed up with a
strike is a different thing. Laborers attacking the profits of
capitalists are out. When a strike is to be quelled, all consuls
work in unison, regardless if only a few months ago they
would rather have liked to cut one another's throats. The con-

sul, doubtless, would have handed Kurt over to the Australian police, or at least tipped them off. A consul is always on the side of order and state authority. A strike is always against the state, if led by the workers. When led by the leaders, one is never sure in whose interest the strike has been declared.

Kurt could make England without any papers, being helped by members of the seamen's union of Australia.

England is a tough spot, since it's an island. An island is always tough. You can hop on it easily. But it is not at all easy to hop off again if you have to do so within a given time. Kurt found himself like in a cage. He could not get off again. He had to go to see the consul. The consul wanted to know why he had left Sydney, or Brisbane, whatever town it was, without going to the German consul to get his papers in shape, and why, in particular, he had come to England illegally. Kurt could not tell his true story. He did not want to. England was in no way safer than Australia. The English would have sent him back to Australia without delay to go on trial there.

Stanislav could not remember exactly what town in England it was where Kurt had gone to see the German consul. When in the office of the consul, where everything, pictures on the wall, labels on drawers and file cabinets, the homely voice of the consul, reminded him of his country, which he had not seen for so many years, Kurt began to cry. The consul took his tears as an expression of the hypocrisy of a bum who wished to gain something by unfair means. So the consul bellowed that he had better cut that comedy because it wouldn't do him any good. Kurt gave him the only answer fit for such a situation. The German language is well provided for such needs. To make his meaning even clearer, Kurt took up an inkstand and hurled it against the consul's head. The consul began to bleed at once and he phoned right to the nearest police-station. Kurt did not wait for the police. He struck down the porter at the gate who wanted to hold him, and off he went out in the street, making a clean get-away.

Kurt had made a mistake anyway in going to the consul. He should have known beforehand that the consul could do nothing for him. He was from Memel, and since he had not adopted according to the regulations of the Treaty of Versailles, that masterpiece of the overwhelming stupidity of brilliant statesmen, no consul on earth could help him. He was neither German, nor a citizen of this tiny little worm of a new nation that does not know, and never will know, what to do with herself. The consul was only a paid servant of the state. He had no power to help a lost sheep get on the road again.

So Kurt was dead now for ever. Nevermore could he see his native country, his parents, his relatives. "All seems so strange and ghastly. But so it is. Let all the political wiseacres try to find out if such things do exist in modern civilization. Of course they won't try, and dismiss even the thought of it by crying out loud that it's an exaggeration if not a brazen lie," Stanislav interrupted his tale.

To Kurt a high official of state had said that his homesickness was only a bum's comedy. A bum cannot be homesick. Refined feelings are reserved only for men and women far up in class, who can take from their drawers every day two fresh handkerchiefs, silk, if you please, or at least genuine Irish linen.

I was homesick. I am homesick. All my struggling and roaming is but a dope to put to sleep my homesickness. It took me some time, and it cost me thousands of achings of my heart, before I learned in full that this thing which is supposed to be your native land, which God gave to you, and which no one, no emperor and no president, can take away from you, this homeland is today canned and put in files of passport departments and consuls' offices. It is now truly represented only by officials with credentials, by men who have the capacity to destroy your true feeling for your country so thoroughly and so completely that no trace of love for your homeland is left in you. Where is the true country of men? There where nobody molests me, where nobody wants to know who I am, where I come from, where I wish to go, what my opinion is about war, about the Episcopalians, and about the communists, where I am free to do and to believe what I damn please as long as I do not harm the life, the health, and the honestly earned property of anybody else. There and there alone is the country of men that is worth while living for, and sweet to die for.

Kurt, the dead boy from Memel, hopped on a Spanish ship which was leaving England exactly the minute Kurt needed a ship most. He could not stay long on the Spaniard. The crew was complete. He had to get off when she reached home. After switching from one port to another in search of a berth he finally, one day when very hungry and desperate, met the *Yorikke* going under weigh. He climbed up and landed a job as coal-drag. The berth as a coal-drag was always to be had on the *Yorikke*.

The *Yorikke* knew nothing about safety devices such as provide for the safety of the working-men in all civilized nations. The *Yorikke* could not have such modern nonsense. Because it costs money, in the first place; in the second place, safety devices are only hindrances to the work that has to be done. A death ship, everybody ought to know, is no kindergarten. Keep your eyes open and look around. If your skin is scorched off, your knuckles smashed, your chin bruised, your arm broken, it's only the lazy parts of your carcass that go off. Work, and work well, and you won't need any means to safeguard your limbs.

The crystal tube at the boiler which served as the water-gauge didn't have the wire screen that is demanded by the law, even in the interior of Afghanistan. One day, while Kurt had the watch in the stoke-hold, this tube burst.

There is on all boilers a valve which, with the help of a long rod, serves to shut off immediately the water-pipe leading to the gauge. As soon as this valve is closed, no steam can go through the broken gauge, and a new gauge-crystal can be set in without the slightest danger to the man who has to do it. There is nothing to it.

But the trouble on the *Yorikke* was that she had no such rod-valve, because the Phœnicians did not have it and so there was no earthly reason why the *Yorikke* should have it. There was only the regular cock directly under the crystal tube to shut off the steam and the boiling water that rushed out through the broken pipe. In less than half a minute the stoke-hold was so thickly filled with hot steam that one could not see the end of his arm, and it seemed impossible for any human being to stay there half a minute longer without being cooked all over.

But that was not to be used as an excuse for the man who had to shut off the pipe. It had to be done, for the steam went down so rapidly that the engine was liable to stall any moment. To bring the steam up again would take two hours. Suppose the bucket was then close to reefs or shoals, the whole ship would be a total loss if owing to the stalled engine the ship went out of control.

Who had to do the job and shut off the pipe? The coal-drag, of course. Who else? The dirtiest and lowest of her men had to sacrifice his life that the *Yorikke* might survive. In the sea-stories and in the pictures these jobs are done, of course, by the skipper himself, or at least by the chief, because somewhere in the background a girl is waiting with a kiss for the great hero. In real life it is always the other way round. It is the soldier, the private, who does it; on the ship it is the dirtiest and the most despised hand that has to do what is called in the log the most heroic deed of the chief.

Kurt shut off the pipe. The steam came up quickly again. The engine had not stopped for a second, and the mate on the bridge had not lost for a minute control of the ship.

Down below, however, Kurt had dropped upon a pile of coal. He had to be carried to his bunk by the second engineer and the donkey.

"I do not wish anybody on earth," Stanislav said, "no matter how much I hate him, to hear once in his lifetime the shrieking and screaming that we had to listen to from the bunk Kurt was in. It went on hours and hours without ceasing for a minute. Never before, not even when I went down with my battle-ship at Skagerrack, had I believed that any human being can cry so long a time without losing his voice. He could not lie on his back, nor on his belly, nor on either side. The skin hung down on his body in long strips and rags as if it had been a torn shirt. All over blisters, some as thick as a man's head. I don't think that he ever could have been saved, even if a hos-pital had been at hand. Maybe it could have been done by putting on his body new flesh some way or other. But sure the doctors would have needed the whole skin of a calf to cover all he had lost. And how he yelled and shrilled! I only wish that the consul who had refused him a passport could have heard his shrieking in his sleep. He sure would never have felt at ease again for the rest of his life, knowing that such a damned worthless little stamped paper as a passport was to blame for such a terrible fate of a young man supposed to have also a soul. But these guys sit at their desk, scratching and filing and polishing their finger-nails and smiling crooked at you if you want something from them—maybe a paper to help you along. They feel so very superior to us working-men. Easy to feel great a hundred miles away from the real life as it is out here.

"Bravery on the battle-field? Don't make me laugh. Bravery on the field of work. Here, of course, you don't get any medals; no mention in the report, either. You are no hero here. Just a bum. Or a communist always making trouble and never satisfied with the conditions as ordered by the Lord himself to help the profits.

"He screamed himself to death. The mate had nothing in his medicine chest to make it easier for the poor devil. We tried to pour into him a cup of gin, but he could not hold it.

Late in the afternoon he was sent overboard, the boy from Memel land. Can't help it, Pippip, I have to take off my cap, speaking and thinking of this boy. Damn it, don't look at me that way, I am not an old sissy. But here you have to sound taps. No getting away from that. Sent overboard like an escaped convict. The second engineer looked down over the rail when he disappeared in the water. Then he said: 'Damn it all. Hell. Rotten business, short again a drag. Wonder when I will ever be complete.' That was his prayer for the boy's last trip. And he was the man whose obligation it was to shut the cock. It's not the fireman's or the drag's business to look after repairs while the ship is out.

"Yes, this was Kurt from Memel. His name is not in the log either. The second had his own name written in as the man who had done it. The grandfather saw the book when he went lifting toilet soap from the skipper's chest. Yes, sir."

41

With the rest of the crew I spoke very little. Most of the time they were cranky, cross, mad at something, sleepy whenever you saw them. In every port they got drunk, drunk as only sailors can get.

To tell the truth, however, I have to admit it was not I that did not speak to them, but they who did not speak to me or Stanislav. We, Stanislav and I, were but coal-drags. A coal-drag is not as high in society as a deck-hand, or, more, the great A.B. These are gentlemen compared with the coal-shovelers, who live in filth, in soot, in dirt, in ashes. You must not touch a drag; you will get so dirty that you won't be clean again inside of a week. Take the bos'n, the donkey, the carpenter. These were the peers, before whom a coal-drag had to stand in awe when they passed by. Capitalists are too dumb, otherwise they'd find some new ideas on how to get along better with the workers. They would make use of the fine social distinctions of the workers for their own benefit. There are even nobles among them—that is, the union men. He who is not fit to join the union is looked upon as a Hunk even if born on the Emerald or right north of Aberrrrdeen.

The bos'n, the carpenter, the donkeyman, and that hang-around of whom I never knew what he really did on board, all these mugs were the so-called petty officers. They were, nevertheless, just as filthy and dirty as we were. None of them had any better experience in seafaring than we had. For the regular life of the *Yorikke* our work was by far more important than theirs. Yet we, the always overtired and over-worked coal-drags, had to serve the donkey his meals on his tiny table in his little hole of a separate quarter. We had to clean up his cave, and we had to wash his dishes. What a great man he was, that we had to serve him! What was his work, anyway? When the ship is under sail, all he does is tinker around without any special aim or anything definite. He smears here a bit of grease on the engine, and there a drop of oil on a winch-shaft; he takes away here a little bit of dirt and puts it there. As the *Yorikke* had only two engineers, he occasionally went on watch in the engine-hold, particularly when the chief felt too tired or not yet perfectly sober, and when the weather was so calm that all the donkey had to do in the engine-hold was to sit on a bench, smoke his pipe, and read true confessions. When the bucket was in port, he was fireman and coal-drag at the same time; and he was in full charge of the winches used to hoist in and hoist out the cargo. For all these reasons he was so great a personage that he had to have his own quarter. He got the same meals we got. But, so as to let us feel that he was a person far higher in social standing than we, he received on Sundays rice pudding with marmalade, well watered by the grandfather to make it last longer and to make it look like more. The donkey also had twice a week our famous prunes in the bluish starch sauce. We received our pudding only once a week, and no rice pudding at all. Such elegant differences are made even in food to show that one person is worth more than another, not for his work or talent, but for his social standing among workers. There sure would be no Cæsar and no Napoleon without these petty officers, foremen and sweat-shop whips, who have one foot on the first rung of the ladder that leads up to the rank of general. Petty officers who come from above are no good; they are failures. The best petty officers are those who come from the ranks, where they were whipped hard only as far back as yesterday. They make the best whippers today. Cæsar can rely on them. They do the job best, and without them he is lost.

Next came the A.B.'s—able-bodied seamen. Then came the deck-hands. All of them were higher in rank than we. Stanislav knew more about sailing than all the three A.B.'s and deck-hands put together. Not only the donkey and the A.B.'s, but even the deck-hands often put on airs when one of us passed by them, as if they were about to suggest that we first had to ask their kind permission. We expected any day that one of these haughty mugs would utter such a demand. Stanislav and I wished they had.

We all were dead. All of us were convinced that we were on our way to the fishes. Funny that even among the dead these fine distinctions of rank and class do not cease to exist. I wonder what goes on night and day beneath the surface of a cemetery, particularly in the cemeteries of Boston, San Francisco, and Philadelphia.

There was, nevertheless, a certain bond that kept us together. We all knew that we were the moribunds. The destiny of all gladiators was ours. Yet we never spoke of it. Sailors do not speak of shipwrecks. It's no good doing that. If you don't want to have the wolf around, then don't call him. Don't even speak of the devil if you don't want to go to hell. We all felt the last day approaching, nearer and nearer. It made us often nervous. Maybe it is the same way that a condemned criminal feels in his cell when he knows the last week has arrived.

We did not like each other. We did not hate each other. Simply we could not and would not make friends or even comrades. But, strange, when in port, none of us ever went ashore alone. We went ashore in bunches of from four to six.

Pirates who had not made a pinch for six months could not look as terrible as we. No sailor of any other ship in port ever spoke to us or said hello. We were too filthy and dirty, too ragged, for any decent sailor to admit belonging to the same honest trade as we. Suppose we tried to speak to other sailors; they never answered. They just hurried away from us as quick as they could. When hanging around in a tavern or in a saloon with dancing dames, we could say whatever we wished; we could insult any other guy that was present. They all pretended that they had not heard what we had said or that it had not been meant for any of them. By the way, this fighting among sailors in foreign ports, seen so frequently in the pictures, is just, like so many other things in the pictures, the bunk. It's a lie all over. Sailors do not fight one tenth as much as sea-stories and pictures try to make the paying public believe. Sailors have more sense than the movie-producers. Evidently no one ever wished to fight with us. We were too dirty and filthy even to be knocked down by a decent sailor. Perhaps he would have felt himself infected. Other sailors just finished their drink, paid, and left. Often they did not even drink, only paid and left quietly. They all belonged to the honest working-class, the fourth rank in a modern state. We had the feeling that we did not even belong to the sixth rank, if such a thing exists in modern civilization. I suppose it does.

There was still another reason, I think, why no other sailor, or groups of them, ever tried to fight with us. They could see that nothing mattered to us. We would kill mercilessly, once entangled in a row. We would tear them to shreds. We would not leave one piece of their clothes good for use. It would have been expensive for them even if they had won the fight. What did we care? Prison or the noose? It was all the same to us. We could not be frightened by any punishment, because we knew what it meant to have six or ten grate-bars out in one watch. We had a Portuguese deck-hand who was only waiting to get a chance to knife a man to death. He had said so, and he had explained it by saying that he was badly in need of a vacation in prison, or else he would die like a dog on the *Yorikke*. He said the worst prison he had ever been in was in a small North African town. But he added that it was still better than to work for the food he got on the *Yorikke*. I am sure there were others on the *Yorikke* who thought the same way and who were waiting for their chance, only they never spoke about it so frankly as did that boy.

The crew of the *Yorikke* was known, let's say notoriously, in all the ports of the Mediterranean, save those of France and Italy, where we were never allowed to go ashore. All the ports of the west coast of Africa as far down as the French Congo were touched occasionally, when the skipper thought it wise to do so, or when some tribe or little nation tried the newfangled ideas of freedom and independence advised by our smart brother Wilson.

Wherever and whenever we stepped into a saloon, the owner would be nervous and eager to get us out as soon as possible, although we threw upon the bar all the money we had in our pockets or in our mouths. Often one of us had all his pockets torn, and in such a case the money was carried in the mouth or, if it was paper money, in the cap. We were good customers. The saloon-keeper knew it. Nevertheless, he did not for a minute let us out of his sight. Every step, every move we made was watched by him.

People in the streets frequently shrank away from us in

horror when we crossed their way. The constant fight of the *Yorikke* to live and to prevent herself from being sent down to ground port was marked in all our gestures and movements. Women grew pale when unexpectedly we came into their path; and women who were waiting for child often shrieked pitifully when they saw us. They pressed both their hands against their belly and murmured prayers to protect their unborn children against the evil, and then they ran and ran without looking back.

Men who were just ordinary townsmen or peasants lost their self-confident manner when meeting us. Some of them plainly showed fear. Most of them just turned their faces away, so that we might not think for a moment that they meant to offend us.

Usually we were followed by one or two policemen, who did all they could not to lose us without coming too close and making it too plain that they were ordered to stay with us all the time we were ashore. Never did they wish us to know that we were under the vigilance of the police. They thought that if we were aware of this we might get wild and lay the whole town in ashes. In many ports there was a rumor that the *Yorikke* had in reality some two hundred men aboard, ready to take any town or any ship on high sea whenever ordered to do so by her master. In these parts of Africa there are hundreds of little ports whose inhabitants are still fed with stories of pirates of the times of the Phœnicians and Carthaginians.

The effect we had upon children was perhaps the most remarkable. Some of them, especially the older ones, cried for their mothers when they met us; some stood lifeless, as if touched with a magician's wand; some ran off like deer. The younger ones, though, stopped in front of us, gazed at us with eyes wide open, as if seeing birds of paradise. Others would follow us, overtake us, smile openly like little golden suns, and frequently they would say: "Good morning, sailor-

man! Have you a fairy ship to sail in?" They would shake
hands and pray us to bring them little princes and maidens
one inch high from the blue Yonderland. Then suddenly they
would give us another look, and they would take a deep breath
and show an expression as if they were waking up from a
sweet dream. Then they would run away and cry without
ever looking back again. It was on such occasions that I thought
that perhaps we were already dead, and only the souls of
children could see us as we really were.

42

The *Yorikke* went her own way—a way which very few
other ships ever tried. Perhaps the skipper knew exactly what
he was doing and what his orders were. From our point of
view, however, it looked as if the *Yorikke* had no schedule
whatever. I cannot recall many times when the ship made
exactly the port it was bound for when it left the last port.
France and Italy we avoided almost entirely. We did not put
in at the greater ports of Spain, either. There we stayed a mile
or so off the port, and the skipper signaled for a boat to take
him in to get his orders and arrange his papers with the consuls and with the port authorities.

For this reason no death ships are known. It's just a yarn
of bum sailors. Death ships belong to the period long before
the American Civil War, to the times when slave-trading was
a great business, and blockade-breaking could make a ship-
owner rich with three successful trips. No, there are no
longer any death ships today. They are things of the past.
Any consul can tell you that. And a consul is a high personage of diplomatic rank. He won't tell you anything which
is not true. No one knows death ships. No government recog-
nizes them. After all, that which is not admitted does not ex-

ist, like the Russian revolution. Don't look at it, and then it disappears.

The seven seas are so full of death ships that you can have your choice of them! All along the coasts of China, Japan, India, Persia, the Malay Islands, Madagascar, the east and the west coats of Africa, the South Sea, South America, coming up as far as the Pacific coast of Mexico, where they land Chinamen and dreams of artificial paradises by the truckload. Money is always useful, no matter how you make it. The point is to have it. As long as you have it, no minister will ever ask you where and how you got it; just rent, or better buy, a church seat, and pay something for the missions in China.

There is still room enough for a couple of thousand more of these beautiful and useful ships. Making immigration restrictions does not help the shipping trade very much. So the ships must look elsewhere for a sound business. One cannot do away with all the bums of the world, because there might be a few artists among them, and writers, or cranky millionaires. So it is close to impossible to check white slavery, just because there might be among the slaves a few wives of men with influence and some daughters of great kings of finance who wish to adventure on their own account. White slavery makes more money for those fine men who are paid to investigate and prevent it than for those who are actually in the trade. One is just as good a business as the other. Difficult as it is to do away with all the bums, it is just as difficult to do away with all the death ships. There are not a few shipping companies who would go broke overnight if they had no death ships. Other companies could not survive boom or depression if they did not send down to the bottom a ship when it is time to do so for cold cash. Honesty is the best policy. But it must pay. Otherwise this saying is as good as the saying about having gold in your mouth if you keep silent. There are some respectable ships among the death ships, just as there are quite a number of rather decent women in the C'mon-up-some-time trade. Since this is so, it would be hard work to find all the death ships. Wherever there is a road or a curb-stone, a bum may exist, regardless of how many bums you send up the river or down to the chain-gangs. After all, there is three times more sea-water than dry land. Therefore there is three times more room for bums at sea than on land.

Certain people think one can find somebody easier on a desert than in the bush, and a ship on the open sea easier than in a delta like the one down at New Orleans. It is, of course, not so. Five ships may go out to find one ship and never find it, not even when its position is fairly well known.

Nobody would ever have found the *Yorikke* if her skipper did not want her to be found. Often he had good reasons to be found, only to be safer afterwards. That skipper knew his peanuts. He could have been invited by the Marquese of Pompshundure and he would never have made a false step drinking his sherry or eating his fruit salad or asking the Marquese to dance the latest blues with him. He knew how to work himself and his old maiden out of any jam anybody had ever tried to put him in. The papers he presented were always in fine shape. Whether they were genuine was another question, which the guy who wanted to get him tight had not the guts to decide. No transatlantic liner could show better papers than he could when cornered.

A Spanish chaser, a gunboat, came up while the *Yorikke* was just bordering the five-mile limit. Suppose the skipper said that the *Yorikke* was outside the limit, and suppose the Spaniard said she was not; the Spaniard wins, because he represents the state. The state is always right, and the individual is always wrong.

Thus it happened. The Spanish gunner signaled with flags and whistles. The skipper did not heed. So the Spaniard got sore and he fired twice the stop-and-stand-by order. The shells fiffed about the mast-heads of the *Yorikke* so that the old maid started to dance, thinking it was still Abukir. The skipper was laughing. Anyway he could not make it and bring the *Yorikke* out of the limit. We were not prepared to choke down the crying throat of the old hussy. Well, the skipper gave the signal to the engine to stop and stand by. The *Yorikke* was within the five miles, no doubt. The skipper pretended to be out. They would have blown us straight to hell if the old man had not stopped.

Aboard they came. Much bowing and begging your pardon and excuses for troubling us. "Yes, sir, excuse me, you are still within the limit. No, sir, we have just taken our position. If in doubt, may we take position together, sir, so as not to leave any question?" "It's all right," said the skipper.

"May we, please, examine your papers? Thank you, sir. Are in order. Only a matter of routine, you know. Would you mind, sir, may we, please, make a slight inspection of the cargo, sir? Won't take long, sir. Half an hour or even less, sir. Acting under orders, sir, excuse me, sir."

Said the skipper: "No objection, gentlemen. Am at your service, gentlemen. But, please, make it snappy. Or I will have to make your government responsible for all and everything. I am short already, gentlemen. We have had dead wind all the time. Go ahead, gentlemen, the ship is all yours." The skipper laughed. He went on laughing and laughing. How this man could laugh! It was a sight and at the same time a feast for the ear. He changed his laughter from the bright and jovial to the ironical, then to the vulgar haw-haw of a fishmarket-woman; then he would chuckle and giggle like a high-school baby. He went through the whole scale and all the shades of laughter, while the officers were diving into the holds or ordering boxes heaved out of the holds to be opened on deck.

Every child on all the coasts of the Mediterranean knew the stories about corned beef from Chicago. Exactly as the husband whose wife is known by all the men in town is always the last person on earth to hear something, so it is with gov-

ernments. Not before the dumbest village idiot has long forgotten it will the government obtain official knowledge that
the whole village was swept away during the flood last year.
So the Spanish government, in the grip of a stern dictator,
finally had word from an office-boy about the lively trade in
corned beef from Chicago.

The officers of the gunner, supported by an experienced
customs officer, went about the holds of the *Yorikke* like ants
about a dead mouse. They were actually looking for corned
beef. And the skipper laughed and giggled so that one could
hear it from bow to stern.

The officers became nervous, partly because they did not
find what they were looking for, but mostly on account of
the laughing and chuckling of the skipper, of which they could
make neither head nor tail. They thought of going straight to
the bottom of things, and they asked the skipper: "Pardon me,
sir, have you any corned beef on board?"

The skipper narrowed his eyes and smiled at them as if he
wanted to make love, and said: "Of course, gentlemen. Excuse
me, please. Por'guese, show the gentlemen to the galley and
tell the cook to let the gentlemen inspect the corned beef from
Chicago."

The officer in charge looked at the skipper for a while, half-
dumb, half-surprised. Then he said, saluting: "Thank you, captain, this will do. I do not want to see it. I am not yet through
here. It will take me only a few minutes more, if you don't
mind, sir."

"Not at all, sir," the skipper said. He bowed and laughed
again.

The experienced customs officer and two men more were
still in the holds below, rumbling about.

The officer in charge went to the hatchway and pointed
out several boxes to be hoisted on deck. The skipper ordered
two of our hands to assist the officers.

Up came the boxes. The officer tapped them all off, some with his hands, others with his shoes, and still others with his closed pocket-knife.

"Have this one opened, please, sir," he asked the skipper.

The skipper giggled, now drawing up his lips in an ironical manner. He ordered the Portuguese, who was ready with tools, to open the box pointed out by the officer.

When the box was open, one could see a row of cans sparkling in the bright sun.

The officer took out one can, then another. So did the skipper; he picked out one and another one.

The officer looked at the label, and the skipper smiled. The officer read: "Van Houten's Pure Hollandish Cocoa. Free of Oil."

The skipper handed the officer one of the cans he held. He laughed right out and said: "Why don't you open this can, sir, to make sure it is cocoa?" His smile became satanical now. I was watching him, and I thought if something should go wrong the old man might be capable of killing that officer like a rat, shut in the others still below in the holds, and try to make off, resting his luck upon the well-weighted safety-valves of the *Yorikke*. Later, knowing him better, I knew he was far too intelligent to do such a thing. He had brains enough to get himself out of any jam, regardless of how thick it might have come. Anyway, his smile stayed diabolical, but it changed again into a light chuckling.

When he offered the officer one of the cans he held in his hand, the officer looked him straight and searchingly in the face. He noted his ironical smile. The officer pressed his lips together and got pale. He seemed no longer able to control his nerves. His hands trembled. He knew something was queer about the ship. But he got angry with himself for finding himself outsmarted by the skipper.

He reached for the can the skipper handed him. Again he

looked the skipper in the face like a professional poker-player. Then, with a resolute gesture, he gave the can to the Portuguese and said to the skipper: "Please, sir, order him to open it." "Go ahead, Por'guese," the skipper said.

The officer thought of corned beef from Chicago and expected to find it in this can labeled Van Houten's Cocoa. When opened, there was in it: cocoa. The officer looked rather disappointed, almost pitiful. But he came to and smiled at the skipper.

He knocked with his shoes against two more boxes and seemed to listen to the echo. He pointed out another box, had it opened, saw the cans with the same labels, pushed it aside, and ordered open the third box. When it was open the skipper looked at it, bent rapidly down, and picked out two cans, apparently at random. He held one of these two toward the officer and said, again using a nasty satirical smile: "Won't you examine one of these, sir?"

The officer looked with a sort of consternation at the two cans in the hands of the skipper, and for two or three seconds he seemed to hesitate. Unexpectedly, however, and as rapidly as the skipper had done before him, he picked out two other cans from the box.

The officer weighed them in his hands. Just when he was about to give one of them to the Portuguese the skipper butted in and said: "Sir, why don't you open this can from the bottom?"

The officer gazed at the skipper, saw his smile, got extremely nervous and said: "No, sir, I'll have it opened from the top." This time the officer had a smile which, no doubt, he thought looked satanical. But the skipper was a far better actor. His smile could look really diabolical, while the best the officer could achieve was a rather silly-looking smile.

He opened the box from the top by having the lid cut off. There was only cocoa in it, Van Houten's Pure Hollandish, Free of Oil.

The skipper laughed out loud. The officer, almost mad with fury, emptied the whole can. Nothing came out but cocoa, and the paper it was wrapped in to keep it dry.

The officer picked out four more cans, opened the lids, smelled at the contents, closed the cans, stood thinking awhile, and then gave orders to his companions below in the holds to come up, the inspection being over.

When all the men had come out and were standing at the rail to go down the gangway to their boat, the officer wrote out the receipts for the damage done, bowed to the skipper, and said: "I beg your pardon, sir, for the trouble I have caused you, but these were my orders. We are, as you know well, at war with the Riff colony, and so you will understand why we have to examine occasionally ships sailing within our waters. Thank you, good-by, and have a lucky voyage."

"All right with me, sir," the skipper answered, shaking hands with the officer, "come again any time you wish, I am always your most obedient servant. Good-by."

Off went the shallop with the officers.

The skipper bellowed up to the bridge: "Get her going. Full steam to get her out of the five. Damn it. Close cut."

He took a deep breath and forced it out with a whistling noise. His laughter was all gone. Now he got pale. After a while he wiped his forehead.

He stood still at the rail where he had said good-by to the officer. Now he crossed over and came near the galley.

"Cook," he hollered, "full after-gale supper tonight, raisin cake and cocoa with plenty of milk, and for each man two cups of rum with extra tea at nine. Come here, get the cocoa."

He took up the various cans the officer had opened, smelled at them, and threw them overboard, save one, which he gave the cook. Then he fingered about the open boxes, picked one out here, and another one there, rather confident in his picking. He handed them to the cook and said: "Of course, special supper for the mess."

"Aye, aye, sir," the grandfather said, and hurried off with the cans.

"Por'guese," the skipper called the hand, "close the boxes and put them back where they came from."

All this time I had been standing at the rail watching this elegant business. I hardly remember a picture which interested me so much as had this procedure. What wouldn't I give to know what went on inside the brain of the skipper when he offered the officer the cans in his hands, and, more, when he suggested to the officer that he open the cans from the bottom! I had more admiration for that skipper than ever before. What a pity, I thought, that the times of piracy are all over and gone for ever. With this skipper I would have gone to rob the whole English merchant marine. It's too late now, with wireless and all that.

Anyway, I thought, something must be done, when I saw those boxes full of cocoa put back in the holds again. One should never lose any opportunity when it knocks at your back door. A few boxes of this Hollandish cocoa mean real money in the next port. All people like to drink cocoa.

That same night, still well filled with the elegant supper, and feeling swell, I crawled into the hold and swiped five boxes.

When Stanislav came below to relieve me, I said to him: "Hey, you smarty, did it ever occur to you that we sail a living gold mine? I am talking of cocoa, you dumbhead. Honorable trade. We can make at least three pounds easy money."

"No such thing as easy money on this trip," he answered. "Still wrapped in diapers, kiddy? It would be a gold mine all right if there were cocoa in these cans. But there isn't. That's the only objection to the gold mine in this case. Are you still that dumb to believe in newspapers, advertisements, and labels? The labels are all right. Only they don't belong to these cans. Haven't you inspected them? Don't dream into your pockets any money so long as you are not through with the inspection.

Haven't I told you a hundred times not to trust in the *Yorikke*, whatever she may show you? If you look closer you will see in these cans only cocoa-beans—beans I mean. But you won't find in any port any soul to buy these beans unless you can sell them at the same time the bean-mills to grind the beans with. If you have got the right mill and you try to grind the beans, they come out: pupp-pupp-pupp-pupp-pupp-pupp, like this, and whoever swallows them won't need any cocoa any more, with milk or without. What an innocent lambkin you are! I don't understand myself how I can get along with such an ass."

I was sure Stanislav was lying to put one over on me. I had seen the cocoa with my own eyes. So had the Spanish naval officer. It couldn't be all black magic.

I simply could not believe it.

Immediately I went up to the bunker and opened the boxes. Stanislav was right. There were cocoa-beans inside. Hard ones, with shiny brass shells. In all the five boxes there were the same kind of beans. I did not find one single can in which there was Van Houten's Pure Hollandish Cocoa. It all was Chicago again. Behind the label Pork and Beans you sure find anything, even bent hoofnails, but no pork and beans.

I closed the boxes and took them back into the hold. I was certainly not interested in the kind of cocoa-beans the Arabians and the Moroccans cook.

The skipper alone, that great magician, knew the word that turned cocoa-beans into emma-gees shells when needed. He was a great master of black magic, the skipper was. Yes, sir.

43

We were half a day out of Tripoli and met with real nasty weather. In the stoke-hold we were so thrown about that most of the time we did not know if we were at starboard or at port side or in which of the four corners and which of the two gangways of the bunkers.

Thrown upon a pile of fuel, trying to collect my limbs, I accidentally looked at the crystal tube of the water-gauge, and I marvelled how such a pretty-looking little thing could kill a grown-up sailor in the horrible way that it had done to Kurt from Memel. I questioned myself for a few seconds: would I jump at the broken tube and shut the cock and in doing so sacrifice my precious life?

I would not do it, I decided. Let anybody who wants to be brave do it. I don't care a tinkling about being brave and being called a great and regular guy.

But who is there who can say for sure what he will do on a given occasion, when no question is asked at all, but has to be answered by a quick move without time to think of what the consequences might be. The fireman might be right under it, and he cannot get away because he is entangled somehow or caught at the furnace door or blinded. Leave my fireman in the mud? Have him yell at me day and night for the rest of my life: "Pippip, for hell's sake get me out, I am boiling to death. Pippip, come get me. I can't see a thing, my eyes are scorched out. Pippip, quick, or it's all over. Pip-pip-p-p."

Just try that and live afterwards. Just try to save your own hide, and leave your fireman lying there whimpering. You hop at it and do it, even when you know that both of you won't stay alive.

On second thought, maybe I would not go. My life is worth just as much to me as is the life of my fireman to him. My life might—

"Pippip, the devil, jump back, don't look, port side and over, jump!"

My fireman howled so mightily that the noise of the engine seemed to be drowned away. Without turning my head or hesitating I jumped over to port and dropped on my knees, because

I had tumbled over the poker against the wall. Simultaneously with my fall I heard a tremendous crash right behind me.

I saw the fireman get pale all over, so much so that even under the thick layer of soot and sweat on his face it seemed to be whitewashed. So I learned that even dead men still can get pale.

I stood up and rubbed my bruised shins and knees. Then I turned round to see what it was all about.

The ash-funnel had come down.

This funnel was a heavy tube made of thick sheet-iron, about three feet in diameter and about ten feet long. In, or, better, through it, the ash-cans were hoisted up on deck to be emptied into the sea. The funnel hung on four short chains against the ceiling of the stoke-hold. The lowest part of it was about eight feet above the floor of the stoke-hold. Perhaps the holes in which the chains were fastened had broken out or rusted away, or the chains had broken. Whatever the reason, the heavy sea we found ourselves in had hastened the break and so the funnel had come down. The weight of this funnel was a ton or so. Suppose someone is beneath it when it falls— he is severed in two, as if cut with a heavy knife, or only his head is cut off, or an arm or a leg or both, or he is cut deep into the shoulder. Who ever would have thought that this ash-funnel would come down? It had hung there since Queen Betsy had her first lover. Why couldn't it stay another three hundred years in its place? But in these revolutionary times nothing is safe any longer; everybody and everything gets restless and wants to change positions and viewpoints. So the funnel drops.

"Yep, fire'm, this sure was a close jump over a razor-blade. Almost got me. I would have been well mashed up. Nothing would have remained for Judgment Day. Well, anyway, I wonder what these guys, sent out at Doomsday to collect all the dead and bring them before the Judge, are going to do with the sailors fallen overboard or shipped over the rail and eaten by the fishes bit by bit—by thousands of fishes? I would like to see how they settle this affair of collecting all the sailors out of a hundred thousand millions of fish bowels."

"That's why sailors are out anyway," the fireman said. "This is the reason why a sailor doesn't care if he swears all the hells he wants to and spits at the seamen's mission."

This time there was no burial with a begrudged lump of coal at the feet, a disinterested tipping of the cap, and the funeral prayer. "Damn it, hell, now I am short again a coal-drag. Wonder when I ever can stay complete for a while."

The water-gauge got its victim. The ash-funnel did not. I would like to know what will be next and who is next? Perhaps it will be that plank leading from the upper bunker to the landing above the stoke-hold. It already crackles rather suspiciously when you walk across. Or if it is not the plank it might be the— What's the use of guessing? The finish will come some way, and likely it will be very different from what one figured.

Next port I'd better step out and skip. I knew, however, that there would be only another death ship after a little freedom. The deads have to go back to the graves, even though they may get at times a mouthful of fresh air to keep them healthy.

Stanislav's and my thoughts must have been somehow in the air. Because when we were in port again, we could not make a move without being watched by the police. At the first attempt to go to the outskirts of the town or to show signs of skipping, the police would have pinched us and taken us back to the bucket. The skipper would have got a bill for the cost of catching two deserters from a foreign vessel. We, of course, would have to stand up for the bill from our pay. And again we would have to be on our knees before the old man to let us have a little advance for drinks.

We tried it again at Beirut. We were in a tavern, waiting for the *Yorikke* to sail and leave us to our fate. But quite unexpectedly, when we felt sure the *Yorikke* had put out and was under weigh, in stepped two guys: "Sailors, aren't you from the *Yorikke?*" We did not say yes or no. We said nothing. But these birds did not wait for an answer. They only said: "Your ship has hoisted the P flag already and is about up and down. You are not going to miss your berth, gentlemen? May we show you the way back? If you do not mind, gentlemen, we are very much pleased to accompany you to your ship."

After we had sadly climbed up the gangway these friendly fellows stood at the wharf waiting until the *Yorikke* was steaming so far off that we could hardly have made it swimming. I say there are really fine folks in some ports, bringing the sailors back to their ships and bidding them farewell as long as they can see the last cloud of smoke.

After all, Stanislav was right: "No way ever to get off again, once on. If you really make it and have luck in skipping the can, they catch you within a day or two and take you straight to another death tub. What else can they do with you? They have to get you out somehow. Can't deport you. You haven't got a country to be deported to."

"But, Lavski, how can they make me sign on? They cannot do that."

"Yea? Can't they? You should see how they can. The skipper, always in need of hands, even pays them a pound or two for bringing you in. He swears that he has signed you on by hand-shake in a tavern, and that he has given you two bobbies advance. A skipper, such a fine man, is always right; the sailor is always drunken and of course always wrong. You have never seen the skipper; neither has he seen you. But he needs you and claims you as a deserter. And don't you try the court. That's the curtains for you. The skipper swears and the birds that got a pound from the happy old man swear, and what of you then? Committing perjury? They fine you ten pounds, and leave you in care of the skipper. Then you work half a year without any advance just for the ten pounds fine the skipper had to pay."

I stood aghast listening to this horrid tale of modern slavery. Those foolish white-slavery acts protect a woman, or claim to do so. Why not a sailor? He cannot wait for the Lord to protect him.

So I said: "Lavski, so help me and bless my lost soul, there must be some justice in this world."

"There is justice in this world. Heaps of it. But not for sailors, and not for working-men making trouble. Justice is for the people who can afford to have it. We are not these people. Everybody knows well you cannot go to a consul. If you could, you would not be on a *Yorikke*. So whenever you come in port on a *Yorikke*, every child knows what you are and who you are. If you could go to the consul, then of course they would have no chance. But your consul is not for you. You cannot pay the fee, and you cannot rattle a hundred-dollar bill among the papers on his desk and forget it there."

"Where is your Danish sailor's pay-book?" I asked.

"Now, look here, you sap. Sometimes I earnestly believe you haven't got any brains at all. A question like that! If I still had that Danish scrap I would not be here. No sooner did I have that beautiful passport from Hamburg than I sold the Danish pay-book for ten dollars American money. For the bird that bought it, it was worth a hundred. He had to get out of Hamburg by all means. You see, I was so sure that I could depend on that beautiful passport. It was just perfect. Reliable like a jane that has got three kids from you and is so ugly that you can't be seen with her in the daytime without feeling sick."

"Why didn't you try your luck with that passport elsewhere, after the Dutch consul had said he couldn't sign you on?"

"Did I try, Pippip? I should say I sure did. I would be the last one not to have on full run such a brilliant front page. I got a Swede. The skipper had no time to take me to the consul, because he was already on his way to put out. When he asked me for my papers I produced my elegant passport. He fingered it, gazed surprised, and said: 'Sorry, sonny, nothing doing. I can't get you off my chest again. Can't make it.' "

"The Germans would have taken you in," I said; "they could not refuse you with that German passport."

"Tell you the truth, Pippip, I did. I got a fine Germ. The pay was dirty low. Yet I thought, well, to begin with, let's stick for a few trips. But when the mate looked at my passport, he bellowed right out: 'We don't take stinking Polacks. Out of here, this is a decent German ship.' Then I got a third-rater Germ. But I could not stand it. Workers, and all those what is called 'proletarians of the world unite,' they are more patriotic than the kaiser's generals ever could be, and more narrow-minded than a Methodist preacher's wife. I hardly ever heard anything else but: 'Polacks out.' 'Won't you swallow the rest of Silesia also, Polack?' 'Even pigs of the German peasants stink less than a Polack.' 'Where is that Polack swine of ours?' They never said it directly to me, right in my face. But I heard it all around, whenever I came in sight. I was often near going over the rail. I sure can stand a lot, but this I could not. So I went to the skipper after the first trip back home in Hamburg. He was fine. He said: 'I know, Koslovski, how it is, and how you feel. I am sorry. I can do nothing about it. You are a most reliable man. Sorry to let you go. But I understand you are going mad or you will kill a couple of the rest. Either wouldn't do any of us any good. I think it is best for you to go and look for a ship which is not German. You sure will find one.'

"Great guys, these fellow-sailors, and sure they are talking all the time about communism and internationalism and eternal brotherhood of the working-class and whatnot. Bunk." I said.

"Now, don't take it this way, Pippip," Stanislav excused them still. "They are educated that way. They can't help it. Was the same with them when war broke out. Karl Marx on their book-shelf, and the guns over their shoulders, marching against the workers of France and Russia. There will still have to pass five hundred years before they won't fall any longer for worn-out slogans. You see, that's why I like it on the *Yorikke*. Here nobody pushes down your throat your nationality. Because nobody has any to play. And don't you think the Russians are so much different. They are as jazzy about their Bolshevik Russia as are the hurrah nationalists of Germany. The Bolshevists shut their doors against hungry workers from the outside as close as do the American labor unions. Dog eats dog, and any devil is a devil for another. I rather go down to the bottom with that sweet old *Yorikke* than eat and live on a Germ ship. I don't want a Germ for a Christmas present, if you ask me."

"Haven't the Poles now a merchant marine of their own?"

"They have. But what good does that to me?" Stanislav asked. "I have it from a first-class Polish authority that I am not a Pole, while the Germs, on the other hand, take me only as a Polish swine. There you are."

44

Month after month passed. Before I knew it I had been on the *Yorikke* four months. And when I came aboard I had thought that I could not live on her for two days.

So I found one day that the *Yorikke* had actually become a ship on which I could live and even laugh. Occasionally we would have a great after-gale supper, sometimes one cup, frequently two cups, of gin. We would have raisin cake and cocoa cooked with canned milk. Sometimes, having picked out for the cook some extra-fine nut coal from the bunkers, he would hand us in return an extra pound of sugar or an extra can of sweetened milk. Whenever we made a port where the skipper did not mind giving us shore leave we were provided with some advance to go and lift a skirt or two, and after that to get well drenched. My mess-gear—that is, the tools to eat with—had become complete. It was, of course, not a perfect unit, for one piece had once adorned a table in a tavern in Tripoli, another had come from a saloon in Smyrna, and another one from Tangier. I had even some surplus, in case one was nipped or got lost.

The filth in the quarters had become thicker, but I was now used to it. In this way the *Yorikke* once more proved an excellent teacher, making it quite clear that the saying: "All civilization is only a thin layer of varnish on the human animal" has a lot of truth in it. The bunk I slept in was not so hard as I had thought when I lay down in it the first day. I had made a pillow out of cleaning-rags swiped from the engine-hold. Bedbugs, yes, we had them. But they are found in all the elegant cities of the world, like New York, Boston, and Balti, and Chic also.

Looking at my fellow-sailors now and then, I could not imagine how it had ever been possible that, seeing them for the first time, I had thought them the dirtiest and the filthiest bunch of guys I had ever seen. They looked quite decent.

Everything became a bit cleaner and more endurable every day that passed. It is like this: You look every day at the same thing, and then you don't see it any more.

No, sir, I have nothing against the *Yorikke*. She was a fine ship. Got finer every day. The crew was not at all so rude and sour as I had thought during the first month.

Stanislav was an intelligent guy, I might even say a real gent. He had knocked about the world a lot, he had seen many things and happenings, and he had gathered experiences such as I only wished every president of the U.S. could have had. The marvel about Stanislav was that he not only saw things but that he saw them clear, through and through, right to their very sources. Nobody could blindfold him with slogans or success yarns. From every experience he had had, from everything he had seen or heard of, he deduced a wisdom and a philosophy which was worth more to him and to his understanding of world, matter, and conditions than the finest and thickest book about philosophy written by a great prof and doc.

My two firemen, I learned, were not like automobile mechanics that understood only their trade, and outside of their trade knew nothing but how far a certain place is, how much gas they use per mile, and what chance you have to win a poker game against the boss who hires and fires. My firemen knew how to talk, because they had learned to think. The A.B.'s and the hands—after knowing them better I found that none of them were the ordinary kind of human bugs. No ordinary man ever came to ship on the *Yorikke*. Ordinary men have their birth-certificates and passports and pay-books in fine shape. They never make any trouble for a bureaucrat. There would be no such thing as the Most Glorious God's Country if half of the pioneers and builders of the great nation could have produced passports and could have passed Ellis Island like the Prince of Wales. Ordinary people can never fall over the walls, because they never dare climb high enough to see what is beyond the walls. Therefore they can never ship on such a peach of a maiden as the *Yorikke*. Really good people believe what is told them, and they feel satisfied with the explanation. Therefore we can be at ease in Nicaragua, and cross the ocean to lick the Germans, and make the bankers the emperors of a republic.

It serves the guy right when he falls from the wall. Let him stay at home in the first place. Freedom? Okay with us. But it must be certified and stamped.

There came a time when the skipper held quite a bit of pay of mine. The question was where and when to sign off. My signing off would not have been recognized in any port. Since I had not brought aboard any paper, the skipper was not obliged to give me a pay-book. Without one, and without being able to prove that I was once born somewhere, the port authorities would have shipped me off on the next death can that put in.

There was left only one kind of signing off. That of the gladiators. Signing off on a reef and going to the fishes' bellies. Still there might be some luck. A sailor without luck should not go sailing. So it might happen that I could reach the coast, somehow. Shipwrecked sailor. Poor wretch. Folks living along the coast take pity on a shipwrecked sailor and take him in and feed him.

Then the consul hears that there is a shipwrecked sailor somewhere. He gets hold of him. He is not a bit interested in the man. He is interested alone in the report how, when, and where the ship was wrecked, and, if you can give an account of it, under what circumstances the ship was lost. "Now, my man, be careful what you say." The report is of great importance, not to the world, but to the company that wants to collect. For if there is no report from an eyewitness the company may have to wait a couple of years to pull in the cash. After the report is made, sworn to, and signed, the shipwrecked sailor gets one pound and the news: "Sorry, since you cannot prove your citizenship, I can do nothing for you. Anyway, don't you worry, an experienced man like you, you will soon get another ship. Quite a few ships put in here. Just hang around."

The ship puts in all right. Yes, sir. The sailor, hungry and sick of sleeping on bales of straw, on park benches, in gateways, in the furrows of cultivated land right near the last house in the town, hops on the ship just getting under weigh. He tumbles to the foc'sle, reads what is written over the entrance of the quarters, and knows where he is again. So he learns that the shipwreck was only an interruption, and, at best, a change in the name of the ship and in the language of the skipper. The fish have patience.

We were at anchor off Dakar. Dakar is a decent port. Nothing doing. Full of French gobs, French marines, French didonks, and French colonial blues, and a lot of French hoppies or dames. But we had no money to look them under. I won't complain, anyhow, because the Arabian janes in Tunis and in Tripoli waiting to see us are just as good. It mustn't always be French. They haven't got any new tricks. The Arabian and Egyptian babies have, and that's that.

Boiler-scaling. That comes right next to setting in fallen-out grate-bars. Boiler-scaling when the fire in that boiler was taken out only ten hours ago and the neighboring boiler is still under full steam. But that's not all. Because it is done right near that section of the funny globe where you say: "Hey, you, look there, see that green painted fence, with an E on it? Know what that is? That is the Equator, or what the scientists call 'the imaginary circle' or the zero meridian." But there is nothing imaginary about it, if you have to scale boilers there.

The imaginary circle. Don't make me laugh out loud. In the first place this fence is white-hot. If you only so much as touch it, your whole arm, as far up as your shoulder, is gone, scorched off like nothing. Put the heavy poker against this fence, and the poker melts like lard. Doesn't leave even a pinch of ashes. No, sir. If you put two thick bars of fine steel one against the other and you hold them on the fence, they get welded into one single piece so that you cannot even see the seam.

"You guys don't know the full story as yet, you dumb-heads," Stanislav said. "But let me tell you what once happened when I crossed the E with the *Vaarsaa*, which was a rather fine Dane hussy. It happened about on Christmas eve, as far as I remember. Now, old *Vaarsaa* got so white-hot while crossing the E that you just could poke your finger or your pocket-knife through the iron hull, and wherever you poked, a hole was left. It was funny when spitting against the hull.

Now, it sure is not decent of a regular sailor to spit against the bulwark of the ship he is sailing on. Anyway, we did it for fun just to see what might happen. Tell you, wherever we spit against the gunwale the spit went clear through and another hole was left. The skipper, who was on the bridge, saw what we were doing and he yelled down: 'T'hell with you damned devils, don't you try to make a sieve out of my ship, or I put you all in irons.' That's what he said. Then he ordered: 'Close all these holes immediately or, hell, I feed you to the sharks.' There wasn't much to it. We just rubbed with a piece of wood over the holes or with our elbows, and the holes closed like you would work with clay or with a fresh custard pie. You see, the hull had gone as soft as dough. The masts really made us quite a lot of trouble that day. They were good masts, all steel tube, see? But in spite of that we worked like young devils to prevent it, we could do nothing to keep those steel masts from bending over like candles you leave standing on a hot stove in the kitchen. We had to work fast to fix tackles high above the mast-tops and to hoist the masts and straighten them out while they were still soft. You see, it was like that, if we had waited until we had crossed the whole E they would have cooled off, and then there would be no chance to straighten them until we docked somewhere around a shipyard. But I tell you, you little birdies, one should never fool around with the E. It's dangerous."

"Now, who would ever do such a nasty thing?" I said. "But I wonder, Stanislav, how come that you, so smart a sailor, could ever ship on a can that had a skipper who would not take the slightest precaution when reaching the E. He must have been a queer miser. Sure, he wanted to save the tunnel expenses like the others who sail four weeks round Cape Horn to save the few pennies the American government charges for using the old Panama Canal. When we made the E on the *Mabel Harrison*, that was what you guys might call a regular ship, such as none of you has ever seen and never will, well, as I said, when we made the E we went right through the tunnel under the ocean, not minding a bit that old fussy Equator at all. Now, in this tunnel it is really cold; you would be surprised to find something so cold straight beneath the E. Not for a minute would you ever imagine that you are sailing straight under the E. It's all well lighted up, almost like day."

"Don't you think that I don't know that tunnel, you puppy," Stanislav said. "We stayed out because the company did not want to pay the expenses. They charge quite a bit. I figure it must be close to a pound a register ton. Sure, they make truckloads of money with that tunnel. But since I have never been in this tunnel I, for the world, cannot make out how the hell they get down the ships the size, let's say, of twelve thousand tons."

"That's easier than you would ever think it is," I explained. "There is a huge hole in the midst of the ocean. Now, the engineers have put through this hole a pipe—'s matter of fact, several pipes; I reckon about twenty or so—to hustle up the traffic. As soon as the ship reaches the entrance to the pipe she bends over a bit and goes in bow first, glides down on well-greased rails. Now, after a while of gliding this way, she finally reaches the bottom, which is a mighty tunnel. There the hands are all ready to get her on a carriage, which is drawn by heavy engines, all running on ten-inch rails. Some tunnels have no rails and carriages. There they have got water in and the ship goes along under her own steam. Here they charge a bit less, but it takes more time and it has happened that ships even sank and were a total loss. Now, when the ship has reached the end of the tunnel it is put in a sort of floating dry-dock and heaved up through the pipe until she comes out again to the open. Here the dry-dock is opened, and off she goes without any damage done by the E. If I had money, I tell you, I would buy only the shares of this company; they pay no less than twenty-two per cent per share. And you can

have the shares rather cheap, because there are people who
don't believe in the company and in the Equator."

"I never thought it would be that simple," Stanislav said.
"My idea was that they would put the ship in a kind of diver's
bell and then haul her down, drag her along the bottom, and
heave her up again on the other side of the E."

"Of course, they could have done the whole job that way
as well," I answered. "But, somehow, I think there must be
a catch in why they haven't done it. Sure, they could not do
it for a pound per ton. Because I figure it must be more com-
plicated working a whole ship with a diver's bell. There
would have been still another way to—"

"What for all hell's sake is going on there?" The second
had put his cone through the manhole and was yelling like
a mad gorilla. "Is this a sewing-circle for an African mission
or what? Are you paid for scaling that god-damned boiler
or do you get your money for shabbering like drunken
monkeys. We will never get the boiler scaled. Turn to it, the
hell, you stinkbones."

"Hey, you grandson of two peaches, you come in here," I
hollered so that the boiler drummed. "What did you say, stinkbones or what? Come in and scale your bitch of a boiler
yourself, you thief. Wait until we are under weigh again, and
then step in the stoke-hold; I swear we'll roast you in the
furnace."

From the thick dust of the scale and from the infernal heat
I was nearly mad. I would have killed him like a louse if he
had come in.

"He won't report you to the old man," Stanislav said, "just
as during the war an officer never reported you for having
spit in his face. They needed you and could not afford to
have you in the guard instead of in the trenches."

In the sweat of thy face shalt thou eat bread. Well, you
who said so, you have never scaled a boiler of the *Yorikke* right
*lose to the Equator with the fire out only ten hours and the

boiler next to it under full steam! It must be done. Boilers have to be scaled or they go up to heaven, taking along the whole crew and all that is left of the ship.

We were sitting inside that boiler as active members of a nudist camp. The walls of the boiler were so hot that we could not touch them with bare hands, nor could we kneel at the bottom without a thick layer of rags under us.

There wasn't such a thing as goggles for boiler-scaling on the *Yorikke*. No goggles were known at Carthage, so why should the *Yorikke* have them? The dust of the scale sprang into your eyes and almost burned the light out of them. If you tried to rub it out it would only pierce so deeply into your eyelids and under them that you would have to pick the specks out with a pin or with a pocket-knife. You feel that you are going mad. You cannot stand it any more and you call on one of the other guys to get them out. He works with his dusty and clumsy hands about your eyes until he gets them clean, but your eyes swell under this torture and they stay swollen and bloodshot for a week.

Even suppose you had goggles, they would not do you any good. The dust darkens them to such an extent that you cannot see where you are.

The boiler inside has to be illuminated for you to see what you are doing, because it is as dark inside as it is in a coal-mine. If you had electric light it would be easier. But on the *Yorikke* we had only the ancient lamps of old Carthage. Five minutes, no more, and the boiler was filled with black smoke so thick that we could cut it like a cake. And the smoke stood as if chained and gummed.

The drumming, hammering, and knocking against the hull inside seemed to crack open your head and mash your brain to powder.

Hardly ten minutes' work and we had to come up and out to get air, exhausted each time like pearl-divers.

We would crawl out and dart under the air-funnel which

reaches into the stoke-hold. The ocean breeze would strike our hot bodies, and then you feel as if a sword were thrust through your lungs. After fifteen seconds you feel like lying naked in a blizzard. To escape this terrific snowstorm, which in fact is only the soft breeze of the tropics, you hurry back into the hot boiler as if hunted, and go to work harder than before with the hope that the harder you work, the quicker you will be out of the inferno.

Before ten minutes have elapsed, however, you have to crawl out again into that blizzard of Saskatchewan, because you feel you are surely going to die if you don't have fresh air.

There is a moment where the nerves seem to burst. It happens when you feel that you have to go out that very second and you see your fellow-man squeezing slowly through the manhole. The boiler has only one manhole. The narrower it can be made, the better for the boiler. Only one man can crawl through at a time. The others have to wait until he is through and fully out. While he is squeezing himself through, which takes a certain time, the hole is entirely closed, and not one mouthful of air can come in. The two men still inside feel exactly like men in a sunken submarine. No difference.

It happened within these few seconds, when Stanislav was just out and I was next, that I looked back on hearing a bump, and I saw the fireman lifeless. With the last breath I had I cried: "Lavski, the fire'm has dropped out. If we don't get him out quick he will choke to death in that poison smoke."

"One minute, Pip—" Stanislav was snapping for air, "let me just catch a noseful."

The fireman was lying somewhere in the thick black cloud inside the boiler. We could not see him at first. But when I crawled back into the boiler I found him lying flat under the lower flue.

It is difficult for a living being to squeeze himself through the manhole. First you put your head through, then one arm, then you bring both your shoulders so far forward that your body takes on the shape of a cylinder. Now you get the other arm out and then you finally squeeze the lower part of your body through. Having tried this half a dozen times, getting bruised and scratched on both arms and shoulder-blades, you can do it rather quickly and efficiently.

To get out a lifeless body is quite a job. We had to take a rope and sling it around the body and under the arms. With another rope we had to bandage the fireman mummy-fashion. After we had him out, his arms and shoulders were well peeled.

Stanislav wanted to take him right beneath the air-funnel into the blizzard. When I saw it I cried: "Lavski, you are killing him. First he must come to and breathe well before we can do that."

We blew into his face, beat his wrists and the soles of his feet, and worked him up with artificial breathing. The heart was throbbing so feebly that we could hardly hear it. But it was beating regularly. We poured water over his head and his chest, and we pressed a wet rag hard against his heart. Whether his face was pale or red we could not make out, because he, like Stanislav and me, looked blacker than a Negro. When I noticed that his breathing was slowly coming along, we carried him under the air-funnel, but put there only his head. The rest of the body we covered with rags. Stanislav had to go on deck to twist the mouth of the air-funnel into the breeze, because the wind had changed.

When we were entertaining ourselves a bit in the boiler, the horsethief was quick to put his cone through the manhole, choke away the little air that came in, and bawl us out. Yet now, when we were in need of somebody to help us and treat us to a good shot, he did not show up, but sat with the chief in the mess, lapping his coffee and blabbing about useless drags and lazy firemen. A cup of gin would have done the fireman good right then, and us too, if only to forget for a minute that grinding of scale dust between our teeth.

We had the fireman coming on fine. We carried him to a pile of coal to have him sit upright. He was still far away somewhere under palm-trees in southern Spain. It took him quite some time to find himself back in the stoke-hold.

"What of all the drunken lousy beachcombers is up again?" The horsethief, that second engineer, had come from the engine-hold, through the famous gangway alongside the boilers, into the stoke-hold, and he was standing right at the corner of the boiler wall, yelling at us, who were still working about the fireman. "You are paid to work here, and not for sitting around and clicking your stinking swear-traps. Get to work, the hell with you."

Stanislav or I could have said: "Look here, sir, the fireman was—"

Yet both of us had, at the same second, exactly the same instinct. And it was the right instinct. Without saying one word we both bent down, grabbed a huge chunk of coal, and gunned it against the face of that pickpocket.

He was almost as quick as we. He had his arm up to protect his face the same moment we flung the lumps of coal. He flew off through the low, narrow gangway. But Stanislav had another big piece of coal ready, and quick as a weasel he was after him and hurled that chunk into the dark gangway with all his might so that it exploded into dust against the iron wall of the side-bunker, and he cried: "You heap of dirty shit, if you ever drop in here again you are going through the ash-pipe to feed the sharks, so help me geecries, and you may spit straight into my face if I don't do it. Now go to the old man and report me and have a month's pay cut off. But if you do, grandson of peaches, there will not be a square inch of skin left sound in your face when we get ashore."

Stanislav had run to the steel door of the engine-hold, which the second had tightly closed behind him. But he listened to what Stanislav yelled through this door, and he took note of it.

All the time we were lying at Dakar, scaling the boilers, the second never came in again and never again said a word even if he did not hear the hammering in the boiler for half an hour. From that day on he treated us as if we were raw eggs. He, in fact, became more diplomatic than even the chief. So the *Yorikke* again had taught me something new, by which I mean: It works wonders for a laborer to have a hammer or a lump of coal at hand to use at the right time in the proper way. A working-man that is not respected has only himself to blame.

After the boilers were scaled and washed we got two cups of gin and a good advance. So we thought things over, went ashore, and gave the port the once-over. I could have stowed away on a French that was making Barcelona. But I did not take this opportunity because I would have left the skipper with my four months' pay in his pocket. I could not afford to enrich skippers. So I let the French sail without me. Stanislav could have got a Norwegian on which he could have gone as far as Malta. He had the same reason not to go I had. His outstanding pay was even higher than mine.

We just roamed about port and looked ships and crews over. Wherever a sailor goes or tumbles, he thinks he is going to meet somebody or something unexpectedly and so have a surprise without paying for it.

45

Looking at ships in port is practically the only thing worth while for a sailor to do after having seen the dames and if he hasn't enough cold cash left over to get his belly wetted. To the pictures you cannot go, because you do not understand the language. So there is nothing better to do than to criticize other ships, their looks, their crews, their grub, their

pay, and to wonder whether it would be better to ship with
this one or that one or stay where you are.

So we came at last to the *Empress of Madagascar*. She was
English. Seven thousand tons or even close to eight; yes, sir.
Seeing her, we thought she might be a fine can to get out on.
A fine shippy. Clean and brilliant, freshly polished over. Almost new. Could hardly have more than four years. The
gilded stripes and lines and patches were still shiny. The paint
like from last month.

"Now, wouldn't she be a peach to have her under your
legs?" I said to Stanislav. "She is so smart she has even painted
eyelashes. Let's have a closer look at her. Trouble is we have
no chance with her."

Stanislav said nothing. He just looked at her as if he meant
to buy her and find out the price for it.

If it were not for the four months' pay I'd have to leave
behind I sure would like to try her. Wonder if I could make
the chief fire me by getting so stiff that on coming aboard
I would go to his cabin and knock him down. Then the old
man might pay me off and keep only half a month's pay for
socking the chief. Or I might go to the old man directly
and tell him I am a Bolshevist, and I have got it in mind to
get up the whole crew, and we would take over the ship
and run her for our own benefit or sell her to Russia. Or I
might go to the skipper and tell him the old story about my
mother back home sick in bed and having an operation and
ask for the biggest advance possible. Once I had this advance
in my pocket, I would watch out for the *Empress* and hop
on when she is hauling anchor. There is still the question of
where she will set me off again, because she cannot take me
with her to England. The British Board of Trade, having so
many thousands of unemployed juicers to take care of, would
be worried to death what to do with me.

Anyway, it costs nothing to work her a bit.

We went into port and there I left Stanislav in a place

he found jolly and needed badly.

Then I strolled back to sweet *Empress.*

"Ahoy, there!" I yelled up, seeing a guy with a white cap leaning against the rail.

"Ahoy yourself!" he answered. "What ye want?"

"Ain't a chance for a fireman?"

"Papers?"

"Nope."

"Naaaw. Sorry. Nothing doing, then, up here."

I had known this before. A pretty, innocent dame like this doesn't take a guy like me up with her. Here I have to bring the marriage license or out you go. Mother is still holding her hand over mousy.

Along the dock I walk, down the whole length of the bucket. On the quarter-deck I see a bunch of the crew squatting, playing cards. I am close enough to understand almost every word they are saying. Now, that's some English they are talking! And on an English can on which the gilded stripes are still sparkling? There must be a ghost somewhere around here. They are playing cards. But they do not quarrel, they do not fight or argue or laugh or swear or accuse one mug of having drawn the wrong card at the right time or the wrong ace at no time, or debate who should have dealt and who not.

Shark-fins and ambergris! What is this? They are squatting as though sitting on their own graves and playing for their own worms. They seem to have the right grub. Look fed all right. Somehow something does not fit. Never seen sailors playing cards with troubled faces like these. Something is queer about the whole safari. A newly born ship. English too. What is she doing here in Dakar anyway? In a port all French—more French, I should say, than Marseille? What's her cargo, anyhow? I'll be— Now, who would believe it? Scrap iron. On the west coast of Africa, close to the Equator. Maybe, she couldn't get cargo on her way home and took scrap iron on for ballast. Makes at least some coin for the company. Home, Glasgow. Maybe they are badly in need of scrap iron in Glasgow. As for ballast, scrap iron is still a better cargo than rocks. Nevertheless, strange that an English bucket with such elegant looks cannot get cargo from Africa to old England or Scotland.

Now, if I hung around here in Dakar a few days, I would find out what's the trouble with that hussy. She can't be a bobtail, can she?

Come to think of it, these birds squatting there are playing cards like deads on their graves. Like deads on— Hello, old masher! Dead ones. But no; it cannot be. It simply cannot be. A dame looking so elegant and innocent, could it be that she is already walking the street? No. No, I am just a bit suntipped. Must be the boiler-scaling. Cracks of scales still in my eyes. I haven't got my eyes clear yet. Seeing things. If I had money to spare, I would go and see the doc.

I walked back and met Stanislav.

"Let's go over to that Norske and have a little talk with them," Stanislav said.

So we went to the Norwegian where Stanislav, yesterday, had made friends with a couple of Danes who came from a section of Denmark which Stanislav knew well. They had a can of fresh butter ready for us to take home. Living like real gents, that's what these guys do. I got a mighty lump of fine Danish cheese extra.

"Now, you two pirates, you are just in time to have supper with us," one of the Danes said. "Sit down on your buttocks and have a real old Danish supper. Quality, and I mean it, and, of course, quantity even more."

So we sat down to a human meal, the kind we had not seen for so long a time that we for a while could not trust our eyes that such suppers still could exist somewhere in the world, and in particular in the foc'sle mess of a freighter.

"Has any of you sailors seen that lime-juicer yonder there?

The what is she? I mean the *Empress of Madagascar?*" I asked
while we were eating.

"Hanging around at the curb-stone quite a bit," one of the
men said.

"Elegant dame," I went on.

"Yip, elegant dame, silk outside, crabs underneath. Better
stay off her."

"But, man, why?" I could not understand it. "Why lay off
her?"

"Silk all right. But if you lift the camisole you might easily
find yourself in a garden full of cauliflowers," the Dane said.

Broke in another one: "She is legal all right. She signs you
on. With honey and chocolate ice-cream. Last dinner every
day. With roast chicken and all the trimmings, and pudding
besides."

"Damn your silly talk," I said impatiently. "Now come along
with the low-down. What's her signal?"

Said the speaker of the house: "You don't look like a John
to me. Rather like a hopper with heaps of salt water inside
the belly. I thought you would guess it for yourself on seeing
her. Well, she is a funeral hussy. Next trip to bottom, with
hell waiting for you."

"Don't you think you are just a bit jealous?" I asked.

"Angel-maker and baby-farmer," the Dane said. "Help
yourself to another cup of coffee. Another treat of beef? Just
stuff it in. We don't have to be misers about milk and sugar.
In the pot. As much as we want. Want to take home another
can of milk?"

"You make tears come into my eyes with such a question,"
I said. "Well, I don't want to offend you, so I will take it."

"Yip, sailor man. She has loaded dead men all right. But
not dead soldiers from France to be taken home to mother
across the pot. Not that. No, dead sailors still eating. But
they may already write home to have their names carved
in the lost sailors' plank in their village church back home.

They can't miss it any more. If you wish to have your own sweet name on a plate in your church, if you have any, just go and sign on. It looks rather distinguished to have right by your own name such an elegant name as the *Empress of Madagascar*. Sounds a lot better than having gone down with an ordinary *Caroline*, or *Clementina Pumpstay*, or *Landshit*. *Empress of Madagascar*, boy, that looks like something great and swell, almost as if you had been her handy boy-friend."

"Why should she try to make insurance cash?" Stanislav asked.

"Simple, honey, like making Swiss cheese around holes."

"She can hardly be out of her diapers three years," I figured.

"Now you got that straight and perfect; I see you can be trusted. Exactly, almost to the day, she is three years old. She was built for East Asia and South American trade to beat the Germans, who are undermining rates again. She was to make sixteen knots at least. The gent who constructed her tried out, it appears, a new model, a new stream line, see, to raise her speed, but with less fuel expenses. As it happened, when she made the virgin hop she could reach four knots only, with asthma. With such a speed any clipper would beat her and she herself couldn't bring in even the pay for the crew, to say nothing of all the other expenses and a profit for the owners. With four knots she was scrap iron. Not even that."

"She could be rebuilt."

"Of course she could. You are a wise guy. But the owners thought of this before you came along and they did rebuild her. Rebuilt her not once, but twice. Each time she came out worse. She has to have the wind at the hams to make four knots now. So she cannot live, and she cannot die honorably. The owners cannot afford to sink her. It would break them. So nothing is left but to cash insurance."

"And you think it will be on her next trip?"

"It has to be. She has tried to cash in twice already within less than three weeks. But she is so bully well that she did not even crack a leak. The first time she went upon a sand-bank. Pretty like a swan she was sitting. I am sure in Glasgow they already celebrated the insurance with champagne. But bad weather came up and with it high water, which embraced the lady and whipped her off fine, off into twenty fathoms, where her old man could not do anything better than steam her off on her way. The second time she tried the game was last week, when we were already lying here. She was sitting smoothly between reefs. Well done by the skipper. He is a smart guy and knows how to navigate a can on a two-inch stripe. Wireless station, of course, was smashed up at the right time, so that the old man had an excuse for not using it. But he had to set flags to keep face and to bake proper witness cakes for evidence. He had tough luck again. Just when he had ordered to lower away the boats, a French coast guard popped up. What that skipper must have cursed when he saw the coast coming! Sure, he had the log already charmed up, and now he had to work the rubber to make it blank again for another fill-in. He had gone between the reefs at low water. The coast sent him, calling by wireless, three tugs. As soon as high water came in again, the tugs got the lady out like on oiled roller-skates."

"And what is she to do now?" I asked.

"Desperation. She has to take her last chance. If she reaches home safely, the Board of Underwriters will sure make an investigation. They will demand a change of skipper. A new skipper has to be worked up by the owners before he is reliable and trustworthy. It may happen that the underwriters back out of her, once she's home again. Then it will be too late for her to make good for her owners. So you see she has to do it on her trip out of here or she can never make it. Around this coast here she must go at it, because it is the safest part, free from the interference of ships rushing in too quick. Here it is silent. Farther north there is too much traffic; besides, there she cannot go off too far from the route, as she easily can do here without arousing suspicion."

I wondered: "Why is she hanging here such a long time?"

"No firemen."

"Silly," I said. "I just passed by her and asked for a chance, saying I am fire'm."

"Got papers?"

"Don't ask herring."

"Without papers she cannot take you. She is English. Rules. Taking in dead ones would look suspicious under these conditions. The investigation might build up a case against her for taking on men without papers who may be inexperienced. She must have good men with clean papers. The firemen were smart. They burnt themselves well enough to be taken to the hospital. Care of the British consul. They know why. Because they are the worst off when she cracks up. The water rushes into the stoke-hold, breaking in the hatchways and gangways, and so they are caught like rats in a trap and cannot get out. They are scorched to death, or drowned, or blown into rags when the furnaces get the cold shower and gun off. The firemen don't have to sign on again, once off. They make time in the hospital until the dame puts out of port."

"How is that bucket to get out without firemen?" I asked.

"Don't you worry, sonny. They are ready for kidnapping, or for shanghaiing, if you like that expression any better."

"Horrible!" was all I could say.

Walking home to our good old *Yorikke*, I could not help thinking of this beautiful ship, with a crew on board that had faces as if they were seeing ghosts by day and by night.

Compared to that gilded *Empress*, the *Yorikke* was an honorable old lady with lavender sachets in her drawers. *Yorikke* did not pretend to anything she was not. She lived up to her looks. Honest to her lowest ribs and to the leaks in her bilge.

Now, what is this? I find myself falling in love with that old jane. All right, I cannot pass by you, *Yorikke;* I have to tell you I love you. Honest, baby, I love you. I have six black finger-nails, and four black and green-blue nails on my toes, which you, honey, gave me when necking you. Grate-bars have crushed some of my toes. And each finger-nail has its own painful story to tell. My chest, my back, my arms, my legs are covered with scars of burns and scorchings. Each scar, when it was being created, caused me pains which I shall surely never forget. But every outcry of pain was a love-cry for you, honey.

You are no hypocrite. Your heart does not bleed tears when you do not feel heart-aches deeply and truly. You do not dance on the water if you do not feel like being jolly and kicking chasers in the pants. Your heart never lies. It is fine and clean like polished gold. Never mind the rags, honey dear. When you laugh, your whole soul and all your body is laughing. And when you weep, sweety, then you weep so that even the reefs you pass feel like weeping with you.

I never want to leave you again, honey. I mean it. Not for all the rich and elegant buckets in the world. I love you, my gypsy of the sea!

THE THIRD BOOK

An old love-song
of an experienced sailor

There are so many ships on sea,
Some do come and some do flee;
Yet none can be so dreadful low
That none is found still further so.

46

I suppose this is a good rule: If you want to keep your wife, do not love her too much. She might get bored with you and run away with somebody who gives her a sound beating twice a week to keep her lively.

My sudden strong love for the *Yorikke* looked rather suspicious, I thought. But having heard right before a hair-raising story of a tough kidnapper, and carrying in one pocket a beautiful can of fine golden Danish butter and a can of milk in the other and a huge lump of rich Danish cheese in my hand, it will be easily understood why I could fall so deeply in love with *Yorikke* and chuck that silken hussy.

Nevertheless, I felt strongly that there was something strange about my growing love for the ragged *Yorikke*. Something was going to go wrong. Maybe the ash-pipe was waiting for me, or the plank across the top of the stoke-hold, or the water-gauge of the boiler. So, with all my ardent love for her, I began to worry and to feel uneasy. Something was hanging in the air for me.

The quarters were stuffy. I could not stand them right now, after having seen the clean quarters of the fine Norske.

"Come on," I said to Stanislav, "let's go off again for a while. We'll stroll along the docks and the water-board until it gets cooler. A fresh breeze is sure to come up soon, likely about nine. Then we go home and sleep on the poop, where it is coolest."

"Right you are, Pippip," Stanislav agreed. "It's near impossible to sleep here now, or even sit around. One feels like getting dumb all over. We might give that little Dutch can a look. Sometimes you meet quite unexpectedly an old friend."

"You don't mean to say you are still hungry?" I asked, laughing.

"Not exactly. But I might get a cake of soap and perhaps even a towel. Things which I really need, and I would sure welcome them."

We hoofed leisurely on our way. It had by now become dark. The lamps of the port could be seen only dimly. No ship was busy taking in cargo or spitting it out. All the ships seemed to have gone to sleep.

"Say, that tobacco the Danes handed us isn't so great when you look closer at it," I said, puffing.

Hardly had I spoken, and I was just turning my head toward Stanislav, when I received a terrific blow on my block. I felt the blow quite clearly when it came down, yet I could not move myself. My legs at once became strangely thick and heavy, and I fell. There was about me a dreadful humming and roaring, the cause of which I could not figure out. Anyway, I was sure that I had not lost my consciousness; at least, I had the impression that I saw and heard everything that was going on around me. That is what I thought.

This sensation did not last very long, it seemed to me. I came to again and rose and tried to walk off. On doing so, I ran against a wall which was iron. All about me it was dark, pitch-dark.

Now, where and what could this iron wall be? I moved to the left. The wall was still there. The same wall I encountered at the right. Also at my back. My head was still roaring and buzzing. I did not know what had happened and what it all was about. From so much thinking and figuring I became very tired. I lay down on the floor.

After some time, when I woke up again, I found the four

walls still there. I could not stand up very well. I staggered
and tumbled. Getting wider awake, I felt that I was not staggering at all, but that the whole floor was swaying.

"Damn the hell and all the devils," I said. "Scram the whole
outfit. Now I know where I am. On a bucket, and she is already well out on high sea. Jolly on our way to hell. The
engine is knocking and stamping in regular time. Must be an
hour or more since the can went under weigh."

It was still dark about me.

With my fists and with my feet I began now to work the
walls to see what would happen. Of one thing I was positively
sure, I was not on the *Yorikke*, because on the *Yorikke* I knew
every nook and corner, and that I might be in our chamber
of horrors was out of the question, for I had had no quarrel
with the skipper in regard to the pay for overtime, and the second would never lay me in. In the first place, he could not
spare so good a drag as I had become during the last four
months. Besides, he knew that he would land in the furnace
the first hour I was out again and below in the stoke-hold.

For a long while nobody seemed to take notice of my bomb-
ing the walls or of my yelling, either. But then a ray of light
fell into the box in which I was. The light widened, and I
saw it came from above. It was a flash-light.

An ugly voice asked: "Finished your snore, you funking
drunkard?"

"Looks like, buddy," I answered. "Hey you, won't you help
me out of here?"

Having said this, I knew where I was and what had happened. Shanghaied. I am on the *Empress of Madagascar*, to be
fed to the fishes and to help sailing-insurance.

"The ole man wan's 'a see ye," the jailor said.

He let below a rope and I climbed up the shaft. Looked to
me as if I was below as far down as the bilge.

"You are a pretty bunch of peach-sons," I said the very moment I stepped into the cabin of the skipper.

"Beg pardon?" the skipper said, with quite a distinguished air.

"Shanghaiers. Man-pirates. Kidnappers. Baby-farmers. Filthy sons of beachcombers, that's what you are, all of you," I bellowed.

The skipper remained undisturbed. He lighted a cigarette and said: "I fancy, my good man, you are still intoxicated. We shall put you for ten minutes under an ice shower to get you sober and to teach you how to address the master of a British vessel. More respect, my good man, when you have the honor to stand in the cabin of a British captain."

I looked into his face and said nothing more. One should not try to catch hissing bullets with bare hands. It does nobody any good, not even the pistol.

The skipper pressed a button.

Then he said: "Sit down."

In came two men. Husky, bully, with horribly crumpled faces, and with the hands of gorillas, they looked like the animal-men roaming wild in mystery stories. The average woman meeting these two birds a quarter of a mile from an inhabited house would have fallen dead on seeing them.

"Is this the man?" the skipper asked.

"Yegh, t'as him all right," one of the two said.

"What are you doing on board my ship?" the skipper asked me. He acted like a judge in an English criminal court; only the wig was missing. Before him there were papers on which he wrote as if he were at the same time his own court clerk. He asked again: "What are you doing here on my ship, and how did you come aboard?"

"That's what I wish to know from you, sir, what I am doing here and how I came to be here."

Now one of the mystery-story animals broke in: " 'Twas t'is way, sir captain, and shoo 'twas t'at. We, my companero an' meshelf, we wae shus like order cleanin' ter hold namber eleven

when wae fall on t'at man in she sleepin' an' much all drunk
from whiskae."

"Well, well," the skipper said. "No more questions needed.
Everything is cleared up. You, my good man, wanted to stow
away on a British vessel with the intention of being taken to
England. I feel sure that you are not in a mood to deny this
accusation. It is a very serious offense under the British law
to stow away on a British vessel with the intention of en-
tering illegally the British Isles. It will cost you no less than
six months' hard labor, perhaps even two years, and deportation. I have every right to throw you overboard, charging you
with intending to blow up a British vessel in the Straits of
Gibraltar and with finding explosives in your possession when
arrested. Of course, as a good and law-abiding British captain,
I would never do such a thing. A man like you ought to be
hoisted up the mast fifty times until you're well skinned, to
remind you of the fact that a British ship is not made to help
criminals run away from the police."

What was there to say? If I had told him what I really
thought of him and what I thought of the social standing of
his mother, the mystery-story animals would have worked me
for three hours. No longer, for I knew that my bones and
my working ability were badly needed. But three hours in
those gorilla hands would sure have been three very nasty hours
for me, and, for the time being, I could not pay them back.

"You are not needed any more, leave us alone," the skipper
said to the huskies.

To me he said: "What are you?"

"Good deck-hand. Painting and brass-polishing, sir."

"You are a stoker."

"No, sir, I am not."

"What is this? You do not mean to lie to a British captain,
do you, my good man? I am informed that, yesterday afternoon, you came around and asked for a stoker's berth, did
you not?"

I did not answer. I only felt sorry that I had made the mistake of saying, the day before, that I was fireman. Had I said I was a deck-hand or a P.S., a plain sailor, they might have lost all interest in my carcass, and I would now be sitting snugly on my beloved *Yorikke*, scaling the second boiler or washing the engine-hold.

I could not wander far off with my thoughts because the skipper said: "Since you are a stoker, you may call yourself very lucky indeed. Two of my stokers have become sick. Tropical fever. You may earn your passage and your bread on my ship. Ten pounds a month, one shilling sixpence an hour overtime when on high sea. Of course, I have no right to sign you on, since you are a stowaway. Upon reaching England, I am sorry, but I shall have to deliver you to the authorities. I shall speak a word or two in your favor in court, provided you obey orders here and do your work well. You may get off with only six months, and of course you will be held for deportation. However, as long as you are here on my ship and you behave as I expect you to, you shall be treated precisely like every other member of the crew. No distinction will be made against you."

I let him have the pleasure of being pleased with his sermon. What else could I do anyway? Nothing; no, sir.

"We may get along fine, provided you do not make any trouble here. If we do not, there will be no fresh water, but plenty of smoked herring. For this reason we would do best to tolerate one another and accept conditions as we find them. Your watch begins at twelve. Watches are six and six hours, because I have no more than two stokers, you included. The two extra hours of each watch will be paid as overtime, at one and six each hour. That will be all. Good morning."

Ahoy, ship! There I was. Fireman on the *Empress of Madagascar*. Well on my way to the wall of my village church. I had no village church, since the last burned down in Chic during the great fire or still earlier. So even this bit of honor, finding my name next to that of the *Empress of Madagascar* on the wall of the church, was denied me.

I might become rich on this tub, for the pay was the up-to-date pay of the British firemen's union. But then there was England with six months of hard labor and two years' waiting for deportation day. The only trouble was that I would never get any pay in my hands. The fishes would get it. Suppose I should have the luck to get away from the reef; I would not get a bob, because I was not signed on. Since I was not signed on, I could not be called to testify in court as to the sinking. So I do not get any money from the insurance, or the board either. I have no proof that I was on the *Empress*. They might even put me in prison as an impostor claiming damages for the shipwreck.

Now, don't you worry, old boy. We won't make England. As to the ground, well, let's have a look at the boats as the best and surest indication of the date.

The boats are ready. Provisions in, and sails, and fresh water. Even gin packed away to keep us jolly. Well, *Empress*, it looks to me the wedding will take place no later than the third day from now.

I have to glance about the stoke-hold to see how I can get out easiest and quickest when the rush breaks in. At the first dim crackling my hearing-flap catches, I shall be up and out so fast that even the devil running after an escaped Presbyterian preacher will get yellow with envy.

47

The quarters are clean and new, reeking with fresh paint and a washing with chloride of lime. Mattresses in the bunks, yet no pillows, no blankets, no sheets. The *Empress* is not quite so rich as she wishes to appear from the outside. It doesn't take me long to know where the pillows and blankets have gone to.

The skipper is smarter than one might have expected. Why send the pillows, blankets, and all such things down to feed the fishes while there is still a market for them?

Most of the dishes are gone also. But enough is left for me to eat like a human being. The meal is brought into the mess by an Italian boy who chatters in a friendly way. The grub is excellent, beyond any criticism. Though I would have thought a last dinner ought to be better. At least it was better at the French fort where I was to be shot as a spy or something.

No rum ever, I am told. The skipper is bone dry and does not give out rum. Being on a ship on which no rum is handed out makes me feel as if I'm sitting in a mission and looking at the silly Bible phrases. How can you walk straight from bow to stern without having some rum laid down in your belly to hold you on your feet?

The mess-boy is calling all hands off duty for lunch.

Two heavy Negroes come in. The drags. Then the fireman comes in. He walks rather heavily and quite swanky.

Now, I have seen that face before. Somewhere. Don't know right now where. Seems to me I must have been once on the same can with him. Wonder who he is.

His face is swollen. Both eyes blackened and blood-shot. A bandage on his head.

"Stanislav, you?"

"Pippip, you too?"

"The same, you see. Caught and caged, and perfect. Looks like we're again in the same stoke-hold," I said to him.

"You got the better of it, Pippip. I took them up. Had a damned fine row with them. Blacked them up and broke them half a dozen fingers. Sure. There is a palm-sized hole in the head of one of them. I got up right after I had the first blow upon my bone. You were lying flat and full out. You got a mighty buzzer under your cap. When I saw you dropping, I bent down the same instant, see. So that blow meant for me in full came on only sidewise. I got up and oared them as they sure never before had been taken. Four they were. But don't you think for a minute that they are still four. Each is only one quarter for permanent use. Want to see them? Go to the port-side bunks. They are still cooling off and plastering all over. I lasted to the last round. But then someone, the fifth, who came in later, got me from behind. I did not know that he belonged. I thought he was rather coming to get me out and give me a hand. So I got a damned hard one on the bean."

"What was the story the skipper told you?" I asked while we were eating.

"Me? There came in two guys telling the skipper that I had been drunk ashore and that in a fight I had stabbed and killed a man, and then I had run aboard the *Empress* to hide and stow away because the police was after me for slaying an innocent citizen of the port."

"Almost what I was told I had done."

"Now," Stanislav said, "on the *Yorikke* we have lost our pay for so many months. Here we will never get a bent penny."

"Won't last long," I said. "Hardly four days. He cannot take her to a better cemetery than the one he is over right now. And be sure it will happen when both you and I are on watch. We two are in boat four. I saw the list in the gangway. The firemen of the watch from twelve to four go into boat four."

"Yep, I know it, I have seen it," Stanislav admitted.

"Got a look at the stoke-hold? How to get out?" I asked.

"Twelve fires. Four firemen. The other two are Negroes. I guess from Kamerun or thereabouts. Speaking a bit English, and quite a bit German. All the drags are also Negroes. Only the petties are white."

"They, of course, will be in the right boat at the right time, especially if they are limeys."

"Telling me. Those men sitting there and eating like dogs, those are the drags of our watch." Stanislav pointed to the two bulky Negroes at the table gulping down their food without any other interest as to what we were saying or doing. Pitiful poor devils they were.

At twelve at night we went below to start our watch. The earlier watches had been served by the donkey, with the help of the Negro drags.

We found all the fires in very bad shape. For two hours we had to work hard to get the fires trim so that they looked like something worth speaking of. Nobody seemed to care here if the fires were going fine or not, or if the steam was holding on, or if it was low to slugging-point. The furnaces were sick with clogged and burned-on slags. The Negroes had no idea how to fire, how to break a fire, and how to clean it. They just threw in as many shovels of coal as the fire would hold, and after having done this they waited to see what would happen to the fire and to the steam.

There are so many firemen, even whites, who never realize that keeping a fire in shape is an art which some men never understand. Working five years before boilers on ships does not make a man a good fireman. If he does not know the art of it, he will be as uninteresting in the stoke-hold after five years as he was when he came below for his first watch.

We had little trouble with grate-bars falling out. The rims were new, therefore wide and strong, so the bars had a good hold on them. One might say it was often hard work to get them out at all, when they had burned away and had to be changed for new ones. It was almost a real pleasure to replace them.

The Negro drags, real giants, with arms like tree-trunks, looked strong enough to carry away on their shoulders the whole boiler and take it up on deck. Yet they dragged in the fuel so slowly that we had to pep them up and curse them to the limit to get sufficient fuel to keep the fires going. Not only were they, despite their huge bodies, unable to furnish the fuel we needed, they were whining all the time that it

was too hot, that they sure were just about to drop dead, that
they were choking and could not get any air, that they were
going to die of thirst and hunger the next minute, and that
their mouths were as full of soot and ashes as if they had
died already and were now swallowing earth.

"Now, just look at these black Goliaths," Stanislav said,
"dying of work which a cabin-boy might do without feeling
overworked. What, compared to this, had we to drag in on
the *Yorikke*? I would like to know what these mammoths
really mean to do with their bones? One arm of theirs is
thicker than my whole chest. Before they get in half a ton
I would drag in six without even so much as wiping my sweat
off. And here they have got the whole coaling-station right
at arm's length. I can't figure that out. Not for ten dollars."

"A pity," I said, "to have to leave behind the *Yorikke* right
now, after we have scaled the boilers and have shoveled in all
the coal from the most distant bunkers. Now comes the easy
time on the *Yorikke*, with fresh fuel filled up right next to the
stoke-hold, and the next five or six days there would have been
sheer pleasure sailing. Shit, damn the *Yorikke*, we have got
other things to worry about. So, what's the good of crying
about a dame you can't have any longer? Maybe she is going
to the taxi dance. What do I care?"

I gazed about the stoke-hold, about all the gangways, hatchways and port-holes.

Stanislav followed my looks and said: "I have viewed
quite a bit already. What we have to do above all is to look
for air-holes where to snap out quickest and easiest. We cannot reach the gangway. That much is certain. Usually they
break off first thing when the crash comes. Just fly away from
the pipes and boilers when you hear the faintest crackling.
The gangway leading up and out is always liable to make a
trap out of which you have no chance to escape. Once up, you
mostly cannot come below any more on account of steam
and boiling water. So better don't try the gangway at all."

When I was through with my inspection I reported to Stanislav: "The upper bunker has got a hatchway leading clear out on deck. We have all the time to keep the way to this bunker clear and the hatchway loose so we can't be caught. I shall take care to fix up a provisional rope ladder, which we'll keep here in good shape."

Stanislav went to examine the way I had told him about. When he came back he said: "You are smart, Pippip. I have to hand it to you. It is the surest and the only safe way out. All right, we will stick to that and make no other trial."

Our work before the boilers was easy. We could have done all there was to do with one lazy hand. We didn't have to worry about heaving out the ashes. The two Negro drags did it.

The engineers never pestered us; in fact, they never popped in. None of them ever complained about the steam-pressure. As long as the engine was still moving, the engineers seemed satisfied. If the *Empress* was speeding or just tumbling along on her way to the last ceremony did not concern anybody.

The funeral could be arranged quite easily in the usual way. Half a dozen good-sized holes drilled into the hull near the bilge. All of them on port side, to make the can lie over softly but surely. The cargo of scrap iron would hasten the effect elegantly. Then it would only be necessary to give all the pumps a punch on the nose. The wireless station would be out of commission accidentally at the very minute the holes begin to suck. Wireless stations do such things. They are not perfect yet. Any shipping board will testify to that and accept it as evidence. A few members of the crew have to go along with the hearse. Otherwise suspicion will arise. The point is, every suspicion has to be avoided. The two or three guys who do the drilling of the holes and the boxing of the pumps must be safe. They are well paid, and if they say anything wrong before the board, they find themselves quickly confronted with three different traps out of which it is rather difficult for them ever to escape again. First, they are accused of being implicated in a crime. Second, they are accused, on account of having been bawled out by the skipper for something, of looking for revenge and trying to get square with the skipper by accusing him of a crime which everybody knows a British licensed captain would never commit. Third, the good old way, taking the guys for a pretty ride. Knowing all this, and keeping it in mind for the rest of their lives, these two or three undertakers keep mum. Anyway, it is not their money that is lost, and other people's money does not hold any interest for them.

There are still other ways. Ways often tried out, and just as safe. Who the hell knows how that bomb with nitro-glycerine happened to be in an innocent-looking case among the cargo? We had better arrest a couple of anarchists and well-known communists, search their lodgings, and find a few similar bombs right under their beds in an old leather bag. The judges and the gentlemen of the board and all the experts who testify in court hate anarchists and communists; they know that all communists do such nasty things, and so the insurance is paid. The judge does not pay. Nor do the gentlemen of the board. The underwriters pay. They also hate communists. So this case helps them to make better laws against communists and criminal syndicalists.

It was not our business to worry about which way it would be done this time. Fact is, we had no time to find out. The whole affair happened, even to us who were prepared, at a time and moment when we least expected it.

48

We had thought the music would start a day later. As it happened, it was only two days after we had been for the first time below before the boilers.

We had just relieved the former watch at midnight, and we were about to break up the fires when there was a terrific bang, and right afterwards a crash. I knew by instinct that the funeral was to take place when Stanislav and I would have the watch. Because then two white men who had every reason to wish the skipper the worst in court or out of court would be done away with. The Negroes, the Portuguese, the Italians from Malta, and the Greeks did not count. They were all tramp sailors who knew nothing about ships.

When the crash came, I was thrown against the furnaces. With the bump that followed I fell back into a big pile of coal.

I had a queer feeling, the cause of which I could not figure out for a second. For a moment I thought that I had gone partly nuts since I felt so strange. But then it dawned upon me that the boilers were standing up vertical, the furnaces above me. So I knew that the bow had gone down and the stern was high up in the air.

All this thinking and reckoning, of course, rushed like a flash through my mind. I had no time to reflect on this or anything else. For some of the furnaces, on which we had been still working when the crash came, had not been closed fully. They now broke open and shed out their fires into the stoke-hold. As only a few furnaces had broken open, I found that I could step out of the mess by jumping between those heaps of white glowing coal and cinders. The electric lights went dim, and almost at the second when I reached the starboard hull they went out. There was still sufficient light in the stoke-hold from the heaps of glowing coal now spilling out faster and faster. I knew that it would be only twenty seconds or so and the boilers would explode. The steam-pipes would bust even before that, filling the stoke-hold with so much hot steam that you could never find your way out safely, because the steam would boil you and make you sightless and utterly helpless.

I did not see Stanislav. I made for the rope ladder leading up to the bunker. It was not necessary to climb up the ladder, because, since the bow was now down I could walk straight into the bunker and out through the hatchway as if on a plain floor.

When I reached the bunker I saw Stanislav already climbing out.

At this very moment when I felt safe we heard a pitiful yell.

Stanislav, with one leg over the hatchway, turned around and called to me: "That's Daniel, the drag. We can't leave him. Guess he is caught."

"Damn it all," I said, "we have to get him."

"Snappy," Stanislav answered, "come in again and get him. But, for all the devils, run or we are finished."

In a whiff we were back in the stoke-hold. The boilers seemed still to hold on for a few seconds. The heaps of fires began now to fill the whole cave with smoke. But they were still glowing and rendering enough light so that we could make out where Daniel, one of the giant Negroes, was lying. With all this smoke and glow the stoke-hold looked like the underworld for ghosts.

Daniel was caught with his left foot under a heavy slab of iron broken off or fallen from somewhere. We tried to lift that slab, but we could not even move it. We tried madly to raise it with the poker. We failed.

"Can't make it, Daniel," I yelled at the Negro; "your foot is stuck and stays stuck."

We tried to drag him out under the plate. We saw we should have to tear him apart to get him out this way. We could not leave him. And we had to go out or we would never make it.

It was then, when the hold brightened up from a flare of the open fires, I noticed the cracking of a steam-pipe, which was bent and upon which one boiler was sinking. The crack just began to hiss, and while not actually seeing it, one could feel that the crack was beginning to widen like the seam of a garment.

"Gadsake," I hollered to Stanislav, "the main pipe is coming."

Stanislav gave it only a glance and yelled at the same time: "Where is the hammer? Get it."

Before he had ended his words I had flung the sledgehammer into his hands. He grasped a shovel and with one mighty stroke of the hammer he flattened out the shovel so that it looked like a crude plowshare with a handle. He set that plowshare against Daniel's knee-joint, put the handle in my hand, and cried: "Hold it this way, hell of it."

I did. With another heavy stroke with the hammer upon the plowshare he cut deep into Daniel's leg. He had to give it two more strokes before the leg was cut through. Now we could drag Daniel out into the bunker and then through the hatchway on deck. The deck, like all other things, was naturally no longer horizontal, but standing up vertically.

Close to the hatchway was Daniel's partner, the other Negro drag of our watch. He had not cared about his brother. He had made his get-away as quick as he could. Now we handed him his crippled pal, and he took good care of him. That must be said.

The whole bow, and with it the forecastle, was under water. The stern was high up in the air. Such a position for the ship had never been tried out at the life-boat drills, which were held every Saturday at two o'clock sharp. Everything about the ship was in a position to which a sailor can seldom find himself accustomed.

The electric lights on deck were still burning. The engineer doubtless had switched the light over from the dynamo to the storage batteries. Apparently the batteries began to draw water, or their fluid had started to leak out. So the lights were getting fainter.

Climbing and crawling about the deck we saw the mates,

the skipper, the engineers, the cook, and a few others whom I could not distinguish. They went about with lanterns and flash-lights, trying to get the boats clear.

I did not see anybody from the foc'sle. They had been drowned like mice in a trap.

The officers, with the help of the galley-boys and the cook, were working hard to get the boats below. Boat two tore off and was, at the same moment, carried away by the sea without a man in it.

Boat four could not be cleared at all; neither could boat six. Boat five could not be reached, and, besides, it was already so heavily battered that it would have been of no use.

So there remained only two boats with a chance to get off.

Boat one came clear. The skipper ordered the men who were to man it. I was not among them, nor was Stanislav. The skipper did not go with it. He was standing on the aft wall of the main-house on midship. He tried to give us the impression that he knew it was his duty to be the last to leave the ship. When such a gesture comes up in the investigation court it looks fine, and it always makes a good story for the sob-sisters. So the underwriters do not feel plucked, and they admit that it was the will of the Lord, against which we can do nothing, and therefore they pay the insurance in full.

Now, all the men still aboard, hanging and crawling against the vertical decks, tried to catch boat three, the last left for use. We got three clear and after much trouble had it jumping upon the waves.

The skipper ordered the manning. Stanislav and I were about to go with the boat, also two of the engineers, the Negro Daniel and his Negro partner, who carried and guarded him. Later there came with us the first mate, a junior assistant, and the steward.

It appeared that the boilers were holding on boldly, obviously for the reason that some of the fires had fallen out and the others lost their strength since, owing to the position of the ship, they were no longer right underneath and within the boilers, but sideways. The stoke-hold, of course, was by this time so full of poisonous carbon gas, heat, steam, and boiling water that anybody caught there would be standing already outside the gate of—well, wherever he had to wait for the trumpets. If the boilers hadn't behaved so well, nothing of the ship or of us would still have existed.

The skipper, after hollering and whistling several times for any man who might still answer, finally ordered the boats to make off. He took his place in boat one. We had an emergency lantern, and so had the other boat. Besides, there were a few flash-lights still in the hands of the officers and the engineers. All together they yet gave only a dim and restless light.

We made our boat clear and pushed off. So did boat one.

The sea was not heavy. A sailor with a good ship under his feet would even have called it a sunshine sea. But it was rough, really rough. One had not felt it while the ship was under weigh. Yet in these small boats one got the feeling of a very lively sea. Close to reefs and rocks in the open the sea behaves in general rather differently from the way it does farther off the reef. While elsewhere the waves may reach a height of only from four to seven feet, near a reef and hidden rocks the waves may reach often three or five times this height, especially when, as often happens, two or three different currents meet at the rocks. The wrecked ship sets up another obstacle to the free movement of the sea, and therefore close to the wreck the sea acts even more unruly.

Taking into consideration these circumstances, it will be easy to understand why those peculiar accidents occurred which changed the whole pile of beautiful plans the skipper had worked out so carefully. It is safe to say that our strange position had never entered his reckonings.

Boat one struggled hard to come clear of the ship. It was a difficult thing to do. It might have been easier in full daylight. Perhaps. In daylight one may get the timing of the waves and try to make off on an outgoing one. Now, when the boat was about twenty yards off and the men were just about to stretch the oars and bring them into the water, a mighty wave crashed the whole boat against the hull of the ship.

Something else happened, right at the same moment when the boat was hard against the hull. One huge part of the ship broke loose and fell with a bang upon the boat, shattering it to uncountable pieces. We heard the cries and yells of the men. But as suddenly as these outcries had appeared, so did they drop into silence. I had a feeling that bang, yells, and boat had been swallowed in one single gulp by a giant sea-monster all at the same moment. Nothing more was heard of this boat. It sure was the most elegant insurance collection, because "even the skipper had sacrificed his life to save the ship." All persons present in court would rise and stand in silence for two minutes in honor of the skipper and his brave crew.

We had managed fine to get out of the crashing and sucking waters near the ship. But we had practically no skilled oarsmen with us, save the first mate. Usually mates do not know much about it, but Stanislav was a first-class man at the oars. I did my best to help him. Daniel could do nothing. He was moaning and begging for a shot of gin to dope his terrible pain. The other Negro had never had an oar in hand any time during his life. The steward was useless. The mate was out of practice. His strokes were brakes rather than pulls. So we could not make any speed.

The mate had a compass. He gave us the supposed direction toward the coast.

The sea was far more unruly than we had imagined. We were tossed high upon the waves and thrown into deep valleys. The oars, so badly manned, did not pull our boat in any given direction. We appeared to circle about the same spot.

Then all of a sudden the engineer said: "Mate, I think we're on shoals or rock. Hardly more than three feet."

"Can't be," the first mate answered. He took his oar and sounded the depth: "You are right, chief. Get out of here, you men, or we go to the devil."

Before he could catch breath enough to say one word more, the whole boat was lifted high up upon a tower-like wave as though it were only a plank. When we were at the crown of the wave, the boat stood still for a fraction of a second and I thought that the wave would go out from under us and leave the boat hanging in mid-air. At that moment another mighty wave caught the boat in its huge fists, whipped it down, and crashed it heavily against the naked rock, and the boat was splintered into a thousand pieces.

No cry was heard, which made me feel sure that the others had been thrown so hard upon the rocks that they must have been left like fleshy rags.

I felt myself lifted up on another wave.

More to assure myself that I was still alive than to cry for help, which would have been silly anyway, I hollered: "Stanislav, have you something to hold on?"

For a short while I heard no answer. But then, his voice still with that twang of a mouth full of water, Stanislav cried back: "Not even a twig. Funk it all, the whole mess. Hey, listen, Pip, I am making back for the tub. Safest place right now. She sure will stay on for a day or two. She won't fall in two yet. Come along. Ride down the waves."

Naturally, he did not say all this in one sentence. The flow of his speech was interrupted by the pails of sea-water which old man Neptune gunned into his swear-hold.

His idea was not so bad. It couldn't be. Because any other idea would have been without sense. I managed to keep my course to that dark tower which could be seen against the dimness of the horizon.

Both of us reached this goal, the dying *Empress of Mada-*

gascar. It had not been easy. Dozens of times we had been thrown back and forth before we finally got hold of this haven in a restless world.

We climbed up, using the bulwark as a gangway. Reaching midship was quite a task, for we had nothing to hold on. We had to go a long way around up to the stern, and from there drop foot by foot until we dropped finally upon the wall aft of the midship-castle. This aft wall now was the deck, while everything else aboard had become steep walls. The two gangways, or corridors if you wish, the one at port side, the other at starboard, were in fact now shafts and no longer corridors. Going down these shafts, one had to climb from door to door, using the door-knobs and hinges for steps. The skipper's cabins and the officers' mess were at the end of the gangways toward the bow, now at the bottom of the shafts.

The *Empress* was standing like a strange tower firmly squeezed in between two rocks. Extraordinary as this position seemed to me then, I learned later that positions like that one have happened before, may happen, and do happen, although rarely. How she could have gone into that position only she could have explained. She stood so solidly that one might have thought she had become part of the rock upon which she had gone to die. She did not shake or tremble. One felt only now and then a sort of rumble whenever a particularly high and strong wave struck her and tried to lift her out between the rocks and throw her over, so as to give her the final shot of grace. At such times she quivered lightly, as if she were frightened of something terrible which she felt might soon take place. But after that she again stood rock-like.

There was no gale. Not even a strong wind. The unusually heavy breakers that came strolling along and pounded unceasingly against the ship seemed to come from a storm-center far away. The outlook was for no heavy weather within the next six hours or so. The sky had been dark all night, without being really black. Just covered over with light, fluffy clouds, which seemed ready to change into mist.

We crawled round to the galley, which was open. We went in and slept there as best as we could.

The sky began to turn gray. The sun came up over the horizon and gilded the sea. Fresh and clean and golden she rose from her bath in the sea and went climbing up the firmament like an invincible warrior for ever fighting against the powers of darkness. I could not recall any time in all my life when a rising sun made such an impression of earthly glory upon me. It made me feel inside happy and proud of being man and living in an age when such a sun was the lord of the world.

We looked out over the sea. Nothing was to be seen. Nobody seemed to have survived. I had no confidence that someone might come along and pick us up. Stanislav felt the same way. All day yesterday we had met no ship and had seen not even the faintest smoke-line of a ship passing in the distance. So we knew that the skipper had brought the *Empress* as far out from the ordinary routes as possible. His two former experiences had taught him to stay away from passing ships and coast guards and patrol-boats. He had hoped and worked for an easy burial, and then a fine get-away for himself and a few men. He had not taken into consideration that he might lose the whole crew of the foc'sle, all the men who were trained oarsmen. The A.B. standing by the helm had been thrown through the front windows out of the bridge and had disappeared. The two look-outs at the bow had gone down before all others. If the boats had been manned as provided for in the boat-lists, at least two boats would have gone off and away without any trouble.

49

By now daylight had become complete. We set out to explore. And for breakfast. We climbed down the gangways.

At the bottom we came into the two cabins of the skipper. I found a pocket-compass and took possession of it. But Stanislav had to keep it, for I had about me no pocket without holes. In the cabin there were two fresh-water tanks for the personal use of the skipper. In the officers' mess we discovered later two more tanks, which were larger than the skipper's. It was likely that we would not run short of water for a month or longer, if, as we were sure, the pumps in the galley would draw water from the ship's fresh water tanks, which certainly still held a thousand gallons. Of course it might be that these tanks had been cracked and were leaking.

On the *Yorikke* we had been familiar with every hidden hold. We could have found on the *Yorikke* the farthest and deepest nook without a glimpse of light. Here it was different. We knew nothing about the ship. But no sooner came the question "When do we eat?" than Stanislav, using his trained sense, found the storehouse. Looking at it, we were convinced that we could live for six months like Balkan kings in Paris. We would not even have to drink fresh water, for the store was well stocked with stout, ale, different sorts of wine, brandy, and a row of gallon-sized bottles with soda water and mineral water. And we had seriously believed the skipper a perfect dry. He would have been the first and only Scotch skipper whom I ever heard of as a dry.

We set up the stove in the galley and fired it. Now we could cook. We tried the pumps. One of them did not draw, but the other brought out fresh water in thick streams. It was cool;

the refrigerator seemed to have worked well until the last minute.

We had an elegant breakfast. Nothing was missing. It was better even than I had ever seen on the *Tuscaloosa*. *Tuscaloosa*, New Orleans, Jackson Square. Well, let us not think. Thinking won't do me any good when I'm on a reef off the west coast of Africa.

After we had eaten and while we were smoking the skipper's cigars, I began to feel slightly sick. Stanislav too seemed not to be at ease.

For a while I thought there must have been something wrong with the food.

Then Stanislav said: "Now, Pippip, what do you know about that? I am getting sea-sick. Has never happened to me since I sailed for the first time on a Fünen fishing-boat."

I became worse than a lubber on his first trip in heavy weather. No explanation could be found. The ship was firmly bedded between the rocks. The heavy breakers thundering, now and then, against the huge mass of the *Empress* made her sometimes tremble slightly, but that could not be the cause of our sickness.

After thinking, Stanislav said: "Now I can tell you what the trouble is with us. It's that idiotic position of the cabin, with the heavy breakers going up and down all the time while we are standing still. Everything is head under foot. See? We have to get used to that position, and after a day or two we will be fine."

"Right you are," I admitted.

We left the cabin, climbed up upon the aft wall of the mainhouse, then upon the bridge, and there the sickness left us, although we still felt funny having a ship in such a crazy position and set in a strange angle against the horizon.

The excellent cigars we were smoking made me a wise man. I said to Stanislav: "You see, it's like this: only what you talk into yourself, only that makes you what you are. What I mean is this, I am sure that as soon as we learn to distinguish all that is imagination from what is established fact we shall realize very remarkable things, and we shall look henceforth at the whole world from a different point of view, without interference from any coined slogans or phrases or cheap ideas. I wonder to what far-reaching results such a change in thinking and general outlook might lead us."

Stanislav did not follow me. I had thought all the time that he was a philosopher of high standing, taking things as they came and making the most of them.

He took up my last word: "Lead. Right you are, Pippip. We could lead the most beautiful life any sailor has ever dreamed of or read about. We have here everything we want. We may eat and drink what we wish, even caviar and Chablis, or a good English smoked herring washed down with two quarts of stout. Nobody butts in here and cranks about what we are doing or talking. But what's all the good of it? The quicker we could get out of here, the better, I would feel. Suppose no bucket shows up, I figure we'll have to do something to reach the coast. Every day the same. That's what you can't stand. I sure do not believe there is such a thing in heaven or under heaven as what is called paradise. For I can't figure where the rich go. They can't go to the same place where the sailors go and all the communist workers. Anyway, I tell you, if there should be a paradise and I was unlucky enough to be shipped there, I would yell the most terrible blasphemies day and night and in the afternoon, just for the sake of being thrown out, so that I have not any longer to play the harp and always sing church hymns with stale Methodist sisters, and with seamen's mission preachers, and with mission librarians, and with those hussies that come aboard looking in the foc'sle for photographs from Spain to confiscate them and then sleep with them after much praying to save sinful sailors. Hell must be a pleasure to get away from revivals and collections for the salvation of the heathen."

I laughed and said: "Don't you worry, Stanislav, you and me, we won't get in there. In the first place, we have no papers, no passports. You may depend on that all right; they ask papers from you when you come to the gate. Stamped by consuls and passport-office clerks with the okay of an Episcopalian deacon. Or else they bang the door right in your face. And don't be short of papers that make a modern citizen, such as birth-certificate, vaccination-certificate, certificate of baptism, certificate of confirmation, marriage license, income-tax receipts, receipts that you have paid your light-bills and for the telephone, an affidavit that you have no connections with criminal syndicalism or Moscow, and a certificate from police headquarters that there are no charges against you still pending. You think what I say is funny. But why the hell does a man need so many papers here on earth if no one would ask for them up there? Doesn't every preacher tell you everything on earth here is only a preparation for the beyond? So are all the papers and passports, only preparations to have them in good shape when knocking at the gate to be let in."

"Now, what you say, Pippip," Stanislav answered, "makes me think. The whole mess we are in does not fit me all right. Everything we have here is too good to last. It can't last, I tell you. I am suspicious of the whole safari here. Having such silly luck as we have, I think there must be something wrong. I simply can't stand by. All looks like as if this good luck and all this splendid grub and drinks has been shipped to us for the simple reason that something very tough is kept in store for you, and they wish to pep you up and fix you well before you get the finale done. I know that feeling. It was plumb sure exactly the same before we went into that fight off Skagen."

"Shucks. Don't talk liver-wurst. You're the kind of guy who spits out roast chicken when it flies into your open mouth, to avoid meeting with tough luck. All nasty things come by themselves. They don't need any help from you. Live your

life when you have it; you don't know a thing what will be
hereafter, and there may be no way of making good what
you lost while still here."

Stanislav picked up his usual good humor. He laughed and
shook off his depression and his German philosophy mixed
with Slav fatalism. He whistled. But right after that he said:
"Damn it, a sailor whistling. Funking hell, I don't know what
is the matter with me. Guess I have eaten too well. I am an old
fool, that's what I am. Never before in all my life did I have
such rotten ideas. Only today. It all started while we were
sitting in the old man's cabin, in his easy chairs, at his table,
drinking out of his glasses, using his mess-gear. And there it
was that I thought: Now we are eating here like real gents,
and right there, below your feet, almost touching them, there
are swimming in the foc'sle all the guys you saw yesterday still
alive. You have only to crawl down through a few feet of
water, smash in the doors, and out they come floating, all
dead, swollen already, with their eyes wide open. They won't
allow us to sit here quietly and eat and drink like kings. They
sure will call the unseen visitor of the ships to come and get
us off the table and join them. A ship is something alive, with
a soul, and therefore she does not like to have in her bowels
dead sailors, who give her indigestion. Corpses as a paid-for
cargo, that is different. That is all right. But no dead sailors
swimming and floating about, and no way to spit them out. I
hate it."

"What can we do about it?" I asked. "Can we help it?"

"Exactly what I mean," Stanislav said. "We can do nothing.
That's what makes it so bad. And look at this: all the others
have gone fishing, while just we two have been left. Just we
two. There must be something wrong somewhere."

"Look here, Stanislav, what's the use of spitting like that?
And if you don't get quiet, I shall change quarters. Yours will
be the starboard gangway, mine the port-side one. And
we won't even say hello when we meet. As long as I am still

alive, I won't listen to such nonsense. There is plenty of time later when we are washed off here. Besides, if you seriously want to know my opinion as to that queer leaving us behind alone—but, boy, there is nothing to talk about. We simply did not belong. We were shanghaied, kidnapped, robbed, stolen. We were not here on our own account. We surely never wished anything bad to the *Empress of Madagascar*. She had never done us anything wrong. So why should we help her to her funeral? And she knows it. She had no reason to do us any harm. That's why we are still sitting here, whereas all the rest of them have gone off."

"Why, for all the funking sons, didn't you tell me this before, Pippip? Of course, you are right."

"I am not your legal adviser. Besides, you never asked me, and you are not paying for it either," I said. "And look here, Stanislav, really you should be less ungrateful toward fate."

"What do you mean by that, Pippip?"

"What I said. You are ungrateful, that's what you are. You need a guy to tell you that. Destiny has made you half-partner of one of the latest issues of His Majesty's merchant marine. She is a bit slow. I will admit that. But so are others which are less beautiful. If somebody makes you a gift of a fine turkey, you wouldn't be so rude as to ask also for the cranberry sauce, would you? You are not only fifty-fifty on this most elegant British ship, you are also half-owner of a store the like of which you won't find in many ports along the coasts of western Africa. Caviar, jam, jelly, golden butter, milk, tips of asparagus, spinach, plum pudding, ten different kinds of soups, meats, fish, fruits, all the crackers you need, biscuits, and then, the honey of all, ale, stout, real Scotch, three brands, cognac, French wine, Italian wine, Port wine, Malaga wine. Man, Stanislav, you do not deserve what destiny has dropped into your lap. You are rich, Stanislav, did you ever realize that? You are a ship-owner. We may form the company right now. I vote for you as president if you vote for me as the vice-pres, yes, siree. I mean it. Has the world ever seen an ungrateful guy like you? Owning an eight-thousand-register-ton ship and then still worrying about the running expenses. I guess I will go below and shake me up a cock. Just feel like."

"That's right." Stanislav was again the jolly partner he had always been. "I am going with you and get drunk. Who knows, a can may hop along and pick us up, and for the rest of my life I would never forgive myself for leaving behind all these treasures without having even tasted them."

So there now began a banquet which could not have been any better for the original owners of the *Empress* when it was newly born out of the shipyard. I think we got mighty soused. Whether we spent at this banquet one day or four I could never figure out. We got sober and drunk, and sober and drunk again. How many times this happened neither of us could tell.

Occasionally, to cool off our heads, we went up on deck and looked around for a passing ship. We never saw one. We felt sure none had seen us, or it would have come close to see what was up with our ship, standing on her head, with her buttocks high in the air.

"We are getting sour weather," Stanislav said one afternoon.

He was right. It came up late in the evening. It was getting heavier and wilder every hour. Looked like one of the worst that came along those parts of western Africa.

We were sitting in the skipper's cabin, which was lighted up by a swinging kerosene lamp.

Stanislav went restlessly to the windows and then back again to his seat.

"What's the rag?" I asked. "You can't do anything about this heavy sea coming up."

He looked at me with a pretty worried face. He said after a while: "Tell you, Pippip, if this weather comes up the way I see it coming on, it is very likely the *Empress* slips off the reef, is thrown over, and goes down with this heavy water-filled bow of hers like gliding off the rails of a shipyard. Then we will have hardly any time to get out of her suck-water. I tell you we'd better look in time how to get off her before she takes us for a ride with no return ticket."

He found about ten yards or so of rope, which he tied around his body to have it ready and with him all the time. I found in a drawer a ball of strong cord about as thick as an ordinary pencil.

"Let's climb up on our deck," Stanislav advised. "It's better for us to sit there in the open than to stay inside. We would be trapped here in this cabin the same minute she makes off, and then we would have no chance to get clear. Being in the open and free to move, there is always a chance of getting away in time."

We came up, and there we were sitting again on the aft wall of the main-house. The gale had become so hard that we had to hold on to the rings and hooks we found in the wall.

Wilder and wilder the gale came up. Breakers powerful as trains at full speed crashed against the main-house. We expected any minute to see the bridge break off and be carried away. The breakers came higher and higher until every third breaker reached us and washed us all over. The skipper's cabins and the mess-cabins were now flooded with water.

"If this weather lasts all night through," Stanislav said, "there will be nothing left of the bridge and fore part of the main-house by the morning. Looks like the sea is quite ready to carry off the whole house on midship. We'd better work before that happens, Pippip. Let's climb up on the aft wall of the stern-house, where the rudder machinery is. Seems the safest place. But good-by, lordly eats and kingly drinks. The rudder-house has not enough left-overs to feed even a young mouse."

"All right with me, Stanislav, let's go and make the rudder-house."

"There is still the probability that, supposing the weather calms down, part of the main-castle will stay. The house does not go off with just one blow. It breaks off piece by piece. We may just still wait an hour before we try to climb up. Here we have a hold, but while climbing we are at the mercy of the breakers; if they whip us at the wrong time, we are all washed off."

So we hung on waiting for our chance to start to climb.

Three gigantic waves, each of them seemingly ten times as heavy as any of those that had licked the *Empress* so far, whipped against the wreck with such a roar that we thought the end of the world was close.

The third of these gigantic breakers caused the *Empress* to rock heavily. She still stood firmly upon the reef, but we had the feeling that she had broken loose, or that one of the rocks between which she had been squeezed had cracked. She trembled as never before. We no longer were sure that she was standing upon the rocks like a tower.

The sea seemed to know that the end of the *Empress* was near and that nothing could save her now from her fate. Dark thick clouds were tossed above us like so many torn rags. The storm seemed to grow into a greater rage so as not to be laughed at by the thundering and roaring waves.

Through these rags of clouds we could see, for a few seconds, the shining stars that, in spite of all the uproar, called down upon us the eternal promise: "We are the Peace and the Rest!" Yet between these words of promise we could see another meaning: "Within the flames of never ceasing creation and restlessness, there we are enveloped; do not long for us if you are in want of peace and rest; we cannot give you anything which you do not find within yourself!"

"Stanislav," I hollered, "the breakers are coming on again. There she goes. The *Empress* is dragging off."

I saw, in the dim light of the stars, the first breaker closing in on the *Empress* like a huge dark monster.

Then it fell upon us. We felt its hundreds of wet claws trying to tear us away from our hold.

With all our strength we held on. But the *Empress* was lifted high up—standing for a while, it appeared to us, at the very peak of the bow—then she made a half-turn and stood quivering and trembling as though in terrible fright or in pitiful pain.

The second breaker leaped at us even more strongly, and we lost our breath under it. I felt that I had been thrown into the sea, but I still had iron rings in my hands, and so I knew that I was still on the ship.

The *Empress* now moaned like a human being dying of horrible wounds. She turned around slightly. High up at her stern she staggered and began to lean over toward port side. We heard her hull cracking and heard hatches or masts breaking away. No longer did she stand upright with her stern straight up toward the clouds. Again she quivered all over. To see the death of a young woman who does not want to die cannot be more painful than watching the *Empress* resist so bravely the onrushing end. Strange it was that although my own end was as close as hers, I felt like a dying soldier on the battle-field who forgets his own death when he sees how painfully his buddy is making off to glory.

Suddenly, almost without knowing it, I roared: "Stanislav, ahoy!"

I did not know for sure if he had yelled also. I think he must have done so, but I heard nothing.

The third breaker came on. It was the heaviest and most powerful of all. It came entirely conscious of its victory.

The *Empress* seemed to have become indifferent already. She showed no reaction any longer. It was as though she had died of fright.

The third breaker roared and thundered and raged. Yet it was a useless comedy. The *Empress* was dead. She did not tremble when this last breaker caught her, nor did she rock or

waver. She lay down ever so gently. The little waves which
run after the outgoing breaker like so many little tails caressed
and kissed the *Empress* when she fell onto her knees and
glided smoothly down into her last berth.

Another breaker rushed on like a hustling undertaker. The
Empress was softly lifted up once more, she was whirled
around in a half-turn, and without cracking or knocking her
hull upon the rocks, she was laid on her side, and with a last
gargle, ghostly against the uproar of the sea, she was buried.

Before she disappeared entirely, I heard Stanislav holler:
"Jump off and swim, Pippip, swim for your life or you will
be caught in the wash down. Get away from her."

It was not quite so easy to swim as Stanislav had suggested,
for I had received a good knock on my arm by a broken mast
or something that had broken loose.

I nevertheless swam with all my strength. A wave had
caught me, and it threw me far enough out of the wash so that
I could make off the sinking *Empress* without being in danger
of being caught by her eddy.

"Pippip, ahoy!" I heard Stanislav yelling. "Where are you?
Are you clear?"

"I am. Come up here!" I hollered back. "Come on here! I
have got plenty room for you. No, here! Here, ahoy. Here
I am. Hold on. Here, here, come on. Ahoy, hoiho!"

I had to holler some time before Stanislav could make out
in which direction to swim to reach me.

After a long while he came close. He reached me. I lent
him a hand and he climbed up where I was hanging on.

50

"Like to know what's this we are sitting on," Stanislav asked.
"I don't know myself. I was thrown upon it," I said. "I

couldn't even tell exactly how it happened. I figure it must be a wooden wall from one department of the bridge. Perhaps from the chart-room. Here are some iron rings set in with bolts and brass handles."

"I didn't have time to look at the bridge cabins closely," Stanislav said, "or else I would know where this wall comes from. Anyway, it doesn't matter what it is and where it comes from. Lucky that there are still some parts on some cans that are still made of wood. Otherwise we should not be here."

I agreed. "Makes me think of the old story-books in which you can always see a sailor or a cabin-boy embracing a mast floating upon the high waves. Nothing doing in times like ours. Masts also are now made of steel. Just try to embrace a broken-off mast of a sunken ship today and see where you'll head at high speed. If you ever see another picture like that in a book or in the movies, just cry out loud that the book-maker or the movie-director is a cheater. Sock him if you can get him."

"My, you have got a nerve to talk such silly nonsense right now under the conditions we are in." Stanislav seemed to be sore at me.

"What do you expect me to do? Mourn about a bucket that went off under our feet? Sing hymns? Say my evening prayer kneeling before the bed? Or cry like mother's baby who has put his fingers in the hot gravy? Hell, who knows where we shall meet within an hour or so? It's now maybe my last chance to tell you what I think about steel tube masts. And, mark my words, that sure is something which ought not to be forgotten, because it is very important indeed. Masts are no longer of real use to make a good story."

Morning was still far away. The night was heavy and dark. The waves were high. We were thrown up and down. Hardly a star could be seen. It was cold. The sea was, on the other hand, lukewarm, as it is in the tropics.

"We are lucky, damn it. Clear off and safe like that," Stanislav said. ·

"To the devil you go with your whining. Beseeching all the guys down at the bottom. You are a luck-killer. Waking up the whole safari to come up and get us. I wonder where you were raised. Unbelievers of heaven and hell. I say hell, that's what I say. And damned we are, all of us. No getting away from the outfit. Shit in the goldfish. If you are sitting pretty, don't yell about it. Knock wood. Oh, why did I ever in all my life put up with a blasphemous sailor like you? I don't understand the Germans at all, why they could ever take a guy like you for a gob. No wonder they could not make Skagen and had to go home. Well, they were saved only by leaving you to the Danes."

"Won't you shut up and let us think a bit to make sure what we are doing?" Stanislav broke in.

"Think? Think? What do you want to think about? Tell me that. Sitting on a broken-off wooden wall in mid-ocean, and at midnight, and you want to think. I only wish I could get a separation so I wouldn't have to see you any more. It makes me sick. Thinking."

"What else can we do right now? If we fall asleep we are finished."

How the world changes. For months and months we had to worry and be troubled about papers and identification cards. Then we had to worry about rats the size of huge cats. After this, or at the same time, we had to sweat and to bleed about dropped grate-bars. And now, all of a sudden, it does not matter any longer if there are passports in the world or if the world can go on without them. What does it matter if grate-bars fall out or not on the *Yorikke*? Sailor's identification cards or not. Whatever a being may own is of no importance, of no concern at all. It is gone and useless. All we have is our breath. I shall fight for it with teeth and nails. I won't give up and I won't give in. Not yet. Not to the ground port.

"My opinion of the merriments of life is different from what we have right here and now," Stanislav broke up my reflections.

To this I answered: "I think, Stanislav, to tell you the truth, you are again ungrateful to destiny. How changeable is human life! Just think. Yesterday you were half-owner of one of the finest ships of His Majesty's merchant marine. You were half-owner of the most elegant store, with caviar, Scotch, and champagne. Now all is gone, and you are fighting with the fish for their eats. What else, what more pleasure do you expect in one lifetime? You cannot have everything. Others have it only in the stories. We have it in reality. Do you want to change places?"

"I don't know exactly. But I figure I might like to change places and rather read stories than live them. And if you talk any more of that kind and don't hold on well to the rings and the handles, you won't even have a chance left to live your stories."

He was right, Stanislav was. As usually he was. I had nearly been swept off the raft. The breakers were not felt as when we were still on the ship. The breakers now just played with us, taking us high up and then down again fifty feet. Often we were for almost a minute entirely submerged. This helped us not to forget that we were still on high sea and not reading a story in bed.

"We must do something about it," I suggested. "My arms are paralyzed. You know I got quite a crack on them. I am losing ground. I cannot hold on very much longer."

"Same with me," Stanislav said. "We have still rope and cords about us. Let me have yours."

I got the cord I had tied around my waist while we were still on the ship, and Stanislav helped fasten me to the rings and handles. With my lame arm I could not have done it alone. This done, he tied himself upon the raft with the rope he had brought along.

We were now ready to wait for the next adventure.

After a thousand hours, or so it seemed, morning came and brought with it a calm day. The sea was still high.

"See any land?" Stanislav asked.

"Nothing I would know of. I always knew that I would not have discovered America, not even if I'd been washed against her shores. Well, I don't see anything. Not even a smoke-line."

Stanislav suddenly made a jerking gesture: "Man, are we lucky? Fine that you picked up the compass in the old man's cabin. Now we can sail."

"Yes, we can sail now," I said; "at least we can now always make out in which direction lies the coast of Africa and which way America. All we need is sails, masts, a rudder, and the right wind. Little, isn't it?"

"Sure it is. But I have got the feeling we are going somewhere else. Neither shore." That's what Stanislav said.

During the forenoon the sky had cleared. In the afternoon it became cloudy again. Before evening a slight mist began to settle over the sea. With this mist the sea calmed down and became rippled.

The vast distances toward the horizon and the immensity of the sea shrank when the mist closed in on us. The sea became smaller with every minute, until we had the illusion that we were floating on an inland lake. As time went on, even this lake narrowed more and more. Now we felt as if drifting down a river. We had the sensation that we could touch the banks with our hands. The walls of mist seemed only to veil dimly the river-banks.

We became drowsy. I dropped asleep and fell into dreams. When I woke I looked around and said: "Stanislav, man, look, there is the shore. Let's get off and swim. It's hardly a hundred yards off. Can't you see? There, right behind that misty wall. I knew we were close to shore."

Somehow, both of us hadn't the will-power to loosen the cords, make off, and swim that stretch to the shore.

I simply could not, hard as I tried, get my thoughts clear and reason things out. There was something in my head or about my head that made my brain feel numb. Almost like being drunk. Or it was like I felt when I was bumped on the head by the shanghaiing gang. I wanted to talk to Stanislav. I only wanted to talk nonsense so as to keep awake. But I could not manage it. I saw that Stanislav was drowsy again and was falling asleep. So I could not resist and I also fell asleep.

I woke up when water splashed into my face. Night had come.

The mist was still upon the sea, which had now become glassy. An indication that the mist might turn to thick fog. But the mist was not heavy. It was only upon the water. High above me I could see the stars twinkling. I thought I heard them calling.

Now I could see quite clearly the river-banks on both sides. We were still drifting down the river. It might be the Hudson or the Mississippi. How we had come there I could not figure out. It caused me pain to think. Then the mist banks opened. Great patches of it fluttered. Through these openings I could now see the thousands of twinkling lights of a great port. What a large harbor it was! It had skyscrapers and many other high office-buildings and apartment-houses. I saw the windows illuminated. Behind the windows there were people sitting and moving about. I saw their shadows. They all went about their own affairs, not realizing that here on this big river two sailors were drifting down helpless and out into the open sea.

The skyscrapers and apartment-houses grew higher and still higher. I had to bend my head down against my neck to see the top of the highest buildings. What a huge city this was that we were drifting by! Twinkling lights far, far away, and close at hand also. The skyscrapers went on growing until they reached the very heights of the sky. So now the lights in the windows looked exactly like the stars in the firmament. Right straight above me, and in the zenith of the heavens, the tops of the skyscrapers closed in upon each other, so much so that they were bent, touching each other. I became afraid that these high buildings bent over to such an extent might cave in any minute and bury me under their ruins. I was filled with a joyful hope that it would happen, and that that way I would be relieved from all the pain I felt, and, more than from everything else, from the thirst. I shook off the thought of thirst and of fresh water. But I could not help it. It came again. In my soul I began praying that the skyscrapers might fall down upon me and make an end of the world.

A terrible fright caught me, and like mad I yelled: "There is a huge port. Stanislav, look! Get ready. Must be New York. Stanislav, can't you see? Wake up! Hell, what are you so slow about?"

Stanislav stirred, woke up, scratched himself, shivered from the cold, shook off his sleepiness, looked around, gazed into the mist, tried to penetrate the veils around us, stared at the river-banks.

He made a gesture as though he had not seen right. He rubbed his eyes over and over again to get the salt out.

Then, having looked around at all sides, he said: "You are dreaming, Pippip. Pull yourself together, old man! That's no lights of a port. It's only the stars that you are seeing. There are no river-banks. How could we be on a river? We are still out on the high sea. You can easily tell it by the long waves. We must be off coast no less than thirty miles. Maybe two hundred. Search me. Wonder if this damn night will never end."

I did not believe him. I could not believe him. I still wanted to get off the raft and swim over to the river-banks. While thinking about how many strokes I might have to make before I would reach the bank I fell asleep again.

Thirst, hunger, and salt in my mouth woke me up.

It was bright daylight.

Stanislav was watching me. His eyes were red as if they were bleeding. The salt water had made my face feel as if covered with an iron crust.

Stanislav was moving his mouth in a strange way. I thought he was trying to swallow his tongue. His tongue was swollen and seemed not to fit any longer in his mouth. So I thought again that he might try to spit it out and relieve himself from this nuisance.

He looked at me as though scrutinizing my face. Blood seemed to run into his eyes in streams. He flew into a rage and yelled with all the might of his voice: "You dirty liar, you dog! You have always said the fresh water on the *Yorikke* is stinking and pesty. You stinking rat, you funker! Water on the *Yorikke* is the finest water in the world, coming from the cool springs of Nampamptantin of Hamtinoa of the springs of the—of the—of the springs—the springs of the pine forest —of the fresh—of the water—of the crystal springs—of wandering in pine forest."

I did not think that he was talking nonsense. It was all clear to me, like short commands from the bridge. I said: "Right you are, Stanislav, good boy. The water on the *Yorikke* was iced water from the pole, and the coffee was excellent. Have I ever said a word against the coffee on the *Yorikke*? I have not. Never will."

Stanislav was working again with his tongue. It looked as if he were in need of breath or as though choking to death. He swallowed and made an effort to press his lips together. He closed his eyes and I thought he would fall asleep.

With a jerk he awoke and yelled somewhere into the far distance without giving me a glance: "Twenty to five, Pippip. Get the hell up and out. Bring the breakfast. Sixty sixflytee ashes cans with ashes coal fuel boiler cans with ashes to be heaved. Heave up! Throw the lever around. Smash the pipe. Get the breakfast. Potatoes again and stinking. And smoked herring sick. The coffee. Much coffee. Much much more coffee.

Where is the coffee? Water. Bring the water, cool the glowing cinder. The water. Water. Water."

"I cannot get up;" I said. "I cannot make it today. I am too tired. I am all in. You have to heave the ashes alone this morn. Where is all the coffee?"

What was that? Now? I heard Stanislav yelling. But I heard him yelling from three miles away. My own voice also was three miles away.

Three furnaces then broke open. Heaps of live coal were falling out. The heat—I could not bear it any more. I rushed up to the air-funnel to turn it round to catch the breeze and blow it down into the fire-hold. Spainy, my fireman, hollered at me: "Pippip, for hell's sake, shut the furnace doors. The steam is falling. Steam is falling. Falling. Falling. All falling. Breaking. Hop away, Pip, ash-funnel is coming down. Smash your belly. Breaking." The steam-pipes burst, and all the steam hissed in the fire-hold, and upon me, boiling me and scalding me. I rushed to the trough in which we kept the water to cool off the cinders. I wanted to drink that muddy water because I was thirsty. Devil, how thirsty I was! But it was all salty and thick. I drank and drank as if I'd never be filled up. The furnaces were still open. I could not shut them. They were too heavy. I had to leave them open. They were high above me, and I saw it was the sun burning down upon me and I was lapping up water from the sea.

I got tired trying to close the furnaces and I fell asleep, dropping into my bunk as if dead. The fireman took up the trough and with a wide swing he threw all the water about the fire-hold. The water drenched me, I awoke, and a wave had come splashing over our raft.

"There is the *Yorikke!*" Stanislav yelled all of a sudden, pointing in some empty space above the waves. His voice was hundreds of miles away. Or my ears had lost the ability to judge distances. Stanislav began to yell louder. I could see it, that he was yelling as mightily as his voice would allow. Yet I could catch it only as a very thin sound, as far away as heaven. "There, there! There is the death ship. She is standing by. The port. Do you see the Norske ship? There she is. All glory. All in golden sun. She has iced water from the fjords. Can't you see, can't you see, Pippip?"

He had partly risen, squatting upon his knees. With both his arms he was pointing into space.

"Where is the *Yorikke?*" I too began now to yell.

"Man, old man, can't you see her? Are you blind? There she turns about. Now standing by. Please, please, can't you see her?"

His voice became pitifully pleading.

"Can't you see, Pippip? The devil, six grate-bars have dropped. Damn the whole shit. Now funking eight. Get me the can with the plum jelly put into the furnace to finish the grate-bars. Where is the coffee? Why didn't you leave me a drop? That's no Chinese laundry soap, it's butter, golden butter, you funking liar. Get me the tea! God damn, where is that coffee again? Eat the whole can of milk in one seat, Pippip. They steal it. All highwaymen. Another shot. Straight, I said; can't you hear me? Off your skirt, you little hussy, sweety! Get the coffee!"

I, not knowing if I was in my mind or out of it, watched Stanislav. It came to me, thinking what power he had, how he fought before breaking down. He hammered the raft with his fists. He worked his whole body, still bound by the rope. He threw his arms and his upper body into all directions, pointing here and there, yelling at me and asking if I did not see the *Yorikke*, once under full steam, then turning about, then standing by and lowering away anchor.

I became indifferent to everything. It began to hurt me to turn my head to see the port or to watch the maneuvers of the *Yorikke* coming up to reach us.

Stanislav, unceasingly watching something on the sea which he believed real, started hollering again: "Hold her, hold her!

Pippip, we are drifting away. She cannot make it after all. I must now get her. All the bars are out now. Do you see the fireman? My fire'm is in the boiler. Where is the water? I have to hurry now to run along and hop on or she makes off."

He worked on the rope with which he had fastened himself to the raft. He had lost his ability to loosen knots. He worked at them like a monkey, not knowing any longer how to pull them open. In fact he tightened himself up more while he thought that he was getting out.

"Where is the shovel? Hell, let's cut the leg for once. Or I am going down. The water is rushing in already." He went about the rope more hastily, yet with still less skill. Of course, the rope, not very strong from the beginning, rubbed and torn constantly against the iron rings and brass handles and worked at with the hard hands of Stanislav, could not last long. It finally began to break and to loosen. With a last hard jerk Stanislav freed himself of his entanglement.

"The *Yorikke* is sailing. She is off. Quick, quick, Pippip! The Norske has iced water. See the guys standing at the rail waving the coffee-pot? I won't stay on a death ship. I won't. I won't."

Stanislav trembled in excitement. He got wilder every minute. His feet were still in a few slings of the rope. He noticed it with the last flicker of his dying mind. He pulled his legs out of these slings. Then he sat on the raft with his legs hanging down in the water.

All this I saw and took note of as if it were happening a hundred miles away and as though I watched it through a field-glass. I had no personal concern in it. Such was my feeling, strange as it may seem.

"There is the *Yorikke*. The skipper is saluting us. See him, Pippip? He tips his cap. Lump of coal at the leg. Why don't you come?"

I stared at him. I could not grasp what he was saying. I could not form his words into an idea. They were just words.

"Hop on, Pippip! Tea and raisin cake and cocoa and after-gale."

Now I saw, he was right. Yes, no doubt, there was the *Yorikke*. Floating above the waters in a sort of majestic silence. She made no wash. I could see her quite clearly. I recognized her by her funny-looking bridge, which always hung high up in the air.

Sure, there was the *Yorikke*. They were having breakfast now. And prunes in a bluish starch paste for pudding. The tea was not so bad. It was even good when there was no milk and no sugar. The fresh water did not stink, and the tanks were clean as if new.

I got busy to loosen the knots of the cord I was tied with to the raft. My fingers, however, did not obey me. They were just fumbling, doing nothing I wanted them to do.

I called upon Stanislav to help me untie the cord. He had no time. He did not even pay attention to my calling him. I do not know how he had managed it, but I noted that his feet were entangled again in the slings. He was working hurriedly to free himself once more.

His yelling and his ceaseless working at the rope had caused his wounds to break open. The wounds on his head which he had received when fighting the shanghaiing gang. Thick blood broke out of those scars and trickled down his face. It did not concern him. He didn't notice it at all.

I tore and pulled at my cord. It was too thick, and it had been tied up too well by Stanislav. I could not break it, nor rub it through, nor was I able to wind myself out snake-fashion. Whenever I thought I had won a few inches, I only found that I was fastened better than before. The water had tightened the cord so much so that the knots were as if soldered. I looked around for an ax, a knife, a shovel. This reminded me that some years ago, on one occasion, I had helped flatten out a shovel to cut a mast which caused a Negro to cry. Anyway, the compass fell into the water again, and I had to fish it out with a grate-bar that was still red-hot. I was still working at the cord. It refused to let me out. This made me think I was wrangling with a policeman who had searched my pockets right in front of the American consul, who asked if I wanted a meal-ticket. The knots of the cord got tighter. This made me mad, and I cursed whomever I could think of, even God and my mother.

Stanislav, quite cunningly, had got his legs again into the water, but was still sitting on the raft.

He turned around to me, but looked not at me but by me. He shook his head. Then he yelled: "Come here, Pipplav Pap Pip. Only twenty yards' run. All sand. Just run. Grates are all out. Water minutes to seven engineer. Get up. Below all full of ashes. Get up. Shake out of it!"

Then the gangway was shrieking: "No *Yorikke*. There is no *Yorikke*. It is all fluttering mist. There is no—no—"

The noise hurt me, and I hollered as loud as I could: "There is no *Yorikke*! It is a hellish lie. There is no *Yorikke*!"

I grabbed the cord with all my strength, because I looked around and saw that the *Yorikke* had gone far away. I saw only the sea. I saw only the waves rolling from horizon to horizon like eternity in movement.

"Stanskinslovski, don't jump! For God's sake, stay on!" I howled. I became terribly frightened. I felt as though I had lost something which I had found and could not have any more, no matter how much I might want it. "Stanislav, don't jump! Don't jump! Stay! Stay on! Hold on! Never give up!"

"She is heaving short. Hauling in. I am running to the death ship. I have to run to catch the *Yorikke* by the buttocks. Running. Running. Hundred yards. Fünen, ahoy! Com'a! Come'a!"

He jumped. He did it. He jumped. There was no riverbank. There was no port. There was no ship. No shore. Only the sea. Only the waves rolling from horizon to horizon, kissing the heavens, glittering like the mirrors of sunken suns.

He made a few splashing strokes in no definite direction. Then he lifted his arms. He went down. In deep silence.

I looked at the hole through which he had slipped off. I could see the hole for a long while. I saw it as if from a great distance.

I yelled at the hole: "Stanislav. Lavski. Brother. Comrade. Sailor. Dear, dear comrade. Come here. Ahoy! Man, ahoy! Sailor, ahoy! Come here. I am standing by. Come on!"

He did not hear me. He would have come. Sure he would. He did not come up any more. There was no death ship. No port. No *Yorikke*. He did not come up any more. No, sir.

There was something very remarkable about it. He did not rise. He would have come up. I could not understand.

He had signed on for a long voyage. For a very great voyage.

I could not understand this. How could he have signed on? He had no sailor's card. No papers whatever. They would kick him off right away.

Yet he did not come up. The Great Skipper had signed him on. He had taken him without papers.

And the Great Skipper said to him: "Come, Stanislav Koslovski, give me your hand. Shake. Come up, sailor! I shall sign you on for a fine ship. For an honest and decent ship. The finest we have. Never mind the papers. You will not need any here. You are on an honest ship. Go to your quarters, Stanislav. Can you read what is written above the quarters, Stanislav?"

And Stanislav said: "Aye, aye, sir. He who enters here will be for ever free of pain!"